PRAISE FOR AGAINST THE WARRING WINDS

"One part fantasy adventure, one part compelling mystery, one part wrenching drama—all of the ingredients skillfully woven into an epic tale that is sure to please fantasy readers. The warring winds are carrying a new voice in fantasy, and you won't want to miss getting caught in the storm!"

— **Wayne Thomas Batson**, Bestselling Author of *The Door Within Trilogy*, *The Berinfell Prophecies*, and *The Myridian Constellation*

"An action-packed adventure that I didn't want to put down. If you like fantasy with a lot of heart, don't miss this one."

— **Angela R. Watts**, Bestselling and Award-Nominated Author of *The Infidel Books* and the *Remnant Trilogy*

"Author C. Jonah Abbott creates a fascinating milieu of magic vs. technology, race against race, and sibling against sibling. Fans of the genre will find the tale a unique take on familiar elements and enjoy Abbott's refreshing voice."

— **Robert Mullin**, Author of *The Wells of the Worlds*

Against the Warring Winds

A Tale of the Elven Rift

C. Jonah Abbott

Anointed Colony Media

Published by Anointed Colony Media, LLC
www.AnointedColonyMedia.com
Greeley, Colorado

Cover art by Mert Genccinar.
Map illustration by C. Jonah Abbott.
Text divider artwork by Freepik.
Cover and interior design by Anointed Colony Media, LLC.

Library of Congress Control Number: 2024924670
ISBN 13: 979-8-9917075-0-3

Printed in the United States of America

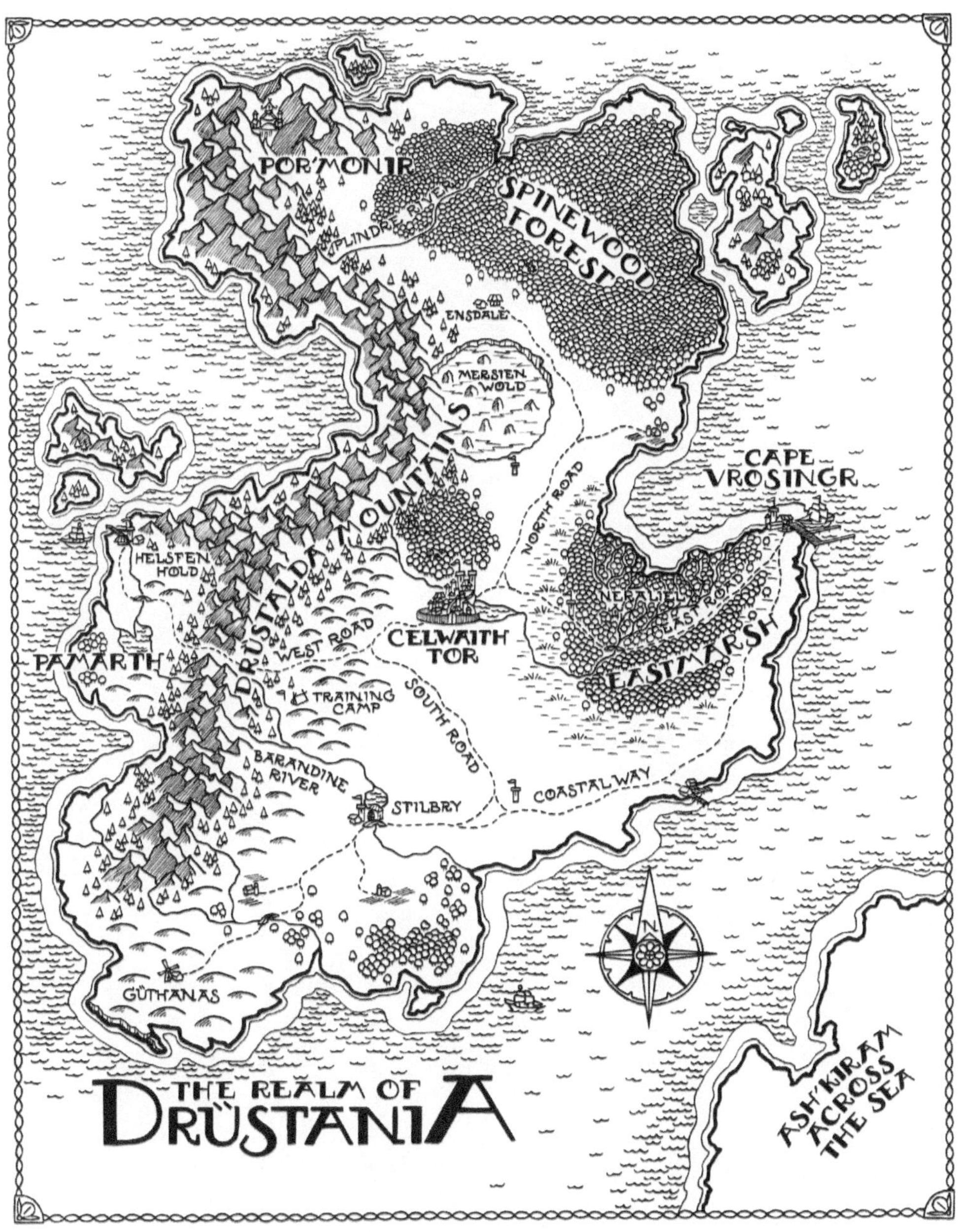

POR'MONIR
SPINEWOOD FOREST
PLINDRE CAVES
ENSDALE
MERSTEN WOLD
CAPE VROSINGR
NORTH ROAD
NERALISLE
EAST ROAD
HELSFEN HOLD
DRUSTALDA MOUNTAINS
CELWAITH TOR
EASTMARSH
PAMARTH
WEST ROAD
TRAINING CAMP
SOUTH ROAD
BARANDINE RIVER
STILBRY
COASTAL WAY
GÜTHANAS
N
THE REALM OF DRUSTANIA
ASH'KIRAM ACROSS THE SEA

For the One True King, pursuer of my soul. Though once I usurped Your throne in my heart, now I yield all glory to You. May those with eyes to see and ears to hear discover Your Truth in these pages.

PRELUDE

I AM ALONE NOW, and the cold breath of the northern wilds bites my heels.

The world has been broken for so long, and rather than desperately trying to mend the pieces, I find that perhaps I would have been better off merely fixing myself. But I am an old man, and I fear this may be my last winter before facing the eternal night. My family precedes me in death, and my voice and hearing have gone, so there remains nothing but my thoughts to condemn me, and my quill to comfort me.

Since time immemorial, there was a stable peace between the two peoples. The elves, known as D'harnir in their ancient tongue, plied their innate magics in healing and creative arts; but the D'salnir, men, were ever strong in industry and battle. For unknown ages, they aided one another in their respective lacks and needs, and society thrived. Men were renowned as builders and protectors, and elves were likewise revered as doctors and alchemists.

If nature asks a question, it also provides the answer, and so it was with men and elves. Each group opposed and complemented the other in equal measures, so that few communities ever became wanting. It was an unparalleled symbiosis of cultures, for the physical and the spiritual came together as one in delicate balance.

But this world is a harsh one, and people have short memories. The waves of time threaten to dash upon the rocks every good thing.

> *— Haron Geled, Last Scribe of the Union*
> *23rd of Hollyn, mid-winter solstice, in the 48th year after the Rift*

ONE

*When adversity comes, it will be silent as
the wind, swift as the viper's bite; woe to
those who are caught unprepared.*

— Codes of Binding 8.27

"NIENA, BEHIND YOU!"

Niena caught the oncoming horse and buggy out of the corner of her eye and seized up in terror. The hooves bore down on her without sign of slowing, and her stomach lurched as she was yanked out of the street by her more observant friend. The cab driver sped past, fecklessly unaware of the near trampling that had occurred.

Trying and failing to regain her balance, Niena bumped headlong into a paisley doublet with ridiculously flared sleeves. The heavyset man to which the gaudy articles belonged swore at her with equally colorful language to mind her place.

Niena mumbled a terse apology, and as she did so her friend, Keordi, took her arm again and guided her away from the scene.

"Are you okay?" Keordi inquired, concern written on her face.

"I'm fine. Just distracted, is all."

"Since when? That's usually my problem, not yours."

Glancing around, Niena noticed again what had caught her attention in the first place. People were watching them, and the stares shifted into feigned disinterest the moment Niena and Keordi came closer than several yards. The annoyance of the watchers became even more palpable now, but the sentiment was the same as before. They didn't think her old, scuffed shoes were worthy of walking on their smooth stone paving slabs.

She supposed they might be right.

Niena hated to admit it to herself, but the disdainful looks at her faded green dress, threadbare handbag, and dingy white gloves hurt. These clothes might not be the finery everyone in the Gilded Quarter was used to, but they were the most expensive things she owned. And for what? She might as well have made the trip in her work things.

Niena reminded herself she wasn't there to partake in frivolity, even though she had precious few afternoons free from the long hours working at the loom. She couldn't hide that she was from the Barren Quarter, nor did it matter anyway. She was there to do business, and no sane shopkeeper would prevent her from spending money.

Niena checked her hairnet to make sure her unruly blonde locks were still in place. "Let's just say there's a reason I don't go to the Gilded Quarter very often," she replied to Keordi without elaboration.

Keordi snatched her arm and locked elbows, immediately affecting a stiff posture and gait that mimicked the pride of the busybodies surrounding them. It was almost comical, because Niena's shabby dress made Keordi's look like a burlap sack, and the latter's dark, tightly curled hair was free of net or bonnet and blowing in the light afternoon breeze.

"Of course you don't, Miss Cresthaven," Keordi said in a posh accent while looking down her nose. "You care too much about what others think of you to have any fun."

Niena couldn't help but laugh at the caricature as they strolled further up the hill. "You don't care enough! Your kind of 'fun' could get us clapped in irons."

"That's why it's useful to have an older brother in the city guard!" Keordi smirked, with a waggle of her expressive eyebrows. "Speaking of, I think he might have taken a fancy to you."

"Kasdan? Surely not."

"All I know is, he asked after you the other day and got mighty antsy when I wondered why."

Niena frowned. Her friend usually saw drama where there was none, but this didn't sound like merely stirring the pot.

She and Keordi had only been three when their families first met. After Niena's mother had died in childbirth, her father, Voster, had moved to the city so his sister, Anise, could care for Niena's newborn brother, Tollan. Keordi and the rest of the Harroway family had welcomed the Cresthavens in, despite the limitations of Celwaith Tor's Barren Quarter, and the two girls quickly bonded.

Kasdan, in contrast, was a couple of years older, and was already working to earn a living while Niena and Keordi were still young. Recently he had been granted a coveted position in the city guard and was now the talk of the neighborhood. Niena had never known him well nor considered him in a romantic fashion, though she supposed his dedication to his family and his work ethic were commendable.

"Then he's going to have to do a lot more than ask," Niena said. "He has to win over my papa first, you know."

"Don't worry, boys are dense sometimes. You can tell him I said that." Keordi flashed another grin and hiked up her skirts. "Come on, we're almost there!" she called, breaking into a run.

Niena couldn't help but shake her head at such endearing brashness before following. She quickly became out of breath while Keordi steadily outstripped her in pace, weaving through the rich folk and paying their annoyance no mind. The brown-skinned girl was impossibly fast—despite being shorter than Niena and racing uphill, too, she noted in annoyance.

The bell tower at the Cathedral of the Winds marked the hour, cheering five times for Niena to power through. She timed her breathing to the rhythm and finally crested the top of the incline. She spied Keordi standing at the end of the street, twisting a frizzy strand of her hair around one finger and tapping her foot in mock impatience.

Niena ducked past another pedestrian and came to a panting halt, drawing still more inquisitive eyes. "What . . . are you . . . staring at?" she called between breaths at the closest onlooker, a woman in a stiff bodice and hoop skirt carrying a floral-embroidered parasol. "Never seen an unstarched dress before?"

Keordi snickered. "That's the spirit!"

The woman huffed and continued on her way, looking oddly as if she was hovering over the paving stones due to the width of her hem.

Niena felt something tickling her neck and realized that in her haste, her hairnet had slipped out of place. She reached up to set it right again, but Keordi had already given it a swift tug and let the flaxen waves tumble free of their yarn prison.

Niena gasped and tried to snatch it back, but Keordi danced out of reach and tucked the net into the handbag hanging in the crook of her opposite arm, laughing mischievously.

Niena rolled her eyes, knowing any attempt to reclaim the hairnet right now would be fruitless. She ran a hand through her hair to straighten it, all the while admitting to herself that it did feel good to spite the scornful looks around them. She shouldn't need to put on airs just to inhabit the same space as the economic gentry.

Though what a space it was. The sights, sounds, and smells of Wraelian Square opened out in front of them. Despite all the preoccupation with image and status here, Niena could not deny the breathtaking beauty of the Gilded Quarter.

On the far side of the square rose an imposing portcullis, beyond which loomed the towers of the royal palace and keep of Celwaith Tor, the capital and largest city of Drüstania. Niena could see for miles beyond since the castle had been built on a solitary rocky bluff, leaving the rest of the city to spill down the gentle slope on one side like a babbling brook.

In the center of the square, on a large, engraved stone pedestal, stood a stone figure of the late King Wraelian, more than twice life-size and wearing a golden crown and graven royal tunic. It held a bronze sword angled down in its left hand, with a silver dove perched serenely on its right. The grand pose drew one's gaze upward, away from the other creature trod upon by the statue's right foot: a cobra carved from black onyx. The precious metals contrasted starkly with the colorless marble in the late afternoon sun.

A handful of city guards had gathered around the statue's base to set up a scaffold in preparation for the statue's weekly polishing and upkeep. The current king of Drüstania, Wraelian's eldest son, Pelendion, insisted on the utmost respect for the legacy of his father's throne, and the people generally obliged as far as Niena knew.

All around the statue sprawled out a host of temporary market stalls and carts in a haphazard maze of a thousand different products. Niena recalled from her history lessons that the square could hold all twenty thousand residents of Celwaith Tor in a pinch, but she found it hard to imagine a crowd larger than what she saw in front of her now.

"What are we searching for again?" Keordi asked.

Niena stepped off the curb to wade into the noisy morass of people. "I'll know it when I see it."

"So, special but not too expensive—that narrows it down."

Keordi's sarcasm was cutting at times because she spoke the truth. It wasn't every day that one's younger brother turned sixteen, and Niena had been scraping and saving for the past six months to give him something he would treasure. She wished she knew what that item might be, but Tollan was difficult to pin down.

"Does Tollan like knives much?" Keordi suggested, pointing out a table filled with weapons, most of them ornamental. The hawker and presumable owner of the stand had a waxed mustache almost as pointy as his rapiers.

Niena wouldn't consider it. "I guarantee none of those blades are as fine as what Papa knows how to make at his forge, or even what Tollan could strike himself given the chance."

"Right, of course." Keordi shot her a quizzical glance. "You know, Voster could merit somewhere better than a ramshackle smithy in the Barren Quarter. People come from the far side of the tor for his repairs."

"I don't think he wants to." A bookseller's tent caught Niena's eye, and they passed by for a brief look. The tomes were well bound and printed for the price, but none were notable save for an imported collection of poetry from Ash'kiram across the eastern sea. Tollan cared more for military history, so Niena directed them to move on. "Papa seems content to stay as long as he's helping the people around him. Though Aunt Anise is as desperate as ever to leave," Niena finished.

"Desperate for a beau, more like," Keordi joked. She pulled them aside for a moment, out of the path of traffic. "What about you, then?"

Niena blinked. "What about me?"

"What do you want to do someday?"

Niena opened her mouth to speak, but no sound came out. She realized that she wasn't sure. Her entire life had consisted of staying above the ever-present undertow of poverty in the city, interrupted every so often by happy moments with those she cared about. Her father, aunt, and brother were everything to her. "I want ..." She glanced around for something to change the subject. "There!"

Keordi cocked an eyebrow, then followed her gaze.

A few stalls over, in the shadow of Wraelian's statue, there stood a little white-haired man with a plethora of glass lenses mounted on his face, hard at work on one of his wares. Surrounding him in a chorus of ticking was a diverse array of clocks and watches, all of which showed the same: five hours and ten minutes after noon.

"You want a clock?" Keordi turned back, squinting in puzzlement.

"For my brother," Niena said, grabbing her friend's hand and tugging her along. "Papa is always chiding Tollan for losing track of time, remember? This would be perfect—both unique and practical."

"If you say so," Keordi said, suspicious of the forced change of subject.

"Excuse me, sir," Niena called as she stepped up to the counter. "I'd like to look at some pocket watches?"

The man held up a finger, cutting off further questions. His elderly hands shook ever so slightly as his tweezers set the tiniest of screws in its niche. He pulled out a matching minuscule screwdriver and tightened it, before hurriedly sweeping it all to one side.

"My apologies, ladies, business has been rather slow today." His white mustache curled up in a chuckle as he stood and dusted off his navy doublet with loose white sleeves. His right eye looked comically large until he raised the lenses on his headgear to examine his new customers properly. "Oh, you two pretty girls are, heh, not from this part of town?"

Niena shared an exasperated glance with Keordi, covering the motion by tucking a few locks of hair behind her ear. "Yes sir. I may be from the Barren Quarter, but I'm looking to buy a gift for my brother, and you look like a skilled clock-maker."

"Well, thank you," the man said, nodding once, "but you misunderstand me. I remember what it's like; I used to live there too until I taught myself mechanics. The name's Aldren, just like the sign!" He pointed up at the brightly-colored billboard behind him, which indeed read *Aldren's Timekeepers*. "And who might you be?"

Niena wasn't sure if she should believe him, or if it was all part of the sales pitch, but she played along. "I'm Niena, and this is Keordi."

Keordi fluttered her fingers in greeting.

Aldren tilted his head in colloquial reverence since he didn't have a cap. "A pleasure. Now, what can I show you?"

Niena described the ideal watch. "Something simple, easy to wind . . . Oh, and durable, especially the chain."

"I think I have just the thing for you," Aldren said as he rummaged through his stock. "It's one of the first pieces I made, but I learned quick it was too understated for most of the—er, clientele around here." He winked and plunked down a watch with a hinged brass lid. There was no glass covering the hands inside, and a dark chain attached to it with a clip that doubled as a winding key at the other end.

"That looks perfect," Niena said with appreciation, but she knew the moment of truth was coming. "What are you asking?"

Aldren scratched his stubbly chin, seeming to measure her up. "Honestly, Miss Niena, you'd be doing me a favor by taking this off my hands, and seeing as you're coming all the way from the slums, I'll give you a discount. Twenty silver."

Niena tried not to show her excitement, as she had brought more than enough to meet the price. But she knew the game and suspected he could go lower. "Can you make it eighteen?"

Aldren must have expected the question and immediately counter-offered with a twinkle in his eye. "Still twenty, but I'll engrave it for you."

Niena cracked a smile and pulled out her coin purse in agreement. It was a fair price, far better than she had expected to find.

The watchmaker placed the timepiece in a vise and picked out a bladed tool from a leather satchel at his side. "Initials?" he asked, spinning the largest of his lenses into place over his eye.

"T. C. for my brother, Tollan Cresthaven."

"Any relation to Voster?"

"I'm his daughter."

Aldren slapped his knee, his face lighting up. "Well, twist my springs. You know, I'd have never been in this business if it weren't for him." He held up the engraving blade and waggled it. "I'm still using the tools he made for me, heh, more than ten years ago now."

Niena smiled, knowing for sure now that she wouldn't be scammed. "Papa always did know how to make friends."

"That he did," Aldren said. "Be sure to wish him well for me."

Niena watched, fascinated, as Aldren confidently but carefully shaved off the top layer of brass to create two perfectly etched letters in the center of the lid. After blowing away the debris, he wound the spring, wrapped the piece up in a small cloth bag, and presented it to Niena with a flourish.

"Now remember," he said kindly, "you'll have to wind it at least once every twelve hours, or it won't keep proper time. Let me know if it gives you any trouble, and I'll fix it free of charge."

Niena nodded, accepting the bag. "Thank you very much, sir."

"Of course!" the watchmaker said with an eccentric bow. "And may I say, Miss Niena, that you have the most stunning green eyes I think I've ever seen in the Gilded Quarter?"

Niena blushed and thanked him again before turning to leave. With concern, she realized her shopping companion was nowhere to be found. "Keordi?" she called out but realized the sound wouldn't carry over the crowd. She raised herself up on her toes and tried to see over all the bobbing heads, but the interference of large hats, parasols, and other extravagance made it impossible.

There was little wonder that Keordi had gotten bored and wandered off. Niena had spent far longer than she intended to with Aldren, but she suspected that few people visited with him outside his business. She felt a bit of a connection with the man since he had worked himself out of the Barren Quarter for over a decade.

Something to aspire toward, perhaps.

Niena hedged her bets and followed her nose in the direction of the fruit and pastry stands. Keordi could never resist a meat pie.

It was not a snack, but rather music that had drawn Keordi away. At the edge of the square, a few ragamuffin kids had thrown together a kind of circus performance with acrobats and juggling accompanied by drum and pipes. More likely it was a scheme to hold the people's attention while other children picked pockets, but that had not stopped Keordi from joining in. She skipped around with the children, smacking a tambourine in time with the light, happy ditty from the piper.

Niena pushed her way through the group of people watching and waved her friend down, gesturing toward the street that would take them back to the Barren Quarter.

After handing the instrument to one of the children, Keordi politely left the circle and met up with Niena. "What's the hurry? Did you find something for your brother?"

Niena unwrapped the watch and showed it off before placing it carefully back in her purse. "No hurry. Just thought we might split something to eat on the way back since I have a few coins left over."

Keordi's eyes lit up. "Maybe a pie?"

Niena laughed as they walked away from the square. She knew her friend too well. "We can stop by my favorite Sunken Quarter bakery on the way back—their prices are still reasonable even with the wheat shortage. That reminds me, we might also pick up an orange for my aunt before we leave. They are so hard to find down in the Barren Quarter, and—"

A flash of light and a deafening explosion came from behind them. Both young women whirled to see rubble flung across the square from the origin of the blast: the statue of King Wraelian. A sizable chunk of marble skidded across the pavement directly toward them, and Niena pulled Keordi aside just in time.

The stone shot past them, only stopped by a wooden cart that immediately splintered in on itself.

Niena's ears rang. The air filled with the acrid scent of black powder and the screams of the terrified and injured. Time seemed to slow as she dragged Keordi into an alleyway, both breathing heavily once under cover. Scores of panicked others rushed past their hiding place, trampling each other in a mad dash to get as far away from the square as they could before there was another explosion.

A man ducked into the alley next to them, inordinately tall and wearing a dark blue hooded cloak. In his haste to escape the mob, he didn't see the young women and collided headlong with Keordi. He slipped on the smooth paving stone and took both of them down, causing his hood to fall to his shoulders.

Niena gasped at the sight, for he was no man at all. The figure had deathly pale skin and ears that came to lengthened points above and behind his temples. Like the elves out of legend.

They locked eyes, and she saw fear in him for only a moment. She sensed a strange, intense pressure in her mind, even as she pressed her body back into the stone wall to show she wasn't a threat. The figure's lips moved, but she couldn't hear what he was saying. After a tense moment, the creature passed by and turned a corner deeper in the alleyway.

Niena took several fast, deep breaths and offered Keordi a hand up from where she sprawled on the ground. "Are you all right?"

Keordi clutched at Niena's arm and tried to steady herself, but her leg gave way and she yelped. "I must have twisted my ankle," she said, holding a hand to the side of her head. A little blood showed from where she had struck the wall on the way down, and her dress had a new rip in the hem to match the others.

Niena draped Keordi's arm across her shoulders to take on some of her friend's weight. "You didn't see the tall . . . uh, man in the hood?"

"What man?"

"The one who knocked you down."

"No, I . . ." Keordi trailed off. "I must have missed it."

That's not possible, Niena thought to herself. He had been in full view of them both. Maybe Keordi had hit her head too hard. On the other hand, the details had started to become fuzzy in Niena's mind as well.

No. She knew what she saw, even if it was impossible.

"Let's get you home and get that scrape looked at," Niena said, helping her friend step back out into the vacated street.

"What about the market? Should we help . . ." Keordi started to ask, but the square came back into view and answered the question.

Wreckage was strewn everywhere, much of it on fire. The paving stones were littered with bodies, some warm with life and others cooling, while guards began to emanate from the palace keep.

"I don't think so, Keordi," Niena said, tears welling in her eyes. She couldn't help thinking about the clock-maker. She thought she could make out the sign for *Aldren's Timekeepers*, crumpled amid the debris nearest the statue. Another few minutes at the stall, and she might have shared his fate. "The guards know what to do. We would get in their way."

Keordi nodded silently, and the two of them hobbled away from the destruction.

TWO

The way of the world is like entrusting knowledge to pupils, only for pride to disregard it. But there remains one who takes the teaching to heart and is blessed.
— Codes of Binding 2.04-05

THE RED-HOT METAL HISSED, held against the cool anvil by a firm grip on the tongs. Tollan struck at it again and again with his hammer, glowing sparks sent flying by each impact. The malleable iron continued to turn under the force, bending around the horn of the anvil until it had formed a pleasing oblong semicircle. He removed it and laid it down flat, where he would even it out and strike the fuller and the toe. In another few minutes, he had the result pulled out of the fire, quenched, and added to a pile of others almost identical to it, all waiting to be polished.

"Good, son," Tollan's father, Voster, encouraged from the other side of the forge, where he was completing a simple hatchet. He insisted on always having a full stock of household tools for sale, and they had sold one to a woodworker earlier that day. "Your speed and accuracy are improving. That's a fine horseshoe."

Tollan puffed out a tired breath. He was sick of horseshoes, but they consistently sold out of them if he didn't churn them out constantly. He never got to work on anything exciting, like blades.

"Thanks," he said a little sourly, careful not to tip his tone into sounding like sarcasm. He had stepped in water hotter than the quenching barrel last week and didn't want a repeat of that disciplinary episode.

Tollan wiped the sweat from his brow and fetched another iron rod. He told himself that he didn't dislike working the forge, that his family was fortunate to have a business in the Barren Quarter that paid for itself and even made slight profits—most of the time. But he was almost sixteen, and he was certain he didn't want to do this for the rest of his life.

A flash of yellow caught his attention as he was heating the metal, and he turned in excitement to see two Celwaith Tor guards on their patrol. One of them met Tollan's gaze and nodded in greeting as they marched past, and Tollan grinned back. He yearned to join the ranks of King Pelendion's finest and wear the Drüstanian crest. Not only would he become a part of the nation's storied military history, but he wouldn't be tempering horseshoes day in and day out.

Tollan's father spoke up, having seen him staring after the mail-clad soldiers. "Don't even think about it, son. I can't meet all the smithy's orders on my own. There's not enough time in the day."

"Only because you set our prices so low," Tollan protested, with a little more force than he had intended. "I've seen what's selling over in the Sunken Quarter, and they charge twenty-five percent more for sloppy craftsmanship."

"That's the price of guild membership, Tollan. Where would the people of the Barren Quarter go for affordable quality wares if not for us? We're needed here." Voster set his tools down and leaned on the fence that enclosed the forge area tacked onto the front of their ramshackle house. "Look at me. Is there anything we need that we don't have?" he asked.

Tollan sighed and met his father's eyes. "No, sir."

His father nodded, a smile tugging up the corner of his beard. "Then I'd say we're doing pretty well. And what's more, everyone around us is doing a bit better too." He reached out to tousle Tollan's hair like he always did.

Tollan recoiled, stepping out of reach. It was patronizing, and he wasn't a kid anymore. "What about the Harroways?" he asked in frustration. "They haven't missed rent since Kasdan joined the guard. Think what we—"

"I said no," Voster spat through his tawny gray beard, his tone emphasizing that he would tolerate no argument on the matter. "It's not worth the danger you would face. That yellow livery would be a target on your back, for some."

"Dad. The worst the Crownless have done in years is hold 'secret' meetings and avoid paying taxes. They aren't a threat—"

Tollan cut himself off when he saw a customer approaching. Probably for the best, as he was letting his emotions get the better of him. That never went well. As his father greeted the potential buyer, Tollan checked his iron to find that it was more than ready. He gripped the tongs tighter with his gloves and lifted the glowing rod from the flames.

He listened in on the conversation as he shaped the metal, surreptitiously rolling his eyes when his father allowed the price of a cast-iron skillet to be haggled down even further from his initial more-than-fair offer. Tollan wasn't heartless—of course, they could offer better prices to those in dire need, but at the end of the day, the smithy was a business. The cost of materials had been steadily climbing in the last few months too.

It was still strange that both Tollan and his sister had grown to be taller than their father, but it was almost appropriate that he no longer looked up to the man physically. Even so, there was no denying that Tollan's father carried a stout muscular strength that neither of his children had inherited. It was the only thing that kept Tollan's wagging mouth in check at times.

A commotion came from further up the street, and Tollan, his father, and the customer turned to see the cause. A young boy, no more than eight, rushed down the hill toward them as fast as his short legs would go. His eyes were wild with either exhaustion or fright.

Voster called out to the boy, recognizing him as a neighbor. "Whoa there, Farby! What seems to be the trouble?"

The kid didn't slow but threw them a few words as he passed. "Wraelian Square's been attacked! Gotta get home!" Farby turned the corner and was gone.

"Attacked?" Tollan repeated, looking at his father in alarm. "What?"

Voster's graying blond eyebrows had beetled into a serious, worried frown. "I don't know, son."

"You think Niena was still there? How long ago did she head out?"

"Hours ago now," he said. "Let's wait and see what else we hear, but you'd best start turning down the forge." He left Tollan to it and returned to business with the alarmed customer so as not to lose the sale.

Tollan would normally have relished the chance to end the workday early, but a cold lump of uneasiness formed in his gut as he tossed the unfinished horseshoe into the quenching bucket. He chided himself but the feeling persisted. They only had the word of a kid to go on, and nothing specific either.

That changed in a matter of minutes as people filled the streets, frantic to return to their hovels. As Tollan gathered the tools and display items to pack away indoors, he overheard hushed words about black powder. *Some kind of explosion, then,* he thought nervously, recalling a book he had recently read on the discovery of the substance.

It wasn't long before a familiar face appeared, but it was not Niena's. "Anise," Voster called, opening the gate for her. "Thank the winds they let you go early today."

"What's the word? Anything?" Tollan asked urgently. His mind raced with possible culprits and motives.

Anise huffed and puffed on account of her corset, supporting herself with the workbench. "Give me a moment, both of you."

Tollan's aunt was more than slightly vain, an irregular quality for living in the poorest part of town and working in a weaver's den. She wore a dress that, despite having once been upper class, had deteriorated such that Tollan suspected Anise had pulled it from a rubbish heap. She had repaired it to some extent, but it remained unflattering.

Voster gathered their remaining materials and gestured with his head for Tollan to hold the door. "Let's get you inside," he said to Anise. "We'll set about making some dinner while you tell us what you've heard."

Anise gripped Voster's arm as he passed. "I know Niena went to that square today—I told her not to, I did. Please, tell me she's here."

Voster shook his head, a pained look on his face. He carried his armload of supplies over the doorstep and into the house.

Anise stared after Voster for a moment, tears forming in her eyes. Tollan had already come to the same conclusion: if Niena had hurried back from the Gilded Quarter, she should have already arrived. The knot in his stomach grew worse.

"She'll be here any minute." Tollan reassured his aunt, still holding the door for her.

Even after Anise had followed his father inside, Tollan tarried to examine the state of the neighborhood. The streets continued to empty as the chaos died down, but the true danger would come out after dusk.

"Oughtn't you to go out and look for her?" Anise asked Voster when he came back up from the basement storeroom.

Tollan kept the door ajar, waiting for the answer. He saw his father's fists clench as he struggled with the decision.

"It would be dark by the time we made it up the tor and back," Tollan pointed out, thinking it made more sense to wait. "And they may well have chosen to come back a different way or go to the Harroways' first. Niena knows to be home by sundown."

"But what if she isn't?" Anise worried.

"Tollan is right," Voster answered reluctantly. "The city is too big, and she may be hiding out somewhere. But if she isn't home by dark . . ." He paused to take down the bow from above the mantle and clenched his hand around the grip. "It won't matter how dangerous the streets are, we aren't leaving her out there."

Tollan swung the creaky door shut and slid the heavy iron bolt into place, to open only when Niena arrived or when they left to find her. His uneasy feeling had subsided now that they had a plan, though the hardest part now was waiting. A mental image of his sister came unbidden, sprawled across the cobblestone, and all color gone from her still, cold face. He refused to dwell on it.

Anise baked some flatbread to pass the time as she told them what she had heard about the destruction at Wraelian Square. The story was mostly second and third-hand rumors, and it didn't make any of them feel better. "Celwaith Tor hasn't seen unrest like this since the Pamarthen raids," she said, puttering about the kitchen. "And then only because no one had faith in King Wraelian to put down the marauders."

Voster paced by the door and listened, while Tollan kept glancing out the window. The minutes ticked by slowly, marked not by Anise's broken grandfather clock in the corner but instead by the lengthening shadows and darkening alleyways outside.

THE WALK HOME WAS painstaking and long, thanks to how much effort it took to support Keordi's leg. They heard the news get passed from door to door ahead of them, and attributions of motive to the anti-monarchist faction known as "the Crownless" abounded. A few noticed Keordi's injury and asked if they had been there or seen anything strange. There wasn't much to tell, since Niena dared not mention the pointed-eared man. She could be institutionalized for claiming to see something so patently ridiculous.

She considered the encounter again. He had looked vaguely like an elf with his pointed ears, though that could not be true. Niena's childhood book of fairy tales had been written over a hundred years ago, and it was obviously fictional. Elves could not turn up one day from the pages of folklore to vandalize the image of a very real king. Besides, the elves in those stories had been small and spritely, not over six feet tall like the mysterious assailant.

In fact, Niena realized, the elf-man couldn't have sabotaged Wraelian's statue, because there had been guards working on it the whole time. Was the real culprit a rogue soldier with a vendetta against King Pelendion, or the royal family?

Niena determined that she would ask her father about the encounter before doing anything else. It was no use wondering about all of it on her own; for now, it was enough that both of them had escaped mostly unharmed.

She shook the thoughts from her head and shouldered more of Keordi's weight, so they could move faster. Luckily, the way home was almost entirely downhill. But before the streets could change underfoot from paving stone to cobble and finally back into dirt, Niena and Keordi were the only ones walking them.

As they entered the Barren Quarter, the sun was perilously close to the western horizon. The buildings here looked precarious in opposition to the planned grandeur of the Gilded Quarter, like they had been constructed of paper and crushed into spaces too small for them. It made the deserted alleys seem positively eerie in the sun's last light.

Keordi's mother was pacing anxiously on the doorstep of the Harroways' small hovel when the two girls turned the corner at last. From there it was a whirlwind of relieved hugs, questions from Keordi's three younger siblings, and doting on her sprained ankle.

Niena had to politely excuse herself from the conversation and the offer of some hot broth for dinner. *Anise is probably worried to the point of nausea by now, and that's if Papa hasn't organized a search party,* she thought. Having said a quick goodbye, she hurried out the door. She was only minutes away from the smithy, two streets over and one up.

She was so focused on the effort of running in her green dress that she didn't see the torchlight flickering ahead of her at the final intersection.

She ducked back into the previous alley, but it was too late. "Hey! You there!" a gruff voice called.

Niena had already spent most of her energy in her homeward haste and her skirt wasn't doing her any favors either. A skinny man with missing teeth caught up to her and wrenched her arm, bringing her to a painful stop. He was no less strong for being so thin.

"Please," she panted, holding up her other arm in supplication. "I'm just on my way home."

"Oh are ya now, pretty thing?" The thin man leered, looking her up and down. His clothes were riddled with holes, through which she could see his filthy yellowed skin. "By the looks of it, yer pretty far from there. We was heading that way, to give yer bloody king a piece of our minds."

Niena blanched. They thought she was from the Gilded Quarter, despite the state of her wardrobe. How ironic that she hadn't dressed up enough to fit in with the upper class, but now was being mistaken for them anyway. Her heart thudded with fear. Images flashed through her mind, stories of what had happened to other women who had been caught outside during the city's bloodiest nights seven years ago.

"What do we have here?" another man said, catching up to them. He fished around in her pilfered handbag with his thick, grimy fingers, taking out the cloth pouch in which the pocket watch was wrapped.

"No," Niena protested, struggling to reclaim what she had saved months to buy. The man jerked it away from her, prompting a round of raucous laughter. She looked around and saw that she was surrounded by at least eight men of varying colors, heights, and builds, and none of them appeared honorable. "That's for my brother! Take anything else you want, just not that," she pleaded.

"Oh, we'll take whatever we want all right," the first man said through his missing teeth, pinning both of her arms behind her and leaning in close enough for her to smell his rancid breath. She tried to recoil, but couldn't.

Niena heard the telltale ring of swords being drawn from their sheaths. "That's far enough," another voice called from behind her, where she couldn't see. "This is an unlawful assembly. Disperse and give the young lady back her things before we're forced to bring you all in."

One of the men guffawed, taking a swig from a dark bottle. "Two lone city guards want to tell us what to do? The ones who let the rich cut our wages every day, then turn around and rob us again with the king's taxes?" He broke it against the wall, splashing liquid and leaving behind a wicked-looking glass shiv in his hand. "Let's toss 'em."

From there, everything went straight to hell.

The skinny man holding Niena abruptly released his grip and joined the fight, leaving her to fall in the muck covering the ground that reeked of refuse and now spilled alcohol. She rolled away from the brawl out of sheer instinct and tried to stand, but her legs were tangled in her skirt. She glanced up while extricating herself, and wished she hadn't.

The two guards were out of their depth, but held their own thanks to their mail and armor plating. At least, until they became surrounded and the burly man who had stolen Niena's bag had his beefy arm around a guard's neck. The others moved in for the kill.

She watched as the other guard's sword cleaved through the miscreant's arm and sent it flying as the man himself grasped in disbelief at his bloody stump. The severed arm fell with a thump and a twitch onto the street, right where he had dropped the cloth pouch during the opening blows.

Niena suppressed her desire to retch and dove for the pouch. Seizing it and kicking the arm away in disgust, she pushed herself frantically to her feet and searched for a way out of the mess.

The enraged group of rioters surged forward past her, seeking revenge for their fallen comrade. In front of her, the man with the broken bottle struck the sword-wielding guard across the face, who went down like a limp fish. She ran for her life, past the downed guard, and out onto the main thoroughfare.

There was the smithy, just across the intersection. The windows glowed with welcoming firelight. She glanced behind and didn't see anyone in pursuit, but that couldn't last long. Holding tight to the cloth pouch and lifting her skirt, she pumped her legs harder.

She barreled through the gate, upon which hung a makeshift sign that read "closed." The still-cooling forge smelled disconcertingly like the smoke from the aftermath of the market. She vaulted up the steps to the front door, banging desperately on the cracked wood.

"Papa? It's me!" she cried, starting to break down. "Papa!"

The door opened, spilling warm lantern light out onto the stoop. Her father collected her in his brawny arms the moment she crossed the threshold, and she melted into them. They stood like that for a moment before he closed and bolted the door, shutting out the raucous sounds behind her.

Niena felt her father's bushy beard against her head in a gentle kiss, and she instantly felt more at ease. Like when she was a child, his embrace could make anything better. "I feared I'd lost you," he said, his voice strained.

Anise bustled down the stairs from her room in the attic, holding a wet handkerchief and still blowing her nose. "Oh, finally! She's not hurt, is she? What happened to your dress?" she pleaded in a dither.

Niena's arms ached where the men had grabbed her. There would be a bruise, but it could have been a lot worse. "I'm fine," she deflected, still holding tight to her father. She smelled of filth and was covered in grime, but it didn't matter. "A bit shaken up. Keordi made it, too, but she sprained her ankle leaving the square. That's why it took us so long."

Tollan leaned around the corner from the kitchen, munching on a piece of flatbread. "See? I told you she would be okay," he said confidently to Anise, but Niena thought she could hear a slight tremor in his voice. She knew it wouldn't be long until the interrogation started —the only thing more boundless than her younger brother's appetite was his curiosity.

"Were you there? Did you see it?" he asked, right on cue.

Niena tucked the cloth pouch away and out of Tollan's sight, finally letting go of her father. "I'll give you the full story later, but I need to talk to Papa alone before I say more. It's urgent."

Niena's father looked at her hard, trying to discern the reason. He squeezed her shoulder and nodded. "All right, let's go downstairs for a moment. Anise, try to make sure Tollan doesn't eat everything before we sit down to dinner."

Tollan frowned, his mouth full of flatbread.

Niena followed her father to the cellar. The house was cramped, but still a better home than most denizens of the Barren Quarter could claim. In other words, the roof only leaked in a couple of places. Anise had decorated with castoff knickknacks from the richer parts of town, and Niena even had her own small bedroom while her father and brother shared one.

The downside was that sometimes, so many deliveries for the forge would come in at once that her father's inventory of ingots, skins, and other materials overflowed from the storeroom into what seemed like every empty space in the house. That wasn't the case tonight though, and even the cellar looked a little bare as the last shipment still hadn't come from Helsfen Hold in Pamarth.

Niena's father sat her down on a dwindling stack of leathers. "What is it, little blossom?" he asked, warmly but with deep concern. "You were screaming at the door—did you run into trouble out there?"

"I'm not so little anymore, Papa." In fact, she had been an inch or two taller than her father for five years now. "Yes, some, but the city guards came and . . . I'd rather not talk about that."

He pursed his lips, and she knew he wanted to press for details on who needed a thrashing. Instead, he regarded her again with his muddy gray eyebrows raised. "Well, 'big blossom' doesn't have the same ring to it."

Niena laughed gently, thankful for the diversion. He always knew exactly what to say.

"If not that," Voster prompted, "what's the matter?"

"You're going to think I'm insane."

Niena's father got down next to her, and placed a thick hand on her knee, disregarding the gunk the dress had picked up from the alleyway. "Try me."

She started from the beginning, showing him the watch, relaying Aldren's compliments, and describing the explosion as they left the square. When she mentioned the hooded figure with elf-like ears, her father's eyes narrowed and his whole body seemed to tense, but he continued listening.

"Then I helped Keordi home and came straight here as fast as I could," Niena finished briefly. "But she didn't even see the creature, or remember that she had been knocked down. How is that possible?"

Niena's father rose from his seat and paced, his face etched with serious contemplation. After a few moments, he got down in front of her and looked her dead in the eye. "I believe you. You did the right thing to come to me alone with this."

"What does it mean?"

Voster covered his mouth, stroking the edges of his beard. "I have some ideas. Don't tell anyone until I say so. Might be best to stay around the house for a while too—Anise says the weavers' will be closed at least through tomorrow, maybe longer."

Niena sighed and agreed. She didn't have a desire to go outside again anytime soon, regardless.

He pulled her in close for another long hug. "A lot of things are going to change in Celwaith Tor after today, Niena. This city's been waiting for an ill gust of wind to knock it down for far too long. We have to be careful."

Niena clutched him tighter, letting a few tears spill down her cheeks and onto his stained work shirt. "I love you, Papa."

He rubbed his hand across her back, his breaths coming deep and even in contrast to her sobs. "I love you too, little blossom."

THREE

Avoid fighting amongst yourselves, and
work out your disagreements in peace.
For peace cultivates loyalty, and loyalty
is your best protection when true
enemies arise against you.

— *Codes of Entreaty 4.09-10*

THE MAN MARCHED DOWN the dim corridor with a scowl plastered on his face, his velvet cape fluttering behind and decorated boots slapping angrily on the floor with each stride. The evening had been long and stressful already, and they were still no closer to discovering the source of the attack.

His stomach shifted uncomfortably, reminding him that he had not eaten. He did his best to shove the yearning aside, as the duties of his station demanded full attention. Despite the late hour, the city guildmasters had demanded an audience with King Pelendion, and so the attendance of Celwaith Tor's jarl was not only implied but mandated. He worked with the guildmasters daily when matters of law conflicted with business, and his birthright as the king's next oldest brother meant that his role was the unfortunately convenient mediator.

Pelendion needed to have a plan to present to the guildmasters for dealing with this threat, but Anseldr doubted that he would. Such brazen terrorism—in the country's busiest marketplace no less—had to be met with decisive action, or else the meeting could quickly spiral out of hand.

Thankfully, Anseldr had already given it a lot of thought.

An attendant brought him a mildly tarnished hand mirror, and in the muted light, he checked that his dark hair streaked with gray was not too disheveled. He settled the silver circlet a little farther forward on his brow, straightened his cravat, wiped the scowl from his face, and nodded. The door groaned like a dying horse as the attendant opened it.

The herald announced him with all the usual jargon, a needless facade of respect at a time like this. "All rise before Anseldr, middle-born of House Arvad, first of his name, crown prince of all the provinces of Drüstania, and jarl of Celwaith Tor."

The five men and women surrounding the room's central semicircular table pushed back their chairs and got to their feet as ordered.

Anseldr waved them back down in protest. "Gentlemen, ladies, after the events of the day and the lateness of the hour, there is no need to keep up propriety for my sake. Please, sit, and I will do my best to answer what questions I can before His Majesty arrives."

Before Anseldr could take his place in the leftmost chair, the group had already begun clamoring over each other in reckless abandon of etiquette. Anseldr supposed in hindsight he had asked for that, and he stared disappointedly back at them in the dim torchlight. It was difficult to parse the words over the noise.

There was Wendebell Farthing, head mistress of the textiles guild, normally pompous and proud of her trade but now the most panicked and hysterical of the group. The broad-shouldered Gadon Sunder sat next to her, pounding a fist into the table and demanding vengeance on behalf of the metalworkers. Finley Croslowe came next, representing the brewers, butchers, and bakers of Celwaith Tor, and though her voice was not as loud, her eyes pleaded for some silver lining of redemption on this terrible day.

But the man on the opposite end of the table was sullen and silent. Anseldr chose to address him first, if only to avoid bearing the news that he knew precious little more than he did six hours ago.

"Lord Denvald," he projected, the others finally quieting to hear as he addressed his second cousin. "We are . . . dreadfully sorry about the loss of your daughter at the square this afternoon. No one here would have blamed you if you stayed with your wounded wife and grieving son tonight."

Marton Denvald didn't look up, instead continuing to stare into the candle flames clustered in the table's center. His eyes were red and raw, betraying the tears that must have wracked him but now seemed strangely absent. His voice was deep and had the slightest shake to it. "Would staying home raise my Serenia to life again, or rain down justice on her murderers?"

The question was met with silence, the chilling weight of the heavyset man's loss leaving the answer obvious and unsaid. As the Merchant Guildmaster, no storefront could open in Celwaith Tor without his signature on a license approving it, and goods were rarely shipped across Drüstania without the insurance offered by membership in his guild. He was one of the most powerful men with royal blood in the country save for the jarls and the king, and yet so quickly he had been brought to the edge of his sanity.

Denvald absently fished a cigar and matches from inside his coat. "I thought not. As impossible as it would be for my daughter to return, I find it more likely than this chamber having any interest in avenging her without my presence."

Anseldr felt the atmosphere of the room turn immediately from sympathy to self-righteous indignation. He fought to keep a wry smile from breaching his face, noticing that even the guards at the door winced at each other. Anseldr had respected Denvald for a long time, but such a bold accusation further endeared the guildmaster to him.

"You mustn't push us away, Lord Denvald," the final figure at the table said to break the tension. It belonged to a man in plain brown robes that nonetheless were made of fine material. "A solitary tree is soon blown down, but together our branches can withstand this storm."

Denvald slammed a meaty hand down on the table. "Enough with your putrid analogies, Empton!"

The head friar of the Cathedral of the Winds shrunk back, chastened by the harsh indictment. Petras Empton deserved it, Anseldr admitted to himself, for trivializing the man's grief with platitudes. Although not a guildmaster, Empton was allowed to attend as the leader of Celwaith Tor's eminent religious charity, so that those who were not fortunate enough to have a trade protected by a guild were still represented.

Denvald clenched the lit cigar in his teeth and pointed a finger at the clergyman before waving it at the rest of the room. "This was no causeless tragedy, and certainly no cursed *tempest*. It was intentional, and we all know precisely who intended it."

"I would not be so quick to accuse," came the voice of King Pelendion from the arched doorway.

Everyone went down on one knee, Anseldr included, with Denvald perhaps a moment behind the others. The herald, having been as engrossed in the unfolding drama as anyone else, stumbled over his words and merely ended with "His Majesty, Pelendion the Third."

The king mounted the small dais at the focal point of the room, gathered his yellow cape, and sat in the elaborate throne-like chair presiding over the meeting table. In the daytime, Pelendion's golden beard would have shone as light streamed in from the tall window behind him, and one could have seen all four quarters of the city spread out below them. But now the darkness outside was littered with flares of burning buildings, and the shadows turned Pelendion's visage equally grim.

"You may rise," he said. Anseldr returned to his seat, as did the others, all in earnest anticipation of what the king might say.

Pelendion looked at each of them in turn for only a moment before proceeding somberly. "I will not keep you in suspense. There are few leads and fewer suspects. And by fewer, I mean none."

The air felt sucked from the room in disappointment. It relieved Anseldr that his brother was the one to break the news, as he knew the guildmasters would not have taken it so well from him.

Pelendion continued. "The hollow base of my father's monument had been filled to the brim with black powder, though how this was accomplished is a mystery. The bodies of all four city guards assigned to the upkeep of the monument have been identified, so we can be relatively certain it was not an inside job." He paused, his expression turning even more sour. "Unlike some rumors that are beginning to circulate."

The surprise was most audible from Marton Denvald. "That alone proves it!" he shouted around the blooming cherry of his cigar, before realizing he had interrupted the king. "Begging your pardon, my liege."

"What does it prove, Lord Denvald?" Pelendion asked sternly, only entertaining the outburst on account of the man's loss.

"That there are those in this city who desire to upset our traditions and do away with the monarchy entirely," Denvald replied, having removed the cigar from his mouth to gesture with it. The others at the table, particularly Gadon Sunder, seemed to agree. "I speak of the Crownless, sire. Those rebels may have been dormant in the last few years, but now and again I hear word of clandestine meetings in Barren

Quarter pubs. Why else would someone destroy such a public symbol of the throne? Why else would someone spread rumors that the city guard—"

"Enough," Pelendion ordered, and Denvald stopped mid-sentence. "My father was a just king, as you should know well. He is remembered fondly, and his defense of Pamarth from the sea raiders has kept the people loyal to our family. If the Crownless are responsible, they risk more people turning against them than towards them."

Anseldr remained quiet, but allowed his face to show agreement. His mind had already plumbed the depths of that rabbit burrow and concluded the same. Not to say that the saboteurs couldn't be the Crownless or someone in league with them, but they could just as well be another foe more elusive . . . and more malicious.

Guildmistress Farthing piped up from between pursed lips, her tone skeptical. "What of the black powder, Your Majesty? That large an amount should have turned up missing. A shipment from one of the ports?"

Gadon Sunder answered first, his hard-edged voice grating across the room. "Not likely. Black powder is easy enough to make for any tomfool with access to sulfur and saltpeter. Besides, the only place in the world with enough powder to fill that pedestal is this castle's armory."

Anseldr noticed the third option, that the guards themselves had pilfered minuscule amounts of powder and filled the monument's base over months, was left deliberately unsaid. Better not to entertain the same line of thinking that the king had already dismissed once.

Pelendion abandoned the pointless mutterings of the rest of the group and fixed his blue eyes on Anseldr's stony gray ones. "You have been extraordinarily quiet tonight, my brother. Tell us your thoughts."

Anseldr's lip twitched. He had intended on waiting a little longer, watching the metaphorical tulaball get passed back and forth before bringing reason back to the forefront. "Very well. Spoken plainly, I believe what we saw today was an act of war, and we should respond in kind."

All eyes around the table widened at the invocation of the word "war," especially the clergyman's. Friar Empton would no doubt be the only one at the table to push back against Anseldr's proposal, but it seemed like the others paid him no mind. That was fortunate.

"It matters little who is behind this attack at the moment," Anseldr explained now that he had complete attention. "It could be our own people from within, or it could be an unseen enemy from without. But if we follow the pattern of events, we begin to see a larger, more organized threat that will soon require military action."

The others remained silent, puzzled regarding the events to which Anseldr was referring. "Please elaborate," Pelendion prodded.

"Think about it. This act of terrorism was committed in the largest marketplace in the country. It hasn't been the first attack on Drüstania's lines of industry and commerce." Anseldr turned to the master of the metalworkers. "Six months ago, Gadon, what came as a severe and unexpected blow to our economy?"

The man stared back at him for a moment, since the answer should have been obvious to anyone in the room. "Our largest silver mine in Pamarth collapsed after the supports were knocked out. No witnesses, just months of work lost and hundreds of dead workers."

Anseldr nodded, allowing the words to sink in. He gestured to Finley Croslowe next. "Then, almost three months ago, there was that unexplained wildfire near Stilbry?"

The woman frowned at the implication. "The locals believe it to have been caused by lightning, but yes, the fire consumed large parts of the three most productive wheat farms that supply Celwaith Tor."

Anseldr would rather she hadn't tried to undercut his point, but he moved on to the other two guildmasters. "And I need not mention the sudden proliferation of bandits and thieves along the roads in the last year, Lord Denvald. But not even six weeks ago, we heard of five merchant ships that had mysteriously vanished en route to Cape Vrosingr, filled to the brim with cotton and other goods from the southern plantations."

Denvald merely puffed on his dwindling cigar, deferring to Madame Farthing's quick reply. "Goodness, what a disaster. Our weavers may not have enough to meet demand for the winter season," she said nervously. "Not only have we lost the massive worth of the goods themselves, but Lord Denvald told me the other day that the cost of building new ships alone outweighs all other payouts this year combined."

Denvald removed the cigar stump from his cheek and mashed it out a little too forcefully in a ceramic ashtray. Any signs of his earlier grief had receded like the glow of the ash. "The Merchant Guild will be limping at least until next year at minimum. We had few enough vessels as it was, and Cape Vrosingr does not have the infrastructure to build as many as we need right away. We will have to ship over land, which takes longer and is more costly."

The attitude of the room shifted at last, and Anseldr knew that his strategy was paying dividends. "So, you see that our society is under assault from all sides. The Crownless may prove to be responsible for this, but if not, these ongoing incidents still seem designed to inspire fear in our people and distrust in our authority."

Pelendion stroked his beard, weighing the merits of his younger brother's arguments. "You present a compelling case. With all these crises coming upon us in mere months without a drought or famine, the odds do suggest a measure of intent. What would you propose, brother?"

"We must ensure that our people are equipped to defend against more open threats once they arise. For they will arise, and the desecration of our father's monument may only be the beginning." Anseldr had been waiting for this moment to strike, and he seized it. "I submit to Your Majesty that a draft of all men between the ages of fifteen and thirty must be proclaimed. Our existing army will train them in tactics and weaponry for five weeks, and then they may return to their daily lives until they are otherwise needed."

"An at-arms militia, ready at the king's call," Marton Denvald said in an enamored hush as Sunder bounced a fist on the table in agreement. Farthing and Croslowe were harder to read, but they seemed not to be swayed as far as their counterparts.

Friar Empton wasted no time in illuminating the pitfalls of Anseldr's plan, under the guise of concern. "Even if I agreed that the portents speak of war, I do not see the logic. Presuming our own citizens are responsible for this sabotage, we would be training our enemies to fight against us. Also, what makes you think the poor can afford to abandon their livelihoods for weeks on end to train in a field somewhere?"

Anseldr had anticipated exactly those reservations. He continued in the same tone as before, though his eyes lingered on the friar in a veiled glare. "To your first point, we have already established that most of the kingdom reveres the royal family. Compared to one hundred years ago, we are in a time of unparalleled prosperity, and an overwhelming majority of Drüstanians credit that to the kingship of House Arvad. Of course, we run the risk of traitors in the ranks, but we must have more faith that those loyal to the crown will outnumber and outsmart our foes.

"As to the poor, I would urge His Majesty Pelendion to consider opening the royal treasury to pay the conscripts for their time." Anseldr nodded in deference to his brother, who allowed him to continue. "It would only be for a month, and the rate of a soldier is a handsome day's wage. This would also help to alleviate the recent stress on the people, what with the rising prices of bread and clothing."

Silence reigned supreme once Anseldr had finished, and with no further objections, all waited in the flickering light to hear the king's word on the matter. It was a full minute until Pelendion stirred and spoke.

"I do not agree with my brother in all of his assumptions, but he is right in one thing," Pelendion said, slow and deliberate in his tone. He stood from the dais and descended, circling the chair, and pointed out the window at the scattered fires below. "The people are afraid, and we must reassure and unify them. I am wary of what unforeseen consequences might come from cutting our workforce by a third, even temporarily; however, Anseldr's proposal would present the people with direction and the financial means to withstand these uncertain times."

Pelendion returned to the table but did not sit, instead resting a hand on the wood grain surface. "As king, it is my right to make the decision, but I feel that all of you have better knowledge of how this action will affect those in your respective lines of work, so I will put this to a vote among the guildmasters."

Anseldr knew his brother too well. Pelendion had taken the coward's way out, appealing to those more informed on the matter and allowing them to decide. Instead, it was in the interest of averting blame, should the result of the decision be regarded poorly in the end. It was shrewd, Anseldr had to admit, though he preferred to be more direct.

Either way, Anseldr's preferred outcome was assured. The guildmasters—like the citizens under them—demanded a response to the attack, and his brother dared not appear inept. Even should the vote fail, Anseldr gave decent odds that his brother would still proceed without the convenient excuse of guild approval.

"Those in favor of training a militia?" Pelendion put forward.

All except Friar Empton answered in the affirmative, with Lord Denvald the most emphatic by far.

THE BEDROOM SUITE WAS pitch dark when Anseldr finally entered, carrying nothing but a lit candlestick. The heavy curtains were drawn over the window, and he could barely make out the silhouette of the four-poster bed and its singular occupant. He didn't blame his wife, Emeline, for turning in without him; it had already been encroaching on midnight before meeting with the guildmasters.

Anseldr moved closer to check on Emeline in the flickering candle flame, careful not to let the light strike her eyes. Her delicate pale face was so peaceful, framed in contrast by her messy dark hair. He looked with longing at the space next to her, but he still had much to do before morning.

He bent to kiss her softly on the forehead, before crossing the room to the far door where his study was located.

Emeline stirred, clearing her throat as she rolled over. "Anseldr? Is that you?"

He kicked himself for waking her. "Yes, love. Go back to sleep, I'll join you soon."

"What time is it?" she mumbled.

"Quarter to one," Anseldr answered, not sure why he was fibbing about it. "I have to write Pelendion's address for tomorrow, then I can sleep."

"Okay," she said, the word stretched into a yawn. "I miss you."

Anseldr winced, remembering how he had promised last week to make time with her more of a priority. It couldn't be helped now though . . . just like all the other times. "I know you do. I won't be long," he lied again, knowing it would take an hour or more in his tired state to decide on the right words for the address.

He stepped into the study and closed the door behind him, wishing for the tenth time that his and Pelendion's youngest brother was here to write the address instead. Stenden was the jarl of the coastal province of Eastmarsh, home to the port city of Cape Vrosingr. Anseldr despised that he had all the benefits of being a jarl but none of the responsibilities that Pelendion tended to delegate downwards.

Anseldr took the candle from its base and lit three more around his desk, illuminating the surface enough to work. As he retrieved ink, quill, and a roll of parchment, he found himself fascinated by the tapestry hanging on the wall over his desk. He had seen it many times before, of course, but in the light of the candles, it seemed to take on a hypnotic quality.

On a background of yellow and gold, the intricately woven image of the Drüstanian crest came alive. A snow-white dove was locked in battle with a coal-black asp, the talons of the former clenched in a death grip around the snake even as the scaly body looped around the bird's shoulders and prepared to squeeze. Other colors faded in and out through the detailed line-work, opposed in contrast to each other but creating a mesmerizing effect when viewed in its entirety.

As he turned over the tapestry to examine the reverse, what became more fascinating to Anseldr was how each color consisted of only one thread, doubled over on itself and the others to make the cohesive whole. If a strand came loose and pulled out, the woven artwork wouldn't just lose that color from the design—the entire image would come undone.

Someone out there was hunting for Drüstania's loose threads, and Anseldr knew they were starting to tug on a few. He only hoped that this enemy was not so far embedded in their society that, like the dove and the serpent, they risked destroying each other in the process.

But which of them was the dove, and which the serpent?

Anseldr shook the ominous thoughts from his mind and returned to the work at hand. He had convinced the guildmasters of the need for a militia, but that was to be expected. The people would be the hardest to win over to his side.

FOUR

But do not let yourselves be taken to obsession and worry. As even the most steadfast rock is beaten down by the tide, so the fears of many lay claim to the fates of all.

— *Codes of Binding 8.28-29*

TOLLAN BLINKED SEVERAL TIMES and stretched. He thought it odd that the early-morning light had peeked into his window without his father shaking him awake yet. He groggily rubbed the sleep from his eyes and looked over at the other bed, made up and empty. His father must have decided to keep the smithy closed and let Tollan sleep in for once.

The change was welcome, if a little jarring. Tollan's father had a strict work ethic that rarely bent or broke for anyone.

Tollan stood, being careful not to hit his head on the low slanted ceiling of the room he and his father shared. He relieved himself in the chamber pot and pulled a leather jerkin on over his work-stained forge clothes. He hurried down the stairs to quell his complaining stomach.

Niena sat in the kitchen nook, dressed in a pair of work breeches cinched around her waist and a billowy off-white blouse that Anise hadn't wanted. She looked tired, and Tollan wondered if her night terrors had come back. She was rapidly paging through a book that Tollan recognized as one of the collections of children's fables they had read growing up.

"What's that you've got there?" he asked, slipping past her. He grabbed an apple that was on the verge of spoiling, like most of the fruit that ended up this far down the tor.

Niena closed the book before he could see what she was examining. The cover showed no title but had a stamped image of some forest sprite peeking out from behind a knobby tree. "Nothing," she replied evasively. "Couldn't remember what happened in one of the stories is all."

Tollan scoffed. "That's hard to believe." He took out his pocketknife and carved a wedge from the apple before plopping it in his mouth. "I thought you had all those fake stories memorized long ago."

Niena glared at him. Apparently, he had struck a nerve. "Just because they aren't historical doesn't mean they don't have value."

"Sure," Tollan groused. "But why read about made-up things when the real histories are twice as interesting?"

Niena fell silent, crossing to the corner bookshelf and gingerly sliding the book back into its gap. *She's acting a little strange*, he thought, but chalked it up to everything she had been through.

"Where's Dad and Anise?" he asked, changing the subject.

"Anise went to talk to her friends at the Cathedral's charity hospital in the Terraced Quarter, to see if they've heard anything more about yesterday. She said she'd be back soon," Niena said stiffly. "I haven't seen Papa since after dinner last night."

"Huh." Tollan swallowed. Maybe his father hadn't turned in at all. Come to think of it, he usually stirred when his father came to bed, and he didn't recall that happening. "What did you talk to him about last night?"

Niena sighed and looked at him with pleading in her eyes. "He asked me not to tell anyone yet, so please, don't ask. I'm still a bit shaken up, and I've barely slept."

"Okay, okay, sorry." He leaned on the kitchen table and cut another slice off his apple, miffed at the secrets. It had always seemed to him that his father favored Niena, so it wasn't exactly surprising.

A mischievous grin replaced his remorseful pout. "Was it about my birthday in two weeks?"

"Tollan!" Niena exclaimed, exasperated. "If I said it was, would you stop pestering me?"

"Well, that means it's not, so no," Tollan answered. He was messing with her at this point, so he didn't keep up the pressure. "We're, uh, all here for you, you know?" He held a piece of the apple out to her.

"I know," Niena said with a nod, finally smiling and accepting the peace offering. "Even if I want to smack you sometimes."

There was a clatter at the door as the latch turned with a key, and Voster came in. He was disheveled, with bags under his eyes that said he had slept less than Niena, if at all. "Morning," he said as he hung up his satchel, his voice hoarse.

Tollan had rarely seen his father in such a state, and it rattled him. He didn't return the greeting.

"Papa?" Niena asked, putting a hand up to check his temperature. "Have you been out all night?"

"No, but I have been awake," their father said as he slumped into a creaky chair at the dining table, waving Niena's concerns away. "I'm fine. I stepped out before dawn to attend to some business and see how the city looked after the riots last night."

"Business?" Niena inquired. Tollan would have asked if she hadn't.

Voster sighed, hesitating a moment before answering. "There's still no trace of our missing shipment from Pamarth. The gatekeepers haven't checked it in, and the Merchant Guild office could only tell me it had been on the schedule. They don't pay much attention to uninsured deliveries."

"Any chance of thieves out west?" Tollan asked. He recalled something he had overheard while delivering a repaired plowshare the previous week. "There's been word of wagons going missing along the road to Cape Vrosingr lately, but that's in the opposite direction."

"Winds help us if that's the case," Voster said grimly. Losing the cost of all that brass and iron would deal the smithy a serious blow, if not put them out of business entirely. Tollan was tempted to state again how much Merchant Guild membership would benefit them through insurance alone but knew it was a losing battle and held his tongue.

Voster cleared his throat. "Either of you had breakfast? I'm starving."

Tollan finished off the core of his apple and dropped it out the window into the compost bin. "Sort of," he said.

Niena stoked a fire from the coals in the kitchen stove. "Anise is out searching for gossip, but we can whip up some flapjacks."

Voster rested his head on his forearms. "Please do," he mumbled.

Niena was just taking the first cakes from the pan when there came a sharp knock at the front door. Tollan set down the batter and went to answer it, but his father held him back and stood. "No, I'll get it."

Tollan thought the precaution was a little paranoid, but then again, things weren't exactly normal. He couldn't remember a time that his father stayed up all night outside hunting season. There was something sinister going on, and Tollan hated not knowing what it was—hated even more that his sister wouldn't talk about it.

Relief showed on Voster's face as he opened the door. "Am I glad to see you, Kasdan. Have you heard anything?"

Tollan followed Niena from the kitchen to greet their guest. He hadn't seen Keordi's older brother in some time, perhaps once or twice since he was selected to serve in the city guard. Tollan had wanted to ask Kasdan more about his duties, though after what Niena had seen last night, he wasn't sure he envied the position anymore.

Kasdan was dressed in simple chain mail and yellow livery emblazoned with a simplistic Drüstanian serpent and dove, complemented by several pieces of mismatched armor and a satchel slung over his shoulder. The vambraces, open-faced helm, and iron shoulder plates had seen a lot of action from previous owners, and the dark-skinned, clean-shaven man underneath would have seemed almost as haggard were he not so young.

"I'm afraid there's not much in the way of news, sir, especially the good kind," Kasdan replied. He looked past Voster and greeted Niena with a sympathetic smile. "I'm sorry you were there to see . . . well, everything," Kasdan said to her after a nervous pause. "I was only able to check on the family for a few minutes last night, but Keordi told me. We're doing all we can to find the culprits."

Tollan watched his sister nod sadly, looking down and wringing her hands. She seemed uncomfortable, though he didn't understand why. "I'm . . . sure they'll turn up," Niena said. "How is Keordi doing?"

"She's been better, and has unfortunately seen worse," Kasdan said, which Tollan thought was an odd statement. "I can't thank you enough for helping her get home."

"Don't mention it," Niena said, smiling at the return to more normal conversation. "She would have done the same for me."

Voster moved out of the doorway and motioned for Kasdan to join them. "Won't you come in? We were about to have breakfast."

"I'm afraid I can't," Kasdan explained, his voice returning to a less personal tone. "This isn't a social call. I'm here on the king's business and have several more neighborhoods to cover."

Tollan cocked an eyebrow. "What kind of business?" he asked.

Kasdan took a small, decorated scroll from his satchel. "All members of the guard were dispatched to canvas the city this morning. I'm supposed to read this proclamation to every household."

Tollan could only remember one other royal proclamation being issued in his lifetime, after King Wraelian had succumbed to poor health and Pelendion had ascended the throne. That was a simpler matter of informing the public about the king's death, but this seemed different.

"Is Anise home?" Kasdan asked.

"No," Voster answered with a frown. "It's just the three of us here at the moment. We'll fill her in when she gets back."

"What's it say?" Tollan asked impatiently.

Kasdan unfurled the scroll, cleared his throat, and began reading. "*His Majesty Pelendion of House Arvad, sovereign King of Drüstania, commands that all residents of Celwaith Tor present themselves before the palace gates this day to hear his declaration against the acts of violence inflicted upon the city. The address shall commence promptly at two o'clock. In addition, an after-dark curfew shall be instated until further notice to prevent more unrest, beginning tonight at sundown. Anyone found to be in violation of either of these orders shall be jailed or fined.*"

"Understood," Voster said apprehensively. "We'll be there."

"Who do you think did it?" Tollan asked before Kasdan could hurry off to his next stop.

"I don't think anyone knows yet, Tollan." He rolled up the parchment again and returned it to his bag. "But there's a lot of people with grudges in Celwaith Tor, that's certain. Now, I need to be going, or I'll make someone a criminal because I didn't read them this blimey paper."

Kasdan went to thread his way back through the forge to the gate, but he seemed to think better of it and turned back. "Hope to see you all again under better circumstances," he said, his gaze lingering a second longer on Niena than the others.

Voster thanked him again and bid farewell. He closed the door and leaned against it tiredly.

A thousand thoughts whirled inside Tollan's head. He would get to see the king today, in likely the most historic moment of his life. Of course, it was on the heels of one of the country's greatest tragedies, but they would be gathering in the square where it all happened—maybe Tollan would be able to spot some clue that the investigators hadn't.

No. The idea that he would bring these murderers to justice was absurd. After a few weeks, everything would go back to normal as if nothing had happened, and Tollan would be stoking the forge and striking horseshoes like always.

The clatter of chipped ceramic plates brought Tollan back to the present. Niena had poured more batter into the pan and was hurrying to set the table.

"Papa?" she prompted, as he had still not moved from the door.

Their father sat back down and rubbed his bleary eyes again. "I guess we're all going to the palace to hear the king say his piece, but hopefully not until after I get a nap. Now please, pass the flapjacks before I pass out."

NIENA HAD NEVER SEEN so many people in her life. The Cresthavens were jostled at every intersection, and there was no slowing down without the risk of being trampled. Her father and Tollan tried to shield her and Anise from the worst of it, but even so, staying together in the sea of people became more difficult as they neared Wraelian Square. Niena didn't want to go back to the site of yesterday's awful events, but there would be no avoiding it.

Quite a few of the buildings along their path through the Gilded Quarter showed the telltale marks of unrest, from broken windows to fire damage. Heavy rain had fallen in the early morning hours, or else she expected the damage to have been far worse. She wondered with a chill down her spine how many of the faces surrounding her had participated.

Niena spotted the end of the street up ahead, where people filed into the square, and noticed something strange. "Looks like every guard in the city is posted at the entrances," she remarked to Tollan over the cacophonous noise of the crowd.

He didn't hear her at first, and she repeated her observation into his ear. "Oh! Naturally!" he hollered. "I suspect a gathering this size might be very tempting for anyone who planned the first attack!"

Niena hadn't considered that, and now wished she had kept her mouth shut. Tollan had pointed that out so nonchalantly like it was obvious, and that worried her almost as much as the logical conclusion.

She couldn't remember another time that all of Celwaith Tor had been mandated to appear before the king at once. Even under Wraelian, most communication with the people came in the form of short missives posted around the city. Niena wondered why an in-person speech was needed, and if the city's population had grown too big for the square to hold them all.

As it turned out, there was barely enough room, including the balconies mounted on the second and third floors of buildings around the square's perimeter. There was no trace of the sprawling market she remembered, either having been destroyed by the blast or cleared away for thousands of pedestrian feet to stand. Even the center of the square was covered over, with children climbing the remnants of Wraelian's statue to attain a better view of the palace than their parents' shoulders.

To Niena's relief, her family had ended up on the westernmost edge of the square, which meant they had the easiest route home once the king's declaration had ended. Or else they would have the first chance to flee, should something more nefarious happen.

She glanced around, trying to spot the Harroway family in the crowd, but it was hopeless. There was no telling where they might have ended up since Keordi's sprained ankle would have ensured they left earlier than necessary. Niena winced in sympathy, remembering how difficult the walk down the tor had been for her. Uphill would not be easier.

"Can you believe it? Someone stepped on my hem!" Anise cried out, bemoaning her needlessly fancy dress.

"I told you not to wear your best clothes, like you always do," Voster said while trying to rub off the worst of the grime. "This is a proclamation, not a royal ball."

"One never knows where or when they'll meet their future spouse," Anise harrumphed.

Tollan snickered, and for a second, Niena's smile was genuine rather than forced. Anise wanted so badly to marry up and out of the Barren Quarter slum district, she had even purchased that old, non-functioning grandfather clock to make the apartment look a little more prestigious for any potential suitors. The idea of being so choosy at Anise's age was laughable to Niena, but her aunt wasn't about to change her ways now.

Long and low horn blasts issued from the parapets far above the gate on the far side of the square. The crowd became still, waiting for the court herald to announce the king's arrival. It was almost eerie, Niena thought, how one man could command the attention of so many.

The royal titles began to be listed, and she saw two figures emerge from behind the herald. She couldn't make out any details at this distance, but the afternoon sun glinted yellow off the figures' foreheads, betraying their crowns. The queen stood back, while the king stepped up to the lectern which held an amplifying trumpet. When he spoke, his words came loud and clear to the farthest corners of the square.

"Good people of Celwaith Tor!" the king exclaimed with strength and solemnity. "It is with great sadness that I have called you here today, in the wake of a tragedy that has shaken our society to its core. I have not witnessed a worse injury to the innocence and unity of our fair nation since the barbarian incursion seven years ago, after which my father managed to drive them back to the western seas."

Niena hadn't even been a teenager and had understood little of what was going on at the time. She remembered how worried everyone in Celwaith Tor had been, as entire fishing villages along the shores of Pamarth had been razed to the ground with no survivors or witnesses to report on the size of the invading force.

She glanced at Tollan and saw him staring up with rapt attention, drinking in the king's words. He had been fascinated with history as a kid and often imagined taking up arms in the great battles that had united Drüstania into a nation. This was no doubt as close as Tollan might ever come to meeting King Pelendion, but Niena couldn't bring herself to enjoy the historic moment in the same way her brother did.

"It was for my father's memory that I commissioned a statue to adorn this very square in his honor, a monument which violently exploded yesterday afternoon when an unknown assailant set off a cache of black powder they had hidden in the pedestal." The king's voice paused, seeming to Niena that he was reluctant to speak the next words into existence. "The explosion . . . claimed the lives of twenty-two citizens and another thirty-seven were severely wounded by the resulting debris."

That many? Niena thought, bringing her hand to her mouth. An image from yesterday of Aldren the clockmaker with all his spectacled lenses flashed into her mind, and she fought to hold back tears. He did not deserve to end his life that way.

Niena's father reached for her other hand and squeezed it, even as he kept watching the king. She squeezed back, grateful for the support.

"Make no mistake," the king said after a heavy moment of remembrance throughout the square. "Such a grievous attack on the great people of Drüstania is an act of war, and it will not go unpunished."

A rousing cheer went up among the crowd, one in which Niena noticed Tollan joined without reservation, but it died down when Pelendion almost immediately continued speaking. "We have yet no knowledge of who was responsible for sowing terror among us. But let me be clear: the heinous, destructive riots throughout the city last night were just as much a crime and no doubt precisely what the perpetrators hoped to cause. This must end."

An uneasy knot formed in Niena's stomach, and she knew the king's next words would not bear good news.

"This is not something I wished for my people, but we have explored every alternative, and the guildmasters are in total agreement with Prince Anseldr on the necessity of such drastic action." King Pelendion spoke the words with conviction, but all could hear the disappointment in his voice that it had come to this. "To protect Drüstania from further threats and acts of violence, I have ordered the creation of a militia for every city and township."

The crowd whispered under their breaths, and Niena strained to hear. Pelendion continued to speak calmly and clearly. "I have approved the royal treasury to be opened, and every able-bodied man between the ages of fifteen and thirty shall be paid a soldier's wage for five weeks. During that time, they shall be escorted to designated locations for military training."

Niena's father clenched her hand even tighter until it almost hurt. *The king means Tollan,* Niena realized. He was almost sixteen, the prime candidate. She turned to look at her brother and saw his face light up in excitement at the prospect. He had wanted this for a long time, and now their father couldn't tell him no.

The crowd became more agitated than before, but Pelendion raised his hands and tone of voice to retain control. "Calm yourselves, please. I know this will bring undue burden to your homes and businesses, but I promise to mitigate that as best I can. While in training, these men will be fed and housed at my personal expense, and after they take the oath, they shall be allowed to return to their normal lives until we have great need."

Even Niena had to admit, it seemed like a fair proposition, and the other families throughout the square clearly thought the same as the noise died down. A soldier's wage was not insignificant, and free food and lodging for a month on top of that was more than generous. It would only be a month, and after that, Tollan would come home.

But her father's hand had still not released hers.

"Believe me, this is the furthest thing from what I wanted for you all," Pelendion said, bringing his address to a close and at least appearing to deviate from his intended script. His voice came across as less sure, but with more sincerity. "But yesterday made it clear that Drüstania is not prepared for conflict of any scale. We have become complacent in the last seven years; we have loosened our security, and I bear the blame for allowing the heart of our nation to be scourged. I ask your forgiveness and your trust as we forge ahead.

"The soldiers posted on the streets leaving the square will document each recruit and give instructions to board wagons bound for the training camps in the western foothills. Everything you need will be waiting for you there or follow shortly after, and anyone who doesn't meet the requirements may return home. Thank you, and long live Drüstania." The king turned from the podium and retreated into the palace along with the queen and his herald.

A few scattered people took up the patriotic chant and echoed the king's last words, but most were like Niena: unsure of themselves and how to react. She glanced at her father and Anise, who looked just as uneasy. The knot in Niena's stomach had become a pit, with the knowledge that Tollan wouldn't leave with them today. The army would take him away now, without the chance to pack or properly say goodbye.

"Can you believe this?" Tollan said breathlessly, his voice cracking. He seemed to be so caught up in the idea that he didn't notice his family's somber mood. "I get to train in combat!"

Their father finally released Niena's hand to place his own on Tollan's shoulder. "Son, this isn't something to be excited about. It's too dangerous."

Tollan rolled his eyes and shrugged off his father. "More dangerous than all your hunting alone in the northern wilds when you were young? No, Dad, this is important. What's more, I'm going to be making the family some better money for a change."

Voster didn't have a reply, standing there in shock as segments of the crowd filtered past them toward the recruitment lines. He nodded slowly and looked away, and Niena could tell he was hurt. Anise had started to cry and took out a handkerchief, but before anything else could be said, the pressure of the crowd around them became too much. They had to start moving toward the exit or be separated by the flow of people.

Dozens of soldiers blocked the westernmost street, each one taking down information and telling citizens where to wait or to proceed. It was an efficient system, and as the Cresthavens were already so close to the exit they might only have a few moments together.

Anise smothered Tollan in a hug that looked more like he was being eaten by a mountain of ruffled fabric. "You come back to us safe,

Tollan," she said quietly, dabbing at her tears. Niena stood awkwardly by as her brother extricated himself.

Her mind flashed back to all the times they had fought and made up throughout their childhood. They never seemed to see things the same way, and Tollan had always known exactly how to push her buttons. Even that morning, when he had done everything possible to get a rise out of her, she would not have wanted anyone else as her little brother.

"I, um, I've never missed your birthday before," Niena said, not sure how to say goodbye. There was not enough time for what she wished she could say—only one group waited in front of them now.

Tollan's face softened a little. "It's okay, Niena. We'll celebrate when I get back. Then you can show me whatever it is you bought yesterday—"

"You," the closest available guard said, pointing to Tollan. "How old?"

Niena clutched at her brother's arm in desperation, but Tollan stepped up. "Almost sixteen," he said proudly.

The guard grunted, glancing over Voster, Niena, and Anise in turn. He made a singular mark on a board in his hand and waved the three of them through a gap in the ranks to the street beyond. "The rest of you may go."

"Wait," Voster said, placing himself between Tollan and the soldier. "My business could go under without my son's help. I'm a blacksmith— he can help me supply the militia, whatever you need!"

Tollan spoke up before the guard could answer. "Dad, stop. I'm going."

Voster took a deep indecisive breath, his fists opening and closing. His voice came out raspy and strained. "Son, there's a lot that you don't know, that I should have told you . . ."

"Tell me later." Tollan went to join the growing group of recruits waiting to load onto wagons. He locked eyes with Niena one last time and smiled confidently before the guards hurried the family onward to make room for the next group.

She tried to look back, and saw other hurried goodbyes among loved ones; scarcely a household in the city would remain unaffected. Peering around the corner, Niena spotted Tollan's mop of dark wavy hair for only an instant before he was gone.

FIVE

Be shrewd should you choose to keep secrets, and wary of keeping them at all. For there is a time when such things must be revealed, and it may not come when you expect.

— Codes of Entreaty 6.11-12

"NAME?" ASKED A KNIGHT with an oblong nose, wearing bright and clean livery and wielding a quill and paper. He waited several moments for a response, then cursed. "Your last name, boy! We don't have all day."

Tollan blinked and realized the soldier was speaking to him. "Uh, Cresthaven, sir," he said. "Tollan."

The guard flipped through a stack of pages and checked a box, verifying recruits against the city registry. The guard didn't even glance at him again and threw a thumb over his shoulder. "Welsevic here will take you to your wagon. Next!"

The named soldier grabbed Tollan's arm a little too roughly and hurried him toward a staggered row of wagons hitched to horses. They stopped next to one on the end, a rickety thing with wobbly wheels.

"Get on board," Welsevic ordered. "We'll head out once all the wagons are loaded, so sit tight."

Tollan didn't realize how tight his seat would be. He took a spot in the front corner of the teetering contraption. The shabby clothes of most recruits indicated they were from the slums like him, but he could see many from the Sunken Quarter, some from the Terraced, and strikingly few from the Gilded.

After what Tollan guessed was three hours, half the open space had been filled with as many wagons as could be co-opted. The last of the crowd had yet to leave the square and the guards continued loading more men and boys despite the carts being full to the brim. Tollan was now forced to sit with one leg hanging off the edge nearest the front wheel.

If this showed the army's lack of preparation for recruitment, Tollan was starting to wonder how bad the training camps would be. And, he reasoned, he shouldn't have expected any better. This had all happened overnight.

"Don't worry, lad," an older voice said next to him. Tollan looked around and found the voice hadn't come from an occupant but from the driver's seat. The livery on his chest was faded and threadbare, and his face was gaunt with a gray mustache drooping over his mouth, but he had kind eyes.

"I'm not worried," Tollan said as the wagon sagged and creaked with the addition of another man. But, he realized, if someone advised him not to be worried, there was usually a reason. "Should I be?"

The man guffawed, leaning over to spit some foul-smelling tobacco on the cobblestone. "That's the spirit. Naw, it'll be rough goin' at first, but you'll get used to it. The first few days is the worst part."

"How do you know?" Tollan asked before he realized the question was a little rude. "I mean, there weren't this many recruits when you joined."

"Too true, boy, but the training's stayed the same," the man said with a wink. "I swore the oath over thirty years back, then served under Wraelian in the Pamarthen raids as a scout. I'm getting too old to fight now, but they keep me around to drive the horses."

Tollan felt a little better, if only from this man's disarming demeanor. "Thanks, um . . ."

"Name's Marlaph, and you're welcome," the man supplied, waggling his mustache. Before Tollan could give his name, Welsevic returned for the last time and slapped the side of the wagon before mounting the seat beside Marlaph. "Oh, looks like we're shovin' off."

Marlaph snapped the reins, and the horses started off to keep pace with the rest of the formation. Welsevic divided loaves of bread among the recruits, eaten before the cart had even left the square.

The long caravan carrying hundreds upon hundreds turned onto the main road which meandered down to the city gate. It was just after sunset, and the streets were dark and empty save for the patrols enforcing the king's new curfew. It seemed odd and melancholy like there should have been people waving handkerchiefs and shirts in farewell.

Tollan had been outside Celwaith Tor to the surrounding farms more often than many of the city's residents, but as he passed through the large wooden gate and out toward the foothills, it felt unnervingly final. Not that he would never see home again, but rather that when he next entered that gate he would be a different person. His childhood was officially behind him.

He settled in for the long ride and tried to keep from feeling sick on account of the swaying, rattling wagon.

NIENA NEEDED A MOMENT to collect her thoughts, to come to terms with what had happened, but she didn't get one. Her father led the way back toward the Barren Quarter at a brisk pace, attempting to stay ahead of the anxious stream of people that continued to emanate from Wraelian Square.

Anise protested, relieving Niena from the urge to complain. The older woman hiked up her skirts even further, unwilling to let her hem be soiled yet again. "Now, hold on, Voster! I can barely keep up in this dress, let alone breathe. What is your blooming hurry?"

Voster's first reply was to quicken his steps as if Anise's question had been a crack of the whip. "We have little time, and I've wasted far too much of it already," he said gruffly, glancing behind to make sure Niena was still following.

Niena's long legs had no problem keeping up with her father and her work breeches allowed for more freedom than her aunt's getup, but she was still finding herself winded. She had never seen him like this. It was unnerving, especially after their discussion the previous evening.

Voster finally slowed when they reached the Barren Quarter, giving Anise time to catch her breath. "I hope . . . Pelendion knows . . . what he's doing," she wheezed. "We don't even know . . . who's responsible for the attack."

Niena's father didn't comment, whether out of distraction or reluctance, she couldn't tell. "Come, we're almost home," he said.

They arrived to the sight of a notice nailed to the front door, haphazard and off-center. Niena tore it down in anger and disbelief and handed it to her father.

"*By the order of Prince Anseldr, Jarl of Celwaith Tor, this smithy is henceforth in the service of the Drüstanian army,*" he read, his eyebrows knitting into a terrible gray storm cloud. "*The owner of this establishment, one Voster Cresthaven, shall be compensated for his time and provided with directions and materials to produce any and all required goods. Failure to deliver or refusal to comply shall result in arrest and imprisonment pending trial."*

Niena recalled her father's words, so long ago, but only yesterday evening. The world continued to change around them, too much and too quickly.

"They can't do this!" Anise exclaimed, snatching the parchment. She turned it over and over again in her hands as if there was something they had missed. "You worked so hard for this place, Voster. They can't just—!"

"I'm afraid they can, and they have," Voster said, his voice quiet and growling. He unlocked the door and ushered them all through, but took Niena aside before she could retreat to her room. "If you'll excuse us, Anise, I need to speak with Niena privately. There's a lot we need to discuss."

Niena frowned, unsure what he meant. It seemed like their family didn't have much of a choice in what was happening.

"Privately?" Anise repeated, indignant tears welling up in her eyes. "Tollan has been taken away, our home has been made the king's footstool, and you want to shut me out at a time like this?"

Voster sighed in frustration and crossed the room, taking his sister's hands in both of his. "I don't mean to, Anise, believe me. I'm beyond grateful for you, ever since I brought the kids back from the northern wilds. Tollan wouldn't have lasted the week without your help, I know that for certain, and you've made this a home to be proud of."

"Then what could you possibly have to talk to Niena about without me?" Anise asked, not buying the compliment. Niena had to agree, it was strange that her father wanted to exclude Anise from such an important conversation.

"I promise to tell you everything when the time is right," Voster replied heavily, looking her dead in the eyes. "But for now, you have to let me handle things. Trust me." He let go of her hands and gestured for Niena to precede him up to the second floor.

Anise lowered herself into her threadbare patchwork easy chair, taking the opportunity to throw one last stinging comment. "You can't blame me for being short on trust. You disappeared for years and didn't even bother to write our mother about your marriage before she passed."

There was a moment's pause as Voster was hurt by the memory. Niena watched him as he struggled not to say something he might regret, but he turned and followed her up the stairs instead.

"Why can't she be a part of this?" Niena asked in a hushed tone.

"You'll see," he replied and brought her into the bedroom that he and Tollan shared.

Niena sat on her brother's unmade bed, the scent of his sweat lingering in the air. Her heart twisted a little, and she wondered if Tollan had left the city yet. When would she see him again? In a month, when Pelendion had claimed basic training would end, or would Tollan be assigned elsewhere? If another prominent attack came, there would be no telling how the king's intentions might change.

Voster's bed creaked as he sat down opposite her. He stroked his beard, which seemed grayer than the previous day. His knee bounced up and down, fidgeting as he usually did when thinking hard.

"Anything could happen to Tollan out there, Papa," Niena said. "I'm scared for him."

"Tollan is smart," he replied dismissively. "He can take care of himself, and he'll be back home in a month." Niena's father looked at her earnestly, and she could tell he struggled to find the right words. "But you're right to be worried. There are far more dangerous things in the world than guardsman training."

Niena glanced toward the window and saw other families beginning to return from the square. "Like what, Papa?"

Voster paused again, and his knee bounced more furiously. "There is ... something I've never told you or Tollan. You both deserved to know, but I thought—hoped—that it would never be relevant."

Niena wasn't sure what to think. Her father had never given her reason not to trust him.

"What do you remember of your mother, Athria?" he asked unexpectedly and without elaboration.

"Almost nothing," Niena said. It was a sore subject for her, and surely her father knew that. "Tollan and I gave up asking how you met her years ago, and you've never told us much. I think I remember what she looked like, and vaguely helping her around the farmhouse."

"Well, you were only three. Do you remember how she died?"

Niena frowned. Last night the nightmares had returned, no doubt spurred on by the stress and fear of surviving the detonation in the square. "I see the manticore in my dreams on occasion, but all I know for sure is what you told us—she died protecting me and Tollan."

"That much is true," Voster affirmed. "What you haven't known is how she was able to protect you." He leaned under his bed and pulled out a burlap drawstring bag concealing an item about the size of a book.

He unwrapped it, and Niena saw her suspicions were correct. It was an old book, with the small leather cover dyed a faded green that must have once been brilliant and stunning.

"I had this hidden away, buried outside the city," Voster said, turning the book over in his hands. "Didn't think I should risk it falling into the wrong hands when we moved here. I retrieved it early this morning once the riots had died down."

That explained where he had been all night, Niena realized. "What's in it?" she asked cautiously.

"Here. It's yours now." He held it out to her.

Leafing through the thick, almost brittle pages, she saw that they were all handwritten. It had to be several hundred years old at the least, she guessed. The first section was written like a journal, with dated entries referring to a "rift." The last half of the book had many smaller passages from something the writer called "the D'harnin Codes."

"I'm sorry, this doesn't make any sense to me," she said, hoping her father would explain more without needing to read through all of it right that moment. "What's a D'har . . . D'harnin?"

After all the stalling he could have mustered, it seemed like Niena's father came out with the truth in a rush. "The D'harnir—or as we might better know them, elves—are creatures that lived among us once, long ago. They used magic for healing, protection, and even agriculture."

"Elves?" Niena repeated. So, she hadn't been crazy. Her mind flitted to the treasury of fables she had paged through that morning, looking for any scrap of information that might explain what she had seen. Tollan had called them fake stories. "Like in the stories we used to read? They're real?"

Voster nodded solemnly. "And as you've guessed, the cloaked saboteur you saw yesterday was one of them."

Niena took a deep breath, trying to reconcile it all in her thoughts. "How did you get this? And where have the elves been for centuries?"

Voster stood and began pacing, as if he couldn't sit still and remember at the same time. "It's a long story, most of which you can read for yourself. The gist of it is that men drove the elves out of civilization into the wilds, where they hid and made new lives for themselves. I found the book in a ruined tower up near Ensdale while hunting one summer, the same one your mother and I eventually rebuilt. The descriptions of geography led me further north into the wastes."

Niena listened carefully, the missing pieces of her father's past finally becoming clear. It was almost unbelievable—except that she had seen an elf with her own eyes. "What happened then?"

"I found them," he said, sitting back down next to her. He had stopped fidgeting. "I found one of the D'harnin enclaves, called Por'monir. The people there were . . . not thrilled with me, as you might expect, and even considered killing me to prevent being discovered. But that's when your mother intervened."

"She was one of—but that makes no sense. That would mean that Tollan and I are . . ." Niena trailed off, stunned into disbelieving silence. It was simply impossible.

"Half-elven," he confirmed. Calmly, gently, Niena's father reached out and took each of her hands in his. He guided one upward to her ear and placed the other next to his own head. "Feel them for yourself."

Niena didn't know what she was looking for until she felt the difference. The upper edge of her father's ear was curved and soft save for the cartilage under the skin. Hers was subtly different in shape and had an almost unnoticeable ridge of rougher scar tissue right along the top.

She gasped and jerked her hands away. She remembered that her brother, too, had a jagged scar in the same place. Her father had always claimed that Tollan fell down a few stairs when first learning to walk, tearing his ear on an upturned nail. But that had been a lie.

Niena stared at her father, her eyes starting to sting with hot tears of betrayal. She couldn't bring herself to say anything, didn't know what to say.

"Your mother believed we had to hide it from everyone, even you," Voster admitted, breaking the silence. "I didn't agree, but she felt it would have put you in danger. We never had the chance to discuss when you should know the truth, so I buried it along with the book. I hope you can forgive me, little blossom."

Niena curtailed the conversation for a moment, lying back on the bed to think and process. She wiped her wet eyes and took a deep breath while holding a hand to her forehead. This had to be some sort of fairy tale fever dream. But it was real, she was here, and the pages of legend now threatened her family's entire way of life.

"What happened next?" she asked past the lump in her throat.

Her father looked away. "When?"

"When you met Mama."

"She was the daughter of the enclave's arbiter, or judge, so she decided to negotiate on my behalf. I had helped save the life of one of their scouts, and his family decided to vouch for me as well, even adopting me as their own. I stayed there for several months, and fell in love with your mother." Voster leaned on his knees with his hands entwined under his nose, looking hard at the far wall but seeing beyond it to his distant past. Niena wondered when he had last thought about it. "When Athria's father found out she had promised herself to me, he was furious. He . . . asked us to leave, and we weren't long on our own until you came along.

"Your mother abandoned her heritage and swore never to use her magic again—she broke that promise to protect you and your unborn brother," Voster finished. He didn't move, a few tears of his own sliding down to catch in his beard. "Somehow she convinced the manticore to leave our farm, but not before it had mortally wounded her."

Niena now knew for certain that this was the truth. Her father seldom cried, not if he could help it. "Why now?" she demanded. "If it was so important that Tollan and I stay ignorant of this, of Mama, why tell me now?" She regretted how confrontational those words sounded as they left her mouth, but she needed to know.

Voster swallowed, his throat tight around the words. "I trusted your mother's instincts. I might never have considered it if you hadn't seen that D'harn yesterday, and if Tollan hadn't been taken from us. It's clear that, whatever peaceful beliefs the D'harnir once had, at least a few are lashing out. And your brother is in danger because of it."

"Why?"

"Why do you think?" her father said, clenching his fists. "You saw what Keordi could not. What does that tell you?"

Niena tried to connect the pieces. The elf in the alleyway had used magic to cloud Keordi's perception of him. Abilities like that could certainly have aided an entire people to remain hidden for hundreds of years. But whatever the spell had done to Keordi had not affected Niena, which meant elven blood made someone immune, or perhaps harder to enchant.

She sat up too quickly and almost whacked her head on the slanted ceiling. "Tollan would be able to see them, too."

Voster nodded gravely. "That, and there are other differences between human and elven physiology. If this comes to war, and Pelendion's men find out the truth, Tollan could be interrogated or even hanged as a traitor. And if the D'harnir discover he can see them, he would be a target."

Niena had thought her family's situation was dire before, but it seemed to be getting worse by the minute. "What can we do?"

"About Tollan?" Voster stood and resumed pacing, arms crossed over his chest. "Nothing directly, at least until he returns from training. We'll have to hope he doesn't call any attention to himself by then." He raised a finger, underscoring what he was about to say. "However, I may be able to influence things less directly."

It took a moment for Niena to realize what her father was suggesting. "You're not serious."

"I may be the only man alive who knows the D'harnir still exist, let alone how to find them. If there's a way I can prevent a war where my son would be fighting on the front lines . . ."

Niena understood the logic, but dividing their family even further at such a crucial time was not wise. "You don't even know if this enclave is responsible for the attack."

"If not, they may know who is. It's all I have to go on." Niena's father paused, fixing her with his tired, bloodshot gaze. "I want you to come north with me."

Niena stared back in bewilderment. "What?"

"We're losing the smithy regardless. Our finances can't adjust to the jarl's demands for work. And given the current state of Celwaith Tor, I think you might be safer out in the wilds with me."

"What about Anise? You would just leave your sister?"

Voster rubbed his forehead, letting out a pained sigh. "She is going to hate me, but that seems like nothing new. It's not the first time she's had to fend for herself. She has the Harroways and her charity friends to lean on. I'll leave her a note explaining as much as I'm comfortable to say, along with the trancheon's share of our savings."

Niena frowned, trying to think of some way to keep the family together. But there was no best option, beyond what could have been if her father had only told them sooner.

"Do you really think Anise would last out there?" Voster asked sadly. "The woman who can't stand her hem getting stepped on?"

"You're right," Niena acknowledged, realizing that he had already considered every concern. She never had a reason not to trust him until now, and she knew he only wanted the best for her and Tollan. If anything, she should be angry just as much at her mother, but that would tarnish the few memories of her that she had left.

Niena stood and crossed the room to her father's side, stopping short of an embrace. "When do we leave?"

Niena's father leaned up to kiss her on the temple, his beard and warm breath tickling as he smiled in relief. "Pack well, little blossom, and pack as warm as you can," he said. "Turn in early. We leave before dawn despite Pelendion's curfew."

Voster left to begin preparations. Niena watched her father go and lingered a moment longer in the bedroom. She decided to make Tollan's bed to internally remind herself that he would be back.

He was a smart kid who worked hard and asked a ton of questions. If Kasdan did well as a city guard, surely Tollan would thrive in such a setting. There was nothing to worry about, she told herself—until the reality of what her father had said came crashing back in.

As she tucked the last blanket corner in at the foot of the bed, Niena remembered the pocket watch she had bought for Tollan, and a wave of sadness overtook her. This would be his first birthday that she had ever missed, and she wouldn't be there to celebrate with him. She almost broke down at the foot of the bed, frustrated at how her brother had been taken from them and fearful about what lay ahead for her family.

But then, like a cool refreshing breeze after a rain, an idea fluttered into her mind, and she held tight to it. Niena might not be able to celebrate Tollan's birthday with him, but her present might.

She hurriedly gathered some paper and an ink quill from her father's end table and returned to her room to write two notes—one for her brother and another for Keordi.

SIX

As a seed must fall from the tree, so must children be parted from their families to grow anew. But sorrow awaits the branch broken before the time is ripe.

— Codes of Binding 1.32-33

NIENA AWOKE IN A cold sweat. The horrific images conjured by her subconscious faded away until she could relax back into her comfortingly real pillow. She regulated her breathing but dared not close her eyes yet.

She had seen the oncoming manticore for the second time in two nights, its spiked tail reared back in midair to strike. The encounter had felt so real, more vivid than ever tonight. The predator's glowing yellow eyes were seared into her soul, and the imagined wind of its huge leathery wings still caused the hair on her neck to stand up.

A shiver traveled down her spine as the creature's inhuman roar echoed in her mind. She knew now that she had heard that horrible sound before, and that time it had been real. But in her dreams, her mother was never there to save her.

A second soft knock came at the door, and Niena realized the first must have been what woke her. "Yes?" she whispered.

Her father's hushed voice filtered through the door. "It's time to go."

It was still dark when they slipped out into the alley behind the forge, the latch closing behind them with a muted *clink*. The haphazard knapsack constructed of blankets and leather straps sat awkwardly against Niena's back, but it was the best that they could have made on short notice.

All was quiet, and the streets seemed fortunately clear of patrols. A chill had come over the city in the wee hours of the night, and Niena shivered. She reminded herself they would soon be overly warm from traveling all day on foot. They crossed the street and turned to follow the next until they reached the Harroway residence, making sure to stop and listen at each intersection before continuing.

On the doorstep, Niena stooped to leave a small brown parcel tied with twine and a folded slip of paper tucked in the top which read: "Keordi—read first." With her most important errand completed, Niena took a deep breath and motioned to her father that they should get going.

A noise came from above them, and Niena winced.

"Psst," a familiar voice whispered through the now-open window on the hovel's second floor. "Hey."

Niena glanced around and checked that the coast was clear, then called quietly up to Keordi. "What are you doing up at this hour?"

Keordi's round face peeked out of the darkness, her eyes glittering like diamonds among clay. "I could ask both of you the same thing what with the curfew. My ankle is keeping me awake, so I have it elevated."

Voster gestured to the street corner and whispered. "I'll keep a lookout. Make it quick."

Niena nodded and turned back to her friend. "I'm sorry. I don't have time to explain. Papa and I are leaving the city."

"Now?" Keordi squeaked, trying to keep her voice down. "For good?"

"I hope not," Niena said. "We should be back in about a month. I left a package and a note on your doorstep that says more." That was almost a lie—the note said precious little in case it fell into the wrong hands. She presumed the note her father had left for Anise was equally cryptic.

Keordi leaned out the window on her elbows to look down at the stoop, her curly hair wild and unkempt. "Okay," she said. "Well, whatever it is you're doing, I hope it's worth the risk."

"Me too," Niena said. "Keordi, I—"

"We have to move, now," Voster broke in, waving urgently as he approached. "A patrol is coming up from Barstow Street."

Niena looked back up at the window, to find it shut tight. "Feel better soon, Keordi," she whispered.

Her father led them on a route that would circumvent the incoming patrol and place them near the city gates. They stuck to back alleys and side streets, and the reek of dumped chamber-pot contents followed them everywhere, especially once they crossed into the Sunken Quarter. As the name implied, it was the lowest point of Celwaith Tor, the furthest from the peak of the stony bluff where Pelendion's castle rested. The residents here would have been as poor as those in the Barren Quarter, except that their proximity to the main gate meant they got more business from new visitors to the city.

A pair of city guards clanked along the main avenue with their polearms and lanterns. Niena flattened herself against the alley wall. Her father crept past and watched the guards to see which way they went.

The guards continued toward the main gate and did not turn aside into one of the side streets. Voster grunted in frustration.

Niena moved up next to him. That was a second close call with the law, and she didn't want to keep pushing their luck. "It's okay. It will take a little longer to go around. A bigger question is, how do we get through the gate without being seen?"

Voster saw an opportunity and quickly ducked out of cover to an adjacent alleyway that still angled in the general direction of the gate. Niena followed close behind, and when they arrived at their new hiding place her father outlined the plan. "The outer walls aren't as impregnable as the keep. They aren't meant to stop a siege, as much as provide basic security. The gatehouse garrison has an outer door, so we need to wait for the right moment to slip through."

Niena frowned. "The garrison? Where the watchmen sleep?"

Her father shrugged. "Best I've got, unless you want to crawl through the drainage ditch."

She scrunched up her nose at the thought of it. If the stench was bad now, she didn't want to wear it for the next few days. But there might not be an alternative way out of the city. "Not particularly."

The last alley spilled out next to the wall, which was tall enough that climbing would be hazardous but not as tall as the nearest buildings. They kept to the shadows as the barred gate loomed ahead. It was a large wooden thing, wide enough to allow passage of multiple two-horse carriages.

To Niena's surprise, it was deserted. Promising, but she didn't trust it one bit.

Sure enough, right on cue, the two soldiers they had passed earlier strolled up from the opposite direction and paused for a moment at the gatehouse. They seemed to be chatting, waiting on their shift replacements to retire for an hour's rest before sunup.

"Move already," Voster muttered, looking nervously at the sky. Telltale signs of the approaching sun gathered in the east, and they would be exposed if it got much brighter.

A deep-sounding knock came at the gate, followed by an unintelligible call from the other side. The two guards looked at each other, then trudged up the creaky wooden stairs leading above the gatehouse where they could address the newcomer.

Niena and her father darted forward to take cover under the stairs. If the gate opened, it would be a good position to slip through unseen. If they could pull it off, that would be much less risky than sneaking through the guardhouse.

"Who goes there?" one of the guards called. "What business have you in Celwaith Tor?"

"Freight delivery for one Voster Cresthaven in the Barren Quarter," a gravelly voice yelled back. "Metal ingots and other supplies."

Niena's eyes widened at her father, surprised by the coincidence. "I guess we don't have to worry about that missing shipment anymore," she whispered lightheartedly.

Voster harrumphed, and the irony was not lost on him. "Eight days late. Ridiculous."

"We're under curfew by order of the king," the second guard said. "You'll have to come back by daylight."

The cart driver protested. "I don't know anything about no curfew. It's almost dawn anyway and this delivery was overdue last week! Open the gate, or I'll wait right here until you do!"

There was silence as the guards conferred among themselves. "Stand by. We just have to *inspect* your cargo, see if there's anything of quality," the first guard confirmed finally, implying by his inflection that they would be helping themselves to the merchandise as well.

Niena scowled. "Why, those conniving, two-faced, greedy . . ."

Her father shushed her. "It doesn't matter now. Time to go."

They sprinted from the stairs to the other side of the gate and listened as the chains ground together. The metal bar lifted, and the gate groaned inwards, providing them cover from the guards' lines of sight.

Two horses led the cart through, and as soon as the back of it cleared the range of the gate, it began to close.

"Now," Voster said, and Niena again followed close behind him. They stooped to stay hidden behind the cart and slipped around the closing gate at the last second.

Niena's father gestured to stay put for a moment, and when they heard the two guards speaking with the cart driver again, they knew it was safe to leg it down the road toward the tree line.

Niena came to a halt once they reached the cover of foliage and panted, leaning on her knees. "That went easier than I expected," she said between breaths. "What are the odds?"

Her father agreed. "We got extremely lucky. Let's take this as a good omen, little blossom. We have a long road north."

Niena cast one last look back at the castled peak of Celwaith Tor, the silhouette becoming visible against a brightening sky. Then she turned and followed her father, each pace further away from her home and all she had ever known.

THE WAGON TRAIN TRAVELED for two whole days, resting briefly at water crossings to slake the thirst of horses and occupants alike. One of the wheels had caved in on itself the second day, and a few hours went to waste fixing it. This meant that Tollan's crew was the last in the train to arrive at the campsite rather than among the first. Tollan grumbled some choice words that would have earned him a belt lash at home as they passed the drivers and empty carts already beginning the return journey.

Tollan's right leg was cramping fiercely by the time they pulled in just after sundown. *I almost would have rather walked from Celwaith Tor*, he grumbled to himself bitterly. *It might have even been faster.*

Barely enough light was left in the sky to see the pitiful complex of mud and tents nestled in the foothills of the Drüstalda mountains. Although the view was more than incredible, Tollan's heart sunk into his toes when he noticed many recruits lying in the dirt around the tents.

There was no room left inside, and it looked like a heavy storm was beginning to blow in from the south.

They were all directed to the mess tent for their rations, which proved to be a bowl of watery stew and two small crusts of bread. Normally Tollan might have groused about it, but after how little they had eaten since the king's speech more than two days prior, as far as he was concerned it was delicious. Afterward came the arduous task of staking out what little comfort and shelter they could find, even as the first drops of rain began to fall.

Tollan wandered to the edge of the camp. There he found an open patch of ground under an evergreen tree that might keep the rain away if the wind was right. He fell to the ground and lay there, happy just to be able to stretch his muscles out. He was beyond exhausted but too cold to sleep.

"It appears great minds think alike," a slightly pitchy voice said nearby.

Tollan opened his eyes and turned to see another recruit in the darkness around the side of the tree. He was leaning against the scrawny trunk and had gathered a bunch of the fallen dry needles into a pile. The boy's limbs were lanky, and his voice sounded young, maybe even younger than Tollan.

"Great minds?" Tollan repeated.

The shadowy figure waved back toward the tents while still concentrating on his pile of kindling. "None of them thought to go looking for their own shelter, they're huddled out in the rain hoping for their turn to go in next to the fire." The boy sighed in frustration and beckoned Tollan closer. "You wouldn't happen to have a knife on you?"

Tollan made his way over and noticed that the boy was dressed in far better clothes, but they had been roughed up with rips, tears, mud, and worse. "What happened to you? Are you all right?"

"Huh?" The kid fixed Tollan with a puzzled look, then looked down at himself. "Oh, that. I did it to myself—a lot of Barreners have it out for people like me. Thought maybe some of them would pass me over if it looked like I had already been beaten up."

"People like you?" Tollan asked, though he had a feeling he knew.

"My family's from the Gilded Quarter," the boy explained as he desperately scraped two flints together against the dry needles. "That alone is enough to make me a target. Those with little always begrudge those who have much." In his haste, he nicked his left hand with the rock in his right and quickly held it to his mouth. "You're sure you don't have a knife?"

Tollan was wary of the boy and unsure how much he should reveal about himself, but he fished out the pocketknife his father had given him on his fifth birthday. "Hand me the flint."

The boy tossed him the rock, and Tollan began striking it against the blade. A few small sparks emerged and quickly became a lick of flame along the edge of the dead needles. With a little coaxing, the pile had lit in earnest and gave off decent heat despite the crackle and pop of the scattered raindrops filtering through the branches overhead.

"Thanks," the boy said, piling on other twigs and needles to keep it going. The new lick of flame revealed his freckled face and equally fiery red hair. "I'm Thaxon Denvald. And you are?"

"Tollan Cresthaven," he answered. He decided not to dodge the inevitable. "I'm, uh, from the Barren Quarter."

"Oh." Thaxon appeared chastened, but not with remorse. It seemed like he wished he hadn't been so forthright with his opinions, not that he was ashamed of them. "Look, I know not all of you are like that, but face it—the only people who hate the monarchy enough to attack the square are not those who have money."

It made a measure of sense, Tollan had to admit to himself. The Crownless did have a reputation from years past, and it was true that the group was made up of the lower class. But Tollan resented the implication that anyone in his circle could stoop that low. "Why are you even out here, since you think so little of the rest of us? I heard a rumor that you rich folk could buy your way out of the militia if you wanted."

Thaxon stood up with a scowl, almost hitting his head on the lower branches, his hands balled into fists. "My sister died in that explosion! And my mother is laid up in bed right now because a piece of that statue took her leg off at the knee." He was panting now, practically sobbing as he poked an accusing finger at Tollan's chest. "If putting up with a little hardship gets me any closer to finding which of you is responsible, I'll do it gladly!"

Tollan realized with a start that he was holding his knife at the ready. He lowered it carefully before putting it back in his pocket. He let the confrontation cool for a few seconds before speaking more calmly. "My . . . sister was there, too. I could have lost her."

The heated glare in Thaxon's eyes dimmed a little. "But you didn't," he pointed out jealously.

"No, I didn't," Tollan confirmed, sitting and adding a few larger sticks to the fire. He leaned on his knees, staring at the ground. "But my mother died when I was born. I never even got to meet her." He almost mentioned his strained relationship with his father, but wondered why on earth he was sharing so many details with a stranger.

The fire sizzled and popped as the rain fell harder, and the wind picked up. Thaxon stacked a few stones to shield the blaze, but there wasn't much that could be done about it. "I'm sorry," he said. "I shouldn't have put all of that on you."

Tollan met the other boy's gaze and nodded. "It's fine. Your sister didn't deserve what happened to her." He hadn't truly understood what the attack on the square had meant; it had shattered the tentative respect that had once existed between the upper and lower classes. The rich blamed the poor, and that blame would only stoke animosity further. "For the record, I think Pelendion is a great king, and I want whoever destroyed that statue brought to justice. We aren't enemies."

Thaxon sat cross-legged next to him and held out a hand. "In that case, how about friends? Great minds should stand together."

Tollan looked at the other boy's hand for a moment. When he reached for it, the grip surprised him by rivaling his own. It was a firm shake, for a pampered rich kid. "I suppose I could use one of those."

The wind picked up at the same time as a fresh downpour, blowing a deluge of droplets down through the tree and onto their already-sputtering fire. Thaxon tried desperately to revive it, but it was no use.

They lay back around the trunk of the tree and shivered, trying to find the most comfortable position in the cold and wet. Still, Tollan thought as he finally drifted off from exhaustion, it didn't seem as cold as if he had been alone.

INTERLUDE I

Splintering Relations
c. 150 – 32 years before the Rift

OVER THE YEARS, THE reasons why the D'salnir and D'harnir became at odds with each other have become hopelessly obscured by petty grudges and hearsay. Many allege the division could have been avoided if only a societal wrong against them had been righted, or if the opposing group had done their fair share. I suppose to blame them for refusing to look deeper would be hypocritical; after all, each of us wants to be in the right. Some of us are just more dogmatic about it.

Others, long since deemed to be crackpots and contrarians, hold that there were those who stood to gain power and wealth from pitting the two groups against each other . . . until the tensions erupted into riots, riots into martial law, and martial law into open war. I am sorely tempted to dismiss this theory out of hand based on the outcome, though I know too well that ambition would drive some men to burn down their own homes if they thought they might gain from it.

Then there are rare souls who believe that perhaps looking for someone to blame for our problems is precisely what splintered our healthy culture. I was still young when those splinters formed, so much of my understanding of the situation comes from my father, Ervan, who remained head liaison to the

D'harnin clans even after war was declared. No one else was better positioned to see how the schism happened, but seeing a cause and having enough influence to stop the effect are a world apart from each other.

According to my father, the troubles started about a century before his time, after men had managed to reclaim most of the wilderness surrounding the southern cities and trade routes. This ensured that both men and elves could thrive without constant threat of attack from predators and wild folk. Having protected their settlements and farms, people were now free to turn their minds to other pursuits. There was a period of great prosperity for both races, where food was plentiful, and science and philosophy boomed.

However, men soon realized through their technological advancements and scientific discoveries that the effects of many of the elves' beneficial abilities could be replicated to varying degrees. As a result, the elves felt that their way of life was being demeaned, and their once-valuable contributions to a balanced society were being made obsolete.

The D'harnir spent long months with their representative consuls trying to craft legislation that would protect their heritage and influence. Two years before my father took office as ambassador to the D'harnir, they succeeded. But many men lost their jobs when those laws took effect, resulting in an effective grudge that spread through the people like wildfire. Men came to see the elves as a weight on society rather than a boon, and the wedge between the cultures was driven deeper.

It was only a matter of time until a spark caught in such a potent pile of kindling. And the fire would consume us all.

— Haron Geled, Last Scribe of the Union
24th of Hollyn, in the 48th year after the Rift

SEVEN

A STIFF BREEZE BLEW across the wet morning ground, and Tollan woke to an uncontrollable shiver traveling the length of his spine. He sat up and whacked his head on a low-hanging pine branch, reminding him with annoyance of his bedroom's low ceiling at home. He groaned and lay back down, and realized he felt even more clammy and tired than when he had fallen asleep the previous night.

He looked around and saw the first rays of sunlight beginning to dispel the mist from the abundance of last night's rain. The boy he had tentatively befriended last night was nowhere to be seen, so he crawled out from under the tree and went to relieve himself.

All the rainwater had turned a nearby creek into a rushing brook, threatening to overflow its banks as it tumbled down the foothills. If Tollan recalled his geography, the water would eventually join the

Barandine River on its way south to the sea, but all he cared about now was his parched throat.

As he finished drinking from his cupped hands, a long and low horn blast sounded from the camp, calling everyone to assemble on the large field next to the insufficient housing tents. A few people stirred and followed the directions, but many had not yet awakened. *Hopefully, there will be more food for early risers*, Tollan thought as he dried his lips on his sleeve and started in that direction.

"Hey! Tollan!" the familiar pitchy voice from the previous night called out as he neared the field.

He scanned the steadily growing crowd of young men and saw the red-haired boy holding his hand up in greeting toward the front. Tollan had thought it was just the firelight last night, but the bright coppery color on Thaxon's head stood out like a vein of iron on a mountainside.

Tollan wove his way through several clusters of recruits and caught up with Thaxon close to a raised wooden structure on the field's edge. It was flanked on both sides by large poles from which hung the yellow Drüstanian battle standard featuring the snake and dove. It looked to Tollan like a rudimentary speaking podium, in which case the two of them would have front-row seats.

"Wondered where you had gotten to," he remarked, clasping Thaxon's outstretched hand.

"Woke up before first light. Too cold to sleep," Thaxon explained, his eyes bright and alert in spite of it. "Asked a corporal some questions while warming up, though."

He started chatting up one of the officers? Tollan thought. Either having a rich family meant better connections, or Thaxon was so personable that he could start a conversation with anyone. "What did he tell you was happening this morning?" Tollan inquired, desperate for more information.

"Orientation," Thaxon said with an infectious smile across his freckled face. "We're going to be divided up into columns for the duration of training. You should be in mine."

Tollan agreed, not willing to lose his new ally so quickly. "Of course. Do you know if there's going to be anything to eat? I'm starving."

Thaxon looked sheepish. "Oh, right. Sorry," he said, and fished out a paper bag from inside his ripped and muddy doublet. "I brought these from home," he said under his breath and stepped closer to hand it off so no one else would see. "Salted pork jerky."

Instantly Tollan's mouth watered, and he surreptitiously stuffed a few pieces in his mouth. "Thanks," he said around the deliciously seasoned mouthful and handed the bag back to its owner.

"Don't mention it. To anyone," Thaxon clarified as he hid the stash again. "I heard the extra tent materials and food rations might not arrive for another several days, perhaps a week."

"A week?" Tollan repeated, recalling his father's delayed supplies. He wondered what was going on. "I know it's important to arm the militia as soon as possible, but I was hoping they would handle the logistics a little better."

"I think there would have been problems even with the best planning," Thaxon said, looking around to estimate the number of people entering the field behind them. "Near as I can tell, there are about two thousand here from Celwaith Tor, and maybe a few hundred more from the outlying villages. Presuming there are similar camps in the other provinces, the supply chain just wasn't up to the sudden strain."

Tollan blinked, realizing the scope of what the whole nation of Drüstania was having to endure. "How would you know all that?"

Thaxon shrugged. "My father is the Merchant Guildmaster. It's his job to know the ins and outs of shipping throughout Drüstania, so he talks about this kind of thing all the time over dinner."

Tollan fought to keep his face stoic. He supposed Thaxon's surname had been familiar during their introduction last night, but his tired mind hadn't made the connection to *the* Lord Denvald. "Makes sense," he said with an understated nod. He couldn't believe his luck to have befriended someone so influential and knowledgeable.

Tollan raised himself up on his toes and looked around to see that the field was beginning to look crowded, but still minuscule compared with the gathering at Wraelian Square. "You really think there's two thousand here?"

"That's my guess. A little less than half of Celwaith Tor's population are men, and at most a quarter of that would be in the right age and health to be eligible for the draft."

The horn sounded again, close enough that Tollan had to cover his ears. The two boys turned to watch an imposing figure in fully decorated yellow livery climb the stairs and step forward on the podium. The recruits fell silent as they saw the elder soldier, save for two or three hooligans that booed and were quickly silenced. Some were not as excited as Tollan to be here.

The man did not immediately begin speaking but rather turned slowly and lingered one by one on those present. His short hair had completely turned gray, suggesting that he was perhaps a few years older than Tollan's father. His trimmed beard hid the lower wrinkles on his face, but his deep-set eyes were accented by harsh crow's feet and an even harsher scar along his left temple.

"Militia recruits: welcome to your crucible," the man spoke into an amplifying trumpet. His clipped, gravelly voice echoed across the field, bounced back by the hills on each side. "A moment which will define you for the rest of your lives."

Tollan was well familiar with the concept of a crucible in the context of smithing, and the idea of being melted down and purified did not much appeal to him. *But,* he thought with an inward smile, *whatever came out of the process was better and stronger.* He would be part of the history he had only read about for so long.

"It is here, on this field and in these hills, that boys will become men, and those who think they are already men will be proven wrong." The man paced the length of the podium, his boots thumping on the wood with each slow, heavy step. "I am Sergeant Major Halvandr Senn, and from this moment until I clear you for return to your homes, I am both your whip and your reward.

"His Majesty King Pelendion has ordered that we take no longer than five weeks to shape you into models of Drüstanian honor and strength. He expects a militia equipped for any eventuality against an unknown enemy, so: gird yourselves for the most grueling month of your heretofore insignificant lives."

More jeers and disrespectful noise rippled through the crowd, spurred by the officer's rude comment. Senn stopped pacing when he had returned to the center of the podium and clacked his boots together to stand at attention. "In my days serving His Majesty's father Wraelian, I spent many shivering nights out in the elements of Pamarth, and we all counted it a privilege to be there. If we did not, there was always the alternative of a swift court-martial and hanging, so I trust that all of you slept well last night."

The recruits understood the warning, and there were no further protests.

Tollan glanced aside to Thaxon, who stood tall and hung on the sergeant's every word. Justice for the death of Thaxon's sister was a far more potent and worthy motivation than Tollan's immature rebellion against his father. His own reason felt petty by comparison, and perhaps it was.

The sergeant major continued. "Today, you will be taught what it means to move and act as part of a unit, and any failure to hold to those standards throughout your service will result in swift retaliation and discipline. You will do everything you are told, and you will do nothing else without the leave of your commanding officer.

"Behind you, there are thirty corporals spaced at intervals along the length of the field." Tollan and Thaxon turned to look, but as they had been in front it was now difficult to see through everyone behind them. "As far as you are concerned, their words are as mine, and my words are as the king's himself," Senn ordered brusquely. "Remember that, and you will do well. Line up in groups, six rows by twelve, and await their instructions.

"For Drüstania." Senn finished his oration abruptly, leaving the rest to his designated officers. He strode down the wooden stairs from the podium, two guards following him back to his private tent. The field of recruits meanwhile devolved into the chaos of men forming ranks for the first time.

Before Tollan could comprehend what was happening, Thaxon yanked him by the arm. They fell in line together, as straight as they could be against the orientation of the podium. Some amount of order began to emerge as recruits found their places in a grouping or found they needed to join another. They wound up along the rearmost edge of a group about halfway across the field, and they didn't have to wait long for their corporal to step forward.

He was not overly tall, but of a stockier build than the Sergeant Major, to the point that his armor appeared stretched around the shoulders. "Column Seventeen!" he bellowed between his imposing mutton-chop whiskers, commanding silence. "I am Corporal Feldram Crandas. You will call me Corporal, or sir. If any of you forget to address me in that fashion, all of you will bear the punishment."

That sounded harsh, but Tollan supposed it was the most efficient way to drill army etiquette into people who weren't used to it. He hoped he wouldn't forget and run off at the mouth, because his fellow recruits would undoubtedly hold a grudge against anyone who caused them pain.

Crandas began at the front, taking note of each recruit's name and leading them in the Drüstanian oath of service. He hadn't even made it through the first row of six before one of them forgot to say "sir."

Tollan wanted to groan but dared not speak without being called on. He caught the same dread in Thaxon's eyes as Crandas ordered them all to sprint to the far hill and back again.

It was going to be a long day.

WITHOUT ANY WARNING, TOLLAN was frightened out of his first sound sleep in the week since leaving home. He flinched at the raucous noise and sat up on his straw pallet, his heart racing. The other occupants of the tent scrambled to their feet as well, knocking heads together in such close quarters. Everyone else realized it a moment after Tollan did: they were under attack.

The torchlight of what had to be hundreds of invading forces filtered through the tent canvas, growing brighter as the enemy charged them with frenzied battle cries. Tollan froze completely in place, unsure of himself or what to do. There had been no orders in case of an attack.

One of the other recruits, quicker on his feet, shoved him aside and made for the tent's closest exit. Tollan recovered and instinctively followed the man, climbing over bunks with little concern for anything but getting out.

But just as he reached the opening, the tent flap was opened wide by their adversaries. Tollan's eyes showed white in terror, and he scrambled back. It was hard to see in the flickering darkness, but the warriors were dressed in all manner of clothing and dark paint, wielding blunt weapons and swinging them at anyone within reach.

Roving bandits! Tollan concluded in horror. They must have come from the east, or worse, they were the ones responsible for his father's missing ore shipment.

"Column Seventeen!" the telltale voice of Corporal Crandas shouted above the pandemonium from the center of the tent, sword drawn. "Stand your ground! Fight back!"

With what? Tollan thought in desperation before remembering his pocketknife.

He never had a chance to fumble it out of his leather jerkin. The enemies pushed farther inside, their weapons raised to cut down Tollan along with the next row of unarmed defenders. He raised his arms to cover his face and felt the club come down hard on his bare forearm. He yelped in pain and tried to grab the weapon with his other hand, but the adversary had already reared back for another strike.

Tollan heard a dreadful ripping noise from somewhere behind him and the pressure of warm bodies at his back lessened—someone must have forced another way out. He fell backward and sprawled across two bunks, staring up at the bandits about to kill for no other reason than because they wanted to. Savage faces bared their teeth, all their eyes wild with bloodlust except for one to Tollan's right—who looked almost comical and had . . . red . . . hair?

Corporal Crandas' whalebone whistle sounded, and the entire offensive ground to a halt. "That was absolutely pitiful!" he bellowed out the newly-opened hole in the tent canvas, sheathing his sword. He kicked a straw pallet aside for emphasis, clearing room for him to pace and point at the recruits who had attempted to run away. "No regard for the lives of your fellow men, or the orders of your commanding officer! You ought to be ashamed of yourselves!"

It was all an exercise. We were never in any danger, Tollan comprehended at last. His heart still pounded, and he didn't hear much of whatever tirade Crandas spouted next. He shuddered in relief at still being alive, but he was also furious that the corporal's ruse came at the expense of restful sleep.

Thaxon came close and extended a hand. Tollan looked at it with disdain but accepted the aid, being careful not to use his bruised arm to lift himself.

"Sorry for the harsh wake-up call," Thaxon said in a hushed voice.

"The first night I win the corporal's lottery to sleep indoors," Tollan growled. Until more tent materials were delivered, only half of the column could fit inside, and Crandas had opted to deal with the problem by casting lots. Might have seemed fair, too, if Tollan hadn't lost the luck of the draw three nights running. "Stop chuckling, it's not funny!" he complained, more loudly than he intended.

Thaxon stifled his snickering laugh, and his painted face dropped to dead serious. "Of course not," he agreed, the corner of his mouth twitching upward slightly.

Tollan had a mind to throw a punch and turn Thaxon's face as red as his hair, but Corporal Crandas turned back around and fixed both of them with a pointed stare. "Anything you would like to say, Cresthaven?"

It begged to be said, and in Tollan's aching, exhausted, hungry state there was no holding it back. As if it wasn't bad enough that he and a few others had been singled out for additional physical training after hours, this mockery of a midnight raid was completely uncalled-for.

"Yes, sir," Tollan said, making sure he had slipped in the deferential address. "I would like to ask what we were supposed to learn from this?"

The tent went silent as the grave. Tollan felt all eyes on him and stood his ground. "Some of us haven't truly slept since Celwaith Tor,

Corporal. We had no emergency plans and nothing to defend ourselves with. So, tell us: what was the point?"

Crandas stalked closer until he stood one pace in front of Tollan, his bushy brow lowered in stern evaluation. "Fetch me a bucket of water," he said, in the quietest tone of speech he had used since training began —but the simmering anger behind it ensured every ear in the tent could hear. "But go further upstream, I don't want any of the sludge you all drink from down here."

"But—" Tollan protested.

"*Now, soldier!*" Crandas ordered, his voice morphing into a roar that no man or child would dare oppose.

Tollan winced and ducked his head, making his way through the uncomfortable bystanders to the outdoors. Every tent was ringed with recruits and blazing torches, showing that the exercise wasn't just for Column Seventeen.

"The rest of you," Crandas said while Tollan remained in earshot. "You'll learn to be prepared for anything when you turn in at night. Ten miles before dawn, down to the crossroads and back! Get moving!"

It sounded like those who had dressed up as "bandits" would also be forced into running the loop. *Good*, Tollan groused.

It was tempting to think he had gotten the better end of the disciplinary stick, but Tollan had a sinking feeling that this chore wouldn't be as simple as it seemed. He weaved his way through the rest of the sleeping camp to the equipment tent, and in the darkness had to settle for a bucket with a broken handle. He tucked it under his left arm, the one that hadn't suffered a blow from an overzealous playacting bandit, and set off.

The grass along the upstream path had not yet been ground into oblivion, making it difficult to follow in the darkness. Still, the further he went from the camp's torches, the more his eyes adjusted to the moonlight. He could hear the rest of the column receding downhill, knowing from experience that coming back up to camp would be the worst part.

Tollan knew he had reached his destination when the path forded the stream. Down on his knees, he dunked the pail into the freezing water and held tight to keep it from getting carried off. Lifting it again was the tricky part, but he managed to keep most of the weight on his left arm while using his right to steady it.

The longer walk back was torture though, and he regretted not searching for a pail that still had some kind of handle. The extra minutes left him wondering what possible punishments Crandas could have devised using two gallons of water.

Tollan set the bucket down outside Column Seventeen's tent flap and cleared his throat. He could see the corporal was still inside, perhaps straightening things up after the failed war games. "I brought what you wanted, sir," he said, standing at attention.

Crandas stepped outside, and in so doing, his foot knocked over the pail. The water sloshed out and quickly drained away to nothing. "Guess you had better get more," he said, and went back inside.

Tollan blinked, then did as he was told. When he returned the second time, he made sure that Crandas accepted the bucket by hand.

The corporal accepted it without a word. He stepped to the side and dumped it out on the ground before handing it, empty, back to Tollan. "Again."

This is insulting, Tollan fumed as he carried the fourteenth load back to camp. His right arm throbbed, protesting the abuse, and a splitting headache was forming at his temples—probably due to exhaustion.

His foot snagged on a rock, and he went down, hard. He clutched at the bucket, but it was no use. It slipped out of his hands.

He wanted to scream in anger, and he supposed that was the point. *The point . . .*

He got up and retrieved another two gallons of freezing water from the stream, and went to Crandas. Before the corporal could take the container from his straining arms again, Tollan tossed it aside himself and stood at attention. "I understand, sir."

"Do you?" Crandas said, stepping close and staring Tollan right in the eye, but he wouldn't flinch. "*What* do you understand, Cresthaven?"

"It is not my place to ask questions, sir," Tollan said in as even a tone as he could muster. "I am to execute my orders to the best of my ability, and leave all other considerations behind."

Crandas stood there quietly with eyes narrowed for several seconds, keeping up the pressure. He finally grunted and turned away. "Now that sounds more befitting a soldier. But if you thought understanding your error was all you needed, you thought wrong."

Tollan clenched his jaw, fighting the urge to speak or move or do anything. His legs shook, weary to the bone. Only he and the corporal were present, and his military career—perhaps even his life—depended on how he responded to the corporal.

Crandas kicked the bucket back over to him and pointed to it. "Keep going until the column returns from their run, then join them for your field exercises in formation."

How long might that be? Tollan wondered, glancing at the sky. There was still no sign of the sun, and judging by the moon's position, he could not have had more than two hours of sleep before the mock raid.

"But don't get comfortable," Crandas continued. "I received confirmation that our additional tents will be delivered today, and I'll make sure Column Seventeen is put hard to work cutting trees for the frames."

"Sir, yes, sir," Tollan said, shoving his questions and opinions down where they wouldn't see the light of day—that is, if the sun ever did finally come up. He saluted and set off toward the stream for the fifteenth time.

EIGHT

Without a mother, a child lacks passion.
Without a father, a child lacks discretion.
Without either, a child lacks.
— *Codes of Binding 1.01-03*

"WHAT BUSINESS COULD YOU possibly have crossin' the Mersien Wold on foot?" the second of the two mounted soldiers asked in disbelief. "The next village ain't for thirty miles, and there's nothin' between here and there except shale and sagebrush."

Niena's father subtly motioned to let him handle the talking. "It's the fastest way to Ensdale from here, last I heard," he said in an innocent, unassuming tone. He tapped the simple longbow slung across his shoulders. "We're planning on doing some hunting in the wilds north of there."

Niena supposed that statement was true enough. She glanced between the two men barring their way, wondering how far out the patrol route extended. She and her father had taken care to skirt the view of the northern watchtower, but they hadn't expected to run straight into more Drüstanian guards.

"Hunting?" the first knight scoffed, appraising the two of them. "There's plenty of good hunting closer to home without risking yourself and, if I might say so, such a fetching young lady."

Niena's teeth set on edge, wanting badly to deliver a retort to the man's clumsy pass at her, but she stayed silent.

"Bite your tongue," Voster said, his tone still cordial but just barely. "I've traveled the Wold many a time, and I know the dangers."

"Have it your way then," the second, ruddy-skinned officer sighed. "Aye, this road will get you where you're goin' the fastest. But it'll be both of your funerals if'n you don't find shelter afore nightfall."

"Thank you for the concern," Voster said. "It's not warranted."

The soldiers clicked their horses' reins and passed them, returning to the northern watchtower. Niena heard the first one mutter something that sounded like "crazy old man" before going out of earshot. She moved up alongside her father, and they continued out into the sparse desert-like crater.

"What did he mean?" Niena asked. "What happens after dark?"

"Nocturnal predators," her father said. "Wild dogs roam the Wold in packs, hunting the rodents that come out at dusk to forage. This time of year, the dry season, they get so desperately hungry that they'll attack anything else that moves, including travelers."

Niena swallowed, her throat dry. "We can't make thirty miles by evening," she reminded him. "It's impossible."

Her father kept moving, not showing a hint of worry. "No, we'll have to strike camp along the way. It's fine—I prepared for this."

The hot late morning sun beat down on them as they kept going, reflecting off the broken stone, and it was all Niena could do to keep putting one foot in front of the other. Although high summer had passed a month ago, the heat had decided to linger with a vengeance. She had a thin scarf around her neck and forehead to keep the sun from burning her too badly, but her sweat had drenched it through.

Niena's father marched ahead of her, setting a pace with which she found it difficult to keep up on the loose rocks. At least she was more able to exert herself than the pampered elites of the Gilded Quarter. The idea of a posh woman and her parasol tottering across the shale made Niena smile, but come to think of it, she would give anything for a parasol right now.

They crested a rise, and Niena was greeted with the disheartening sight of the same broken stone stretching as far as her eyes could see. Sharp outcroppings rose out of the flat wastes like the backs of great tortoises, all of it sprinkled with patches of nasty shrub-brush and cactus plants. She estimated it would take them the rest of the day to make it even halfway to the horizon, where the edge of the enormous valley curved upward.

She wasn't willing to keep moving yet. "What are we even doing here, Papa?" she asked, her doubt getting the better of her.

"You mean the Wold?" he clarified. "It's the most direct route north, like I said."

"No," Niena answered. "You don't even know if this enclave is responsible for the attack. What if we're going all this way for nothing?"

Voster stared northward, his eyes plotting the easiest course through the shale. "All the better if this is news to them. They may be more willing to help us, to keep the elven race secret. Though, knowing your mother's family, I find it likely that Por'monir is involved in some way."

Niena considered that, in light of what the book her father had given her said. She hadn't gotten far in reading it, only attempting a few pages in the waning light once they set up camp each evening. She gathered that the D'harnir were a pious people who held to their traditions and did not pursue revenge. That didn't track with current events, so at least one of the groups in hiding had abandoned the old ways and decided to lash out.

"And what do you expect to happen once we get there?" Niena pressed, raising an eyebrow. She took out her water skin for a few sips before carrying on. "You'll convince them to give up their crusade?"

Her father shook his head, still gazing pensively to the north. "I don't know, little blossom. There's nothing else I know to do. If we don't try, many people will die at the hands of killers they can't even see—and maybe Tollan along with them."

That wasn't reassuring, even if it did seem logical. Niena had been wrestling with the same ideas since leaving Celwaith Tor, letting them percolate in her mind as they journeyed northward. Each time, she had come to the same conclusion, and it frustrated her that her father didn't know any more than she did.

She wished she didn't feel so useless.

Niena took another swig from her water skin, and her father interrupted her. "Go easy on that," he warned. "All the fresh water here is deep underground, so what we have will have to last through tomorrow. Let's keep going. Daylight is wasting."

Niena stowed the skin away in irritation and followed her father down the other side of the ridge, continuing ever northward. Occasional respite from the sun came as it descended and cast shadows of the many outcroppings across their path, but after several more hours, the coming night underscored their need to find shelter. They hunkered down and made camp against one of the hulking mounds of rock, so they would have something at their backs.

"Look," Niena whispered, pointing toward a small, skittering movement about ten yards away. "What's that?"

"That is a belvint," Voster said, leaving his pack next to her and readying his bow. He nocked an arrow and waited for the creature to stop moving as it stood up to munch on the seed pods of a nearby spiky shrub. The string released, and the arrow whistled straight into the tiny rodent's neck. "Decent eating for small game."

Niena looked at her father in awe. She hadn't known that he was such a good marksman. "When did you learn to do that?" she asked.

"I used to tan my own leather instead of ordering it," Voster said with a smile. "Living in the city, hunting became less necessary, but once you know the feel of a bow, you never forget how to use it." He went to go retrieve their dinner, leaving the weapon behind next to her.

Niena admired the curved wooden weapon with a new appreciation, noticing the notches above the wrapped leather grip that aided in arrow placement and aim. It seemed simple enough. "Teach me," she said when her father had returned with the dead belvint.

The creature turned out to be no bigger than a squirrel, with no tail and larger diamond-shaped ears. Voster pushed the arrow through the rodent's limp back and out the other side, the blood dripping onto the stone at his feet. "Are you sure you want to learn? I remember how tender you were with animals growing up."

Niena's stomach turned a little at the sight of the belvint's dead, glassy eyes, but she wouldn't be deterred. "I guess I feel like I'm weighing you down out here."

"Not at all," her father replied through pursed lips. "It is a worthy skill, to be sure. But the bow has to be treated with respect—an arrow can just as easily kill a person as one of these animals."

"I understand, Papa," Niena said, acknowledging the weight of the responsibility. "I will."

"I can't teach you anything tonight. It'll have to wait until we're in better country," Voster said, reaching into his sack for some dirty rags and a medium-sized glass bottle filled with clear liquid. "But since you want to be useful, take these and spread them in an arc about twenty paces out."

She took the bottle and uncorked it, recognizing it from their old kitchen stores. A strong, sour aroma rose from the opening. "Vinegar?"

"The unpleasant smell should keep any coyotes or wild dogs away, and dull traces of our sweat or this belvint's blood," he explained. He splayed the rodent out on a rock and drew out his knife to clean it.

Niena didn't stay to see the rest of the gruesome process and walked the perimeter as she was instructed. She dropped a vinegar-soaked rag every so often and hoped it would be enough to protect them. Her father had assured that they would be passing out of the Wold tomorrow, but a lot could happen in a night and a day.

She shivered from the drastic drop in temperature now that the sun was down. The wind had picked up as well, a wind that might carry their scent to predators lurking out there in the wastes.

Niena placed the last pungent rag, and her ears caught the sound of a howl off in the distance. Dozens of others echoed in reply, all over the desert landscape. She hurried back to her father's side, just as he was trying to get some brushwood to kindle in a hollow formed by pieces of shale.

"Sounds like their hunt's begun," Voster said calmly. "Here, help me shield the flame."

They cooked the belvint in eerie silence, watching and listening for any movement close by. The waxing moon came out from behind some wispy clouds, and the resulting contrast kept them from seeing phantoms in the landscape. Finally, Niena's father stamped out the fire and poured the last of the vinegar on it before giving her slightly more than half of the food.

The tough, gamy meat wasn't enough to fill her stomach, but it was hot and fresh. She ate it quickly and curled up in her blanket next to her father to conserve their body heat as he took the first watch. She found it hard to get comfortable with the rocky outcropping digging at her back, and the occasional howling of dogs kept her from drifting off. Even if she did sleep, she wasn't sure that her nightmares wouldn't come back again; the roar of the manticore woke her more nights than not.

Niena sat up, remaining huddled next to her father. He stiffly scanned the horizon, with his hand resting close to his hatchet and even closer to his bow. She followed his gaze and saw a handful of dark shapes speeding across the landscape, heading west.

Niena held her breath as the creatures drew closer, but they did not slow or change direction toward the campsite. The vinegar had worked, and the dogs continued on their way.

She felt her father tense. He stood to look southward, behind them. Niena gathered her blanket around her and followed suit. It didn't take her long to spot what had captured her father's attention.

"What is it?" she asked in a whisper.

"Fire," he said. The speck of orange light was visible above the edge of the valley, near where they had entered the Wold. "It has to be the watchtower."

"A beacon of some kind?" Niena thought, puzzled.

"No," Voster replied gravely. "It's been attacked. The tower is burning."

Niena hugged her blanket close around her shoulders to ward off a chill. No common bandits would raid a Drüstanian watchtower—it would be too much work for too little reward. No, this meant that the D'harnir were on the move, and if they were taking out key military placements . . .

The elves intended far worse than a little chaos and terrorism.

When they were both seated once more, Niena's father drew her into a comforting—though not quite relaxed—embrace. "So," Niena whispered, drawing his mind to other things. "Where are we headed tomorrow?"

He stroked her hair, keeping his eyes focused outward on the night. "With any luck, we climb out of the Wold and come back to more hospitable lands. The day after we will restock our provisions in Ensdale and continue north."

"Ensdale," Niena repeated. Aptly named for the last stop on the North Road, there would be nothing but harsh wilderness beyond. "Isn't the old farmhouse not far from there? I'd like to see it."

Voster shook his head. "No. It's a fair bit of a detour into Spinewood Forest, and we can't afford the time."

That seemed a weak reason to Niena, and she knew there had to be something else. "Why? We're ahead of schedule and making good time, right?"

"For now." Voster sighed and scratched at his beard, which needed a trim. "Niena, for the last decade and a half I have tried to put that part of my life behind me because it hurt too much to think about. I loved your mother more than anything, and after losing her, the only thing that kept me going was making sure I didn't lose you and Tollan as well."

Niena lay back down and breathed into her blanket for extra warmth. She knew she should trust her father's word, but her few memories of her mother were shrouded in fear. Maybe returning to the farm would stir better ones. "At least you got to know her," Niena said.

Niena's father remained silent, and for a moment she thought he hadn't heard. But at last, he bowed his head in resignation. "Yes," he whispered, his voice tight. "I suppose I owe you that much."

ENSDALE PROVED TO STILL be a small town, though it had grown into a hub for hunters and farmers all over the northern reaches of Drüstania rather than the cozy country hamlet of sixteen years ago. Few lived there year-round, but many routinely passed through or stayed for a season. Niena and her father fit right in on that count, and no one questioned their business.

They spent the last of their silver on restocking their provisions and buying a fishing line, having left the rest of their money with Anise. "If we weren't on our own before, we are now," Voster said quietly as they left the merchant store. "Everything north of here is wilderness and mountain glaciers, so living off what we can hunt and forage will be our only option."

"It's a good thing we're here in late summer," Niena remarked, tearing into a loaf of bread. It had been ten days since leaving home, and finally having fresh baked goods again was a delicacy in and of itself. "I bet everyone in Ensdale gets snowed in come winter."

Her father shrugged, appearing to be lost in his memories of the place.

Niena followed him out the far side of town, and they cut northeast across a meadow toward the forest-covered foothills in the distance. There were no more roads to follow since they all culminated at Ensdale, but there were a few game trails. Niena was thankful the wild underbrush hadn't grown so thick that it threatened to trip her.

Niena had to retract her gratitude in short order, however, as it soon turned to brambles and thorns that grabbed and pinched at them as they tried to proceed. Her father pulled out his hatchet to hack the worst of it out of their way, but it was slow going.

"Now you see why it's called Spinewood," Voster said between strokes. "Although, the forest has grown outwards more than I would have thought in such a short time." He pointed out a small but nasty-looking purple flowering vine. "Careful of those. Poisonous."

Niena steered as far clear as she could but took a moment to remember what it looked like. "As in, it might kill you 'poisonous'?"

Voster chopped most of the way through a small tree and pushed it down with his foot. "As far as I know, it doesn't affect humans, but it makes elves dangerously sick. Your mother and I found that out the hard way when we settled here. I have no idea what it would do to you."

Niena didn't ask further questions, reminded of her elven blood and what it meant. She had been living a lie. There were threats and difficulties in this world that she had never known and might never understand now—what right had her parents to keep that knowledge from her? If it hadn't been for her encounter in the square, she would still be ignorant.

An uneasy feeling settled in the pit of Niena's stomach. Maybe her father had been right—they shouldn't go to the farm. She wasn't sure that she wanted to know more about her mother after all. She just wanted it all to be over as soon as possible, so that their life could go back to normal.

"Papa," she spoke up, but he cut her off and pointed ahead.

"There," Voster said. "That's the old barn . . . or at least it used to be."

Surrounded by young trees, with one growing straight up through the roof, a small barn stood in a state of rapid decay. The wild foliage had taken root, and the rotting wood was so covered in vines it appeared to be more of an oddly-structured thicket than a building.

"I built that myself after you were born," Voster said with a sweaty smile, re-energized by the sight of the old farm. "The house is a little farther ahead."

Niena followed halfheartedly, knowing that turning aside now would serve no purpose. Having some shelter would be better than none, she reasoned after noticing the sun's low position in the sky. The waning sunlight filtered through the forest's dark leaves to make a dappled pattern across the spiky underbrush. If Niena hadn't been preoccupied, she might have thought it beautiful.

And then, she saw it. The remains of an old stone tower sprouted from the forest floor like yet another tree, truncated at the top by a gently slanting roof. The east side of the house had fallen in, leaving crumbled masonry scattered about. The vines had been unable to find purchase on the stone, so it stood aloof and largely untouched by the surrounding morass of flora except for the broken wall.

The sight captivated Niena with a strange attraction, and the unease in her gut waned. But as her father cleared a path to what was once the doorstep, she fell to her knees, overcome with dizziness and clutching her head. Visions flashed through her mind, horrible things that she had only seen in cloudy nightmares. She saw them clearly now.

One image overtook the others: a manticore, spattered in blood and surrounded by disemboweled pigs in a pen on the east side of the house. The beast had the muscular body of a lion, leathery wings of a bat, scorpion's stinger, and a long, curving neck leading to its face—a dreadful human-like face with pointed teeth and glowing yellow eyes. It was more vivid and more real than anything Niena had ever dreamed, and she couldn't help but feel in her heart that she was about to die.

The manticore flapped once, twice, the wind washing over Niena's prone form as it raised itself up to strike a killing blow.

The scene before her abruptly changed. Niena was now inside the house, looking out from the collapsed wall in the east side of the house. Her mother, Athria, stood tall before the monster, cradling a heavily pregnant stomach with one hand—the other was outstretched as if she could hold the beast back with sheer will. She chanted, shouting words in a tongue that Niena couldn't understand. Behind her mother, a much younger visage of her father picked himself up off the ground and brandished a sword.

Niena stared at the strength and beauty of her mother, and for a moment it drowned out the fear of the enraged manticore. But the D'harnin spell Athria cast was not enough to hold back the beast, and the terrible point of its tail shot forward to pierce her shoulder. Niena shut her eyes tight, but that didn't keep the vision from continuing to flood her mind.

Mercifully, the image shifted again, this time to Niena's father holding a blood-covered newborn boy with pointed ears. It was Tollan. The manticore was nowhere to be seen, but Niena somehow knew it had flown off after striking down her mother. Athria lay in the grass and mud nearby, her lifeless eyes staring as dark red blood pooled around her.

Niena came back to her sense of reality, finding that she was hoarse from screaming and hyperventilating. She felt her father shaking her gently, and heard him calling her name. She fought against the memories, if that was in fact what they were, and it felt like mentally treading water. At last, it grew easier, and she came out of it.

She sat up, dizzy and panting, clutching at her father's arms for stability. "Papa, Papa," she said repeatedly.

"I'm here, little blossom, I'm here," he assured, holding her tight and stroking her wavy hair. "What happened? Are you all right?"

Niena kept her eyes shut, not wanting to trigger another wave of the visions. "I . . . I saw Mama," she said.

Voster looked around at where they sat in relation to the crumbled house. "Yes. She . . ." He trailed off and swallowed hard. "She lay right here, and I had to deliver Tollan as she was dying. I tried to protect her, but in the end, she protected me."

"*Us*," Niena corrected, opening her eyes. "She protected all of us."

"That's right," Voster said. He choked tears back and hugged her tightly to his chest. "I'm sorry, I never should have brought you here. There's still so much I don't know about the D'harnir—I had no idea you would see all of that again."

"No, it's all right," she reassured him. "You didn't want to come, and I insisted." They hadn't been the joyous memories she had hoped for, but seeing the events for herself was, in a way, both more intense and less frightening than her nightmares' portrayal of them. Her mother had fought against the manticore, using her elven gifts, and that sacrifice showed Niena more about her mother's heart than any of her father's stories.

Niena stood with her father's help, still dizzy but knowing they didn't have much time before the sun set. "What now?" she asked apprehensively.

"I had hoped to get here a little earlier in the day, but all the undergrowth slowed us down," Voster said, standing next to her and looking the ramshackle house over. "We can try to find another place to stay the night, but this would be the most protected."

Niena hated that idea and thought surely he did too, but she didn't feel up to traveling anymore that day. She reluctantly agreed and followed him inside the door that had fallen off its hinges.

The inside looked even worse than the exterior but still appeared structurally sound. The place looked like it had been ransacked by looters years ago so that anything able to be carried off and used had been.

Voster crossed to the empty double bed frame and lingered a moment. Niena watched as his own painful recollections flickered for an instant across his face, but he pushed through and got down on hands and knees to inspect the floor underneath. "Yes!" he exclaimed. "It's still here. Help me move this."

Niena was surprised that the looters had never checked under the bed, one of the most obvious places for hiding things, but understood when they had lifted the heavy frame and leaned it against the opposing wall. A handful of boards in the floor didn't appear to be particularly loose, especially with the bed placed on top of them, but they weren't fastened down either. Without moving the bed, there was no reason to think something might be hidden there.

Using his knife to slide down along one side and flip up one of the boards, Voster took them out to reveal a diminutive wooden chest. It was about two feet long but short enough to fit in the space between the foundation stones on which the floor rested. He lifted it out and sat there, fumbling with the latch in his eagerness to inspect the contents.

There was very little in the chest, Niena noted while her father sorted through it. He pulled out a curved dagger, a set of desiccated clothes, and a piece of jewelry, all of them without identifying markings but appearing quite foreign in design. "What is all of this?" she asked.

"The last remnants of Athria's heritage," Voster said wistfully. "When your grandfather, Wirvanen, wanted us to leave Por'monir, he instructed that no trace of her past life be taken with her. She was given nothing but these plain clothes and the dagger with which her ears were shorn."

Niena's eyes flitted to the last item. The necklace was simple but elegant, with the pendant consisting of a teardrop bead suspended in a silver design. The bead was a bright blue, perhaps made from chalcedony or lapis, and was fastened at the top so that it dangled freely. "I don't think I've seen anything like it before," Niena said.

"You wouldn't have," he said with a sad smile. "It was the only thing that your mother took with her despite your grandfather's wishes. She used to wear it while we still lived in Por'monir, and told me it was made to resemble her family crest. She decided to hide it all away in the early days, but now that we're here, I think you should have it."

Niena regarded the pendant with respect and placed the cord around her neck. It felt heavier than she expected, accompanied by a feeling of strange tenderness and connection that washed over her. Despite the brief flashes of vivid memory outside, there was little she could remember of her mother's voice or demeanor. But now, her mother felt closer than she could ever remember.

Voster gathered the boards and replaced them in the floor, while Niena took the dagger and strapped it to her pack.

Out of the corner of her eye, in the failing light outside the crumbled section of the house, she thought she saw a figure past the denser trees. It looked vaguely human, but it might have been an animal.

"Hey!" she called. "You!" She rushed down the uneven doorsteps and around the side of the house.

There was no one there—not even the receding sound of rustling leaves and branches.

Voster hurried up behind her. "What did you see?" he asked, scanning for movement among the trees.

Niena stood there for a moment, puzzled. She knew she had seen something, but whatever it was had vanished. "Maybe a trick of the light. I thought I saw someone."

Voster grunted, his eyes narrowed. "If the number of people passing through Ensdale is any clue, Spinewood might be more well-traveled than it appears. Still, we have nowhere else to spend the night."

Niena nodded and turned back, spotting a cairn that she hadn't seen from the other side of the house. She went over and looked down at the place where her mother was buried. The stone had faded, but her father's painted inscription could still be read: *Tynathria, loving wife and mother.*

She touched the pendant she now wore, and imagined her mother watching over them. She thought of Tollan's birthday in two days and prayed to the winds that Keordi and Kasdan would be able to get him his gift in time. The reason Niena and her father had ventured into the wilderness came flooding back to her. "I won't let anything happen to my brother, Mama," she whispered, choking up. "I promise."

Voster knelt and rested a hand on the inscription. "It's . . . been a long time without you, Athria," he said, tears falling on the stones. "We miss you."

They sat in silence together for several minutes, mourning their family's loss and resolving not to lose another.

Daylight was fading fast, and Niena didn't notice when her father stood to ready their beds for the night. She found it difficult to turn away, but when she did her heart felt lighter and driven with purpose.

Niena ate a simple meal with her father in her childhood home, and when she slept there were no more nightmares.

NINE

Integrity is like the sweetness of a blackberry in the heat of summer: hidden in the common thorn bush, but a worthy reward for all who find it.

— Codes of Binding 3.11

"I'M GONNA WHACK YOU, string-bean," a stocky recruit of about twenty-five named Ruger threatened. He had gained control of the makeshift fighting ring almost an hour ago, and had proceeded to win against every challenger since. "Just like last time you stepped in to fight me."

Tollan chose not to acknowledge the taunt but grimaced at the memory of being trounced in less than ten seconds. He gripped his staff tighter in the proper posture and bounced on his heels, running through the proper sequence of strikes and footwork in his head. It was near the end of the day, and he was dead tired, but he desperately needed a win.

Off to one side stood Corporal Crandas, with his whistle clenched in his teeth. Surrounding the three of them in a large circle, the other seventy members of the column expectantly cheered for the fight to begin. Other circles of recruits could be seen dotted around this side of the muddy field, as those columns scheduled on rotations for fighting practice battled it out among themselves.

Crandas raised his hand, commanding silence among the onlookers. After a few tense moments, he quickly lowered his hand and piped a short note on the whistle.

Tollan went hard on the offensive, knowing the only way to maintain the upper hand as the weaker combatant was to keep Ruger off-balance. He feinted at the ankle to prompt a parry, but he changed the angle of his swing and glanced the staff off in a different direction, using the momentum to continue past. Keeping his footwork light in the cloying mud, he lined up an attack on Ruger's backside.

This time, Ruger's blocking staff connected solidly with the strike. Though the man's reflexes weren't as swift this time, he swiveled at the waist enough for a strong deflection. The impact sent a shock up Tollan's arms and gave Ruger enough space to reposition his weak footing and devise a counterattack.

Now Tollan was on the retreat, finding it all he could do to block Ruger's relentless assault. He gritted his teeth and backpedaled, annoyed that he had allowed himself to be boxed in by such a strong opponent. He looked for openings to duck out of reach and start again, but none were given.

There was no escape. Tollan panicked and his defense finally broke. Ruger's staff forced its way through and landed hard against the back side of his ribs. He dropped his own weapon and fell to the ground, nursing his side. The blow hadn't broken the skin, but it would leave a bruise.

The whistle sounded a second time for the end of the match, and the cheers of the other recruits made it clear they hadn't been rooting for Tollan.

Ruger laughed obnoxiously, and Tollan fought to retain his composure. "Barely an improvement, Cresthaven. I would have thought after two weeks you would have stronger form."

That clinched it. Tollan would not continue to be derided by his peers. In one smooth motion, he picked up his staff and swung it upward at Ruger's jaw. The blow rattled the man's face, and he spat out a chunk of tooth.

"Is that strong enough for you?" Tollan quipped.

"Why, I oughtta—"

Crandas' whistle cut in, blowing harsh high-pitched notes between his down-turned mutton-chop whiskers. "Enough!" he called, coming to stand between the two combatants. "Cresthaven, two demerits for dealing a blow after the match ended. Yorvikson, two demerits for deserving it."

Tollan used his staff to get back to his feet, feeling the pressure on his bruised ribs. He didn't feel too sorry about lashing out, considering Ruger had also been disciplined—Tollan counted that as at least a draw, better than another loss. A few hours of hard labor was a small price to pay for a little justice.

"Sir, yes, sir," Ruger said, already standing at attention. "Won't happen again, sir."

Suck-up, Tollan thought, but kept his face respectfully stony. "Sorry, sir. I have no excuse."

"I should hope not. Come with me, the both of you," Crandas instructed, then turned and spoke to the rest of the column. "Pair off and go back to practicing your forms and patterns until I return."

As Crandas led them away from the main group, Tollan caught sight of Thaxon. The red-haired boy raised an eyebrow at him in concern.

Tollan waved him off, motioning that he was fine and would catch up with him later. He would enjoy whatever Crandas had in store for them more than getting beaten by any knucklehead with a wooden stick. Tollan's bruises still hadn't fully healed from the "bandit attack," and the blow to the ribs he had endured made him wonder if there would be anything left of him after training.

It baffled him. All the others had outpaced him in strength and speed, including Thaxon, despite Thaxon being of a similar thin build and several inches shorter than Tollan. Some people were naturally better at certain things, Tollan supposed, but he barely passed most of his tests except for marksmanship. He excelled at that.

The problem was that Tollan never had enough energy to keep up, which was especially apparent in sparring. He felt like he could collapse at any time and sleep for a week. He had been able to recuperate some once the fabled delivery of tent canvas and rations arrived, but it seemed food and better sleep could only do so much.

"What duties do you have for us, sir?" Ruger asked, his voice a chipper model of the perfect soldier. Tollan fought to keep from rolling his eyes at Ruger's obvious ingratiation attempt.

Crandas didn't slow his pace and spoke up as he marched them toward the treeline on the opposite side of the muddy field. "The sacking of the Mersien Wold watchtower seems to have put a rush on our deliveries from the capital. You will be helping to construct an armory tent to house your weapons."

Tollan almost tripped over himself. Moving from sticks to blades hopefully meant they would be receiving proper mail and plate armor as well. His bruises might finally have a chance to heal.

"All the smithies of Celwaith Tor have been slaving away to provide everything we need to outfit you grunts upon your return, and our first meager supply arrives tomorrow," Crandas continued. "Only enough to train with, so get used to sharing gear."

That news was more sobering. Tollan wondered if any of his father's wares would be among the deliveries, and felt sure he would be able to discern by quality if they were. Then again, if the blacksmiths were all rushed to produce as much as possible in a short amount of time, many of his father's telltale practices might have been thrown out for expediency's sake.

They passed the last column on the field's edge and found where two dozen other recruits were cutting down and splitting trees as discipline for acting out. Crandas pointed and told Ruger to join the saw team. "Stay a moment, Cresthaven," Crandas clarified. "There's something I want to address."

Oh no, Tollan thought, watching an unenthused Ruger take his place with three others at the handles of the giant saw blade buried in a great oak. "What else have I done wrong, sir?" he asked, preparing mentally for the worst. He had been on his best behavior ever since the night with the bucket, and couldn't fathom what this was about.

The corporal shook his head. "You haven't. But I have had my eye on you for a while now. In almost every measure you are falling behind the rest of the column."

"I'm sorry, sir, I'm doing the best I can," Tollan said. He had wondered when his performance would become an issue. The last thing he wanted was to be expelled—it would prove his father's caution correct.

"I know you are," Crandas replied. "That's why I'm going to be working with you more closely."

Tollan looked up in surprise.

"Not everyone is capable of physical strength, but you have shown that you take direction well and apply initiative despite your rocky start," Crandas said. "You coordinate well with others, at least when you aren't being antagonized. You take plenty of hits and get back up, even if you can't always dish them back."

Tollan remained at full attention. It felt good to be recognized, but it also felt like an underhanded compliment. "Thank you, sir, but . . . I won't last long in a fight if I can be so easily overpowered by men like Ruger."

"Strength is irrelevant if you out-maneuver your opponents." Crandas rested a gauntlet-covered hand on Tollan's shoulder. "You can think and adapt quickly, Cresthaven. Use that to your advantage."

"What of the forms and patterns, sir?" Tollan asked, confused.

"Convention is for understanding the basics of attack and defense, and based on what I've seen today you've learned those well." Crandas smirked and clenched his other hand into a fist. "I want you to remember all of that, and then do whatever it takes to come out the victor. Warfare isn't always about playing by the rules. That makes you predictable."

"Warfare?" Tollan repeated. "You think it will come to that, sir?"

Crandas narrowed his eyes. "I'm no clairvoyant, but if you ask me, the winds are blowing in worse fates than anti-monarchist terrorism."

Tollan didn't like the way that sounded. Crandas clearly believed the Crownless were responsible for the statue bombing, which made sense on the surface. But Tollan knew the amount of black powder needed to cause that much damage was hard to acquire and harder to smuggle into place, suggesting either an inside job or a powerful outside threat. He wasn't sure which would be worse for his country.

Tollan saluted, placing his right fist over his heart. Whatever the case, he would serve the crown. "Sir, yes, sir. Drüstania can count on me."

Crandas dismissed him to join the work team. "I expect to see you winning your fair share of sparring matches soon, Cresthaven."

"WHAT WAS ALL THAT about earlier?" Thaxon asked when they finally caught up again over dinner. "You gave Ruger what he had coming."

Tollan groaned painfully as he lowered himself to the ground with his bowl of watery stew and bread crusts. His hands had several new blisters forming after shaping tent supports and armor stands all day. "It was nothing, Thaxon. I just lost my temper."

"Oh, come on." Thaxon dipped his bread in the broth and stuffed it in his mouth. His expensive clothes looked ten times rattier than they had that first day, but much more defined muscle hid underneath now. "You were extra quiet last night and this morning," he said around his mouthful. "What's eating you?"

Tollan glanced around to see who was in earshot, then sighed and leaned closer. "If you must know, today's my birthday."

"What?" Thaxon slapped him on the shoulder in happy surprise. "Why didn't you tell me sooner? We should celebrate!"

Tollan scoffed. "Celebrate how? If you haven't noticed, the sun is down, and I'm too exhausted to do anything fun. We have nothing to eat but mystery stew and old bread, and stream water to drink."

"Not all." A mischievous glint appeared in Thaxon's eyes.

"What do you mean?"

"Don't worry about it—meet me out by the tree in half an hour," Thaxon said in a conspiratorial tone. He hurriedly slurped down the remainder of his stew and sped away.

Tollan took more time finishing his food. He felt uneasy about his friend's clandestine plans, but after two weeks of training alongside the boy and setting aside a few minor annoyances, he trusted him.

It was rather nice to have someone to confide in. There hadn't been anyone like that for Tollan back in Celwaith Tor. The occasional acquaintance had come and gone, but he had always been stuck working the forge and rarely met new faces, let alone had the time to become good friends.

Tollan took his bowl to the stream and rinsed it out before returning it to the mess tent. The food had not improved as much as he might have hoped, but the portions were at least decent now that the camp received regular supplies. He had no idea what Thaxon could have found to celebrate his birthday.

The moon peeked out from behind wispy clouds as he meandered his way over to where he and Thaxon had spent their first night. Two silhouettes stood there talking in hushed tones as he strolled up.

"Thaxon? That you?" Tollan called.

He was quickly shushed by the figure on the left. "Yes, it's me. Not so loud."

"Cresthaven? You're who we did this for?" the figure on the right grumbled. "I can't believe this."

Despite the whispers, Tollan recognized the voice as Ruger's. The blood drained from his face, and he thanked the darkness for cloaking his fear. "Um ... Sorry about this morning," Tollan fumbled, trying to keep his voice steady. "Whatever this is, it wasn't my idea—I swear."

Thaxon produced a dark glass bottle from its hiding place inside his tattered doublet. "Ruger's family owed ours a favor for canceling their debt to us, so it seemed fitting that he be the one to help me procure it."

Tollan liked the implications of this less and less. There could only be a handful of places where they would get such a thing on short notice, and none of them were good. "Where did you get that?"

Ruger crossed his arms, evidently unhappy with the turn of events but going along with it. "As it happens, Sergeant Major Senn keeps a case of the good stuff stashed in his tent. He must enjoy a good nightcap after a long day of bossing people around."

Tollan blanched at the implication. "How would you know that?"

Thaxon shrugged. "My family might happen to own a winery down south, and I might have helped unload the delivery, and I might have recognized the label. Here, take it," he said, holding out the bottle. "You only turn sixteen once."

Tollan backed away and held his hands out defensively. "No. I can't take part in this. Your bright idea was to steal from our commanding officer, the only person here who could have us hanged for treason?"

Thaxon motioned downward violently with his free hand. "Keep it down! He doesn't even know it's gone, and once he does, it could have been the fault of any one of two thousand men here."

"That's not the point," Tollan said, incensed that his friend would even do such a thing, let alone enlist the help of someone like Ruger.

"Oh, so you want to be a perfect little soldier now?" Ruger hissed, his tone biting and all too familiar. "When you can't even win a sparring match?"

Tollan had been goaded into doing the wrong thing earlier today, and it wouldn't happen a second time. "I have to turn the both of you in," he said with no small amount of trepidation. "You can come and confess, and maybe the sergeant will go easy on you since there wasn't anything else taken, but . . ."

Thaxon crossed the distance between them and clutched his arm in urgency. "No, please. I had no idea this would be such a problem for you. I just wanted to do something for your birthday—we can put it back in Senn's tent. No one has to know."

Ruger came closer, his mere presence threatening. "Make the smart choice, Cresthaven."

Tollan hesitated, hating that he even needed to think about the decision. He would feel like a traitor if he didn't tell the sergeant what had happened, but he understood that Thaxon hadn't done it out of malice. It wasn't in his character, or at least it didn't seem to be.

He reached out and took the bottle from his friend. "I'll return the wine, and I won't mention any names. If the wind is blowing our way, the sergeant won't press any further since there was no harm done."

"Oh, for the love of—" Ruger started to shout, but brought his voice back down. "You really think it's going to be that simple?"

Thaxon released Tollan's arm and gestured for him to go. "If that's how you want to handle it, we're not going to stop you."

"We're not?" Ruger repeated.

"No." Thaxon had regret plastered all over his face when he met Tollan's eyes. "I truly am sorry."

Tollan nodded before trudging back toward the camp, wine bottle in tow. He did not look forward to speaking with Senn, but there was little doubt in his mind about the right thing to do. Still, he hated that it was Thaxon who put him in this position.

He marched up to Sergeant Major Senn's tent, the only one in the whole camp with a single occupant. A lone soldier stood guard and eyed Tollan warily as he approached.

"What business with the Sergeant Major?" the guardsman asked.

Tollan showed him the bottle. "Returning some of his property, sir," he answered. "I believe it was stolen from him."

The soldier turned with a clink of his chain mail and rang a small bell hanging outside the entrance flap. "Come," Senn's voice called.

The guardsman nodded and ushered Tollan into the tent.

It was furnished well, for a canvas enclosure on what used to be grass. A lantern stood in the corner by a desk and set of drawers, and a proper bed with a mattress lay nearby on a wooden frame. Several boxes stood stacked in the opposite corner, and Tollan could see the wine crate from which the bottle had been pilfered peeking out from the side.

Tollan stood to attention, staring straight forward, and held the bottle in front of him. He thought he would figure out what to say by now, but nothing came to mind.

"Your name, soldier?" the sergeant prompted, rising from his desk where he had been writing. He was dressed in the same armor he had worn during orientation, and the polished, perfect fit intimidated Tollan.

"Cresthaven, sir."

Senn's eyebrow raised almost imperceptibly to the name, and he examined his visitor more closely. His close-cut hair and narrowed eyes bore down on Tollan in judgment. "Well?"

Tollan presented the bottle. "I believe this is yours, sir?"

The sergeant accepted it, appraising the label with interest followed by an angry frown. The cursive lettering spelled out the vintage *Barandine Red*, underneath the sign of the Denvald crest. "Indeed, it is. You had better have a good reason for possessing it," Senn said, his voice hard.

Tollan crossed his fingers that his admission would be enough. "It was stolen from you, sir. Someone in my column knew it was my birthday today and apparently decided to give me their ill-gotten goods."

"Do you have any idea who could have done this?" Senn asked, setting the bottle down on his desk with a heavy *thunk*.

Tollan held his breath for an instant. He would not lie to protect his friend, but he also did not believe that Senn's retaliation would be fully just. "I have some idea, sir, but motives point in opposite directions. It could be someone who bears a grudge and is attempting to frame me or someone who genuinely wanted to celebrate my birthday." It was an awkward half-truth to tell, but he remained at attention and didn't waver. "I thought it best to return the bottle to you as soon as possible, sir."

Senn nodded, observing Tollan for a moment longer. The silence grew oppressive before he spoke again. "It seems Corporal Crandas was right about you," he said. "I planned to discharge you on account of your shortcomings, but we need as much loyalty in this militia as we can find."

Tollan refused to let his face show any sign of emotion, either elation at his plan working or apprehension at how close he came to being muscled out of the army.

"Your honesty does you credit, Cresthaven," Senn continued. "I confess to not noticing the wine had gone missing, but I shall be addressing my personal security more closely in the future."

"I'm glad to be of service, Sergeant Major," Tollan said, feeling the tiniest twinge of guilt for his lie of omission.

Senn still did not dismiss him, however. Tollan's heart sank, hoping he would not be questioned further.

Senn crossed to the drawers alongside his desk and opened one, pulling out a messy parcel of brown paper. "Your name reminded me— this came for you yesterday. I'm told that a Celwaith Tor guard named Harroway had to cajole the duty officer to let him accompany the supply caravan and deliver it personally."

Tollan's eyes widened, breaking his previously stoic face. It had to be from his family, but he couldn't believe that Kasdan had gone to so much trouble on his account.

"A delivery like this is highly irregular, and as such is also highly suspect," Senn explained, handing him the wad of packaging material which Tollan could now see had been opened. "It was not deemed to be dangerous."

Tollan didn't much like the fact that a personal gift had been rifled through, but he could empathize with the need for security. After all, there had been no word of any concrete suspects in the bombing of Wraelian Square, so scrutiny would be the best policy. "Yes, sir," he answered and accepted the parcel.

"You will inform me if you find out anything more about the identity of the thief." Senn turned back to his desk to resume the work that Tollan had interrupted. "You're dismissed, Cresthaven."

Tollan bowed and left the tent before breathing a long sigh of relief. The guardsman outside looked at him strangely but didn't say anything.

Rather than return immediately to Column Seventeen's darkened and crowded tent, Tollan remained in the torchlight a moment longer to inspect his gift. He peeled back the outer layers of the parcel to reveal a small cloth pouch and a folded note. He opened the pouch first and found a charming brass fob watch with his initials engraved on the covering. The handmade face inside was simple but readable. The chain concluded in a clip that doubled as a winding key.

He couldn't imagine how much it had cost and thought it might be the most expensive thing he owned that his father had not made himself. He assumed it had been purchased from the Terraced or Gilded Quarters—and come to think of it, the pouch resembled what Niena had carried home from the market that day. She would have needed to save for months to buy such a piece.

Tollan wound the springs as tightly as they would go and listened to the soft *tick, tick* as the second hand began to turn. He unfolded the wrinkled off-white parchment.

> *Dear Tollan,*
>
> *I hope this is able to reach you in time. I wanted to make sure your sixteenth birthday would be something special, and now that has been taken from us. But they can't take away what we mean to each other as a family. Remember that.*
>
> *After the attack, Papa said a lot of things were going to change in the coming days, but I didn't realize what he meant by that. I expect you'll be going through a lot of changes yourself right now, and I hope that becoming a soldier is everything you always wanted.*

This watch should help you count the hours and days until we are all together again. Be sure to wind it twice a day, and think of us when you do. I look forward to hearing what stories you bring back from training—we might have a few of our own to share as well.

Happy birthday, little brother.

Niena

Tollan wasn't sure what his sister meant by the last part, but it refreshed him to hear Niena's encouragement. Touched by her gesture, he resolved to abstain from poking fun at her so often.

He supposed he shouldn't be surprised there was no note from his father or Anise as well, but he felt disappointed by it all the same.

He picked his way back through the camp and put the note and the watch into his jerkin's breast pocket, making sure to clip the chain to the inside. It would hang there, ticking, as a reminder of what he protected as a soldier in King Pelendion's service.

"Well?" Thaxon whispered from the bunk beside Tollan's when he returned. "What's the word?"

Tollan tried to settle himself in without waking any of the others. He suspected that Thaxon would have been asleep if not for anxiety. "You're both fine, at least for now. The sergeant didn't ask that many questions."

Thaxon lay back on his pallet, relieved. "Thank the winds."

Tollan allowed himself to relax as well, taking a deep breath and letting it out slowly. "That was a very stupid thing you did."

Thaxon looked at him, his eyes barely visible in the darkened tent. "Are we . . . still friends, then?"

"Of course," Tollan replied. Everything had turned out for the best, but that wouldn't always be the case. "Just remember that our oath to Drüstania and the king comes first, always."

TEN

When defending others, there is nothing more honorable than to stand your ground. But when defending yourself alone, wisdom and cowardice often make for strange bedfellows.

— *Codes of Entreaty 4.24-25*

"THIS CANNOT CONTINUE," Pelendion fumed, pacing back and forth across his private chambers in the dim candlelight. "First, the attack on the square. Then, the northern watchtower burns down without a trace of the guards stationed there, to say nothing of the arsonists responsible for the blaze."

His wife, Coranna, dressed in a plain nightgown rather than queenly fashion, gathered the bedclothes tighter around her to ward off the ill news.

Pelendion's strides ceased beside the bed, and he rested a comforting palm on his wife's blanket-covered knee. His hand was steady, but his voice betrayed a deeper unease. "And now, Outpost Heron to the east has suffered the same fate, while caches of new weapons being transported from Cape Vrosingr have gone missing."

Anseldr met his brother's sunken, tired eyes. He thanked the winds that at least Emeline was not present for this, but Pelendion had insisted at this late hour that whatever Anseldr had to say would be heard by the queen as well. "That is the situation as I understand it, my liege," Anseldr confirmed, careful to use the honorific to defuse the coming argument. "I believe we must draw conclusions and act accordingly."

Pelendion shook his head gravely, allowing his wife to clasp his hand. He did not leave her side, but his furrowed brow indicated that his mind was elsewhere. "I refuse to believe that it has come to open civil war. Don't you find it odd that there have been no taunting messages, nothing left behind? We ought to have more faith in our people, Anseldr."

"Perhaps, but each new attack causes our people to have less faith in *us*," Anseldr countered. The prince's silver circlet felt cold on his sweaty brow as he attempted to stay calm. There could no longer be any doubting the identity of their unseen enemy; it had to be the Crownless, as no other group had a known presence in every hold or the organization to accomplish assaults of this scale. "It was an entire outpost this time. The Crownless don't need to raise a flag for the nation to know who is responsible. More than thirty soldiers are either missing or dead, and what consolation can we give their families?"

"What would you have us do?" Pelendion asked after a long pause. His silent wife glanced nervously between them. "Sergeant Major Senn informs me that the new recruits are proceeding on schedule. Until we have any leads on the current location or intent of these terrorists, the recruits should be allowed to return home and resume work. The royal treasury cannot afford to employ such a large militia indefinitely."

"Your Majesty, the safety and security of our cities and towns should be our first priority." Anseldr rolled up the confidential missive concerning the loss of Outpost Heron and tapped the parchment against his palm. "Once word of this spreads, the people will need to know that they aren't next. As jarl of Celwaith Tor, I intend to set up checkpoints at the city gate and between the four quarters to monitor our citizens and newcomers for any suspicious activity. Curfews will prevent any late-night gatherings or riots. And lastly, I will recommend that all other holds in Drüstania follow suit to present a unified front."

Pelendion's bearded face had grown darker in skepticism and apprehension with each sentence Anseldr uttered. "You would restrict our people's freedoms to that extent? When there is still so much we do not know about the situation?"

"That is precisely why it is prudent, my king," Anseldr continued, spreading his hands and bowing to appear less threatening. It was important that his point got through, far more important than his pride. "The measures will only be temporary, for I imagine most illicit or rebellious activities would either become apparent or die down quickly under those conditions."

Anseldr could see little of Coranna's face in the darkness, but it seemed from her posture that she agreed more with him and less with her husband. *Good*, Anseldr thought. *At least someone is listening.*

"You would need to triple the numbers of the city guard for the scale of what you're talking about," Pelendion said after a moment of heavy thought, leaving his wife's side and coming closer.

Anseldr anticipated his brother's misgivings yet again. "I suppose it's a good thing we trained a standing militia," he said softly. He glanced at Coranna and noticed he had her full attention. He had to make his words count double, as she could be the deciding factor in their discussion. "I understand your misgivings, brother, I do, but the situation is more dire than the view from your throne. You are managing our entire country, but I am responsible for the citizens and businesses here, in this city. I truly believe that taking these measures will alleviate the rampant fear in the streets and, ultimately, help us to bring these terrorists to justice."

Pelendion crossed his arms over his chest, signaling he had come to a decision, and it was final. "What some see as security, others may see as oppression. You will give our enemies more reason to feel their rebellion is justified. I cannot condone this."

"I am not asking if you condone it," Anseldr said, careful to ensure his voice bore no hint of defiance. "I am asking if you forbid it." The difference was minimal, he knew, but everything hinged on it. He would not disobey the expressed orders of the king, but if he only risked his brother's private disapproval, that was another matter entirely.

Pelendion had opened his mouth to reply when Coranna gently cleared her throat behind him. "For what it's worth, Pel," she said, her wispy voice drifting out from under the covers, "I agree with him. Maybe you should let your brother take the lead on this. You can always step in if it bears no fruit."

Anseldr kept himself from smiling. Not that Pelendion never went against his wife's wishes, but she did often help him to see reason through his own biases. Anseldr counted himself extremely fortunate for her presence during the discussion—the little input she gave had been potent.

When at last Pelendion's posture relaxed, victory was assured. "Very well, Anseldr," he said, a measure of annoyance leaking into his tone. "Do what you think is necessary to protect Celwaith Tor. But," Pelendion held up an index finger, "do not overstep your bounds by involving the other holds. If your plan proves effective, I'm sure the jarls will implement their own versions soon enough. Stenden especially."

Anseldr bowed his head in acquiescence. "You have my word, Your Majesty," he replied. It was an acceptable bargain, one that functionally changed nothing. As Pelendion had noted, their younger brother often modeled himself after Anseldr's ideas, sometimes even to his detriment. Stenden, along with the port city of Cape Vrosingr, would almost certainly be the first to follow Celwaith Tor's shining example of security.

"Well, it is late, and I have many logistics in the morning to attend to," Anseldr concluded, bowing again to the king and queen respectively. "Good night."

Pelendion grunted. "As if sleep will come easily now. Good night."

Anseldr reached for the doorknob but stopped short of turning it. Another thought occurred to him. "There is one more thing that could help us."

Pelendion heavily took a seat on the edge of his bed, perhaps mentally cursing the ongoing midnight interruption. "What?"

"Do you remember my old friend, Darakh Shi'ev?"

"Wasn't he the Kiramet prime minister's son when we were children?"

"The very one. Ambassador Seriah Le'shom approached me yesterday, rather out of the blue. Darakh has evidently become one of Ash'kiram's most renowned inventors in recent years. When word of our nation's unrest reached them across the sea, he inquired about bringing us a proposal of sorts."

Pelendion's eyes narrowed. "What kind of proposal?"

"Merely business, or so I'm told," Anseldr replied, a statement that was true at least in the strictest sense. He suspected there would be more than business involved, however, since he had been in detailed correspondence with the inventor for much longer than he let on. "He has recently invented a weapon that he believes will help us deal with a potential insurrection. It is, as near as I can describe it, a small cannon that can be operated by hand."

"Hard to believe that's possible," Pelendion said after the shock of the idea had worn off. But his bushy blond eyebrows raised in interest.

"Still, if we could purchase such a weapon in large enough quantities, our outposts would have a significant deterrent to any further attacks."

Anseldr nodded, glad that his brother could at least see the sense in such a useful development. "Precisely, my liege. At any rate, with your permission, I intend to ask Shi'ev to bring a prototype with him for a demonstration. It may turn out to be nothing, or it could make an end to our troubles in short order."

"For no small price, I imagine."

"The royal treasury is not so low on funds that the purchase would be irresponsible," Anseldr said out of caution. His brother had always been reluctant to trade with other countries because he thought Drüstania's reliance on outside resources would weaken the nation's economy. While Anseldr could see the logic, sometimes the advantages of trade outweighed the risks. "Besides, the Kiramet have been begging to import their goods directly for years. With our merchant fleet out of commission, we need someone to help fill the gap in the supply chain. I'm sure the ambassador could negotiate far better prices with Shi'ev if we finally agreed to sign a trade contract, or even just relax our tariffs."

Pelendion sighed and rubbed the bridge of his nose, clearly worn down by the exchange. "Tell this Shi'ev that we will hear his offer," he said in a softened voice. "I will consider it, but I will promise nothing more tonight. Thank you for bringing this to my attention—I know from experience that Celwaith Tor has many interests within its walls, and it is not easy to balance them all."

Coranna, likewise, gave Anseldr a nervous smile from her side of the bed, showing gratitude in her own quiet way.

"Of course," Anseldr said, pleasantly surprised at the recognition. Perhaps his efforts to aid the country would turn out rather well for a change. "Anything for the betterment of Drüstania." He bowed to both of them, then turned on his heels. The room fell into darkness as

Pelendion blew out the last of the candles an instant before the door swung closed.

Anseldr paid no mind to the rows of kingsguard lining the hall, though their armor clinked as they came to attention. The prospect of the job ahead reinvigorated him, and he retired to his study rather than his bed for another sleepless night.

NIENA'S ARM SHOOK AS she drew the bowstring back to her cheek, betraying the weariness of her muscles and the chill of the brisk morning air. She sighted down the arrow's shaft, locking onto her target: a large red squirrel perched on an oak branch twenty yards away. It was just close enough that she felt confident.

"Steady, steady," her father coached from behind. "Good form, don't overthink it."

The vapor of her breath disappeared as she held it for a steady shot. With a *twang* and a sharp whistle, the arrow lanced toward its target— only to miss at the last instant when the squirrel bolted around the trunk. The arrow glanced off the bark and sailed back down to earth.

Niena frowned, discouraged. It had been the better part of a week since they left the old farmhouse, and she had yet to bag her first kill. She did pretty well with stationary targets, but unfortunately, they weren't trying to hunt trees.

"It's okay, little blossom," Voster said to cheer her up. "By my eye, you would have killed it, but that's the trick with animals—they're unpredictable. You'll get something soon."

The squirrel peeked out from its hiding place and flicked its tail at them in annoyance.

"I suppose," Niena said halfheartedly. She slung the bow across her body and started after the arrow. "I'll be right back."

Voster resumed stamping out the fire and prepared to pack their remaining supplies. "Don't take too long if you can't find it, we need to keep moving. I think we might be close today."

Niena covertly rolled her eyes. He had been saying that for two days now. She wondered how well he remembered the area, but then she felt guilty because she knew she wouldn't recall every detail of their trip twenty years from now.

She took off at a light jog past the squirrel's oak tree, looking for any hint of the arrow's yellow fletching poking through the forest floor. They were much farther north, so the going was easier than their brief jaunt through Spinewood Forest. Instead of thorns, the underbrush consisted of seasonal shoots and ferns that could hide almost anything from view.

It has to be around here somewhere, Niena thought. She widened her search in a spiral from where she had lost sight of the arrow. When that proved unfruitful, she turned her gaze upward to see if maybe it had lodged in another tree rather than the ground.

She came up short as she spied something moving, at the base of the hill where a creek gently trickled. An enormous stag bent his majestic rack of antlers down to drink, and it hadn't seen her.

Niena crouched down to hide herself in the ferns and quietly readied the bow. She couldn't believe her luck; the stag was not much farther from her than the squirrel had been, and so much larger that it would surely be impossible to miss.

She nocked a second arrow and drew back the string, the creak of tension barely audible. The animal shifted, and she spied the best shot to the heart.

The stag's ears pricked up, and it stopped drinking to look down the creek, wary of its surroundings though Niena had given it no reason to be. It looked as though it might bolt, but she would not let it happen this time. She took a bead on the stag's neck, and let the arrow loose.

Her aim was low, but not by enough to matter. The arrow pierced deep behind the creature's foreleg and likely through a lung. The stag let out a startled grunt, thrashing about in pain until it bolted away upstream with the last of its strength. For a second, Niena worried that she had missed, but the animal fell with a splash to the water's edge.

"Papa, Papa!" Niena called in excitement as she hurried down the hill toward the stag. "Come quick!"

Niena's father shouted back, but she was too far away to hear precisely what he said. She crossed the creek to inspect her kill more closely. The buck's front half lay on dry ground, but the hindquarters had fallen in the babbling water. She slung her bow across her back and gripped the animal's antlers with both hands, attempting to drag it out. It budged, but she had only moved it a few inches by the time her father arrived with both their packs.

He stood on the other bank of the creek, gaping. "You took that down?"

Niena tugged on the antlers again and looked pointedly at the yellow fletching and wooden rod sticking out of the deer's side. "No, an arrow just fell from the sky, Papa." She grinned. "Can I get a hand here?"

Voster laughed and hopped the creek. They finished moving the beast and he inspected the shot. "A clean kill, Niena," he observed. "Well done."

Niena smiled. "Thanks, Papa."

Voster worked the arrow free, causing a gush of red to flow out and color the stream. The biting iron scent of blood filled the air, and Niena had to look away. "You hit the heart," he confirmed, washing the arrow a short way upstream and handing it back to her. "I don't know how much of this meat we'll be able to take with us, but the antlers and skin will be useful for . . ."

Niena frowned, wondering why her father trailed off. "What is it?"

"Shh!" Voster held a finger to his mouth, listening. The forest had gone quiet, save for the wind and the running water.

No, Niena realized with a start. A distant raspy sound grew closer and louder with each moment they listened.

"Oh, hell . . . Upstream, run now!" her father barked in a harsh whisper and urgently tugged at her arm in that direction.

"What?" Niena shouldered her pack and trusted her father's instincts, following as fast as she could. A bend in the creek bed loomed ahead between two large boulders. *Papa is scared enough to abandon the kill,* Niena thought grimly as her boots threw back clumps of soft dirt. *What is that sound?*

The noise behind them became more distinct, the audible flapping of many pairs of wings. Grating screeches called from the air. Niena glanced back at the dead stag as she rounded the bend, and saw the carcass covered in vicious-looking crimson birds. They pecked and tore at the raw venison with their serrated beaks, guzzling the flesh down in chunks as the resulting blood turned their feathers a deeper red.

A chill ran down Niena's back, and she pumped her legs faster. Clawcrens were the scourge of the wilds, hunting in garishes of fifteen to twenty that picked bodies clean in minutes regardless of whether they were living or dead. She had read about them but never seen them —and indeed, most people who got close enough never made it back alive.

The uphill run took its toll on Niena's breathing, and her father pulled ahead. If he hadn't been so quick on the uptake they would have been swarmed. The trees appeared to thin out over the next rise, which would make running easier without tripping on rocks or roots.

A chorus of spine-tingling screeches came from behind, even closer than before. Niena risked a glance and wished she hadn't. The hunger of the clawcrens had not been sated by the stag, and they were eager for their meal's next course. The birds swarmed between the gap in the boulders and devoured the distance behind Niena and her father.

"They've seen us!" Niena shouted in panic. The clawcrens were only yards away, and there would be no escaping them now.

Voster crested the rise and threw his pack aside. "Dive, Niena!"

Dive? She thought she had heard wrong until she clambered up the rocks and saw the pond's surface disturbed by her father's kicking legs. The topography had formed a natural dam, with the water filling in a small gully that tipped over the edge to become the creek.

The clawcrens tore at her pack, and she didn't have time to discard it like her father had. She fell in and pushed herself as low as she could, holding her breath and crawl-swimming to deeper water. The pack helped her stay down without bobbing to the surface.

She couldn't see anything in the cloudy water, not her father or the fish or even whether the birds had passed by overhead. It felt like forever, even though it must have been only a few seconds, and her lungs began to burn for want of air. She had to surface.

Niena could see the sunlight filtering through the hazy water and thought if she sat up, she could poke her mouth out long enough to take another breath. Giving herself a countdown, she followed through and immediately felt a sharp pain on her cheek. She cried out and yanked her head back under before more of the clawcrens could take a bite. They circled overhead, waiting out their prey.

She rubbed her cheek. Even underwater, she felt it slick with blood. The peck had taken some skin, but it could have been far worse. And in a couple of minutes, it would be. She already felt the burning in her chest again, the desperate desire to breathe with the knowledge that if she did, Tollan would never know how she had died.

Although, drowning might be better than being torn to pieces by a dozen hooked beaks . . .

The water churned suddenly, like soup being stirred in a pot, when something large impacted the surface. The force pushed an unprepared Niena back toward the bank, and when the water retreated her head breached the surface.

She gasped in all the air she could, coughing and wondering why she hadn't been attacked yet. She scrambled back into the water but stopped, frozen in fear at what she heard and saw before her.

Over the center of the pond, an enraged manticore battled with the clawcrens for dominance. Several of the birds fell into the pond, shredded by claws or cleft in two by the creature's spiked tail. In Niena's visions, it had been dusk, and the manticore's countenance had been shrouded. But now, in the daylight and fighting for its life, the manticore appeared even more terrible and revolting. It spiraled in the air with a rhythmic flapping of its wings, carving through the cloud of red birds with vicious abandon despite its injuries.

A now-familiar roar cut through the air and shook Niena to the core, though it hadn't been this terrible in her dreams. She felt the deep rumble even in her chest, and she couldn't breathe, couldn't even think. She clutched at her ears, trying to block out the sound, but it tore at her skull. The mental pressure reminded her of when the elf in the square had tried to enchant her memory, but this was unrefined, brutish, and painful. The relief when it ended was overwhelming.

Niena held a hand to her temple, stumbling over her own feet as she tried to put distance between herself and the creature.

In Niena's peripheral, she saw her father rise from the water further down the bank, hatchet drawn. He swung it blindly, expecting to be mobbed by the crimson birds even while coughing up water. When that didn't happen, he wiped the water from his eyes and gasped at the carnage unfolding above.

Half of the clawcrens had already been dispatched. One of the remaining birds, cleverer than the others, darted in close to the beast's neck and tore out a hunk of flesh and fur. The beast roared again, this time in pain. Niena fell to the ground, writhing at the awful sound.

Voster, unfazed by the noise, hurried to the bank and snatched up his pack from where he had ditched it. Still holding his hatchet out defensively, he reached down to urgently shake Niena's shoulder as the infernal roar stopped. "Push through it, little blossom! We have to leave, now!"

Niena still held the sides of her head. "It ... hurts," she said, allowing her father to help her up. The water continued draining out of her pack and clothes, making it easier for her to follow him. Her mind flitted to the green leather-bound book, which was surely drenched by the lake water. With any luck, its sturdy construction and thick pages would be enough protection.

Niena's father half-guided, half-dragged her toward the northward treeline. The forest thickened quickly on that side of the lake, providing their best chance of escape. "Move, girl, move!"

Niena shook the lingering effects of the manticore's roar from her mind, and quickly got her feet under her. Behind them, the monster's pointed teeth ripped out another clawcren's throat, and the three remaining birds decided another meal was not worth the trouble. Rather than chase those morsels, the manticore turned its glowing eyes after more satiating prey.

Father and daughter barely escaped into the thicker forest as the creature rapidly gained on them. Niena thought they might be safe, due to the manticore's size, but instead it tucked its wings in and slipped between the trees. It bounded across the forest floor like a great serpentine cat, spiked tail writhing and claws tearing into tree bark with each one it passed.

Voster charged ahead even faster, seemingly ignorant of the weight of his pack across his shoulders.

It was all Niena could do to steady her breathing while keeping up with her father's breakneck pace.

The manticore continued to gain on them, albeit slower than before.

The trees thinned out into a rocky ravine, giving the manticore enough room to spread its wings and push off into the sky again. It lined up for a swooping pass at them and roared. Niena fell to her knees at the painful sound, and her father yanked her back to her feet.

They had nowhere else to run. The ravine walls boxed them in, and there was nothing between them and certain death.

Without warning, the forest floor ahead gave way under Voster's feet, and Niena could not stop her momentum. Her heart leaped into her throat as she tumbled head over heels into darkness.

ELEVEN

And so, there are various kinds of strength, none of them immune to any other. As a tree splinters when struck along the grain, so a deft thought can disarm a giant.

— Codes of Entreaty 3.16-17

TOLLAN HADN'T THOUGHT IT possible to get more blisters than what already covered his hands and feet, but every few hours he collected or burst another. The sloppy one-size-fits-all armor brought in from the overworked Celwaith Tor smithies proved instead to be quite ill-fitting. But most of the recruits figured out ways to nip and tuck their overlarge plain yellow tunics around the worst offending edges. What quickly became untenable, though, was sharing one uniform between five different men, resulting in the most rank stew of body odor imaginable.

Sergeant Major Senn had decided to split up each column further, so that smaller groups could march and train against each other in full armor for two hours at a time, while the others continued with regular exercises. Corporal Crandas assigned each subgroup of twelve in

Column Seventeen a leader, and Tollan and Thaxon had the half-expected misfortune of being placed under Ruger.

"What was that supposed to be, Cresthaven?" Ruger demanded after a failed simulated charge, yanking his helmet off and chucking it to the ground at Tollan's feet. "We almost had that one, if your flank hadn't buckled!"

Thaxon stepped in front of Tollan, sticking up for his friend even after the incident with the wine. "You pushed through and left us behind! We couldn't keep up, and Twenty-One's team forced us apart."

Ruger shoved the red-haired boy aside, along with his objection. "It's your job to keep up on the battlefield, Denvald! We are only as strong as our weakest link, and teacher's pet here is a liability to the unit—I don't care what the corporal says."

Tollan didn't react, and instead he stood there silently to take the verbal abuse. The worst part was that he knew Ruger was right. He should have been drummed out of the army, if not for Crandas' recommendation to the sergeant major.

As the training wore on, it became painfully apparent that while everyone else gradually improved in physical endurance and skill, Tollan fell further and further behind his marks. It didn't make sense that he should be so far behind the average man, but any condition that might be impacting his physical health was far from obvious.

"Anything to say for yourself, Cresthaven?" Ruger spat, standing almost nose-to-nose with him.

"No, sir," Tollan replied evenly. He had long since learned how to mask his distaste. "We should have kept pace with you."

Ruger—or rather, Acting Lieutenant Yorvikson—looked even more peeved that he had gotten an apology rather than a reaction. His antagonism had only increased since the wine incident, perhaps viewing Tollan as a spineless kiss-up who had been rewarded, rather than a soldier who thought for himself. "Get ready, Cresthaven," he ordered, cramming his helmet back on. "You're taking point this round, arrow formation. We'll see how you fare carrying all of us on your puny shoulders."

Tollan swallowed and accepted the red band which would mark him as the leader. As the tip of the V-shaped offensive push, all the pressure would be focused on him when they broke against the opposing column's defenses. It was a punishment that would make the rest of the group angry at him and him alone if he failed. But it also meant that he set the pace, and provided that Ruger didn't break formation and push ahead of him, Tollan thought it possible that they might break through to the far side this time.

He wondered if he might get lucky and have the double horn blast during the exercise, signaling the training rotation. Curious, he reached in behind his breastplate and pulled out his pocket watch to check the time and wished he hadn't. An hour remained before they could change stations, and this would be over long before then.

The other eleven members of the group formed up behind him, the left flank of six led by Ruger. Thaxon steadied his shield behind Tollan's right shoulder and nodded to signal the right flank's readiness. Across the field, their twelve armored enemies slammed their dulled polearms into the ground twice, indicating that the exercise should commence.

Tollan held his breath for a split second and shouted. "Charge!"

He knew the rest of the group was champing at the bit to move faster, but everyone remained together to advance at Tollan's pace.

But the extra time it took to cross the field gave Column Twenty-One a chance to restructure and reinforce their position. Tollan watched the enemy lines shift, doubling up in the center of their formation but leaving the edges more exposed. That left a core group of six soldiers, with "wings" of three on each side.

He raised his blunt sword, directing Ruger and Thaxon to lead their flanks left as they closed in. The arrow shape swung wide and then back inwards, aiming not at the center but instead at the weak point where the single file diverged. That would enable Ruger's side to deal with the smaller, divided group of three before aiding the right flank to push through.

Tollan's legs strained to keep up the pace he had set, but he could not turn back now. Ten paces from contact, he raised his shield and barreled forward, his teammates close behind.

He used his sword to shove past the nearest defending polearm and put the full force of his advance into the edge of the first enemy shield. The shock of impact traveled up his arm and into his shoulder, but the angle of entry gave him the advantage of leverage.

The opposing soldier buckled, slipping to his knees in the mud where Tollan swiped his sword lightly across his chest. He stopped fighting and backed away from the engagement, feigning death in the ongoing war game but not wanting to be trod upon.

The skirmish had favored Column Seventeen so far, but their lead would not last. Tollan glanced to his left to see Ruger making quick work of the remaining enemies on that side. On his right, however, Thaxon's flank had been halted in its tracks and was fighting to hold its ground. Two of their number fell, creating gaps that the enemy could exploit.

Tollan clashed swords with an enemy in the back row, then motioned with his shield and called back to Ruger. "Swing around behind them! Pincer maneuver!"

Either Ruger hadn't heard him or chose not to, and a couple of his men peeled off to reinforce Thaxon's line instead. They needed it, but the tactical error would only prolong the inevitable. Thaxon himself was now tied up fighting the enemy leader, and the remains of Column Seventeen's formation had descended into chaos.

Tollan growled and blocked another blow with his shield. They had been so close, but their odds now looked grim.

He broke off his attack since he hadn't been doing any good, and ran as fast as he could to Thaxon's aid. His heart pounded and sweat poured down his face, plate armor bouncing up and down on his thin frame with every step.

But he could not get there in time. The enemy lieutenant shoved Thaxon's wooden shield wide and landed a glancing blow to his helm with a heavy *clank*. The boy fell backward and lay still.

Tollan was livid. The rules of mock engagement stated that head blows were off-limits, but without officers or referees watching, the rules rarely applied beyond a warning to "be careful."

"You!" he shouted, trying but failing to make his adolescent voice sound more threatening.

The lieutenant spun and locked eyes with him, a man with several missing teeth who appeared as though he should have been too old for the draft—or at least had aged poorly. Tollan thought for a second that he recognized the man as one of the town drunks but wasn't positive. At any rate, he wasn't drunk now, and he'd had plenty of practice fighting even before recruitment.

Tollan pulled up short, standing defensively in front of Thaxon's horizontal form. As he eyed up his opponent, he nudged his friend with his boot, which elicited a slight stirring and a groan. The rich boy would recover.

The opposing leader raised his sword, a green sash hanging from his elbow, and charged toward them.

Not much for conversation, then, Tollan mused.

Tollan side-stepped with his shield as cover, forcing the man to over-commit to his attack. That bought him a little time, but not much. He glanced around at the rest of the battlefield to make sure he was clear of other distractions and saw with surprise that his team had rallied.

Ruger finally caught on to what he needed to do and circled the rear with two teammates, and the resulting miniature assault had downed over half of the enemy grunts. That tipped the balance in the offense's favor.

We might have a chance, Tollan thought as he locked swords with his opponent. His arm strained and pushed, but he couldn't overcome the hardened older man. He lifted his shield over his head and ducked under the warrior's arm, narrowly avoiding a hit to his chest which would have put him on the sidelines.

So few soldiers were left in the skirmish that it began to look more like a sparring match. The disqualified recruits stood around watching the outcome of the survivors with bated breath.

Ruger and one other remaining soldier from Column Seventeen, Gwever, teamed up and tagged the next-to-last opponent in the back, leaving them, Tollan, and the enemy lieutenant on the field. But rather than help win the day, they both backed off and watched with the rest.

"What are you doing?" Tollan yelled, batting away another strike and backpedaling. "Help me!"

Ruger grinned, and he and Gwever touched the tips of their swords to each other's chests, effectively taking themselves out of the rest of the match rather than coming to Tollan's aid. "Whether we win or lose depends only on you, Cresthaven!"

Tollan paled in embarrassment as a good portion of the group laughed. Thaxon wasn't there to stick up for him this time either, as he still lay off to the side, holding his head.

If it had been difficult for Tollan to win a fight in his everyday clothes with simple sticks, it would be ten times harder with chain mail and heavy blunted swords. No one knew this better than Ruger, who had quickly gained a reputation as the column's best swordsman. By the end of the third week, Tollan still hadn't won a single match—though he had come close a few times, and that was enough to keep him pressing on.

Ruger meant to humiliate him yet again, but this time allowed someone from another column to do his dirty work. But Tollan would not dare allow a loss—if the enemy had broken the rules to hit Thaxon, he would have to break them better.

Tollan had an idea, risky but possible. He danced away from his enemy and backed up several paces, ignoring the jeers and sizing up his opponent. The older man stalked him with a toothless grin, having every reason to be overconfident of his impending victory.

Tollan quickly undid the two buckles on his forearm, chucked his shield at the man, and lunged forward.

The soldier flinched away, using his own shield to knock aside the distraction before predictably striking again at Tollan.

Noting the angle of the incoming blow from his right, Tollan reached up with his free left hand. He caught the bloke's sword along the cross-guard and did nothing to stop its momentum. Instead, he held on tight as the blade continued its hasty arc. Tollan fell and slid through the mud on his knees. He fought to maintain his grip.

Caught by surprise, the green-sashed leader tried to yank his sword away but found that it had already been released. The unnecessary effort threw him far off balance, giving Tollan the perfect opening to swipe at the back of his knees. The older man went down, landing in the muck.

Before he could recover, Tollan lifted his sword again, this time with both hands. He brought the flat of the blade down as hard as he could, right on the chain mail between his opponent's splayed legs.

The man let out a howl of pain and crumpled inward to the fetal position, abandoning his sword in the mud. He lay there moaning and cupped his groin with his hands.

Tollan forced himself back to his feet, panting and full of adrenaline. The bystanders went quiet in disbelief, and all that could be heard were the sounds of other skirmishes dotted over the training field.

The sound of a whalebone whistle called them all to attention, and Tollan noticed for the first time that Corporal Crandas stood off to one side, watching. "Well done, Cresthaven! Very well done."

"Thank you, sir." He must have returned early from monitoring the rest of the column—it was too early to rotate stations, but he wouldn't argue if the corporal made an exception. Archery was next, something Tollan proved halfway decent at.

Ruger marched up and waited to be acknowledged.

"Yes, Yorvikson?" Crandas said begrudgingly.

"Sir, the last blow was unnecessary and cruel to the other team," Ruger protested. "Cresthaven was not playing by the rules."

Column Twenty-One's lieutenant finally stirred from his humbled place on the ground. He refused to meet anyone's gaze as he returned to stand with his comrades. He looked pitiful, and Tollan was tempted to smirk.

"Neither were you. Nor the other team, for that matter," Crandas retorted, his brow creased. "I would have named victory regardless of the outcome of your little stunt, with no small thanks to Cresthaven's adaptable strategy. But even worse is that you didn't check on your downed teammate when you had more than one chance to do so."

Tollan felt a chill run through him as he remembered Thaxon. He whirled and saw him lying twenty yards away without his helmet. He rushed over to his friend's side, not caring if he got demerits for disrespecting his corporal. "Thaxon, Thaxon! I'm sorry, it's all my fault —are you all right?"

The red-headed kid groaned as he propped himself up onto his elbow. "Other than blacking out for a bit and waking up with a splitting headache? I'm fine."

It sounded to Tollan like a concussion, which was much more serious than fine. Thaxon needed rest, and possibly treatment. "Come on, we've got to get you to your bunk. I'll see if I can find ginger root, maybe some turmeric—"

"Hey," Thaxon interrupted, grinning.

"What?"

"You showed Ruger. That was impressive, what you pulled off back there," Thaxon said as he glanced toward the others. Crandas was still dressing down Ruger, though it seemed like he might wrap up in a minute. "You finally won a match, sort of."

Tollan nodded, not fully believing it himself. His hare-brained move had succeeded by sheer luck. "Yeah, I guess I did. Thanks."

He helped the aching Thaxon to his feet and supported him as they slowly made their way toward the tents on the far side of Crandas and the others. Tollan saw the gathering begin to break up, and both subgroups headed back to rejoin their respective columns.

"Corporal!" Tollan called when they were within earshot.

Crandas came and helped carry Thaxon. "What's his condition, Cresthaven?"

"I'll be fine, sir," Thaxon insisted.

Tollan ignored him and answered anyway. "Concussion, I think, sir. He lost consciousness."

"Bedrest it is, then," the corporal said. "We'll be one short at the assembly, but that can't be helped."

"Assembly, sir?" Thaxon asked, his words ever so slightly slurred. "Is that where everyone is going?"

Tollan looked around at the rest of the camp and saw the entire two-thousand-strong force beginning to stir from their assigned places.

It would take a while to recall the groups still on their daily run up the nearest mountain, but clearly whatever had happened was important enough to assemble all the columns at once.

"Indeed, Denvald," Crandas confirmed, picking up the pace. "Sergeant Major Senn has ordered that all troops report to him on the field at three o'clock this afternoon. Urgent news from Celwaith Tor."

Tollan's heart skipped a beat, then realized he probably shouldn't be excited about the prospect. Urgent news was rarely ever good. He hoped Niena was all right. "What kind of news, Corporal?" he asked, not expecting much of an answer.

Crandas let Thaxon's feet down outside the open flap of Column Seventeen's second tent and sighed. "I suppose you both will know soon enough, but it's better that Denvald hears it now from me rather than secondhand. There's been another attack, this time wiping out one of our larger outposts on the East Road. The attackers seem to be circling the capital, so Jarl Anseldr has ordered all troops from Celwaith Tor back from training early to assume their posts. Whether you're ready or not."

So training had been cut a week short. Tollan couldn't say that he minded, though it frustrated him now that he was finally starting to overcome his natural weaknesses. He supposed the rest of his training would have to be more hands-on.

"The outpost was found completely deserted, the buildings torched with few signs of struggle," Crandas clarified, reminding Tollan of what had happened to the northern watchtower not long before. "The Crownless are becoming bolder with each of their successes."

None of them said anything more for a moment, the silence broken only by the bustling of the other columns' preparations. Thaxon leaned a little harder on Tollan's shoulder, before breaking the quiet. "What should we do now, sir?"

"You? Rest, and nothing else," Crandas replied. "I don't know when we're moving out, but I want you recovered as much as possible before then. Cresthaven, help him remove his armor and get settled, then join us on the field to receive the sergeant major's orders."

"Sir, yes, sir," Tollan and Thaxon acknowledged, almost in unison.

And with a final nod, Crandas turned on his heel and marched off to gather the other seventy members of Column Seventeen.

Tollan sat his friend down on the nearest bunk and began stripping off pieces of armor, starting with unbuckling the shoulder plates.

Thaxon exclaimed, "What happened to your ear?"

Tollan's hand flew up, feeling the right side of his head. Had he been clipped in the fight as well? "Am I bleeding?"

"No, I'd just never noticed your scar before," Thaxon answered, leaning to get a better look.

"Oh, that," Tollan said, turning his attention back to his armor. He could see why it would be alarming, as his ear was missing an odd chunk and the skin folded over where it had been stitched. "Accident when I was little—took a tumble and my ear caught on a loose nail. It's nothing. Are you feeling any better?" he asked.

"Not really." Thaxon swiped an arm across his face to remove the sheen of sweat that had settled there and stuck his leg out for Tollan to remove his armored boot. His stark red hair had grown out since they had met and now looked far more ragged and unkempt. "Sounds like we're headed home soon though. How does that make you feel?"

Tollan wasn't sure if he was being honest with himself. He yanked hard on the boot, and it came off with a *plop*, emitting a horrible odor. He covered his nose and threw it aside. "Me and my dad aren't on the best of terms," he said simply. "I miss my aunt and sister well enough, but I don't know how he will react to my new position."

"Oh," Thaxon replied, lying back on the bunk. "Well, if there's any trouble, I'm sure I can convince my family to help you out."

Tollan nodded. It was a nice gesture, but they belonged to such different tiers of society that it hardly mattered. Besides, they were fellow soldiers first, and friends second. He began to gather the scattered armor but turned back to Thaxon before he finished.

"You know I don't hold what happened with the wine against you, right?" Tollan asked. Things hadn't been the same between them since that night, and he suspected that had prompted Thaxon's offer.

"You don't?"

"Not at all," Tollan said, and he meant it. "I understand why you did it, and you don't have to make anything up to me. You've been a good friend—the best."

Thaxon smiled, then winced and pressed a hand to the side of his head to assuage the headache. "Well, apart from that first night. I practically accused you of killing my sister."

Tollan chuckled and shook his head. "We were all on edge then."

The silence turned awkward, so Tollan finished picking up the rest of his friend's armor until his arms were full. "Try to sleep now, Thaxon. You'll need to be at your best when we face the Crownless. I'll see what herbs and roots I can find and brew you some tea after the assembly."

Thaxon had already shut his eyes tight, but he smiled in agreement. "Thanks," he whispered.

Tollan left the tent and headed for the armory, thinking about what dangers might lie ahead for them both as protectors of Celwaith Tor—and how soon those dangers might present themselves.

TWELVE

*Pain and suffering may be constants in
the short days of the living, but woe to
the one who inflicts them on another
without necessity.*

— Codes of Entreaty 1.08

VOSTER LANDED FIRST, AND Niena followed with a painful *whump* on top of him. She looked around in distress, unable to see anything except the light from the unnaturally-shaped hole they had fallen through maybe fifteen feet above them. The outline suggested a trapdoor, but the floor beneath them was covered in mounds of dried grass.

A weighted net fell out of the darkness behind them, pressing them into the cushioned floor and restricting their movement. It was indeed a trap, but if it was meant for hunting it was oddly designed not to kill. Niena tried to squirm free, but she could find little traction or leverage.

"That could have been a lot worse," Voster said, his voice muffled by the awkward way he was positioned beneath her.

"Are you sure it isn't?"

"Fair point," her father mumbled, trying to shift his weight. "Do you hear that?"

Sure enough, the sounds of distant shouting, heavy footsteps, and whistling arrows echoed down to them. The enraged roar of the manticore passed by overhead, causing Niena to wince in mental pain, and the rhythmic flapping of wings gradually dissipated.

After a short time, the voices came closer, and a wide rope ladder appeared over the pit's edge. A handful of figures climbed down, and with a chill, Niena immediately noticed their height and deep blue hooded cloaks. They were all too familiar.

The first two of the D'harnir stepped off from the ladder and chanted over them with outstretched hands. Niena recognized the telltale pressure on her mind once more. It was still a physical ache, but far less piercing and intense than the manticore's roar. It was more . . . refined, purposeful, like it had been in the alley outside Wraelian Square.

The sudden urge to yawn came over her, but she stifled it. "I'm sorry, I don't understand what you're saying," she spoke up from where she lay trapped under the net. "Can you set us free? Please? We fell into your trap being chased by that . . . thing."

The elves, now joined by two more, abruptly ceased their incantations and stared at her in shock. Voster, who hadn't moved or said anything since before the arrival of the newcomers, began to snore loudly. It was obvious to Niena now that they had been casting a sleeping spell on both of them.

None of the four individuals responded to her question and instead whispered among themselves. One of them gestured in Niena's direction, indicating they did not know what to do with someone who could resist their spells. *Good,* she thought. *Might buy some time for us to explain.*

The group seemed to come to an agreement, and three of them spread out around the chamber. The fourth, bearded and dressed in the same dark blue save for a gray patch over the left shoulder, took a dagger from his belt.

"No, wait!" she said, struggling but still unable to move. She panicked and offered the only thing that came to mind: "My necklace!"

The D'harn moved in to get a closer look at her. He reached through the net and grasped the pendant still hanging around her neck, then glared at her in recognition. "How have you come by this?" he asked in a thickly-accented voice.

"It was my mother's," Niena answered. "She was one of you."

This time, the D'harn took a rough hold of her hair, lifting it to examine one of her ears.

"Ow!" Niena yelped. "Would it hurt you to be more gentle?"

"Hmph. You have been shorn, but the bone structure is there," the elf commented, ignoring the pain he had caused. He stepped back and gestured to his compatriots, but never took his eyes off Niena. "You are a halfblood—almost unheard of these days."

"I'm not a threat to you, I promise," Niena assured as the others removed the stone weights from their fasteners at the corners of the net.

"That has yet to be seen. Do not think of running—I have archers covering the opening."

"We came here looking for you," Niena countered, finally given the space to wriggle free of the trap. Her joints cracked as she got to her feet, and she made sure to hold her hands away from her body so as not to appear aggressive in any way. Her pack dribbled the last remnants of lake water onto the floor of the pit. "Why would we run?"

The captain, if that's what his cloak's gray patch signified, appraised her with his blade still in hand. She examined him in return, spying his pointed ears under the dark blue hood. His extremely pale face was broken by his deep-set blue eyes and a well-groomed reddish-brown beard with flecks of gray throughout.

"You have tenacity, I will give you that. Not many women would dare traverse the northern wilds without more protection than an old man." The D'harn tilted his chin toward the slumbering Voster. "Who is he? Father, perhaps uncle?"

Niena chose not to confirm or deny anything else until she knew a little more about their captors. Surely her blood entitled her to a dialogue, not an interrogation. "Will he be all right?" she decided to ask instead.

The captain's eyes narrowed. "If you mean to ask whether he is currently unharmed, then yes, he is only sleeping. Our magic was once used for the sole purpose of healing and growing crops, but current events have required us to devise more . . . defensive means. If you are asking whether he will remain in such good condition, well, that part is up to you."

If the elves now resorted to threats, that did not bode well.

Niena was about to explain the purpose of their visit when the rest of the patrol stripped the pack from her father's stocky form and lifted him to his feet, still snoring. Even with his pack removed, they struggled to carry him.

The captain's eyes widened in surprise and joy when he saw Voster's face. "No. It cannot be," he said under his breath, moving closer. "Now it makes sense."

Niena blinked, amazed by the sudden change in the elf's mood. She hadn't considered the possibility that this captain may have known her father, but she snatched at the opportunity. "His name is Voster Cresthaven, and I'm his daughter Niena. I take it you've met before?"

The captain nodded, his countenance grim as he examined the sleeping man. "The years have not been kind to his appearance since our paths last crossed. Here," he said to his companions, "lay him up against the side of the pit. I'm going to wake him."

"Is that wise, sir?" the apparent youngest of the D'harnin scouts asked. "He could easily overpower all of us. We would have to . . ."

"This man once saved my life," the captain said harshly. "Do not question me." Once his orders had been followed, he closed his eyes and waved a hand over Voster, whispering in the same odd language as before. Niena tried to make out some syllables, but they were completely strange to her.

Voster groaned, a moment before his eyes fluttered open in confusion. He scrambled to sit up, snapping back to reality as he saw the D'harn standing over him. He squinted, and Niena saw the recognition dawn in his eyes. "What is—Tollan? Is that you?"

Niena blinked. What was this, another trick of D'harnin magic to make her father think one of the elves was her brother? "Papa, what are you saying? This isn't Tollan."

Niena's father gestured for her to help him up. "No, Niena, this is an old friend. Your brother is named after him, as a matter of fact."

"What?" Niena gripped his forearm and helped get her father's feet under him. "But you said Mama picked Tollan's name."

"She did," Voster said with a smile. He wrapped the elf captain in a bear hug. "I never would have met her if this D'harn hadn't almost died in a riverbed northwest of here."

"Emphasis on almost," the elder Tollan said, good-naturedly clapping Voster on the shoulders. "Tynathria named your son after me? I'm touched, though it saddens me to say that is no longer my name. Druinor chose to honor me with the name Tolvanen before he passed on, ten years ago now."

"Oh. I'm sorry for your . . . our . . . loss," Voster said solemnly before turning back to a confused Niena. "Druinor was the Junir clan's elder— he adopted me into the enclave, and was always good to me and your mother."

It didn't explain much, but Niena was hungry for any information about their assailants. She glanced at the onlooking D'harnin soldiers and saw they were just as bewildered and apprehensive, so at least she wasn't the only one left in the dark.

"How is Tynathria?" Tolvanen asked. "Has she adapted to human life?"

"It seems that both of us have had to bear our share of loss," Voster said after a strained pause.

"I see," Tolvanen said, stricken with guilt for asking. "That is ill news. Druinor had always hoped that your union might be a sign of better things to come between men and D'harnir. But most of the changes in the enclave these last two decades have been for the worse."

"How do you mean?" Niena asked. "By my understanding, things weren't that great between us to begin with."

"She has her mother's wit," Tolvanen said to Voster before turning to address her. "You are correct, Niena. Suffice it to say that . . ." He trailed off, sounding like he meant to continue but instead pivoting to a different thought. "Perhaps it would be better for you to see that in person. The city is a half day's ride from here. We can be there before evening."

The youngest D'harn gripped Tolvanen's arm and took him aside. "You are taking them to Por'monir? You know Shilvand would not approve."

"Enough, Hemilhet," Tolvanen corrected. "I take full responsibility for their actions. Voster already knew the enclave's location—if he had wanted to hurt us, he would have done it long ago. Should you disagree, take up your case with the arbiter when you return. Shilvand is your clan's patriarch, after all."

Niena glanced back and forth between the captain and the young soldier. Back in Drüstania, such insubordination would not have been tolerated in the military. Tolvanen was frustrated with it, that much was obvious, but judging by his lack of surprise it was commonplace for orders to be questioned among the D'harnir. Perhaps they had a much looser structure of authority, she reasoned.

Hemilhet caved instead of doubling down. "You can be sure that I will," he said, intending to have the last word but merely sounding impudent.

Voster stepped in, trying to defuse the tension. "Hold on, Tollan—uh, Tolvanen. I don't want to provoke my brother-in-law any more than necessary. Tynathria and I were banished from Por'monir, as you might recall."

Tolvanen shook his head, a slight smile tugging at his cheek. "By Wirvanen, not Shilvand. I know you would not have come all this way with your daughter unless it urgently concerned the D'harnir and our enclave. I do not doubt that your brother-in-law will hear your case, if only for the sake of his sister's remembrance."

Niena sneaked a look at Hemilhet, who had ceased any direct defiance even though a frown still boiled on his face. "Shouldn't we tell you why we're here, and then you can decide to take us to Por'monir?" she asked, confused.

"Not if we want to make it to the enclave while the council is still in session," Tolvanen said shortly. "Fill me in on the way." He clapped his hands, and Niena spotted the silhouettes of three more cloaked D'harnir around the pit's edge, all brandishing bows and arrows.

Tolvanen cupped his gloved hands around his mouth before shouting upward. "One of you, ready two of the horses at camp. Quickly."

The soldiers above acknowledged the order, and the others below finished resetting the trap under Tolvanen's supervision. Niena took the brief opportunity to sort through her pack and discard anything ruined by the lake water. Most of the provisions had been spoiled, but she supposed that didn't matter if the elven city was so close. She dreaded to see the condition of her father's book, but to her surprise, it wasn't in her pack. "Papa, the book," she said, looking at him in alarm.

Her father smiled and drew it from inside the top of his bag, which had remained dry on the lake's shore. "Here—I was in a hurry when you downed that stag and must have put it in mine."

She accepted it back with relief, shouldering her belongings in time for Tolvanen to usher them up the rope ladder. Once everyone climbed out of the hole, the elven soldiers lifted the trigger mechanism into place and lowered the trapdoor slowly back on top of it. With a few smears of mud and debris around the edges, Niena couldn't tell it was ever there. The D'harnir had clearly come to rely on more than their magic to remain hidden.

"Continue our scheduled patrol patterns and check the other perimeter traps for wild game—or other intruders," Tolvanen ordered when the archer had returned with two horses as instructed. "These two may have been followed by more than a manticore. Meanwhile, I will personally escort our guests back to Por'monir. Paltarin is in charge until I return. Voster, Niena, mount up—daylight is wasting." He grabbed hold of the nearest horse's elaborate saddle horn and swung his leg up and over, the dark blue cloak billowing behind.

Voster mounted first and heaved Niena up behind him. She had never ridden horseback before, and the ground looked further away than it should have. She clutched at her father's back for dear life when he clicked the reins, and they lurched forward. He knew precisely how to handle a horse despite never needing one in the city.

"I apologize for seeming harsh back there when we first pulled you from the trap," Tolvanen said after the other elves were out of earshot. He led the horses slowly up a rocky incline. "Many younger Protectors are more zealous than they should be, and it is easier to command their respect if I play along. But you are safe with me, and Por'monir is not far."

Niena briefly touched the pendant hanging from her neck and felt a bit calmer. *We're almost there, Mama,* she thought with both excitement and trepidation.

"We understand," Voster said with a curt nod. "Thank you."

"I also thought it best that we discuss some things away from mixed company," Tolvanen said. "So now, tell me: apart from the magnificent fauna you've encountered, what brings you this far into the northern wilds?"

NIENA'S BREATH LEFT HER in awe as they crested the final rise. A valley spread out below them, a wide grassy plain sprinkled with green but having mostly turned yellow. The edges were filled with now-familiar pine and cedar trees, and the valley walls came together on the far side below a great snowy mountain, closer than its peers on the horizon. Perched partway up the mountainside, almost directly opposite where their horses stood, there rose a walled city carved from stone.

Tolvanen whispered a short incantation toward Niena and her father, and she might have reached for her dagger if not for the smile on his face. "Can you see it this time, Voster?" he said, pointing. "Right there, at the end of the gorge under the treeline."

Voster's frown of concentration cleared from his forehead. "Ah, yes! You weren't kidding—the enclave has grown by at least half since I left."

Niena cleared her throat, eyeing Tolvanen with suspicion. "What was that for? The spell just now?"

The elf regarded her strangely. "You could see past the wardcasters' spell before I shielded you? Intriguing."

"Wardcasters?"

Her father elaborated. "As a defensive measure, many D'harnir trade off shifts in a perimeter around the city. They cast a large spell in unison that blocks the sight of the enclave from the minds of outsiders. Like what happened with Keordi."

"So, any trespassers that fall into the Protectors' pit traps will be enchanted to return home with false memories of an unfruitful hunting trip, " Niena said, admiring the ingenuity of the D'harnir. "And if they happen to avoid the traps, they still can't see the city. Clever."

"But you can block the effects of illusion spells from your mind entirely," Tolvanen said excitedly, then looked away. "I am sorry, half-bloods like yourself have been unheard of in hundreds of years, so it is curious to me. Such thorough immunity to our spells might mean you have the ability to cast as well."

Niena frowned. As long as she could see through whatever wool these elves might try to pull over her eyes, she had no interest in anything more. "I'm not interested."

"As you will." Tolvanen turned back to his horse, chastened by her response.

Niena's father patted her knee. It felt patronizing. He of all people should understand her hesitation since he had hidden the truth of her heritage from her for so long.

Besides, the last things she wanted to consider were similarities between herself and the D'harn that had attacked her home. And although Tolvanen had looked genuinely surprised by the news, his uniform and cloak resembled the terrorist to an alarming degree.

Her father might trust Tolvanen excessively, but Niena had to be more objective for both their sakes.

Tolvanen clicked his reins and led them down the wooded slope as quickly as their horses could safely tread. The sun was descending, but they still had a good portion of the day left. "The Council of Clans will be in session for another hour or two at most," he said as they reached the grassy plain. "We must hurry to ensure you receive an audience with them today—you may not be allowed a second chance to deliver your warning."

"I may be rusty in the saddle," Voster said, "but I'll manage. Hold on tight, Niena."

Niena wrapped her arms around her father's midsection and felt his thighs brace for the sudden jolt forward. With a "Hyah!" from Tolvanen, the chill northern wind became even colder on her face, and her loose blonde locks streamed behind her.

The first few hundred yards were painful, but Niena learned quickly to sway with the horse's movements and not against them. As the mountain city loomed larger ahead, the enclave's placement struck Niena as strategic. The mountainside perch was precarious, but it was also such an unlikely place to build that few would ever stumble across it by accident, as long as the wardcasters blocked it from sight. It also gave Por'monir the perfect vantage point, as anyone on the city walls would be able to see attackers coming from miles away.

Their horses had to slow once they reached the gorge on the far side and started up a switch-backed trail leading up. Niena saw no guards posted along the path, and none presented themselves before they at last approached the tall city gate. Despite its height, the intricately designed wooden doors were so narrow that their horses would have to enter single file. Windows, or rather slits, were hewn from the stone above and to either side of the gate, and a voice called out to them from inside.

"Tolvanen! You abandon your assigned post and bring the accursed humans to our doorstep?" The accent was even thicker than Tolvanen's, to the point that Niena had difficulty making out the words. She wondered if the lookout was using the common tongue for their guest's benefit, or perhaps the D'harnir only used their ancient dialect for casting spells.

Tolvanen raised his hand in a peaceful greeting. "They are not accursed! They are old allies now returned to us with an important message for the Council of Clans."

"What message?"

Tolvanen seemed to have expected the question. "Many humans were killed in their capital city when a D'harnin saboteur used magic. They are preparing for war as we speak." It was an over-simplification, but they couldn't exactly shout all the details through a window.

There was no reply for a few moments as the lookout came to a decision. Niena looked back down the way they came and gasped—no less than twenty-four elven archers had materialized from the sides of the gorge and blocked off their escape.

There was no going back now.

After another minute, the doors creaked and moved with a low grinding sound. Despite the symmetrical designs on the face, the doors did not split down the middle and swing outward as Niena would have expected. Instead, the entire assembly slid aside, deeper and deeper into the stone wall until the opening was revealed. When it groaned to a stop, Niena saw that the mechanism was driven by a series of large stone gears, stronger and sturdier than the gate appeared at first glance.

Tolvanen dismounted first and led his steed through the narrow gap. Niena's father followed suit, helping her down and giving her the horse's halter. "Don't speak unless they ask you something directly," he said in a low voice. "And don't mention your brother unless I do, just in case. Let me handle the talking."

Niena nodded, thankful that she wouldn't be put on the spot. She stuck close behind her father as they crossed the threshold into the enclave city of Por'monir.

The scene within matched the scene without. A large group of Protector archers held their bowstrings taut, every arrow tip pointed at the perceived threat. Another D'harn stood among them, the only one with no weapon drawn. His uniform had the same patch of gray on his shoulder as Tolvanen, but his face appeared far younger. His hair was straight, strikingly black, and cropped shorter around his ears instead of hanging long like many of the other elves.

"Gilbrannen," Tolvanen said, giving the opposing leader a raised hand in greeting. "It is fortunate you were on duty at the gate to meet us."

The D'harn's frown did not falter, and he paid no direct attention to Tolvanen. He looked the newcomers up and down with suspicion. "I would not be so sure. Who is this human?"

"Ah yes, I forget," Tolvanen said with a measure of forced cheer. "This was before your time, though you should have heard the story. This man once saved my life, and married Shilvand's sister. He comes with his daughter, a halfblood."

Gilbrannen's eyes widened. "You were banished," he said to Voster. "You know the punishment for returning."

Niena's stomach turned, and her father squeezed her hand for comfort. She was painfully aware that enough arrows were pointed at their chests to kill them many times over, but she had a feeling that the punishment Gilbrannen mentioned was not as straightforward as death.

The silence was broken by the wind whistling through the stone buildings. A few D'harnin faces peeked out of windows or over the edges of their roofs to see the commotion.

Voster cleared his throat. "I had no intention to come back unless I was invited. But Por'monir is in grave danger, and I would not allow harm to come to my wife's people, banishment or not. The city of Celwaith Tor was attacked—"

"Yes, Tolvanen explained enough," Gilbrannen said, cutting off any further discussion. "Spare the details for the Council. They will judge the veracity of your story, and the arbiter will decide if it is worth commuting your sentence. Now, surrender your weapons."

They did as they were told. Niena reluctantly handed over her mother's dagger and hoped it wasn't the last she'd see of it.

Gilbrannen gave a hand signal, and the surrounding archers lowered their weapons. "Make no mistake," he growled, "you are not welcome here. Tolvanen and my men will accompany us to the Hall of Meeting—do not attempt to speak with anyone else along the way."

"There's no need for—" Tolvanen started to say, but Voster cut him off.

"Thank you." Voster spoke calmly but cautiously and gave a half-bow from the waist. Niena followed suit a second later. "We'll do whatever you need of us. You have nothing to fear."

After a tense moment, Gilbrannen nodded. A couple of Protectors came and took the horses away. Gilbrannen singled another D'harn out and sent him ahead to inform the Council of their coming. The rest of the soldiers gathered around the newcomers, three deep on all sides. "We will see," he said and started walking.

Niena took in her surroundings as they climbed upwards through the enclave's streets, committing all of it to memory in case they were ever allowed to return home. The buildings were either hewn from rock or constructed from cedar and pine logs, with a few consisting of both techniques. Much more care and precision were used to make even the mundane things, so that it all was beautiful in form and function. Even so, there was little color save for the occasional laundry hanging in the alleyways, which were all different shades of blue.

The streets and open spaces were largely deserted before they turned each corner, but she caught glimpses of several elven families. The parents had fear in their eyes as they herded various children inside before bolting their doors, and Niena took pity on them. She had not yet finished the book her father had given her, but if half of that history was true, then the D'harnir had every right to be afraid.

Her father had spotted them too. "Tolvanen," he said, "I see a lot of children. How are you feeding your people up here on the mountain?"

Tolvanen leaned closer as they continued walking. "That is the other reason we have the pit traps. We domesticate the local elk and mountain goats and farm them not far from here. Using magic, we've managed to make them happy and docile, and they feel nothing when the time comes."

Niena caught a whiff of venison from one of the chimneys. She wasn't sure how she felt about magically deceiving a creature to its death, but she supposed it was better than typical butchering of domesticated animals.

She wondered if some D'harnir thought humans should be treated the same way.

"Why do you do that? Use magic on them, I mean?" Niena asked.

"It is Mishenna," Tolvanen answered with a confused frown, stopping in his tracks. "Have you taught her nothing of her heritage, Voster?"

Her father's shoulders tensed. "She is new to all of this," he said in a cautious tone. "I've started with what little I know."

Tolvanen grunted, and they kept walking.

"I've been meaning to ask," Niena said, "What is Mishenna, and how is it different from the Codes? You've mentioned it several times and I don't understand."

"I suppose it might seem odd if you have not grown up with it," Tolvanen admitted. "Mishenna is the standard that we all strive toward in living out the Codes. It is a name for our way of life."

"Okay ... So the Codes say to enchant your animals before you butcher them, and if you do that, you're following Mishenna."

Tolvanen chuckled. "In a manner of speaking. One particular passage tells us to avoid causing unnecessary pain, and most of us apply that even to animals."

"Most?" she pressed.

Tolvanen paused. "The largest generation since the second exile is reaching adulthood, and they have little concern for Mishenna or the Codes. I worry that our ways and morals will be lost if something doesn't change."

Niena considered this. The D'harn she had seen in Wraelian Square hadn't appeared that young, but then again it was hard to tell the ages of most of the soldiers surrounding them. "Why is that?" she asked.

"A question for another time," he said. "We are here."

Niena looked up, surprised to find they had come to the apex of the enclave. They had circled the base of a promontory that looked out over Por'monir and the valley below, and seated there at the head was an immense curved longhouse constructed entirely of wood. The roof was painted a dingy gray-blue, but the frame and doorposts were stained a deep red-brown. It was the most visually stunning building in the settlement by a wide margin, and the care and craftsmanship seen further down the mountain were here outdone tenfold.

Two of the Protectors hurried ahead to open wide the double doors leading into the large structure. As they all passed through, Niena's eyes caught on the carved relief etched into the door frame. It was a feathered bird, with heavily detailed wings extending down and around the hall's entrance. The bird's head looked more like a common pigeon, but the reddish stain used over the wood reminded her more of the blood-soaked clawcrens from earlier that morning.

She found it hard to believe their harrowing escape from the manticore was only that morning. She steeled herself, knowing that they could be entering into another life-threatening encounter now—but this time, willingly.

Niena blinked, the brightness of the hall's interior surprising her. The late afternoon sun streamed through windows on either side of the vaulted ceiling. A railed balcony ran the length of both walls, and a fire pit roared in the center of the room with the smoke leaving through an open skylight. At the other side, a long table surrounded by seven chairs faced outwards, and seven elders watched the procession with grim expectation.

The center chair was the tallest, and although the occupant's face appeared young, apart from a hint of gray-black flowing back from a widow's peak, his hair was white as salt. His clothes were not ostentatious, but hints of lavender embroidery made them seem more regal than the other elders at the table.

It could only be Shilvand, arbiter of Por'monir and Niena's uncle.

"It is you," he said, once the two guests had been brought before the Council. "After all this time, I had begun to hope . . . But no, I cannot imagine my sister would let you come alone to Por'monir if she still lived. Am I correct?"

Voster's beard fell to his chest. "You are. She died in childbirth."

"A pity," Shilvand said. "A common fate among illicit unions such as yours. She might have been with us today if not for you."

Niena's stomach churned at the comment, and she fought against the urge to glare daggers at the arbiter. He might as well have wished she didn't exist. Despite the family connection, Shilvand knew nothing of her mother if that was the first thing to come from his mouth.

Another member of the Council spoke up, an elderly woman with her hair pinned back behind her pointed ears and deep lines through her face. "But Tolvanen would not have been."

"Peace, Matriarch Molenia," Shilvand commanded. "I am well aware of your clan's involvement in past events, and it does not provoke trust."

Tolvanen stepped in front of Voster and Niena and took a knee. "Arbiter, you know that I have served the Protectors and our enclave with honor my entire life. I would not endanger our home and families by bringing them here except in great need. If what Voster's daughter told me is true, we have more to fear from our own than from a human who has only ever proven loyal to us."

Shilvand turned to regard Niena more closely for the first time. His sudden scrutiny unnerved her, but his expression softened after a moment. "You do have more of Tynathria about you than just the necklace," he said. "What is your name, halfblood?"

Her father subtly nodded for her to answer.

"Niena," she replied.

"After the spirits of the forest," Shilvand mused. "Your mother always did love the trees. Tell us, Niena, why you and Voster have disturbed our city today."

Niena panicked. She thought her father was going to do all the talking—she hadn't had time to prepare anything.

"It happened almost three weeks ago now—" Voster started, but never got any further.

"No," Shilvand said firmly. "I asked her to explain."

Niena composed herself, remembering her father's command not to mention Tollan. She didn't know why, but she trusted him anyway. "I, um . . . To tell the truth, I didn't even know you D'harnir were real. Papa never said a word about it until the day I saw one of you. In Celwaith Tor."

The Council all exchanged alarmed glances. As Niena told the rest of her story, their faces ranged from sympathetic to skeptical. She related the similarity of the saboteur's clothes to the Protectors' uniforms, and how she seemed to be immune to the effects of the saboteur's spells. "After I told Papa what I'd seen, he insisted on coming here to warn you."

"Warn us of what?" one of the patriarchs asked. "It sounds like you were the only witness."

"To warn you that there are D'harnir who do not share your isolationist ways," Voster supplied, steering the conversation away from a grateful Niena. "I don't know whether this terrorist is from here or another enclave if one even survives. But our king is readying Drüstania's troops for war, and any activity that may draw attention to the mere existence of Por'monir is dangerous—for all of you."

Shilvand sighed, his speech hesitant and begrudging. "The attacker is almost certainly from Por'monir. Some time ago, several members of the Protectors abandoned their posts and were not heard from again. It is not unreasonable to assume that they are unwisely taking matters between D'salnir and D'harnir into their own hands."

The admission surprised Niena. It didn't sound like it would help them much unless the elves were motivated to help hunt down the perpetrators, but it was encouraging that Shilvand chose not to withhold the information.

"For hundreds of years, all the D'harnir have remained hidden," Voster asked. "Why are things changing now?"

Tolvanen's clan elder, Molenia, spoke up again. Her raspy voice bore a tinge of regret. "Our clan has historically been one of the most pious families in the study of and adherence to the Mishenna, and there was once a Junir educator in every classroom." While she spoke, she kept looking back toward Shilvand as if to gauge his reaction. "But as our family's numbers dwindled, the other clans took it upon themselves to teach the meaning of the Codes to their children. Now, the younger generations bear much unrest and covetousness in their hearts toward humans, believing the southern lands are theirs by right."

Shilvand's eyebrows, every bit as white as his hair, drew together in a stern look. "We have already discussed this at length as a Council, Molenia. The Junir are not the only clan capable of interpreting the

Codes. There have always been multiple schools of thought, and now students have the chance to weigh all viewpoints."

Molenia's wrinkled lips pursed downwards. "Perhaps they should not have the chance if they use it to circumvent Mishenna."

Niena glanced back and forth between the two speakers. Based on the bored reactions of the other members of the Council, this was nothing they had not heard before. But the elder on the rightmost end of the table was no longer tolerating it. "Enough. This debate is pointless."

Shilvand composed himself and turned back to the matter at hand. "Indeed. Voster, you broke the terms of your banishment to bring us this news, and I'm sure some of us here are appreciative. But I, for one, am unsure what you expect us to do about it."

Niena clenched her jaw, dreading what that meant.

Her father was equally taken aback. "You aren't going to send anyone to apprehend your rogue Protectors?"

"Why would we?" Shilvand asked as if it was obvious. He crossed his arms, the dusty blue sleeves draping over the armrests of his chair. "If they should happen to be killed, your kind will only know that we exist, not where we live. And if they are caught, they are well-versed enough in the ancient tongue to slip away easily."

Niena's heart continued to sink into her shoes. The worst part was that Shilvand's reasoning made sense for the elves not to get involved.

She and her father had come for nothing.

"In my sister's memory," Shilvand continued, "and because you risked your lives to bring this message, I will pardon you this once for coming unbidden to our city. But should you return to Por'monir's lands again, the consequences will be on your own head."

Voster took a breath as if to speak, but Shilvand raised his index finger. "You will leave matters concerning the D'harnir to the D'harnir. And if you value your daughter, you will both live out your lives in ignorance of us." He paused as most of the other elders around the table nodded in agreement, then he lowered his hand. "Be thankful my father Wirvanen has passed into the eternal night—he would not have been so forgiving."

The Protectors, as if they had been given a signal, moved to escort Voster and Niena from the hall. Under other circumstances, Niena might have spoken up or resisted, but there was no point. They had lost, and they would go home with nothing to show for it.

"Hold!" Tolvanen called out beside them, and the Protectors released their captives' shoulders. "Arbiter, I must ask. May I accompany them to the southern lands? I can ensure their safe journey and perhaps find a trace of our rogue soldiers to bring them back."

Niena's hope kindled again, even as Shilvand's brow furrowed in annoyance. "If you choose this, Tolvanen," the arbiter said, "you choose exile. You will be shorn, you will swear never to use magic among humans, and you will never again be welcome among the D'harnir."

"No," Niena's father said, his voice raspy. She knew he was thinking of her mother, when she had made the same choice. "We will be fine. Stay with your people, Tolvanen."

Tolvanen looked past Voster to consult his clan's matriarch. Niena caught the subtlest of nods from Molenia, and a faint smile of approval flickered across the lady's lips.

"I am only here today because of this man's good heart," Tolvanen said to Shilvand. "It is a debt that I will never be able to repay, but if I can protect his family by seeking out these traitors to Mishenna, I will. I swear by the Codes that I will never use magic as long as I am exiled."

"So be it," Shilvand said. "Gilbrannen, strip him of his uniform. Othniel, perform the rites."

Tolvanen removed his cloak and hood before handing them to Gilbrannen. His reddish brown hair was tied back in a ponytail at the nape of his neck. His clothes underneath were simple, a light drawstring shirt and leather breeches. "Get on with it," he said, squaring his shoulders.

Another D'harn came forward, carrying a sheathed curved dagger not dissimilar to the one in Niena's mother's belongings. The Council looked between themselves, clearly bewildered by the sudden change in events. But if Molenia wasn't going to protest her kinsman's choice, they wouldn't either.

"I'm not sure I want to see this," Niena whispered, and her father wrapped her in his arms to keep her from seeing the worst.

But she could still hear it. The unsheathing of the blade, the slice of flesh, and Tolvanen's pained groan. Niena winced, and wondered why there weren't incantations to dull his senses now. Surely a person's hurt was worth more than an animal's. As if on cue, the D'harn named Othniel began chanting in their ancient tongue.

Niena's curiosity got the better of her squeamishness, and she turned to look. Othniel's hands came away from the sides of Tolvanen's head when he had finished the ritual, and she could hardly believe the result. Under a smear of blood, Tolvanen's ears looked exactly like a human's, with the skin folded over to achieve a fully normal curve instead of a point.

The D'harn named Othniel cleaned the dagger blade and handed it to Tolvanen. It was now his only possession other than the clothes on his back.

Afterward, the three of them were forcefully escorted down through the city to the gate where Voster and Niena's weapons were returned to them. It all happened in a blur, and Niena couldn't take her eyes off Tolvanen's ears. Where once there were elegant points, there would now always be a scar.

Like her own.

"Why would you do that?" Voster asked as they began the trek back across the field. "What about your family?"

Tolvanen smiled, shaking his head. "I never made a life bond like you, Voster, and so I never had children. My nieces and nephews will miss me, but if your son—my namesake—is in danger, I am bound by honor to help you. Molenia will tell them what happened."

Niena was still in shock, only putting one foot in front of the other out of habit. It was almost sundown, and they would have to make camp as soon as they left the valley. The elves were the furthest thing from hospitable, she thought with a glare back toward the city gate.

The walk back to Celwaith Tor would be a long one. But, she reasoned, Tolvanen would not have exiled himself if he didn't have ideas on how they could track the ones who attacked Wraelian Square.

It wasn't the solution they hoped for, but at least they had found help.

They all walked in silence, none having the appetite for conversation. Once the sun passed the horizon, the darkness increased exponentially. Their visibility worsened, to the point where they had to mind their steps a little closer.

"The trees are just up ahead," Voster said. "They won't be the best shelter, but at least the cold wind won't be at our backs the whole—"

He didn't finish his sentence, because Tolvanen shushed him and brought the group to a halt. The D'harn scanned the surrounding darkness.

"What is it?" Voster breathed.

"I heard something."

Niena gasped and pointed. "There!"

A handful of dark figures left the treeline and spread out as they approached. Niena couldn't make out anything but jagged silhouettes against the starlit grass only fifty yards away. *Perhaps it's an elven patrol returning late*, Niena hoped to herself.

"Greetings," Tolvanen called tentatively. "Who goes there?"

There was no reply. A moment later, a heavy cloth bag dropped over Niena's head, and she was forced to the ground.

INTERLUDE II

The End of Civility
c. 32 – 0 years before the Rift

NOW, I CAN BEGIN to speak from experience. I was still a young boy in the early years of their rise to power, but I remember well the tense discussions about the Macula Society around the dinner table. My father, Ervan, would come home later and later from the embassy, looking more tired with each passing day. I understood little at first from his voiced frustrations and my mother's attempts to calm him, but I listened, and I learned.

The Macula Society was a collection of scientific zealots who championed their flawed vision above all else, and believed that men needed to throw off the shackles of elf-kind in order to progress. At first, they were merely a fringe group composed of inventors and businessmen who had missed out on fortunes because of laws protecting elven trades, but as the years wore on, more people began to agree with them. By the time I was a young adult, they had formed a political party and succeeded in winning a significant minority of Parliamentary seats.

Rumors swirled that the zealots would soon have enough sympathizers to abolish all elven protections, and justified hatred began to grow in the hearts of many D'harnir. Their Codes taught against any violent action as recompense for wrongs, so they chose instead to protest by drastic means. My father *pleaded with them to reconsider, but all houses of healing shut their doors to human patients the following week. The sick and injured lined the streets outside, and still they refused to open without assurances from Parliament that laws protecting them would not be abolished.*

The Macula Society, however, followed no code—and the fact that elven physicians refused to work played right into their hands, as it proved a need for non-magical means of healing. There would be no negotiation, but instead a mockery of justice. In the middle of the night, members of the Macula rose up to overthrow the government while their supporters ransacked D'harnin homes and stores.

Halfbloods and those who had worked with and defended the interests of the elves, including my father, would be targeted next.

— Haron Geled, Last Scribe of the Union
25th of Hollyn, in the 48th year after the Rift

THIRTEEN

A farmer will always be blessed. For what greater satisfaction can there be than to live in the open countryside by the produce of one's own hands?

— Codes of Binding 4.19-20

IT WAS ALREADY HALF past seven when Anise left the warehouse, a long two hours after the usual end of the workday. They had extended her sewing hours so that she worked an extra twelve every week, but her daily wage had remained the same. Anise would forfeit what she had rightfully earned that day if she didn't work as often and as long as the owners wanted.

No doubt they had decided to punish her for Niena's sudden absence leaving gaps in their production line. But it wasn't as though Anise had known Voster would up and take the girl away in the middle of the night. She thought her brother had left such folly behind in his younger days, but instead it was the same sad story: Anise was left behind to pick up the pieces of the life they had shared.

Anise hiked up her patterned skirt and hurried down the side street towards the intersection, hoping she had the time to stop before curfew and buy food for the next few days. She glanced at the sky and decided she ought not risk it; the summer solstice had long passed, and the days were growing noticeably shorter.

The grocers and bakers had probably sold out anyway, Anise groused to herself as she approached a mass of people waiting in lines. Many of the farmers and traders that supplied the capital's markets had decided it was not worth the trouble to bring their wares. The odds of wasting half the day waiting to enter Celwaith Tor—only to be turned away at the gate—were simply too high.

The jarl's new checkpoints continued to make the once-mundane into a needlessly complicated mess for interior citizens as well. There were too few guards to man the stations adequately, resulting in long lines and longer waits until the army recruits returned to bolster the ranks.

"Excuse me," she said and stepped lightly through a gap in the crowd toward the only women's line on the far side. Her elbow collided with someone's ribs, and she apologized.

"Stay in your lane, *Lady* Cresthaven," the bloke spat through chipped teeth. She recognized the dingy man as Sunken Quarter's cobbler, who in his younger days had once tried to court her. His breath was rank with alcohol. "Your prince come for you yet?"

The other men surrounding him laughed hysterically, while Anise ignored it and kept moving. She had slipped out from under the executioner's blade by refusing his advances, and no mistake.

She took her place at the end of the long, winding women's line. She fiddled with her handbag while she waited, making sure she had all the necessary identification paperwork ready to present. Plenty of familiar faces could be seen in the lines of people returning from their workday, but few of them were friendly. Most spotted her dress and either rolled their eyes or glared in jealousy.

Anise was always aware of being grossly overdressed for her job and commute, and sometimes it did draw unwanted attention her way—but at least it was attention. She remembered what it was like to be invisible, and she preferred this. *Dress on behalf of who you would like to be,* she often told anyone who asked, *and you might find one day that you already are.* Sure, it sounded condescending and sentimental, but it was at least a little encouraging, wasn't it?

Never mind the fact that she had not once in twenty years rose in the morning to find she was rich enough that her taste in clothes actually suited her station. But the whole performance had become her routine, and she wasn't changing it now.

"Next!" one of the Drüstanian soldiers at the checkpoint called, and Anise realized that it was her turn.

In hurriedly removing her papers from her handbag, however, the parchment logging her movements caught on the latch and spilled free. She reached out, but a sudden gust of wind blew it beyond her fingertips and through the hastily-erected wooden checkpoint to the other side.

"No!" she called out in alarm, causing heads to turn.

A leather glove snatched it out of the air, halting its headlong journey into the alleyway. "Ms. Cresthaven!" the young voice of the guard said in recognition. "You should be more careful with these—it could take up to a week to issue you new ones."

"Kasdan, you are a sight for sore eyes," Anise replied, thankful that he had been there. Another guard might just as well have let the paper fly past and turned her away. "I'm sorry. I've been in a bit of a haze today."

Kasdan accepted the rest of her papers and handed them all to the clerk, who began authenticating and recording everything in triplicate. "Have . . . you heard from Voster or Niena?" Kasdan asked hopefully.

"That's just it," Anise said. "It's been four weeks now, and not a single word. The jarl's men at the smithy still suspect my brother to be one of those Crownless goons, and they think I know something about him leaving that night."

Kasdan frowned, watching as the clerk wrote down the date and time on Anise's file, then did the same on her copy. "I know, it's awful. I'll try to put in a good word, have them go easy on you."

"No, please," Anise said frantically. "Don't draw attention to yourself or your family. They're seeing conspirators behind every bush. I'm lucky enough to be allowed the attic, even if the army uses the rest of the smithy. I'll be fine."

"If you say so," Kasdan said, accepting the papers back from the clerk and ensuring they were complete. "I don't know whether to hope Voster returns soon, since I'm assured he will be arrested for desertion the moment he does."

That only scratched the surface of Anise's own worries. She accepted her papers back with a tight grip and deposited them safely back in her handbag. "I have no clue why they would leave so suddenly," Anise said. Her feelings had shifted from anger at first to sad resignation. She thought they had been a family, that they would always look out for each other.

"I'm sorry, Ms. Cresthaven, but you'll have to keep moving," Kasdan said, standing aside and waving her through the barricade. "The good news is that Tollan is due back any day now—I'm sure he'll come to see you the first chance he gets."

Anise stood up straighter. "What? But he still has at least a week left!"

"They've been recalled," Kasdan shouted over his shoulder as he went to retrieve the next person's documents. "No time to explain!"

Anise stood there a second longer, processing the news. She would have to get the attic in order. Or, she wasn't sure, maybe Tollan would be staying at the garrison.

A commotion rose up on the other end of the barricade. A livid man cursed up a storm at one of the clerks. "My papers were stolen! I have to get home to my kids tonight," he pleaded.

"Sir, you have to calm down," a guard said apathetically, perhaps having seen the excuse one too many times. "I can send a man to check on them, but you'll have to stay in the brig until your identity can be verified and a new seal issued. Come with us."

"Like hell I will! I'm coming through!" the man shouted, and attempted to force his way past the barricade. A handful of soldiers crowded in to apprehend him.

Not waiting around to see how the altercation turned out, Anise hurried away. She knew it was best to keep her head down and go unnoticed; the man would have to learn that the hard way.

She walked back to the smithy in silence. It crossed her mind that with Tollan and the others returning, the city guard would no longer be stretched to the breaking point. Properly staffed checkpoints meant Anise's day would run smoother, but also that they might be closer to ending this nightmare.

Things had finally begun to look upwards. Anise allowed herself to smile for the first time that day.

TOLLAN BLINKED, HIS ATTENTION snared by a parchment posted on the garrison wall. A familiar portrait stared back at him that sent chills down his sweaty back. He could hardly believe it, but he also couldn't argue with the printed text below.

WANTED, it read. *Voster Cresthaven, blacksmith. Reward of one hundred silver for any information leading to his arrest.*

"What are you looking at?" Thaxon asked, sidling up next to him through the crowd of waiting soldiers. When Tollan didn't answer, he took a closer look and raised his fiery eyebrows. "Wait. Cresthaven? Is that ..."

"My father," Tollan confirmed, a sick feeling in his stomach.

Thaxon shook his head. "What could have possibly happened in three and a half weeks to turn him into an outlaw?"

Tollan had an idea, the only thing that made sense. He just never thought that his father would have gone through with it. "He's ... stubborn. It's possible he decided to leave town rather than let his business be conscripted in service to the crown."

"But ... that's treason," Thaxon said, lowering his voice to a whisper.

"I know." Tollan turned away from the poster and looked in frustration at the recruits lined in front of them. He flipped out his pocket watch and checked the time—he needed to get to the smithy. "What's the hold-up? We've been waiting for hours."

Thaxon shrugged. "We'll find out soon enough. At least we're out of the sun now."

The caravan of wagons had arrived at Celwaith Tor around noon, but they hadn't been allowed to proceed through the main gate. Instead, the soldiers filed through the garrison at a snail's pace. Judging by how many men still trailed behind Tollan and Thaxon, the inward procession would continue until late into the night.

It was after sundown when they finally reached the front of the line, greeted by a short, balding man in yellow tunic who lacked any armor. "Name?" he asked in a hoarse voice. He flipped a few pages and ticked the roll call once Tollan gave it.

"Your identification," the little man said, jerking a slip of paper at him with the royal seal stamped in wax onto the center. "This is in your name and will allow you to move about the city unhindered as a member of the Drüstanian guard. Do not lose it, and report to your primary precinct checkpoint at dawn tomorrow."

Checkpoints, Tollan thought with apprehension. He accepted the paper and continued through, waiting a moment in the empty street so that Thaxon could catch up to him. He examined the paper while he waited, and found it had an expiry date in thirty days. So, either they anticipated the crisis to have passed by then, or they would need to reissue later. Either way, it seemed like far more security than was necessary.

Thaxon strolled up behind him and clapped him on the back. "Well, whoever these rebels are, they aren't going to try anything now."

"Perhaps," Tollan said. "But if they never try anything, we'll never be able to catch them. I would prefer to live my life without showing this seal everywhere I go."

Thaxon nodded, considering, but Tollan didn't let him answer. He was anxious to get back to the smithy and find what was left of his family. "I guess this is where we part ways. I need to get back home."

Thaxon gawked at him like he was a madman. "What are you talking about? If that wanted poster is for real, you can't go home. The king will have paid someone else to work your family's smithy for armor production. You're going to need another place to stay."

Tollan hadn't thought of that, but it made a dreadful amount of sense. "Yes, Thaxon, but I couldn't—"

Thaxon swatted at him, cutting off any argument. "You can, and you will. We have plenty of extra space in the Gilded Quarter. My father travels often to Cape Vrosingr, so it wouldn't be an imposition. He would probably be honored to have the family of one of my fellow soldiers stay in the guest rooms—that is, as long as we wouldn't also be harboring a fugitive from the law."

Tollan was uncomfortable with being considered a charity case, but he knew his friend didn't think of it that way. It would be the perfect answer to their problems in a worst-case scenario. "I appreciate the offer, but I need to know more about what happened first. My aunt and sister could be out in the street right now, or worse."

"All right, we'll find them, and if they need a place to stay, they have it," Thaxon replied confidently. "Lead on."

Tollan acquiesced to that much with a modest smile of gratitude. He would appreciate the company.

The two young men walked together up the main street, empty save for the trickle of returning recruits. They turned up the hill from the Sunken Quarter and had to show their identification to patrols a few times since they weren't in uniform. The streets became more and more grungy, an aspect of the neighborhood which was familiar to Tollan, but positively repulsed Thaxon.

"People actually live in these conditions?" he said, incredulous at the leaning slums.

Tollan shrugged. "It probably looks worse than it is in the dark. The blacksmith shop is a little better off than this, so my family is . . . was, I suppose . . . really fortunate."

Thaxon didn't reply and followed him through the checkpoint barricade into the heart of the Barren Quarter. Once the guards on duty saw their seals, the boys were waved through without any record-keeping delays.

As Tollan rounded the last corner, he caught sight of the smithy down the street, lit up by several torches and the forge itself. Four figures stood there with different tools, still hard at work even after sundown and all of them dressed in Drüstanian yellow.

Tollan crossed the street with Thaxon in tow and raised a hand in tentative greeting. He held out his official seal as they approached. "Um, excuse me? Who's in charge here?"

A hulking bruiser of a man with a heavyset brow looked up from heating a blade in the forge and motioned for one of the others to take over for him. "That'll be me, what's it to ya?" he asked with a frown at their identification.

"Wondering if you can give us some information," Tollan said, trying not to seem cowed by the man's height and bulk. "We just got back from training with the militia. This is my father's smithy."

The man snorted. "Not anymore it's not. What's his face—Cresthaven—skipped town after everything, so we confiscated it to keep the place running. Jarl's orders."

Tollan's stomach twisted into a knot. It was true, then. His father had gone, without trying to get in touch or letting him know. He didn't know why he was surprised; there hadn't even been a note from him with Niena's present. "What about the others? My sister and aunt lived here, too."

"Don't know about no sister," the blacksmith said, turning back to his place at the forge. "Place was deserted except for the strange old bird who lives in the attic."

"Anise?" Tollan asked, perking up. "She's still here?"

The blacksmith waved him off. "How should I know? Go check for her yourself. She comes and goes since we don't need that room for our things."

One of the others unlatched the gate, and Tollan slipped through into the crowded yard. Thaxon followed him up onto the doorstep, but before they could go in, the blacksmith called to them. "Don't touch anything in there! We've organized the place how we like it," the man barked, and returned to quenching his steel.

Tollan noticed from the steam that they used water for quenching, and while that would usually work with good materials and hard labor, it could create imperfections or even hairline cracks throughout the blade. He considered speaking up to say that his father always used oil to quench his blades despite the higher cost, but decided against it. It wasn't his job anymore, and they could cut as many corners as they liked.

He hesitated a moment before opening the front door, not sure what he would find inside. It sounded like the army had taken over the entire house for their operations, and with four workers they would be running through a vast amount of supplies. By comparison, his father usually had difficulty keeping his stock confined to the cellar.

Thaxon clapped him on the shoulder. "You okay?"

"I don't know, I just . . ." He swallowed, and turned the latch. "Yeah. I will be."

The house was not really in disarray, but instead it had ceased to be a house and become an oversize closet. Almost all of the open space was taken up by invasive stacks of anything you could imagine a smithy would need, but mostly steel ingots and leather which still smelled of cow. Few of the Cresthaven furnishings remained, and those that did were unobtrusive things like wall decorations.

They passed the place where the broken grandfather clock had once been, and the bookshelf now filled with spare tools instead of adventurous pages. Tollan felt an ache in his heart and kept moving, squeezing past the stores and on up to the second floor.

There Tollan and Thaxon found more of the same, although a few more familiar items remained than downstairs—presumably because it was easier to leave some items there rather than move them. The two boys passed over the old bedrooms and continued to a rickety narrow staircase in the corner. Tollan ascended and knocked tentatively on Anise's door, while Thaxon hung back on the landing below.

There came a startled racket from the other side. "Oh, what now?" Anise's annoyed voice called out as she undid what sounded like half a dozen deadbolts. "Haven't you bothered me enough already what with taking over my home—"

The door opened, and she stopped short of what she might have said next, completely dumbstruck. Tollan pulled her into a hug, happy to see a familiar face after so long.

The emotional silence lasted all of two seconds.

"Tollan!" Anise exclaimed, as if she couldn't trust her eyes and hands. "By the winds, Kasdan told me you had been recalled, but I didn't expect you back so soon! I mean, not that I'm not happy to see you because I am, but . . . Oh, it's all gone wrong, and I don't know what to do."

"I'm here, Anise," Tollan said, holding her tightly. She was shaking. "It's going to be okay. They cut training short since several outposts have been sacked—they need us to defend the city now, whether we're prepared or not."

Anise's breathing relaxed, and she stirred from the embrace long enough to pull out a ratty handkerchief and dab at her teary eyes.

"Now," Tollan said, desperate for answers. "What on earth has been happening the last three weeks?"

Anise gathered herself together, then noticed Thaxon waiting awkwardly on the stairs. She beckoned him up rather than answering the question. "Who's this you've brought with you, Tollan? Come in, both of you." She retreated into her room and shuffled things around. "I expect this might take a while to talk through."

That's when Tollan noticed the state of the attic. What had once been a neat and orderly bedroom with a slightly leaky, pointed ceiling was now an unmitigated disaster zone. Dishes, books, rugs, chairs, and any other items Anise could carry up from the lower floors by herself had been crammed inside. The only remaining space consisted of a narrow walkway between Anise's bed and the door.

Thaxon's eyes widened in shock as he came up behind Tollan. He had likely never set foot in a peasant home before, and this was not a good first impression of them. "Blimey," he whispered under his breath. "The entire house crammed into one room."

Anise hurriedly tried to find seats for the two boys, making a larger mess in the process as she checked under piles of belongings.

"This is Thaxon Denvald," Tollan introduced. "He was in my column during training and lost his sister to the Wraelian Square attack. Thaxon, this is my Aunt Anise."

Anise found a wooden chair underneath a pile of possessions, and greeted him as she slid them off with a crash. "It's a pleasure, Thaxon," she said, as if there was nothing out of the ordinary. "I'm sorry for your loss—did Tollan mention that his sister was there that day?"

Thaxon nodded. "He has, and thank you for your sympathies."

Anise gestured to the two chairs she had unearthed and plopped down herself on the edge of the bed. "Please, sit down. I imagine you're both tired from your travels."

Tollan sat closest to his aunt and let Thaxon stay nearer the door if he found the squalor unseemly and wanted to make a quick exit. "Now, Anise, don't keep me waiting any longer. I got a gift and letter from Niena on my birthday, but she didn't mention leaving town. In fact, she said she would see me when I got back. What is going on?"

Anise sighed, and lifted the edge of her mattress to pull out a sheet of paper not unlike the one that had come with Tollan's pocket watch. She handed it to him, tears welling up in her eyes again. "They left in the middle of the night after the draft. All your father left me was this."

Tollan opened the letter slowly, taking time to read each line.

My sister,

You have every right to be angry with me. This is one hell of a way to repay you for all you've done for me and the children. But I pray you can bring yourself to trust me when I say I had no choice.

Tollan's life is on the line, and possibly many others. If all goes well, Niena and I will return in a few weeks, and if not . . . Well, that's why I'm leaving you our savings. I hope it's enough to keep you on your feet once they take the smithy.

I know I haven't always treated you like it, Anise, but I do care. I'm so grateful that Niena and Tollan have you in their lives. You are their aunt, but you have been like a mother.

Tell no one, and stay safe.

Your brother,

Voster

Tollan set the letter aside and leaned on his hand, eyes closed in tiredness and deep thought. Had Niena known about all of this when she wrote his birthday note? She had said that a lot of things would change, but that was so cryptic it could apply to anything. It struck Tollan as odd that their choice to leave was motivated by concern for his life.

Tollan sat up and faced Anise. "Do you have any idea what he means here, that my life is on the line?"

Anise blew her nose and shook her head. "Not in the slightest, unless he means the dangers of being in the militia. But even my brother wouldn't be fool enough to try abducting you from training."

Thaxon broke in, appalled that the idea was even being discussed. "Ma'am, that kind of talk borders on rebellion. The king should allow you to have your home back once the army is properly outfitted. At least, provided your brother can prove he had a legitimate reason for leaving when he was needed."

"This *entire* family supports Pelendion's reign," Anise said, chastened by the boy's warning but also mildly insulted. "The Arvad house has always done well by Drüstania, and if you think we have anything to do with the Crownless . . . you are not welcome in this house." She turned back to Tollan, expecting him to chime in.

He smiled awkwardly, not appreciating being placed in such a position. "Yes, well . . . If neither of us know where Niena and Dad are, we can't wait for them to get back to worry about the future. And we can't stay here," he said, gesturing to the state of the house.

Thaxon nodded. "Right. Both of you are more than welcome to stay at my family estate in the Gilded Quarter until things get settled." He seemed put off by Anise's rougher edges, but not enough to retract his earlier offer.

Anise held a hand to her mouth, stunned. "Wait, you said your name was Denvald?" She paused, now recognizing the name. The implication caught her genuinely off-guard. "But . . . why would you do that for us?" she asked.

"Because Tollan and I are both soldiers in the service of Drüstania," Thaxon replied matter-of-factly. "What weakens one of us, weakens all of us. In addition, ma'am, your wardrobe suggests that you know some proper etiquette, so I'm certain my bedridden mother would appreciate someone to chat with."

Tollan smiled, liking the idea more and more. "Not to mention, now we would report to the same regiment."

"I hadn't thought of that," Thaxon agreed. "We might have never seen each other if we were posted on opposite ends of the city."

"So, Anise?" Tollan asked. "What do you say to living in the Gilded Quarter for a few weeks?"

"I think you know the answer!" she exclaimed in excitement. "That sounds more than splendid, Thaxon—it is Thaxon, right?"

He nodded.

"I must admit that I had you figured all wrong," she said, beginning to search for anything she might need. "Oh, I don't have anything nice to wear! And what about the curfew?"

"Don't worry about all that," Thaxon said, pushing himself to his feet. "My mother has spares of everything, and our seals should get us through the checkpoints easily even at this late hour. We do need to leave soon, though."

Tollan mentally smacked himself, realizing that he and Anise had been so preoccupied that they had kept Thaxon from reuniting with his own family. "Of course, you're right. Just the essentials, Anise."

Anise had both of them carry a few small things down to the street, and Tollan made sure to tuck the note from his father in his pocket. He didn't know how he would find any answers while manning the city's checkpoints, but let the winds take him if he didn't try.

"Hey, Thaxon?" he said while they waited outside for Anise in the light of the forge. The new blacksmith's men were still hammering away, close to ten o'clock according to his pocket watch. The neighbors surely hated that.

"Yeah?" the red-haired boy acknowledged.

Tollan met his gaze and smiled, absently winding the spring on his birthday present. "Thanks. I don't know what we would have done without you."

"Think nothing of it," Thaxon said with a shrug. "Whatever might be your father's reason for leaving, it's clear that you're far more loyal than that. I'm honored to call you my friend."

FOURTEEN

The teeth of feral beasts rend the flesh,
but long-held animosity rends the soul.
— Codes of Entreaty 5.17

NIENA SAT ALONE, STARING blankly at the latticed door as she listened to her stomach growl. She didn't know how long it had been since she was dumped in this underground cell, but it must have been days. No one had brought her anything more to eat after an initial plate of bread that was now long empty. The jug of clean water they had left with it only had a few ounces in the bottom. It added salt to the wound of being detained and separated from her father.

The cell itself was cramped and dark except for a strange kind of oil lamp which emitted light but burned with no heat. The place was furnished with a wooden bench, a couple small furs for warmth, and a bucket in the corner for a privy. They were spartan quarters, and the elves taking her pack away meant she had nothing to do but count the pebbles on the ground.

She absently twirled her mother's necklace pendant between her fingers, the only possession her captors had left her. Niena bitterly wished she had her father's green leather-bound book—she hadn't finished it yet, and it seemed like she was just getting to the good part of the histories.

She assumed her father and Tolvanen languished in similar chambers not too far away, but she never got a response when she called out. Either the underground passages went on for miles, or else they had taken many unnecessary turns in the maze of tunnels to confuse the captives. There was little chance of finding her way back out on her own, even if she could escape out the solid metal door.

And then it would be another week or more by foot to return to civilization, which without weapons or rations could well be a death sentence.

Niena heard booted footfalls echoing up the corridor, and debated whether she should call out to whoever it was before they moved on. But the sounds grew louder, and she could see a figure approaching the cell.

Finally, Niena thought. *At least they aren't going to let us starve to death in here.*

The keys jangled, and the door swung open. It was an elf, confirming her suspicions of who had abducted them last night. She found that she recognized him from the previous day: it was the gate captain named Gilbrannen.

She wasn't sure how D'harnir aged, but he appeared to be perhaps a few years older than her. He was dressed in all-too-familiar dark blue and carrying a tray, presumably of whatever leftover slop they had decided to feed her. The lamp caught his light brown eyes and kindled them to a striking-gold against his pale skin and black hair. "I convinced them to let me bring you some better food," he said.

Convinced them? Niena thought suspiciously. If he was trying to get her to lower her guard, he was being too obvious. "Why would you do something like that?" she asked.

The D'harn set the tray down on the bench next to her. "Regardless of your mother's poor bonding choices, Niena, you are still my blood relative. You do not deserve ill treatment."

She kept her tone cool and disinterested. It sounded suspiciously like a ruse. "Oh? What relation?"

"Distant cousins at most," he answered. "My branch of the Falir clan split off from yours a century ago, though we share the name. You may have met my first cousin, Hemilhet?"

The name immediately called to mind the brash young D'harn in Tolvanen's patrol who had given them so much trouble. "Oh, him. I can see the resemblance in your demeanor," she said dryly.

We haven't actually left Por'monir then, Niena reasoned. Shilvand had saved face by appearing to let them go, but instead he had always planned to keep them from returning home. Who knew if the story of several Protector soldiers going rogue was even true?

Niena frowned skeptically at the food. It wasn't much, but there was some dried meat, fried vegetables, and a flat round biscuit. It did smell good, and her stomach gurgled again.

"You should eat before it gets cold," Gilbrannen prompted.

Niena picked up the plate and utensil. She decided that if they wanted to kill her, they had far more creative ways of doing it than poison. She speared a potato and began to eat. "Your patriarch's not been the most hospitable, Gilbrannen, so I can't say it's a mystery why my mother seized her chance. Did you know her?"

"No, I was only a couple years old when she left. I understand why you would think that though," he said, spreading his hands apologetically. "Shilvand is . . . protective of the enclave from outside influence, given our history. Which you know a lot more about than I would have expected."

She put down her biscuit. "What do you mean?"

Gilbrannen reached inside his tunic again and brought out a familiar book wrapped in green leather, holding it gingerly. "It is a remarkably balanced historical account for being written by a human," he remarked. "Although many of the sayings of wisdom in the second half are severely flawed translations of our original codes."

Niena frowned. Of course, the elves had gone through their things, but she didn't like Gilbrannen waving it in her face. "Papa said that book was why he came this far north in the first place. I haven't finished reading it yet, but I guess that such a book would be a danger to you."

"Shilvand would either lock it away or burn it, certainly," Gilbrannen said, holding it out to her. "But I see no harm in letting you keep it for now. You are not going anywhere."

Niena accepted the book and put it behind her. "Thanks," she said before stuffing a piece of salted pork in her cheek.

"If you want, I can bring some other books as well. Most of ours are written in D'harna and wouldn't mean anything to you, but we do still have some in the common tongue. Might help you pass the time."

"Why are you doing this?"

"I told you."

Niena slammed the empty plate down on the tray, rattling it. "No. Enough with the games. No one else even knows the elves exist outside folklore and wives' tales. We are not a threat to you."

Gilbrannen laughed, the last reaction she would have expected. "It is a good thing you didn't call us elves during your audience with the Council yesterday. Many of them consider using anything other than our people's ancestral name as an insult."

"Elves, D'harnir, whatever." Niena dismissed the distraction. "I want to end this conflict before anyone else gets hurt, so Papa and I can go back to our normal lives. What will it take?"

Gilbrannen sighed, and paced back and forth. "It's not that simple. We only know for sure of two, but there could be at least half a dozen other D'harnin enclaves scattered around Drüstania. At least, there used to be that many."

"Don't try to pin this on anyone else," Niena said, getting to her feet. She jabbed a finger at him. "Your agent could have killed me that day in the square, and he was dressed in the same shade of blue that you wear now."

Gilbrannen winced, and she could see that she'd struck a nerve. He checked behind him to see if anyone was listening out in the hall. "All right, I guess you deserve to know. A handful of our best fighters were responsible, and they didn't desert. Shilvand sent them."

Niena clenched her teeth. That much had been obvious, though she hadn't actually expected him to admit to any of it. She waited expectantly for more.

"Originally, they were sent to Celwaith Tor and the surrounding lands, to spy on your people and possibly prevent any northward expansion." Gilbrannen paused, perhaps deciding exactly what to say. "That changed when we discovered scouts from another enclave had been doing the same reconnaissance for several generations already.

"With their information, we understood how truly fragile human society is. With a few strategic nudges in the right weak places, we could accelerate your culture's inevitable fall before finally returning to our rightful lands."

Niena listened with rapt attention. She could sense that this at last was the truth—at least in part. "Where is this other enclave?" she asked.

"I will not in good conscience tell you that," Gilbrannen said with a castigating frown. "There are women and children there, just like Por'monir. We are few enough as it is."

"You have no qualms about killing human women and children," Niena fired back, remembering the grisly sight of the aftermath at Wraelian Square. "Why should King Pelendion care about yours?"

"That is . . . not fair," he said. He looked hurt by the accusation. "We have always been the physically weaker race, and even with our magic we are unable to stand against humanity. It is why we were driven out and killed the first time. Shilvand believes it is time for the D'harnir to take back what is rightfully ours, and the only way to achieve that is by turning the might of men back on itself. Put every man at each other's throat, and we would be free to rebuild our civilization once civil war had run its course. Their rubble would be our foundation."

Niena fell silent, hearing truth in what Gilbrannen said. It was an ambitious plan, but one that made sense given the elves' position and deep-seated resentment. "Do you believe in that?" she asked, speaking up again.

Gilbrannen turned away, and she couldn't see his expression. "There are many who believe it goes against every tenet of Mishenna. But the Codes are meant for the D'harnir to govern between themselves, not men. That is why the rest of the enclave cannot know. They wouldn't understand what is necessary."

"What if you came forward?" she asked. "What would happen?"

"The Council would be convened, as only they can bring collective judgment on an arbiter, and Shilvand would deny any allegations. All the other secret police would testify against me, and I would be banished or locked up for the rest of my life. I and my parents could lose everything."

"That's harsh, toward members of his own clan." Niena began to realize just how intricate and dangerous the situation was. She sincerely doubted that either she or her father would be able to stop further elven attacks, especially if another enclave was perpetrating them. They needed to do what they could to protect Tollan from home—his training would be over in a few days. "Speaking of which, does Shilvand intend to let us go?"

"Unlikely," Gilbrannen replied, his voice emotionless.

"It's just that we were supposed to return to Celwaith Tor next week at the latest," Niena pleaded. She didn't expect anything to change, but if Gilbrannen's sympathy for her was real, he might be willing to break them out. "Who knows what has happened since we've been away."

"More than enough, if our recent reports are to be believed," Gilbrannen said. "Several of your cities have locked down and installed checkpoints, making it difficult for our agents to move anywhere inside without significant planning."

"Well, that's good at least," Niena muttered.

"Why the urgency to get back?"

"It's nothing. Didn't want to be away for so long."

"I will see if Shilvand's mind can be swayed, but we would not have locked you up if he was not already adamant." Gilbrannen picked up the tray and made to leave, then thought better of it and turned back to her. "May I . . ."

She warily sat down again, next to her book. "What?"

"May I see your ears?"

It sounded like such an odd request, but Niena supposed it wasn't. She was reminded of the way Tolvanen had roughly pulled her hair aside in order to get a look. Gilbrannen could have easily done the same, and she would have been able to do little about it, but instead he had asked. She reached up and tucked her blonde locks out of the way on one side, and nodded for him to come closer.

He leaned in, a little closer than she felt comfortable with. "Fascinating," he said, tilting his head this way and that. "That is an extraordinarily skillful shear. If your mother hadn't sworn to abandon the use of magic before your birth, I doubt there would even be a scar."

Niena chuckled. "You should see my brother's—" she stopped herself as a chill went down her spine. She had promised her father not to mention Tollan at all—had she just screwed everything up?

"Your brother's scar?" Gilbrannen asked, seemingly oblivious to the blunder.

"Yes," Niena continued, fighting to sound casual. "My mother died in childbirth, so my father had to cut them. They aren't quite as . . . tidy."

"I can imagine," he replied. "Thank you for indulging my curiosity, Niena." He locked eyes with her one last time as he stepped outside and turned the key with a click. "It is interesting to know that you are not an only child like myself." The clipped march of his boots echoed away, growing faint.

Niena mentally kicked herself. He had been playing her the whole time. He had given enough information to make her buy his act, but there wasn't anything specific she would be able to use against the elves. She had fallen completely for his ruse. Or had there been something in the food? She didn't know if she was immune to all the D'harnin tricks.

How much of what he had told her was even true?

She picked up the book again, but couldn't bring herself to open it. Instead, she curled up in the filthy corner and tried to keep the tears in her eyes from spilling over.

GILBRANNEN BRISKLY MARCHED BACK through the labyrinthian tunnels, feeling rather pleased with himself. The Cresthaven girl had proved to be more resistant to probing than he had anticipated, but that had also been true of Voster. The herbs he had used to season the meat and vegetables had helped the process, but he had still needed to give away more information than he wanted before she let her guard down. In the end though, it had paid off.

Niena was indeed clever, and could prove to be more dangerous than she appeared. But even though she now knew the truth of their arrangement with the Neraliel remnant, it would matter little if she remained locked up underground.

The upward-sloping tunnels opened out into a large natural cavern, peppered through with artificial support pillars. At the far end, a spiral staircase ascended upwards through the rock, until it met the rough, mineral-slick ceiling.

He looked out at the cavern as he climbed, an open space which always made him uneasy. The bulk of Por'monir sat directly above, and the place might have already collapsed ages ago if his ancestors hadn't discovered it and built the supports. The cavern and the maze of tunnels they had since delved continued to serve as the perfect staging area for their plans, versatile but hidden from D'harnir with weaker dispositions.

Then he had reentered the enclave, and gave the password to two of his distant relatives guarding the Hall of Meeting's hidden passage. The two were Protectors like Gilbrannen, but their coded response revealed they served his father's secret police, the Dast'rel. They both knew who he was, but when dealing in their amount of secrecy, abiding by the rules became paramount. He left them to dispose of the tray from Niena's meal while he reported to Shilvand.

The Council of Clans was in closed session, but it didn't matter. He pushed open the double doors into the artfully-constructed wooden sanctuary without concern. As the largest family in Por'monir, the Falir clan had supplied the office of arbiter for ten generations, and since Gilbrannen was part of the arbiter's clan, he would be forgiven the breach in propriety.

The family elders had all been talking in semi-urgent tones when Gilbrannen entered, but silence fell over the hall as he approached. Shilvand's frown was piercing. "What is it, Gilbrannen? You know that we are not to be disturbed until the elders have come to a consensus."

"A personal matter that needs your attention, Patriarch," he replied in an unwavering tone, ignoring the inquisitive faces of the other D'harnir. "I would not have come if it was not urgent—"

Shilvand interjected. "Whatever it is, I will deal with it once the Council is adjourned. You should know better. Go to my chambers and wait for me there."

"Yes, Patriarch." Gilbrannen bowed in farewell, doing his best to appear remorseful before the elders' amused faces. Shilvand meant to appease them by turning him away, but the meeting would be ended in relatively short order now that the arbiter knew Gilbrannen had news.

Gilbrannen excused himself from the Hall of Meeting, hearing the murmuring of conversation begin again as the doors swung shut behind him. He trudged up the elaborate twisting staircase to the second floor, where the patriarch lived and slept—alone, ever since his wife's passing. The furnishings were made of simple materials, but the greatest of care was put into the smallest details.

He greeted two more Dast'rel positioned at the entrance to the suite, and they let him in to wait. Few not related by blood to the Falir clan were admitted into the Dast'rel, mostly because any surreptitious meetings could be swept under the guise of "family business." There were some, like Tolvanen's meddlesome Junir clan, who suspected more to their secrecy, but most believed only what their lying eyes told them.

He relaxed into a cushioned chair, upholstered with elk leather and stuffed with goose feathers, positioned by a large circular window. The view of the valley outside was stunning, though Gilbrannen couldn't make out the sea to the east as he could on a clear day. Instead, he watched the streets of the enclave and waited, contemplating what he had learned from Niena.

At last, after almost an hour, Gilbrannen heard the sound of bustling people leaving the Hall of Meeting, and then Shilvand's footsteps outside the door. The patriarch burst into the room, annoyance plain on his face.

"I apologize, we should have adjourned long ago," the white-haired D'harn explained. "Most of the Council do not know how to drill to the heart of a subject—or perhaps they merely enjoy the sounds of their own voices too much."

Gilbrannen stood out of respect for his patriarch. They knew each other well, but he was still mindful of his station. "What did they need to address this time? I was under the impression that yesterday's unwanted guests had been discussed and done with."

Shilvand sighed and sat across from Gilbrannen, motioning for him to return to his chair. "Some of them worry that Voster was right and Por'monir may be in danger, despite our defenses. On top of that, there are also concerns that the harvesters are not producing enough grain for the enclave to make it through the winter without rationing."

"Do you think any of them suspect?" Gilbrannen asked.

"Not at all," Shilvand said. "Molenia even suggested that we should be putting a portion of our produce away for times like these, if you can believe it. Saying we've grown too dependent on using magic to stimulate our farming when needed."

The idea was humorous, since the Falir family had already been doing that very thing in secret for the last several seasons. The act of siphoning grain away to store underground was likely what caused the elders to be concerned about their dwindling supply in the first place. "I suppose they will all be surprised to know the Dast'rel have already taken care of all their problems."

Shilvand absently pulled at one of his sleeves before steepling his hands across his lap. "I sincerely hope they will not have to find out. If they do, it will be because we have reached the worst-case scenario. But enough about that, what is this urgent business? Have there been complications with the prisoners?"

Gilbrannen shook his head. "No complications, but a few positive developments. Tolvanen refused to speak when I checked on him; I suppose he is now beginning to regret his decision to join Voster in exile. It was fortunate for us though. He was getting too curious of Dast'rel movements of late. After what happened, his family won't suspect we had anything to do with his disappearance."

"Yes, I know," Shilvand said, tapping his fingers together impatiently. "What of Voster and his halfblood daughter?"

"Voster was likewise unforthcoming. I did not use a spell to glean more from him because what he chooses to lie about first may be more valuable. The girl, however . . . she let slip some information that may be of more immediate interest to you."

Shilvand leaned forward in eagerness. "Ah, I knew you would have the best results with her. Voster's reluctance to teach her about our kind will work to our advantage. What have you learned?"

"It seems that Niena was not the only halfblood offspring of Tynathria," Gilbrannen said. "She has a younger brother."

Shilvand's countenance darkened. "I did not think it possible to be more disappointed with my sister's choices, but I am always proven wrong. Not only does she run off with a human and die apart from her people, but she has *two* mongrel children. This begs the question: why would Voster's son not have come here with both of them or even in place of the girl?"

"I wondered that myself. But then I thought back to the reports we received from our agents," Gilbrannen reminded the patriarch. "The human king commanded that all males over the age of fifteen be taken away and trained for battle."

Shilvand's face lit up, seeing the connection. "And based on Niena's age, you believe her brother would be old enough."

"Precisely," Gilbrannen said with a smile. "And if we pressure her correctly, we can use that connection."

Shilvand considered the possibilities, staring out the window at the late summer shadows. "The city checkpoints have temporarily frustrated our sabotage efforts, and it will only get worse. But if we can get a source of information on the inside, learn their methods, we can prolong our operations indefinitely."

"And continue stoking the fires of division," Gilbrannen said, encouraged that his idea had met with approval. "Niena will not hesitate to help us if we threaten her father. I'm sure of it."

"Brilliant," Shilvand said, standing from his chair and approaching the window, now looking south toward the lands of men. "Take her and a few of the Dast'rel by horse to meet up with Silmon near Celwaith Tor. Use all speed by the hidden ways, and you should arrive within a week."

"Yes, Patriarch," Gilbrannen said, doing his best to hide his excitement. He had long wanted to join the agents on the front lines, and now he had a pivotal mission. He rose, but before leaving he had one more question. "Has there been any word from Neraliel?"

Por'monir's allied enclave Neraliel was hidden deep in the swamps along the coast to their southeast, surrounded by inhospitable marshland infested with reptilian and amphibian terrors. Men avoided going through if they could, which made it the perfect hiding place for the D'harnir.

Shilvand stayed at the window, his white hair shining the same shade as the clouds outside. "A runner returned with a message this morning. Crates of weapons are being escorted from Cape Vrosingr to Celwaith Tor, to supply the capital's garrison for the new recruits. Now that the human outpost along the eastern road has been removed, Silmon will be able to safely lead Neraliel's warriors to hijack at least one of those shipments as it passes through the swamps."

"A dangerous opportunity," Gilbrannen mused. "But I suppose Silmon has experience with such risky assignments."

"Indeed, he does," Shilvand said, finally abandoning the view to turn and regard the younger D'harn with harsh concern. "You, on the other hand, do not. I have never trusted you before with a mission so crucial to our resurgence."

The truth of the patriarch's words struck home. Although Gilbrannen had acquitted himself well as a guard captain, he knew that was a far cry from what he was about to do. "I am grateful you believe I am ready—"

Shilvand cut him off, not acknowledging the statement. "Gilbrannen. You know that I have no children and have not re-bonded with anyone since. You are calculating, bold, and bearing unwavering loyalty to our cause, in the same ways I had hoped my son would be. The reason I had not sent you to join Silmon before now is because I wanted to keep you safe."

Gilbrannen blinked, amazed that his patriarch would say these things. He had always looked up to Shilvand, but it humbled him to know that the esteem was mutual.

Shilvand continued. "Make no mistake. Niena and her brother could be the key to dealing a decisive blow, one that brings the entire Drüstanian culture crumbling down. But they could also be what undoes generations of careful preparation. Our family's wardcasters are not prepared for outright war. Everything depends on remaining hidden until we are strong enough. And that means, for now, that everything depends on you."

Gilbrannen met his patriarch's scrutinizing gaze with confidence. "I will ensure your plan succeeds. I will not fail you."

Shilvand nodded, appearing satisfied. He folded his arms, his embroidered gray sleeves hanging down like banners of war. "Then be gone, and be well."

The door to the suite closed behind Gilbrannen, and he hurried on with his thoughts in a whirlwind. He had much to prepare before setting out for Celwaith Tor, including checking on his parents. They couldn't know his mission, for secrecy's sake, but he needed to tell them he was going away. If Niena's brother was as useful a source as they believed, Gilbrannen could be far from home for a very long time.

But perhaps, if the war in Drüstania reached a tipping point, he would be an eyewitness to the devouring fire that would cleanse the world of men. He would pay any price to be a part of D'harnin history like that.

FIFTEEN

The dealings of deceivers are unknown even to themselves, for they have replaced the world with a forgery. The truth shall come upon them and strip them destitute in their weakest moment.

— Codes of Entreaty 6.01-02

TOLLAN RAPPED AT THE bedroom door, this time more forcefully with the knuckles of his leather gauntlet. "Come on! We're going to be late—we're on special detail today, remember?"

Thaxon groaned something unintelligible from the other side, and the rustling of cotton sheets suggested he had rolled over. In his defense, it was still dark out, and the bedding at the Denvald residence was the softest Tollan had ever known, but they needed to get a move on. The two of them might have gotten lucky by getting assigned day shifts, but that meant sleeping in was an unheard-of luxury.

When Tollan didn't hear anything more, he turned the knob and barged in. Thankfully, the door hadn't been locked. "Thaxon—"

The red-haired boy was up and awake, if just barely, sitting on the edge of the bed and wiping at the corners of his eyes. "Do you mind?"

Tollan looked at the nearby easy chair, which still had Thaxon's uniform draped over it from their late return the previous evening. At least they weren't sharing uniforms between dozens of men anymore like during training. He pulled out his pocket watch and shoved the face in Thaxon's. "You've got ten minutes before we need to be out the door, and that's pushing it," he said.

"All right, all right," Thaxon said, peeved but reaching for his trousers. "I'll meet you downstairs. Grab me something from the kitchen."

Tollan rolled his eyes, but assented. He left Thaxon to it and headed downstairs, passing his own room on the way. Even four days after moving in, he still couldn't believe that the Denvalds had let him have an entire room to himself. He wondered what Niena would think of it all, but the reminder of her absence made him sad. She and their father still hadn't returned, and he was no closer to discovering why they had left.

Not that he'd had much time to investigate beyond stopping to see the Harroways one evening. The note Niena had left Keordi was about as cryptic as Anise's and offered no new information, but at least Tollan had been able to thank Kasdan for delivering Niena's birthday gift.

Tollan rounded the curved banister at the bottom of the stairs and cut through the dining hall. The mouth-watering smell of frying bacon drifted through the air from the kitchen. Lord Denvald sat at the head of the table in a heavy robe, drinking a steamy cup of tea and reading a book. He was normally puffing on a cigar, but not this morning.

"Ah, Tollan," he said, looking up. "Good morning, soldier."

"Good morning, sir," Tollan replied, not wanting to be rude but also hoping it didn't turn into a long conversation. "Is everything all right? You normally aren't up at this hour."

Denvald closed his book violently, making a deep clapping sound. Tollan wondered if asking such a thing was in poor taste given their different classes, but the elder man didn't seem annoyed at him particularly. "Yes, just a disagreement with Lady Denvald. I'm leaving for Cape Vrosingr in an hour, so I didn't see any use in going back to bed."

"Will you be there long, sir?" Tollan asked, wondering what could take the merchant guildmaster that far from the capital.

"Unfortunately, yes," Denvald said, hoisting himself from his chair. "The jarl insisted that my guild's fleet spend the last couple weeks ferrying new weapons from the Pamarthen foundries around the coast to Cape Vrosingr. Bringing the weapons over land would be too long and dangerous, while the port is both safer and faster. Anyway, because our ships were diverted from their assigned schedules, it is going to take a while to sort out the bookkeeping and pick up the slack. All of this on top of rumors that the king is considering a trade agreement with Ash'kiram . . ."

Tollan nodded, unsure what to say next. It was difficult to read into how the man felt about two peasants staying in his house, but the guildmaster clearly felt comfortable enough with Tollan to discuss the particulars of trade. Then again, there had been a distinct pall over the home since Tollan and Anise had moved in, and it was entirely possible that few people had taken an interest in Lord Denvald's work recently.

Tollan realized he might be overthinking it, as always. Lord and Lady Denvald had lost their daughter only a month ago. That sudden change would be difficult for any family, aristocrat or not.

"I expect I will be gone before your aunt rises," Denvald continued in a cautious tone, "but can I count on you to pass on my gratitude to her? Letaccia has not left the house since the massacre, and her friends have stopped coming around. It has brightened her days immeasurably to have someone else to speak with who isn't her servant."

Tollan smiled. To be sure, Anise had settled in almost too well at the Denvald house. She had always said that she was meant to be rich, and the way she carried on, he almost believed it now. She even looked the part, after Thaxon's mother had passed down a couple of older dresses still in good repair. "I will make sure to let her know, sir."

"Thank you," Denvald said. "I'm sorry; you were passing through and I prattled on. What was it you needed?"

Tollan cleared his throat. "No, sir, it's all quite interesting. But Thaxon and I have to leave shortly, so we don't have time to sit for breakfast. Would it be possible to—"

"Say no more," Denvald said, clapping his hands. A footman appeared to sprout from nowhere and bowed. "Please pack up some of the bacon they're cooking in the kitchen and send it with our resident soldier here."

The footman bowed again and proceeded through the door to the kitchen.

"You must not be posted in the Gilded Quarter today if you're leaving for your shift so early," Denvald commented, prompting more detail.

"No, sir, you're correct," Tollan said with a hint of pride in his voice. "We're on special assignment today down at the city gates."

"I'M BORED," THAXON SAID under his breath so only Tollan could hear.

Tollan shook his head. He admitted, working the gatehouse for a day had sounded far more glamorous. Instead, it wasn't that much different from the average checkpoint, with two main caveats: it was much, much busier, and far more people got turned away. "Look at it this way: at least we don't have to sleep in the gatehouse like the regulars do."

Thaxon scrunched up his nose, barely visible beyond the guard of his helmet. "I suppose. But we haven't even gotten paid once yet for all our work."

Tollan sighed, and pushed his loose vambraces back up his arms. He couldn't argue with that. It was disheartening that most of the army hadn't received their promised wages, but their commanding officer had assured them they would be paid in full by week's end.

Thaxon stepped forward to accept the papers of the next delivery cart, and passed them to the clerk who had a hefty stack of ledgers going. The line of people waiting to get inside the city stretched away until it was no longer visible around a bend in the East Road.

Tollan continued standing at attention, his eyes scanning for any suspicious movement or nervous habits. So far, in a week of alternating checkpoint and patrol duty, he hadn't caught a single person without their identification and travel pass. Thaxon witnessed a brief scuffle at one of the new checkpoints the other evening, resulting in two unwise citizens being hauled off to jail for a few days, but otherwise the city had been quiet.

He wouldn't let his guard down though, or allow himself to become lulled into a false sense of security. The sooner they found the root of these attacks, the sooner everyone could go back to normal, and all the ridiculous tracking papers could go away.

Toward mid-afternoon the crowd thinned out to the point that Tollan and Thaxon had a few spare moments between travelers. It made the heat of the sun beating down on their armor even more unbearable, since the lack of work meant they had nothing else to distract them.

Tollan cleared his throat and took a swig from the canteen of water hanging at his belt. "Do you mind if we take a detour on the way home?"

"Sure." Thaxon pulled off his open-faced helmet to shake out his sweaty hair and scratch the back of his scalp. "What did you have in mind?"

Tollan drew his iron sword from its sheath. He could tell it was too brittle from the moment it had been issued to him; either too much carbon had been added to the steel, or it had been quenched in water, or both. "Thought I might go back down to my father's old forge and tinker for a few hours, if they'll let me. This sword is painfully low quality." One of his vambraces picked that moment to slide down his arm again, and he chuckled. "And my armor needs altered, if you haven't noticed."

Thaxon raised his eyebrows in awe. "I'll probably just try to snag one of the better ones coming in from Pamarth. I wish I had a skill like yours though."

"You play the cithren."

"A musical instrument is not the same as making a sword from scratch," Thaxon said with a scoff, but Tollan could tell he appreciated the encouragement. He shoved his helmet back on, and pointed out the open gate. "Uh oh, look alive. Here comes official business."

Four guards accompanied the approaching cart, not counting the driver, all in Drüstanian yellow. Crates were piled high in back, strapped down with tricord bands. The reins clicked, and the two horses pulled up short.

Tollan looked around, but the other guards on duty stood off to the side or above the gate, ignoring the newcomers. He and Thaxon would have to check them in, if no one else did. "State your business," he said stoically.

The driver spoke up, his voice dry and almost monotone. "Delivery to the palace armory from the port at Cape Vrosingr. Weapons from Pamarth." He leaned down to hand Thaxon a customs form with a merchant guild seal, and his motions seemed to Tollan a little stilted or stiff.

Thaxon looked it over before giving the form to Tollan. "Checks out."

"Well, don't hand it to me, hand it to—" He looked behind him. The clerk was nowhere to be seen. Must have run off unannounced to take a leak. Typical. He went over to the covered desk and picked up the quill, incensed that he had to do a job he was never trained for. After a few moments searching, he found the right entry log and took down the identifying information. "And you all have your personal seals?"

In unison, the soldiers took out their identification and writs of passage. Tollan rubbed his temple—it felt like a headache had welled up out of nowhere. He took the papers from Thaxon, and wrote the names down in what he hoped was the military transit ledger.

The papers were in order, so he circled the desk and began handing them back to their owners. The guard trailing the right rear side of the wagon caught his attention, on account of being so tall and pale. His uniform looked ragged as well, with a large tear in the yellow tunic under the arm.

"How did that happen?" Tollan asked curiously. "You should get that patched up while you're in town. There's a good tailor over on . . ."

He trailed off, his head throbbing again. The soldier mumbled something quietly, lips barely moving, and for a split second instead of the tall, pale soldier Tollan saw a stout bearded man from the south, with yellow tunic in good repair. He shook his head, and the vision faded back to the pale man.

"What's the trouble?" Thaxon called to him.

Tollan stared at the soldier in front of him, his heart racing. "I'm going to have to take you into custody, sir," he said.

The guard stopped his strange whispering, and suddenly broke into a dead run heading deeper into the city.

Tollan took off after him, hearing Thaxon whistle for the others to close the gate. He glanced back and saw the driver slump down in his seat while the other accompanying guards fell to the ground. He'd never seen anything like it, but at least the wagon wouldn't be going anywhere.

The loose armor bounced up and down on Tollan's chest with each heavy pace as he ran after the rogue guard, steadily gaining. The yellow-dressed figure stripped off as much of his own armor as possible while on the move, presumably to make himself faster and blend in with bystanders in the street.

Up ahead, the pale man ducked into a side alley to avoid going through a checkpoint further up the street. If Tollan was right, the alley doubled back. He chose an earlier turn, planning to cut the impostor off.

Drawing his sword, Tollan pushed himself still faster to be right at the corner when his quarry came barreling around it. Sure enough, he had guessed right, and the man came to a skidding halt.

Before he could run back the other way, Tollan lunged forward and kicked him to the ground. Instead of staying down, the impostor rolled and came up holding his own sword, which he had not discarded.

Tollan fell back under the onslaught, struggling to parry. The man's fighting style was unlike anything he had trained with, making it impossible to predict.

One of the blows connected with the flat of his blade near the cross-guard, and it shattered.

A defenseless Tollan landed flat on his back in the dirt, holding out the stump of his blade.

"Who are you?" Tollan panted.

The pale-skinned figure shook his head, a few brown locks falling out of the cloth band that circled his head. "You'll never know," he said tauntingly, and stabbed forward with his blade.

Tollan rolled, fumbling as he tried to get back to his feet.

The sounds of other guards came clattering up the alleyway, and the impostor broke off his attack with an exclamation like a curse, though not one that Tollan had ever heard. The adversary charged the wall, vaulted off it, and caught a window ledge which he used to swing upwards onto the slanted roof.

Thaxon and two others caught up just in time to see a few lone shingles falling to the filthy street.

The impostor was gone.

Tollan sighed heavily, cursing his luck and his flimsy sword.

THREE STRAW-FILLED EFFIGIES ROSE from the gladiolus patch, their burlap faces dull in comparison to the surrounding garden. It was almost golden hour, and the sun's rays caught the many varieties of colorful flowers perfectly. Anseldr resolved to spend more time here to appreciate the sights and smells; the palace gardener deserved more recognition for her talents.

Although the royal garden normally embodied peace and tranquility, this evening was substantially different. Coranna attempted to plug her ears and cowered behind the king's shoulder. Anseldr's wife, however, was not as visibly shaken. Instead, her fingers dug into his upper arm like the claws of a felinx in anticipation.

With a crack like a lightning strike, the head of one of the effigies exploded backwards in a hail of dust and straw. Anseldr winced as his ears rang from the sound, but thankfully the garden wasn't very enclosed.

Darakh Shi'ev raised the weapon back to vertical, a wisp of smoke issuing from its barrel. Without saying a word, he held it out to the king.

"Remarkable," Pelendion said, gingerly taking the precision-machined miniaturized cannon and examining the trigger and hammer mechanism. He sniffed at the lingering scent of black powder in the air. "It pulls easier than a crossbow."

"Yes, Your Majesty." Shi'ev's olive-skinned face smiled congenially, a feature common among those from Ash'kiram. His black suit had accents of dark green and was tailored to be much more form-fitting compared to colorful Drüstanian fashion. "It does take more time to reload, and if not cleaned correctly the residue will prevent a consistent ignition. But, in my humble opinion, the increase in lethality and accuracy more than compensates."

Anseldr already knew the information from his correspondence with Shi'ev over the last several months, but he asked anyway. "What is the range?"

"Our factories maintain the strictest quality and consistency checks," Shi'ev answered with pride. "Every single rifle that has been fire-tested was capable of hitting a man-sized target consistently over one hundred yards, more than double that of a well-made crossbow."

Pelendion raised his eyebrows approvingly, turning the weapon in his hands to admire it from all angles. Anseldr couldn't remember the last time he had seen his brother so enamored with an object. Pelendion pointed to a metal loop attached to the end of the barrel. "What is this for?"

Seriah Le'shom, the Kiramet ambassador to Drüstania, reached into the crate that had housed the sample weapon and pulled out another item wrapped in scarlet cloth.

"One innovation for which I cannot claim credit—it was my assistant, Adwin, who suggested the alteration," Shi'ev said, accepting the parcel from the ambassador. He gingerly unwrapped it to reveal a single-edged blade with no handle. "This pike can be fastened to the end of the rifle to be more suitable in short-range combat."

Before Shi'ev had even fastened the shiny steel to the barrel, Anseldr could tell that his brother was hooked. "May I?" Pelendion asked, trying and failing to mask his eagerness.

"By all means, sire," Shi'ev said, retrieving another paper cartridge filled with a tiny approximation of a cannonball and a precisely-measured amount of black powder. He showed the king how best to reload and, after tamping the ammunition into place with a ramrod, cocked the hammer and gestured to the burlap dummies. "Simply rest it in the crook of your shoulder, look down the barrel, and aim using the crook of the raised sight."

Anseldr noticed the palace staff were now gathered around the outskirts of the garden, drawn by the noise of the first blast. He opted to cover his own ears this time rather than suffer the ringing, and Emeline and Coranna both followed suit.

The hammer sprung forward, and the recoil caused Pelendion's arm to shudder. Even so, the bullet buried itself into the leftmost dummy's shoulder.

A smile spread across Pelendion's face, and he charged the faux enemy line. With relish, he plunged the pike blade into the packed straw torso and drove the whole effigy to the ground. He released the weapon, and it stayed upright, poking out of the pile of burlap.

A smattering of applause swept through the gathered onlookers.

"How much for five thousand of them?" Pelendion asked, breathing heavily but still beaming with exhilaration.

Le'shom and Shi'ev traded glances, and the lady ambassador fielded the question. "We are prepared to offer a competitive price since this will mark the beginning of such a historic trade agreement between our two nations. And as a token of our good faith and desire to do business, the first two hundred units will be our gift to Drüstania."

The ladies and a few onlookers gently gasped, and Anseldr couldn't help but smile at the shrewd move. Perhaps this was the encouragement his brother needed to finally see they needed Ash'kiram's help to put down this rebellion, regardless of how low the royal treasury might begin to run.

Shi'ev went to retrieve the rifle from the burlap cadaver, bowing to the king as he did so. "That shipment is awaiting your signature in the bay at Cape Vrosingr as we speak," Shi'ev said.

Pelendion drew himself up and sobriety returned to his bearded face. "The prevention of yesterday's intended attack on this very palace is cause to believe the tide is turning. But we are no closer to discovering the source of this unrest, and we need to empower our soldiers to fight back when the opportunity presents itself."

"I agree, my liege," Anseldr said. "I have no doubt that if our men were equipped with these rifles, the saboteur would have been killed or captured." He would not sully his tongue with the words *I told you so*, but this was as close as he could come to it.

Besides, Pelendion knew already that if it hadn't been for Anseldr's security measures, the terrorist's cart of Pamarthen weapons would have made it all the way to the royal armory. Considering that the weapons crates had instead been filled with a copious amount of black powder, it was possible for the palace to have caved in once detonated.

But the attack had been averted, and that black powder could be put to a much better use.

Pelendion nodded stoically toward Anseldr, acknowledging the support. "Therefore, in light of our current crisis, Ambassador Le'shom, Mr. Shi'ev, it is my duty and honor to reopen negotiations with you concerning a trade contract between our two nations."

Another smattering of applause, this time joined by Anseldr.

"That is welcome news, Your Majesty," Shi'ev said, placing the rifle back inside its travel crate. "I understand Seriah has had a preliminary agreement written up for years now, waiting for such a time. Perhaps we could start there and redact portions until it meets with your approval?"

Pelendion agreed and ushered the visitors inside to review terms over a feast in their honor. Suddenly remembering their many different errands in preparation for the banquet, the many spectating palace servants bustled off to complete them. The king and queen led the procession to the banquet hall.

Anseldr and Emeline were the last to retire indoors, as he wanted to take her aside and admire the last few minutes of the sunset together. Though he immediately found himself looking more at her than the view. Her hair was pinned up, and a few stray wisps at her temples framed her rosy cheeks.

"I suppose that went better than anyone could have hoped," Emeline said with a coy smile, leaning against the railing edge of the garden terrace. "Except you, of course. The king should be honored to have such a brother. I doubt Stenden would dare to be as outspoken for the betterment of the kingdom."

The wind picked up, and although it was not cold Anseldr felt a chill. He turned from the view and drew his cape closer about himself. "I think Stenden has more fortitude than you give him credit—"

Anseldr frowned. He saw a strange shadow in the corner of the gabled roof, but as he looked closer it vanished. It was just an instant, but enough to cause him not to finish his thought.

"What is it?" Emeline asked, following his gaze.

"Thought I saw someone up there for a moment," Anseldr replied, shrugging it off. "It's nothing."

He took her petite hand in his and led her back through the garden to the waiting banquet.

Hours later, after all bellies were full, and the trade contract had been finalized and signed, Anseldr returned to his desk to peruse the reports of yesterday's encounter once again. The words of Tollan Cresthaven fascinated him, the boy responsible for unraveling the plot. Anseldr thought he recognized the boy's surname, but couldn't place it.

Cresthaven's description of the escaped terrorist was haunting, and implied he could wield some kind of hypnotism over people. Anseldr had never heard anything like it, in legend or real life.

Unfortunately, the seemingly trance-inducing powers were so strange that it didn't rule anything out. The Crownless could still be responsible if they had discovered some secret of mind control. Or it might be that some foreign entity had spurred on the Crownless. Or else the Crownless could be a convenient distraction from the true threat to his people.

Nevertheless, it was a lead, and he intended to follow it. Anseldr resolved to have the city guard start rounding up street magicians and fortune-tellers for questioning. He had always found their tricks and card readings a bunch of bunk, but if these hypnotic abilities were possible, they would be the ones to know. With any luck, they might find their saboteur among them.

A tentative knock came at his office door, and Anseldr immediately knew it was Emeline. "What is it, love?"

The door cracked open, and his wife stood there in her frilly nightgown. "The Kiramet inventor is here to see you," she said. "He claims it's urgent."

"Shi'ev?" Anseldr put down the parchments and stood. "I'll go out to him."

"Don't be long," Emeline said, a pleading look in her eyes. "It would be nice to fall asleep next to you for once."

"I'll make sure of it," he said, though he didn't know if he would have control of that. He kissed her on the forehead, then brushed past her into the corridor. "This should only take a minute."

Shi'ev waited for him outside the jarl's chambers, still dressed in his clothes from the demonstration and banquet. Anseldr ushered him into a small foyer, and motioned to keep their voices down. "Old friend, it is good to see you in a less formal setting, but it is quite late."

"I know. But given that Le'shom is leaving for Ash'kiram in the morning, I needed to discuss this with you now," Shi'ev whispered. "I may have a way to expose your enemy once and for all."

Anseldr was more than intrigued. "Do tell."

"First, I need to know more about what happened at the gate. I have heard rumors throughout the day, but I was hoping you would fill me in."

Anseldr hesitated for a moment about how much he should reveal, but he had known Shi'ev since they were boys. The man's father had been the Prime Minister of Ash'kiram twenty years ago, and the two boys had become fast friends. Ever since, they had sent each other letters at least once a year, but more frequently as of late.

Besides, more eyes on the problem could only help. "What you have heard was probably accurate, though I'll get you a copy of the reports. To be honest, Darakh, we don't know what we're up against. We took the guards accompanying the shipment into custody and held them in separate cell blocks for questioning. Their stories are all the same: they don't remember anything since leaving Cape Vrosingr with the cargo. They were on the road one minute, and then they woke up here in the capital prison."

"So, either they all agreed beforehand on an incredibly hard-to-believe story, or they are all telling the truth." Shi'ev said, his dark eyes staring at the candle-lit chandelier in contemplation.

"It would seem so," Anseldr agreed. "I even pulled the service records for each of the soldiers, including the missing one whose uniform was worn by the leader. They have all been in the army between two and five years with exemplary records and no demerits. It is unlikely they are traitors to the king."

"Do the eyewitness reports note anything strange?"

Anseldr related the most relevant of the Cresthaven guard's statements, and Shi'ev's eyes narrowed with each revelation—not in surprise, but like his suspicions had been confirmed. "Have you heard of such things before?" Anseldr asked.

"Not in modern times," Shi'ev answered ominously. "Long ago in Ash'kiram, there used to be a creature called a drakaina. Are you familiar?"

The name stirred in Anseldr's memory. "Some kind of horrible hybrid between a woman and a dragon, wasn't it? I always thought they were fictitious."

"So did we," Shi'ev confirmed. "But almost a decade ago, an explorer found an emaciated corpse of one in a cave uncovered by the desert winds. Preserved for hundreds—if not thousands—of years. Since then, it has been hidden away in our historical archive, and I have been one of the few scientists allowed to examine it in exchange for my silence on the matter. It is authentic."

"This is all interesting, but what does it have to do with what happened at the gate?"

Shi'ev sighed, clearly hoping Anseldr would have put the pieces together himself. "The traditions say that the drakaina had immense power over the minds of men. By some trick of their voice or their mind, anyone in their presence could be entranced and led away to their doom. Most who encountered them were never seen again."

Anseldr couldn't deny the similarities, but he failed to see the relevance. "The saboteur was a man, tall and pale according to the report, without scales. I doubt your drakaina had anything to do with this."

"No, not ... the drakaina," Shi'ev said more loudly before remembering his surroundings. He quieted his tone again, though his frustration had become evident. "Even in our legends, there were no males of the species anyway. But the drakaina may not have been the only creature with that power, and there is still much that we don't know about the world."

Anseldr had to concede the point. At the least, it made as much sense as any other idea. "Perhaps. But how would we ever know? At least sedition can be proven by physical evidence."

"That is true," Shi'ev admitted. "And if my plan works, you may be able to obtain that evidence—one way or the other."

Anseldr wrapped his fleece robe tighter around himself and folded his arms. He had a feeling he knew what the inventor was about to suggest. "Enlighten me."

"As I happen to know, you have had periodic troubles with bandits along your main roads between the holds. Many shipments have gone missing, but there wasn't any rhyme or reason to the lost merchandise." Shi'ev paused. "Am I correct?"

The question was better answered by Lord Denvald as the merchant guildmaster, but it sounded right. "Yes."

"I have a theory. Whoever your adversaries are, and if their attempted infiltration was not an exception, they could be specifically targeting more heavily-guarded shipments to gain better materials and armament."

The logic tracked, especially since they would not need to risk life and limb to steal the goods. And now Anseldr could guess what Shi'ev's plan entailed. "Ah, that would allow us to bait a trap for them. Continue."

Shi'ev laid out the rest of his plan. With some sleight-of-hand, they would be able to deliver the first shipment of two hundred rifles to Celwaith Tor in an unmarked, unguarded cart. The presence of an armed escort would draw the terrorists instead to an empty wagon— empty, that is, save for more Drüstanian soldiers. With luck, there would be too many soldiers for the adversaries to enchant, and it would be easy enough to obtain evidence about their identity or base of operations from corpses or captives.

Anseldr bit the inside of his cheek, mulling over their options. "That might work, as long as my brother agrees. But we'll need soldiers that are familiar with the situation and can recognize any hypnotic effects—the two from the gate should suffice. Might even promote Cresthaven to lieutenant and have him lead the unit, seems to have a strong head on his shoulders for one so young."

Shi'ev nodded. "That sounds like a wise course of action. With your permission, I'll inform Ambassador Le'shom of the plan before she leaves in the morning so that the rifles are not sent from Cape Vrosingr prematurely."

"You aren't going with her?"

"I was hoping to remain in Celwaith Tor a few more weeks to peruse the royal library. You have several rare books that I would enjoy the chance to study."

"But of course," Anseldr reassured him. "Feel free to stay here in the visitor's suite. Perhaps I can find the time to join you and catch up at a more reasonable hour."

"Indeed," Shi'ev said, now abashed concerning the hour. "And with that, I shall bid you good night."

Anseldr showed his old friend out into the corridor, so he could at last retire to his bedchamber. Judging by Emeline's deep breathing, she had already fallen asleep.

He felt guilty as he climbed under the covers next to her, but he shrugged off the feeling. It had been a productive day for the jarl, all things considered. In the morning, he would set a plan into motion that would reveal the identity of Drüstania's foes once and for all.

SIXTEEN

No matter how wise, an argument will not sway one whose mind is set in their errant course. Their only reproof is that which you cannot give them: experience.
— *Codes of Entreaty 4.07-08*

NIENA'S INTERNAL CLOCK WAS completely bewildered now. She could not discern the time of day this far underground, and when she did sleep it wasn't for more than a few hours at a time. More than once she wished she had brought the pocket watch she purchased for Tollan, and she worried what her brother might think if he returned from training to find only Anise.

But at last, despite the cool clammy air, she felt exhausted enough to fall into the deepest sleep she had achieved since arriving in her cell —which, of course, meant that the D'harnir would choose that moment to rudely awaken her. The actual time didn't matter anymore, because it certainly still felt like the middle of the night.

At first, she struggled with the D'harnir, the adrenaline rush going to her head. They tied her hands in front of her with a rough woven cord, but left her alone once she was on her feet. She grabbed her father's book, which they surprisingly didn't try to take from her.

"What's going on? Where are you taking me?"

She received no response beyond a shove toward the open door of her cell. Maybe she would get to see her father, even if just for a little while.

The two guards hustled her out into the maze of underground corridors she remembered from before. They ran into no one as they turned one corner, then another, and finally the delved tunnel opened out into a cave. It was natural, but with a flat path carved through the mineral towers that had dripped down from the ceiling over thousands of years.

Similar lamps to the one that had illuminated her cell had been placed periodically along the route, shining a dim bluish light most of the way to the next one. Niena could see that the cave turned a corner up ahead, or at least the path did, but the chamber was so tall that the light did not extend to its roof.

The D'harnin soldiers picked up their pace now that they weren't closed in by walls and tight corners, forcing Niena to keep up. Not far past the bend and down an easy slope stood a handful of horses accompanied by three more D'harnir. One of them looked up from packing the saddlebags, and the lamplight caught his face well enough for Niena to recognize Gilbrannen.

Niena couldn't hide her disdain, reminded of her ridiculous blunder the day before last. *Or was it the day before? A handful of sleeps ago, anyway.* But the person she desired to see most wasn't anywhere to be seen. "Where is my father?"

Gilbrannen reached out to try to calm her down, but she wasn't going to fall for his tricks again. She took a step backwards and bumped into one of the guards escorting her, who grabbed her arm tightly. It reminded her unpleasantly of the drunken men who had accosted her in the streets of Celwaith Tor, except these individuals were sober and all the scarier for it.

"Voster will be perfectly safe in his own cell," Gilbrannen replied smoothly. "But you, Niena ... You can help us achieve our goals in Drüstania."

Niena wrenched her arm free of her captor. "And what makes you think I would help you murder more innocent people? I thought causing harm was forbidden to you."

"Only unnecessary harm," Gilbrannen retorted, and the other soldiers chuckled at Niena's idealism. "And how we fight *is* necessary. Men have thrived for centuries by consigning us to unexplored or unwanted scraps of wasteland. If we did not make war from the shadows, we would never survive."

"Wars are fought in the open, where both parties know what's at stake and who their enemy is," Niena corrected, her voice gaining a hard edge. She raised her father's book, clamped tight between her tied hands. "You think any human alive today has a clue what was done to your people that long ago?"

"That matters little. Most of Por'monir knows nothing of our efforts," he said, turning back to his saddlebags. "Their complacent piety would keep them from understanding what has to be done. But once the kingdom of Drüstania falls from within—"

Niena had heard more than enough. "Why would I ever care now?" she interjected, on the verge of shouting. "I might have sympathized with you, once, but you've twisted your circumstances into a crusade, a mockery of justice," she said, using words she had read from the histories. "Your quarrels are not with the men of today."

"I suppose I cannot expect you to think otherwise," Gilbrannen spat bitterly. "You have been raised all your life in the oblivious privilege of humanity, despite your blood. Remember this conversation when the ambitions of men prove you wrong. They always have, and they always will."

"This path will result in the destruction of the D'harnir," Niena said, her voice now low and threatening. "And you will have only yourself to blame."

Gilbrannen whirled and stuck an angry finger in her face. But rather than continue shouting, he lowered his hand and smirked. "We will see. I would prefer that you believed in what we were trying to accomplish, but you will help us in our cause regardless."

Niena's stomach twisted as she realized he was right. She couldn't refuse.

Gilbrannen motioned for one of the guards to remove her bonds, and he produced a knife to cut her free. "Voster will remain here in our custody the entire time, and Shilvand will have few qualms with killing him should you not comply."

The cord which bound her wrists fell away, and she rubbed one gently where it had chafed.

"I would advise you to be more careful of your words and actions, Niena," Gilbrannen said, crossing his arms over his chest. "Your father's life depends on it from now forward."

Niena knew she had no choice, not really. It proved an obnoxious repeating pattern in her life: she was never the one in control. But she could not allow them to hurt her father.

But how many other lives might be lost if I help them? the quiet thought in the back of her mind asked. She seized onto the words "might be" with a vengeance. Nothing was certain about the future. She just needed to keep her father alive as long as possible until she could think of a way out.

But she resolved, then and there, she would not kill for the D'harnir, no matter the cost. She would do anything they asked, but she would not live the rest of her life with blood on her hands.

"What do you want me to do?" Niena asked, the rebellious streak sapped from her.

"Wise choice," Gilbrannen encouraged as his men loaded up the last of the supplies and mounted their steeds. "We know your brother would have been drafted into the Drüstanian army. You're going back to Celwaith Tor to make contact with him. Once there, you will be our informant about troop movements, checkpoint protocols, and any other useful information he happens to come across."

So, it *had* been her innocent mention of Tollan that tipped them off, Niena realized bitterly. *All of this could have been avoided if I had kept my mouth shut.* Even then, Shilvand might have decided to kill her and her father if they didn't prove useful in some way. It infuriated her how unclear the morality was among the D'harnir, and especially among Shilvand's secret police.

"Just so I know," Niena said, "what are you expecting of me, and how do you determine failure?"

Gilbrannen nodded, climbing up onto his horse and looking down on her. "If you miss a scheduled meeting, Voster dies. If you tell anyone and our operation is discovered, Voster dies. And if you go too long without giving us good intelligence—"

"Papa dies, okay. I get the picture." Niena crossed to the last available horse, again intimidated by the size of the beast. She placed the book in the saddlebag and gripped the horn to vault up and over the horse's back. Thankfully, one of the other guards led her horse, because she did not want to admit that she had never ridden by herself before.

She would have to learn by doing.

NIENA'S BACKSIDE AND LEGS ached, and it was all she could do to keep holding on to the bouncing saddle beneath her. The trees whizzed past in the evening light, making it hard for her to see their surroundings. It was doubtful she would recognize any landmarks, anyway, having spent little time as an adult outside the city.

Gilbrannen and his men had forced her to travel underground for leagues and leagues, and when they finally emerged into the sunlight northwest of Ensdale, it felt like a weight had been removed from her shoulders.

As far as Niena could tell, none of their horses' breeds were built for speed but rather endurance. It was a potent combination with the mysterious spells of the D'harnir, which they spoke over the horses during breaks every half hour or so. Niena tried to make out what they were saying and replicate it, but could never catch more than a few syllables. In any case, their steeds always seemed vastly rejuvenated after these rest stops, and they could keep up long-distance sprinting paces for far longer.

It wouldn't have surprised Niena to know they were crossing Drüstania in record time. If they had been able to travel by main roads, she would wager they could have reached their destination in five days. Instead, when they stopped tonight, it would be a week since they had left Por'monir, cutting how long it had taken her father to travel the same distance by more than half.

She tried not to think about her father, trapped back in his cell underneath Por'monir. She hadn't seen him or Tolvanen since they were first incarcerated, so it was possible that the elves had already killed him and were lying to squeeze more information out of her. If that was the case, she supposed it was working.

The elven riders came over a small rise, and the sudden shift of direction nearly threw Niena from her saddle. The group slowed and came to the edge of a small bluff that rose out of the surrounding trees to give them a better view of the land. In the distance, peeking through the hills, a great cliff rose up. The keep of Celwaith Tor sat like a pointed crown on top, shining with the last light in the west.

But Gilbrannen wasn't looking at the city. Instead, he scanned the landscape, looking for something. "There," he said, and pointed out another outcropping to their southwest. Not a bluff, but a natural bridge hollowed out by a spring underneath.

The perfect place for a hideout, Niena realized. Deep in the woods but with elevation and a fresh water supply. She patted her horse Evwoin's neck, reassuring her by touch that she would be able to eat and drink soon.

Gilbrannen led them away from the overlook and picked up the pace again, until they stood below the towering arch of rock. He dismounted and cupped his hands to his mouth, giving a series of odd whistles that sounded vaguely birdlike, but also like no bird Niena had ever encountered.

No sooner had Gilbrannen completed the set of trills than a handful of D'harnir melted out of the surrounding trees, dressed in clothes that matched the shades of the foliage and rocks almost perfectly.

Niena shivered a little. These elves had mastered the art of blending into their surroundings even without magic. She had no doubt that any men to come wandering into these woods would either be handily disoriented and directed away from the cleft in the rock, or would die before ever knowing they were in danger.

"Gilbrannen," a voice called from behind them. This D'harn was dressed in the familiar dark blue cloak of Por'monir, hiding most of his face. "We received no word of your coming. Did you happen to meet our messenger along the way?"

"No, Silmon, we did not," Gilbrannen said, clasping the other D'harn's forearm in a gesture of kinship. "But I am eager to learn what urgent information you have sent. Was your attack on the royal armory a success?"

The D'harn called Silmon paused a moment before answering, ducking his head in apparent shame. "I regret to inform you that the operation failed, stopped before we could even pass the checkpoint at the main gate. I take full responsibility."

Gilbrannen fell silent, seeming to Niena like he wanted to wring the agent's neck but instead clenching his hands into fists. "We should go inside, and you can explain how this possibly could have happened with our safeguards in place."

Silmon bowed his head in deference. He turned and gave hand signals to the camouflaged soldiers, at which point they faded back into the trees to remain on watch. Silmon's eyes then came to rest on Niena, frowning at her unpointed ears and pinker skin tone. "Who might this be?"

Now that she could see his face, something about it was unsettlingly familiar. With a gasp, it came to her. "It's you! You're the one who bombed Wraelian Square!"

The D'harn didn't even acknowledge her, but instead turned and challenged Gilbrannen. "You intend to lecture me about safeguards and risk-taking when you bring a human woman right to my doorstep?"

Gilbrannen cut him off, moving to stand between the agent and Niena. "You have no authority to question this. She may appear human, but she is not—at least entirely. Her father is our captive, and her brother is a soldier in King Pelendion's army. Perhaps the information she can glean for us will be worth more than your failure."

Niena wanted to speak up, as she hated people talking about her in her own presence, but she knew that would only make things worse. If she could hold out, they would release her to go back to the city, and she could consider her options. Anything she did would have to be subtle to keep her father alive, but at this point any freedom from constant observation was better than none. She kicked her foot up and over the saddle and dropped rather inelegantly to the ground behind Gilbrannen.

A chastened Silmon led them along the water's edge and up into the deep natural arch, while the other soldiers took their horses' halters and followed. They all crossed the water at its shallowest point and went deeper into the hill, where a chamber housed a small fire ring and a bunch of bedrolls. The horses continued past to be placed in stalls carved out of the rock, invisible to passersby.

Gilbrannen pointed for her to sit in the corner. He turned back to Silmon, both their faces lit from below by the newly blazing campfire. "Now, tell me. Neraliel supplied you enough black powder to destroy half the keep and possibly take out the king himself, but you bungled it. Explain yourself."

Silmon kept his tone even and calm. "The scouts from Neraliel halted the shipment in the swamps and were able to take control, but there was a casualty among the humans. I decided the best solution was to dress in the fallen guard's armor and go in myself with the others under my spell."

Niena leaned on her knees, laying her head downward to appear that she was sleeping and not listening, but keeping her eyes cracked open to watch.

Gilbrannen paced impatiently. "A foolhardy plan to begin with. It would be difficult to wrangle the minds of four other men in addition to masking your own presence from anyone else. Our magic is not without its limits, even for someone as talented as yourself." He sighed in frustration. "What happened next?"

"I cannot explain it," Silmon said, shaking his head. "It went smoothly until they handed our papers back at the gate, and one of the guards suddenly ordered me detained specifically. I was forced to flee on foot. This guard seemed to barely be affected by my illusion spell."

Gilbrannen's pointed ears perked up at that turn of phrase, turning to regard Niena. "Well, I think we know who that was."

Tollan. Niena drew in a hopeful breath. What were the odds he was the one posted at the gate that day? If it had been anyone else, the saboteurs would have slipped through unnoticed. But that meant Tollan had returned from training, so she could talk with him when she arrived and explain what he had seen. Finally, everything could be set right.

Silmon stayed silent, preferring not to preside over his own execution. Niena couldn't say she blamed him, but was secretly rooting for him. If the D'harnir could make such large mistakes, there was still hope they could be defeated.

"Unbelievable," Gilbrannen fumed. "It is beyond comprehension *why* you would go in alone. The first rule of a successful plan is flexibility."

"I am aware," Silmon said. "I was overconfident, and I jeopardized the operation."

"Not only that," Gilbrannen said, dismissing the confession with a wave of his hand. "Your failure has torn our plans apart at the seams. Now, Celwaith Tor guards will be on the lookout, checking the contents of all shipments against the manifest. And if anyone over there has the mental acuity of a flea, they will now know that the anti-monarchists are not behind these attacks."

Silmon tried to speak again, but Gilbrannen wasn't having it. "No. You will be demoted, and I will take over this forward outpost until such time as Shilvand indicates a replacement. Let us hope for your sake that Niena here provides some way to salvage the situation."

Niena looked up, having heard her name. Both elves stared at her. "What about me? I thought I was just another pawn for you."

Gilbrannen smiled, and it looked almost genuine for a moment. "You are. But you are more useful—we don't have to bind your thoughts using magic."

Niena snorted, then stood and dusted herself off. She felt grimy, not just because she hadn't fully washed herself since before arriving in Por'monir, but due to the way she was being used. "You couldn't enchant me even if you wanted to. That's why you had to resort to threats and blackmail."

"Enough," Gilbrannen said. "We have had this debate already, and it tires me. You know what you have to do, and you know what will happen if you do not. In two days' time, five hours after noon, Silmon will meet you in the shade of the tor by the lake. You will pass on any information you have learned, and devise a better meeting place inside the city walls."

"Fine," Niena said, her voice clipped. "I'll leave in the morning." It was already after sundown and curfew would be in effect, so there was no use trekking the few miles to Celwaith Tor tonight. Niena claimed one of the bedrolls and pulled out her father's book in the light of the campfire.

She had already finished reading it for the second time, including the few excerpts of the Codes. But the elves didn't know that, and reading made a good cover as she considered how best to explain everything to her brother tomorrow.

SEVENTEEN

Bonds made in harvest time and plenty will surely fall away, but a brother forged by drought and hardship will be ever-present.

— *Codes of Binding 4.25*

"YOU'RE GOING WHERE?" ANISE exclaimed, placing a self-righteous hand over her chest. "But you just got back from training last week!"

"And that's not all," Thaxon said excitedly, not bothering to repeat the orders for Anise's benefit. "They promoted him to lieutenant, and I'm going with him!"

"What?" Thaxon's mother, Letaccia, said, sitting more upright in her bed. Her amputated leg was hidden under the covers, and Thaxon said she rarely got up anymore so she might seem more normal. "That is marvelous news. To think that both of you are so young and being trusted with an important mission like this!"

Tollan sighed. If there was one thing he hated, it was being fawned over for no good reason, and Anise and Letaccia were the headmistresses of fawning. "It's really not that important a post, your ladyship," he said, cautious of his words. Tollan had been expressly ordered not to speak about what he had seen at the gate, much less the details of their sting operation. "We're simply escorting a shipment of new weapons being imported from Ash'kiram. Should be fairly routine."

"Hogwash," Letaccia said dotingly, her graying red hair leaving no question as to the origins of Thaxon's fiery locks. "Those weapons could be what prevents a civil war. From what I've seen of you, I daresay such a promotion couldn't have been given to a better boy—unless, of course, it was Thaxon here."

"Mom," Thaxon groaned, embarrassed.

"I would be lying if I said it wasn't dangerous, though," Tollan said, not willing to sugarcoat the situation even though he couldn't tell his aunt and their hostess the truth. "There's been a lot of bandits along the roads, and Outpost Heron was recently sacked. Odds are good they will try to accost us."

Tollan suspected they had been chosen with an ulterior motive as well, not just because they happened to have been at the right place at the right time. Tollan and Thaxon weren't important enough to worry about what might happen to them. If they came back with proof of the Crownless, all the better, but if they were overwhelmed and captured or killed on the road, it would be no major loss to Celwaith Tor. But he kept that bit of thinking to himself.

Anise had fallen silent until now. "I, um," she started, then cleared her throat. "May I speak with you privately, Tollan? That is, if it's alright with Lady Denvald?"

Letaccia waved them off. "Please do. I want to spend some time with my son before he saves the country from what happened to my dear Serenia."

Tollan winced, being reminded that he needed to tread carefully when discussing these matters around the Denvald home. For Thaxon, this mission undoubtedly felt more like an opportunity for vengeance rather than walking into the jaws of an unknown beast and hoping it doesn't bite down too hard.

Tollan bowed to Letaccia in proper form before placing a hand on Anise's shoulder and guiding her out into the hall. "Thank you, your ladyship," Tollan said, and closed the door behind them.

They kept proceeding down the corridor until they could speak out of earshot of the others, near the grand spiral staircase that led down to the atrium. Tollan still found the sheer size of the house unnerving. He turned to his aunt and asked in a whisper what was the matter.

"The matter?" Anise bit back at him in a huff. "Your father and sister still haven't returned from who knows where, and you're stepping headfirst into the lion's den. You've never had to lead before, or spent much time beyond the city walls ... it's a harsh world out there, Tollan."

"That's the point. I have to step up. I'm not a child anymore," Tollan said, hurt by her assumption. He glanced aside and saw one of the servants carrying a tray of tea up to Letaccia's room, and didn't say any more. He let the apron-wearing maid pass and turned back to Anise with a pained expression. "What do you want me to do? Refuse? The commissioner said my orders came down from the king himself."

"Well, no, I ..." Anise trailed off, her eyes watering. "I don't want to lose you, too."

Tollan wrapped his aunt in a hug, and let her cry it out. "It'll be okay," he said, realizing that those words could turn out to be a lie. He wasn't sure he sounded convincing and changed the subject. "Besides, you'll still be here tending to Lady Denvald—she even offered to pay you for your time, right? You always did want to live in the Gilded Quarter."

Anise sniffed back some of her tears. "I suppose I have the know-how, but winds above if that woman doesn't half annoy me most days."

Tollan chuckled, but steeled his face as the hug ended. "I won't be gone long. Two days out and two days back, and maybe nothing will happen. We leave in the morning."

Anise began heading back to help serve the tea. "You make sure to see me before you leave. No matter how early it is."

Tollan nodded. "I will."

He fumbled with the cool metal fob in his pocket as he watched his aunt go, wondering if he would ever see her again. Or, he thought as he pulled the watch out to look at the engraving, if his father and Niena would ever come back from their mysterious errand on his behalf. Obviously, they had intended to return by now, but there could have been complications . . . or worse. As Anise had said, they lived in a harsh world.

But Tollan couldn't think about that right now. He stifled the part of himself that needed to know the why, and set about the how of being a good soldier.

He descended the spiral staircase and clicked open the metal cover on his watch to compare it with the Denvalds' huge and intricate grandfather clock in the atrium. This one worked, unlike Anise's old rubbish heap find.

His watch was a few minutes slow. He hadn't been winding it as often as he should have.

With a pop and a twist of the key, he wound the watch's mainspring tightly, set the hands, and resolved that whatever awaited them in Eastmarsh, he and Thaxon would come out on top. They had saboteurs to catch.

THE ROAD TO CAPE Vrosingr was long and boring, as the terrain around them changed little in appearance or elevation most of the way. The

East Road sloped gently downward all the way to the sea, or rather the vast level swamps that had been partially cleared and filled in to make way for commerce. Before it had been completed, the route to Cape Vrosingr swung two days off course to the south to avoid the fetid pools.

A couple of familiar faces joined them for the trip, including Ruger Yorvikson, of all people. He still seemed to resent Tollan, but masterfully hid it most of the time. As the commanding officer, Tollan had the authority to issue any orders to any soldier that he wished for the duration of the trip, so none of the men wanted to get on his bad side and risk walking the entire way. That helped, because Tollan wasn't sure enough of himself to know that he would follow through on any disciplinary action if he was challenged.

Tollan arranged for his men to assume the watch in shifts of two hours between stops. As there were a dozen soldiers plus the driver, they would all trade out so that four guards would be walking alongside the covered wagon at any given time. Four hours riding and two hours walking seemed good for everyone, and at roughly eighteen hours of travel in the first day, the equal division ensured the men wouldn't squabble about it.

At least, that was the plan, until they found out how hot and smelly it got inside the covered wagon. Even if Tollan hadn't counted himself among the guard rotation to lead by example, he would have needed to walk at least as often, or sit up with the driver, just to clear his head. But as they proceeded from the plains into the marshlands, Tollan became more and more uneasy. The sounds of the swamp were completely foreign to him, and the stench and humidity soon became as unbearable inside the wagon as the biting insects were outside.

They stopped for the night in the remains of Outpost Heron. Several soldiers were already there, overseeing repairs to the main building. There was enough shelter to accommodate them through the darkest hours of the night, but in the morning, they exchanged horses and continued on their way.

Nearing noon, Tollan found himself with Thaxon setting the pace in front of the wagon, while another two guards brought up the rear. Tollan had tried to keep conversation to a minimum in the wagon as he didn't want his men thinking he played favorites, but they could talk more freely out here.

"Ugh, can't believe we haven't seen anything yet," Thaxon bellyached as they marched. "If these bastards are lying in wait for an armed convoy, they should have seen us and tried something by now."

Tollan shook his head. "No, they're smarter than that. They know that wagons proceeding toward the cape are usually empty. The return journey is when we'll have to keep our eyes open."

"Right," Thaxon said, still scanning the trees for anything out of the ordinary. "So, Lieutenant, sir, how are you feeling? Holding up all right?"

Tollan cocked an eyebrow, and waved in thanks to a civilian transport headed the other direction which had pulled over to let them pass. "Other than almost constant stress and self-consciousness over every decision I make, it's fine."

"Not really any different from before, then." Thaxon smirked.

Tollan punched him in the arm for the insult. "That was out of line, soldier," he said with a touch of sarcasm. He reached down and slid his sword halfway out of its scabbard to show it off. "At least they replaced my sword with one that isn't as cheaply made. But the armor still needs work—nothing I try on fits right."

"That's because you're thick in the head, not in the shoulders," Thaxon offered, and ducked out of the way of another punch.

"You better watch it," Tollan warned mockingly. "Or I'll have you walking the whole way back."

"You wouldn't dare." Thaxon rolled his eyes. "My father would hear of it. Which reminds me, my mother said he should still be in Cape Vrosingr when we arrive. Think we might run into him?"

Tollan shrugged. "It's possible. The cache of weapons we're escorting would have to be checked in at the Merchant Guild customs office, so I'm sure he will be involved."

Thaxon walked a little closer to keep his voice hushed. "What are they, anyway? One of the palace servant girls told me it's like a tiny cannon."

Tollan had been briefed before his team had left Celwaith Tor, and technically the information was still classified, but Thaxon would find out within the day anyway. "That's the gist, but I don't know precisely how they work yet. We will each be authorized to use one for the return journey to give us the edge over any attackers."

Thaxon grinned, clearly thrilled with the idea of being one of the first to use the new weapon against their enemies. "Will we get to practice with them?"

"Not as much as I would like to," Tollan answered. "We'll be walked through all the functions and upkeep, learn how to aim them, and then we'll have to be on our way." He fished his pocket watch out to check the time. "Speaking of, looks like our shift will be finished any minute. But before we go back inside—what's this about you talking to one of the palace girls?"

Then it was Thaxon's turn to throw a lighthearted punch, and Tollan sidestepped with a laugh.

It was late afternoon by the time they crossed into Cape Vrosingr. Situated on the coast, it was less a proper city and more a huge sprawling dock that happened to have all the necessary amenities. The jarl's estate towered above the other rooftops, making it known where the king's youngest brother, Stenden, resided.

It wasn't obvious where to go, but the driver had made the trip before, and Tollan sat up with him to take in the new sights.

They rolled up in front of a long building with a tall, slanted roof and the words "Merchant Guild" painted in cracked, faded white pigment across it. Looked pretty downbeat, Tollan thought, but he supposed the weather along the coast might tend to be more extreme. Past the building, only a couple moored ships sat at the vast dock, and beyond that the sea stretched out to the horizon.

Tollan had never seen the sea before, nor any body of water larger than the lake at the base of Celwaith Tor. It smelled different too, with the salt mist turning the air sour. It was awe-inspiring and daunting at the same time, but he didn't have time to appreciate it.

A representative came out to inquire about their business, and once he was satisfied, the large sectional doors rolled back to admit the wagon. The building proved to be an abnormally huge warehouse, stacked tall with goods brought from all throughout Drüstania and being shipped to the next buyer. Tollan had never realized until now how many goods came to the capital by boat—and this was one of several such warehouses. The amount of money exchanging hands had to be enormous.

His soldiers trundled out of the wagon and lined up in two rows, where Tollan took his own place in front of them all. A familiar figure emerged from the offices at the far end of the spacious chamber.

"Lieutenant Cresthaven!" Lord Denvald called out as he crossed the vast space. "Imagine seeing you here, and in officer's garb no less. Congratulations on the promotion. I trust your journey was uneventful?"

Tollan bowed, and his men followed suit. Thaxon was a little slow on the uptake, having never needed to bow before his father.

"Lord Denvald, sir," Tollan greeted the man, a little more stiffly than he would have in the home. "Thank you for taking the time to square the shipment away with us personally. Yes, nothing to report on the way here, but if our enemies are watching the roads they surely saw us coming."

"Good, good," Denvald said, puffing on a strongly-scented cigar as he often did. He nodded in fatherly approval at Thaxon. "Ambassador Seriah Le'shom informed me of your intentions before returning to Ash'kiram, so we have all your needs ready to go. I'm glad they've chosen you and my son to look into this—they couldn't have chosen two brighter lads."

Tollan detected a note of jealousy in the compliment, not unlike Letaccia's quip that Thaxon should have been the one promoted. Perhaps he, too, thought his son was more befitting the rank. "We simply hope to serve our country by retrieving these new weapons, and if the winds are right, to expose this conspiracy against the king."

"Just so." Denvald gestured toward the back of the warehouse. "I have the crate of arms and ammunition for your team ready right over here, if you'll follow me. The others are already loaded in the unmarked civilian transport that will precede you back to Celwaith Tor. Your men are free to make themselves comfortable in the staging yard and unhitch the horses for the night."

Tollan saluted the men, giving them leave to do as the guildmaster had suggested. He marched after Lord Denvald, who brought him to a sturdy wooden crate over three feet long. Peeling back the lid revealed thirteen metal rods mounted on wooden stocks, and a strange assembly where the two were fastened.

Tollan picked one up and handled it. It was surprisingly heavy yet easy to hold, and a leather strap was attached to the stock and barrel for carrying. "So, this is what all the fuss is about. How does it work?"

Denvald smiled eagerly, and held out a small, wrapped paper cylinder. "The Kiramet call it a rifle. This is what you load it with. Tear it open, dump the black powder down the hollow barrel, tamp the metal sphere down after it with the included rod, and it's ready to fire. The same rod can be used in tandem with cloth and oil to keep the barrel free of obstructions or buildup."

Tollan examined the trigger assembly, and realized the mechanics were simple but required higher precision than any blacksmith could produce. If anything was even slightly out of place, pulling the trigger might instead blow up the whole contraption in the user's hands—and given the quality of Tollan's last sword, he wasn't thrilled about the odds.

"You will want to carry it loaded for the journey home," Denvald admitted. "Ambassador Le'shom told me it isn't ideal, but if you are ambushed, you will not have time to properly load a bullet. There is also a pike attachment for the loop below the barrel in case the enemy gets too close."

Tollan nodded, an uneasy weight settling in his stomach. Carrying loaded weapons meant they would need to be careful not to shake or bump them, which could cause a premature firing. It dawned on him that by this time tomorrow, he might actually have to use the weapon in a life-or-death situation. "All right. Let's get these moved outside so my team can figure them out before sundown."

Lord Denvald tucked his cigar in his cheek and clapped to get the attention of a handful of warehouse workers. Once the crate was being moved, he gestured for Tollan to follow. "The real shipment will leave at first light tomorrow, followed by your own marked and armed wagon a quarter-hour after. In case they get wise to our ruse, your men should hopefully be close enough behind to drive off any attackers from the other wagon."

"Very good, sir," Tollan said, eager to wrap up the formalities as they were not his strong suit. "We shall be ready to do our part."

Denvald went and greeted his son while Tollan helped the rest of his men set up makeshift targets against a fence. They would be aiming at the ground so that they wouldn't cause any injuries at the docks—or worse, spring a leak in one of the ships. When that was prepared, Tollan gathered everyone including the wagon driver in a line by the weapons crate, and tried to get Thaxon's attention. They would have little enough practice time with the rifles as it was, and Tollan didn't want to repeat himself.

Lord Denvald held out his hand to his son, and Thaxon shook it. "Best of luck out there, lad. I'm proud of you."

Thaxon smiled, his red hair hanging down rakishly over his forehead. "I have to go, Dad."

"Ah, yes," Denvald replied, regarding Tollan with a look of warning. "Who would have thought the two of you could become so crucial in this investigation?"

"Not I, m'lord," Tollan said. "I'll do my best to keep your son safe. You have my word."

"See that you do," Lord Denvald said, and clapped his son on the shoulder once more before returning to the bowels of the Merchant Guild warehouse.

"Don't think too much of it," Thaxon said under his breath. "Losing my sister Serenia has been tough on all of us."

Tollan wanted to say he could relate, but he couldn't. His father and sister going missing was easier to live with than knowing Niena had died. He couldn't even imagine how that might feel. Instead, he put a sympathetic hand on Thaxon's shoulder and called all the men to attention. They scrambled to their feet from various states of repose and fell in line.

"Listen up," Tollan said, holding up the new weapon and demonstrating like he knew what he was talking about. Being in command seemed to mean faking confidence that others believed in, and he only hoped he faked it well enough that they all survived tomorrow.

THE COVERED WAGON SLOWLY wobbled along the treacherous road through the swamp, while the nerves of its occupants were stretched thin. The air was just as oppressively thick as before, but it had taken on a much more ominous feeling when they could be ambushed from behind every tree.

Tollan had taken to sitting up next to the driver with his loaded rifle across his lap, ready to aim and fire at a moment's notice. It quickly became tedious and tiresome to remain so pent-up in fear, but he couldn't afford to relax or become less alert. He continued checking his watch and calling out the shift changes, but time seemed to slow to a crawl. It had rained in the morning and afternoon, but now the sun had come out for a few hours in the evening and all the moisture was evaporating as a thick mist.

Thaxon walked out in front of the wagon as before, this time accompanied by a recruit named Danvar who had almost been too old for the draft and somewhat resented the fact that he hadn't been born a few months sooner. Both of them held their firearms gingerly, not trusting that they wouldn't go off unintended. They scanned the hazy trees and standing water for movement.

"Up ahead!" Danvar called. "There's something on the road!"

Tollan squinted, peering into the mist, and finally spotted it as they drew closer. A jagged shadow poked up out of the raised dirt and gradually possessed more detail. A chill ran down Tollan's back as the shape resolved into shattered planks and split wagon wheels: the remnants of the shipment that had gone ahead of them.

There was no trace of the driver or the nine crates of rifles.

The enemy had outsmarted them.

"Everyone out, now!" Tollan shouted back into the wagon while readying his rifle. "There's been a—"

Off on their right, a mossy embankment suddenly raised itself out of the water, and Tollan realized it wasn't a mound of land at all. It was a trancheon, a giant toad-like creature bigger than a horse. In the moment it had taken him to realize that, the trancheon had spat out its tongue and wrapped it around Thaxon's waist.

"No!" Tollan shouted, and reflexively aimed his rifle at the creature.

The harsh whistle of arrows sounded from the trees all around and above him. One of the horses neighed in pain as an arrowhead sliced past Tollan's shoulder to strike deep into its neck. Another found its place in Danvar's chest, and he went down. They were surrounded, and the attackers began picking them off one by one as Tollan had feared.

He pulled the trigger—but it was too late. The metal ball buried itself in the toad's thick hide, but did nothing.

The last he saw of Thaxon was his outstretched hand being sucked down the trancheon's gullet.

EIGHTEEN

Monarchy submits all to the whims of one, swayed by ambition; democracy subjects all to the whims of most, swayed by fear. But the council of elders keeps all accountable to their own clans.

— *Codes of Binding 9.05-06*

BY MID-MORNING NIENA STOOD in line to enter the main gates of Celwaith Tor, and it was the longest line she thought she had ever seen. Gilbrannen had reviewed her mission in detail before she left, to ensure she knew how to contact Silmon outside their normal contact schedule. She had hurried out of the elven hideout with a minimum of threats toward her father, but now the restless crowd restrained her to a snail's pace.

Niena touched her mother's necklace, frustrated that Gilbrannen had confiscated the green leather book as she was leaving. It was the only thing she might have shown Tollan to prove her outlandish story, and now he would have to believe her words alone.

With his skeptical nature, though, she wasn't sure if he would.

When they had finally passed the bend in the road, Niena hopped up on the back of a wagon to see what could be holding them up. The gate appeared to be open for admittance, so she was no closer to figuring out the delay. The farmer who drove the wagon gave her a stern scolding for her troubles. She apologized and went back to waiting anxiously.

She reached the gate about noon. The farmer's wagon in front of her took a mortal long time as the city guards searched it and checked the contents against the paperwork, but they finally cleared it and waved Niena to the desk.

The clerk, dressed in yellow livery but without the plate armor of the other guards, glanced up at her from his logbook then back down. He was still writing in the details of the delivery wagon. "Papers?" he snapped.

"What?"

"Your papers." The clerk put his book down and frowned at her. "You need identification and a signed statement of your business to be allowed in the city. Where have you been the last five weeks?"

Niena realized how much had changed in her absence. She and her father had seen the northern watchtower burn, and there must have been other incidents as well to cause such paranoia—justified though it was. "Um, I'm sorry, I've been out hunting in the northern wilds with my father. I live here, in the Barren Quarter."

"Likely story," a nearby guard said. "Where is your father then? What about your hunting wares?"

The clerk sighed. "I'm sorry, I can't let you in without identification. That's it. If you want to file a request for residency, we can do that, but you'll have to return in a week and see if it's been granted."

Niena stood there in shock, her mouth slightly ajar. She couldn't even bring herself to say anything in protest. She walked reluctantly back the way she came and wondered absently if she would be able to find her way back to the D'harnin encampment by nightfall. If she didn't make her first rendezvous with Silmon in two evenings, it would be over for her father.

"By the winds, Niena, is that you?" a voice called from the gatehouse as she passed.

She whirled, and saw the most welcome of sights: a familiar face that might be able to help her. "Kasdan!"

He rushed down the stairs and over to her. "What seems to be the matter? Won't they let you in?"

"No," Niena said, and explained the situation. She didn't want to, but she told the lie again about her father spending the season hunting and trapping up north, and added a bit about being sent back to check on Tollan. "Is he in the city now?" she asked.

Kasdan winced. "I'm afraid you missed him. I've seen him once since he came back from basic training, but last I heard he was promoted to lieutenant and sent to Cape Vrosingr early this morning."

"What?" Niena said in absolute bewilderment. "How? Training wasn't supposed to end until, when, yesterday? And he's been promoted?"

Kasdan gestured for her to calm down, sympathy in his dark eyes. "The short version is, they ended training early due to Outpost Heron getting sacked. From what I understand, Tollan was instrumental in uncovering a plot on the palace armory, hence the promotion. And now he's been assigned to backtrack the terrorists to their source."

Niena held a hand to her forehead, the worry and disappointment washing over her like a flood. This was just her luck, after all she had been through. "Will he be back?"

"I don't know," Kasdan said earnestly. "You'd have to ask the commissioner. Your aunt might know more—she and Tollan have been living in the Gilded Quarter with the family of one of Tollan's mates from training."

Niena raised her eyebrows. Had the city turned upside down in only a month? "What? I mean, that's . . . great and all, but what happened to the smithy?"

Kasdan lowered his voice, his tone bitter. "The jarl confiscated it for the army effort. Oh, and your father's a wanted man now, so wherever he is he may want to stay there awhile."

"I didn't realize things could get so much worse," Niena murmured.

"Aye, you don't know the half of it. The grain doles have been running dry, and the security checkpoints make bringing in food too costly and time-consuming for most farmers to bother with. The whole city is starving, unless you're rich or have connections. But you didn't hear that from me."

Kasdan cleared his throat and spoke in a normal register again. "Here, let's get your temporary papers in order and find Anise. I'll talk to my commanding officer and see if he will let me escort you."

"You have no idea how grateful I am, Kasdan," Niena replied, her voice a little shaky. She could tell in the way his eyes lingered on hers that Keordi had been right—he was smitten with her. But would he still feel that way if he knew what she really was?

No, she couldn't be distracted by that right now. She needed to take the most important things one step at a time, and maybe one day she and Kasdan would be able to have a nice, long talk about his intentions.

The process at the check-in office was easy and straightforward with Kasdan vouching for her. She was issued a temporary identification that allowed her to move about the city until it expired in a month, when she would need to apply for a longer stay with proof of either residency or employment. *What a nightmare*, she thought.

But at long last, she was given leave to enter the city. Her first inclination was to turn down the fastest route back to the Barren Quarter, then remembered Kasdan was taking her someplace in the Gilded Quarter. "Lead the way," she told him, and he did.

They passed through several checkpoints with few delays since Kasdan's identification allowed them to skip the long lines. The alleys were littered with lean-to shelters, either merchants unable to leave the city because it would mean opening their stalls late the next day, or people now unable to pay their rent and evicted by their landlords. Niena assumed the reason the guards didn't round up the homeless at night was because there wouldn't be enough room in prison if they did. Kasdan was right—the overbearing security measures were causing the city to fall apart at the seams.

Trying to get her mind off the squalor, she cleared her throat and asked Kasdan a question that had been sitting in the back of her mind. "Were you able to get the package to Tollan in time?"

Kasdan grinned proudly as they walked up the hill out of the Sunken Quarter, the buildings turning gradually to more and more expensive construction. "I had to convince my commanding officer to let me accompany one of the supply carts out to the foothills, but I got it done. Tollan even stopped by the house a few nights ago to thank me, and I saw his new watch. A pretty nice piece—I'm sure it wasn't cheap."

"It wasn't. I saved for months," Niena said with a genuine smile. Her heart glowed, happy that at least something had gone right in all this mess. "And how is your family? Is Keordi's ankle healed?"

"It's been difficult since Mum was temporarily laid off from the fruit market, but we've been surviving on my guard wages," Kasdan said, appreciative that she asked. He turned off the main road, suggesting that they had almost arrived. "Keordi's almost back to normal, though the ankle does give her trouble if she's on it all day. She's been a little sulky ever since you left—I'll tell her you'll pay them all a visit soon."

Kasdan stopped in front of a gaudy, multi-story house that took up most of a city block. Pillars supported a part of the upper floor that jutted out over the portico. "Here we are."

Niena almost fell over. She recognized the house, having walked past it several times with Keordi. "This is where Tollan and Anise have been staying? The Denvald estate?"

"I couldn't believe it either," Kasdan said with a shrug.

Niena looked at the ornate door, then looked back at her armed escort. He did have a good heart, and she couldn't imagine why she had overlooked him before. "Thank you, Kasdan. For everything. We . . . I owe you so much."

Kasdan looked away, hiding a blush. "You'd better knock."

"Don't leave yet. Wait here, please," she said, and approached the enormous house. She felt so alien walking up to the elegant, decorated door. She timidly reached up to knock, but realized just in time that there was a rope next to the door attached to a bell, which she rang.

The door opened, and a valet appeared in the gap. He looked Niena's tattered pants and baggy shirt up and down, clearly wondering what the hell she was doing on the doorstep. "Yes?"

"Is Anise Cresthaven in?" Niena inquired after an awkward pause, hoping she didn't look too much like a vagabond.

"Just a moment," came the stiff reply, and after a minute's wait Niena could hear Anise's high-strung voice wondering who could possibly be calling specifically for her.

The reunion was an emotional one, but fraught with anxiety for Niena. She dared not explain the truth behind her father's disappearance, and if she did try, she would never be believed. Even worse, if Anise did believe it, she might bring the information to the authorities, which would spell certain death for Niena's father. She hated to lie, but there was no alternative that she could see for now.

Anise could sense that something was up and that she wasn't being told the whole truth. Niena deflected by asking if there was any spare food that could be given to Kasdan in thanks for all he had done. He politely declined, but Anise wouldn't hear of it and bustled off to supply him with the day's leftovers and some bread and fruit from the pantry.

Niena thanked him again and, once Anise had showed her the amenities and retrieved a fresh change of clothes, she quickly beat a retreat to a washroom. "Couldn't have you meeting the lady of the house looking like you came off the moors," Anise said, and began pouring the boiling water for a hot bath. "But don't think you've gotten out of telling me all you and Voster have done since leaving—that was a rotten thing of you to do, slipping out in the middle of the night like that. You had me worried sick."

Niena felt horrible about it, but she could only say that she was sorry and that it couldn't be helped.

"But why?" Anise asked, frustrated. "Oh, never mind for now, you're probably exhausted. I'll leave you to your bath. Come find me when you've finished."

Once the door was shut and Niena had her privacy, she stripped her sweat-caked clothes off and placed her mother's necklace carefully on the cabinet. She stepped gingerly into the luxurious water, and couldn't help but sigh in ecstasy, but the pleasure of washing off all the grime was short-lived.

She sat there in the tub, hugging her knees to her chest and rocking back and forth. She had been pushing herself for so long and so hard, and now that she had the space and time, it was all she could do to stop from crying. But she wouldn't let herself—the only thing she had control of right now was her emotions, and she wasn't about to abandon that too.

Niena stood, her body calloused from her travels but clean, and dried off with a towel. She put on the casual gown Anise had left for her and cinched the belt around her waist, then draped her mother's pendant back around her neck. She stared at her reflection in the mirror, thinking that the woman staring back looked different than she remembered. Her image was hardened, more resolved somehow.

She had work to do. And there might still be someone who would believe her story, enough to turn the situation to her advantage.

"YOUR MOTHER WAS A what now?" Keordi said, standing opposite Niena and staring back with the most incredulous look plastered across her face. Her frizzy hair was bunched up in a knot behind her, but plenty of it had still escaped.

"Hush!" Niena hissed. Keordi's mother and younger sister were downstairs in the kitchen, but the drafty Harroway house carried all kinds of sounds. "Keep it quiet. You heard me right the first time."

Keordi obliged in volume, but her tone was still that of snarky disbelief. "I was giving you a chance to rethink what you'd said. Your mother was a magical creature from bedtime stories?"

Niena sighed. She didn't know why she had expected anything else, even from her best friend. She had hoped for a little more willingness to listen, but she had to admit that the whole situation sounded impossible. "Look, I know it sounds like I've gone and jumped headfirst off the tor, but I swear I haven't. This is real."

"All right, okay," Keordi said, but her concerned eyes still said she didn't buy it. "Can you at least tell me what your mother being an elf has to do with leaving town in the dead of night? Your note didn't clear any of that up and your aunt was beyond worried. We all were."

"I'm trying to get to that."

"And while you're at it, tell me why you couldn't have explained it all before you left. We might have been able to help you."

Niena stood to leave. She knew Keordi had some lingering resentment from how they had parted ways, but the insinuation that she had deliberately abandoned her friend cut deep. "I hoped you would trust me, since we've known each other so long. Look, if you aren't going to take my story seriously, I should just go."

"If you can't give me a serious answer," Keordi replied from her place at the window, "maybe you should."

Niena stared blankly back at her, a heavy weight descending on her chest. So that was how it would be. She turned to flee downstairs, but stopped on the landing when Keordi spoke up again.

"We used to share everything, Niena." Keordi shook her head and refused to meet Niena's gaze. "There was no secret either of us had that the other didn't know. Why are you shutting me out?"

Niena's hand rested on the corner of the wall, the bare dry wood threatening to leave her a splinter as a parting gift. She took a breath to start her story again, but stopped short. "I'm not," she said in irritation. "If I was lying, I would have come up with a more plausible story. Look, just, don't tell anyone else?"

"I wasn't going to anyway," Keordi affirmed. "I would hate for you to wind up in the asylum."

"I'm done," Niena said, and began quickly descending the leaning stairs. "Goodbye, Keordi."

"You're the one who left town in the middle of the night, only to come back a month later spewing nonsense!" Keordi called after her. "What was I supposed to believe?"

"You were supposed to believe your friend," Niena said over her shoulder, and nothing else needed to be said.

It was an awkward silence as she entered the kitchen heading for the door, since Keordi's mother and sister had heard the last few words.

Mrs. Harroway had just placed a pot of soup on the burner, using ingredients that Niena had brought down from the Denvald estate kitchen. Mrs. Harroway spoke up, her husky voice sweet and inviting despite the obvious disagreement upstairs. "Oh, Niena, I was hoping you would stay for supper. We've been eating better the last few nights than the whole last year, and I wanted to thank you."

Niena stopped shy of the door, hand on the latch. "Not tonight, Mrs. Harroway, but you're welcome. Don't mention it."

"Anything I can tell Keordi, later?" the kindly woman asked, wringing her large hands.

Keordi's much younger sister, Maivey, stood off to the side chopping an onion for the stew. She glanced between her mother and Niena, then back to her onion.

Niena cleared her throat. "No, sorry. I have to be going."

Mrs. Harroway looked disappointed, but didn't press. "All right, dearie, just know that we're here for you. Take care."

"Thanks, Mrs. Harroway," Niena said, wishing it was true. She waved at Maivey before stepping outside.

She looked up at the sky, noting the sun's placement. It was later than she had expected. If she wasn't careful, she would miss her rendezvous with Silmon—she didn't even have time to go back to the Gilded Quarter first.

She ducked back in to ask Mrs. Harroway a question. "Actually, there is one thing. Do you have a bucket I could borrow?"

They did, and Niena set off with the promise to return it to Kasdan the next day along with some extra scraps from the Denvald pantry. She had to cross the Barren Quarter and the Sunken Quarter to get to her destination, passing through all the checkpoints along the way, and she only had perhaps an hour and a half until the appointed time.

She needn't have worried. With the workday still in full swing, the checkpoints had only a few people waiting in line. Her empty bucket drew some odd glances from the guards, but they didn't question it as she drew closer to the water gate.

It wasn't much of a gate, in comparison to the main entrance to Celwaith Tor. However, it did allow for two lanes of foot traffic to proceed up and down a series of carved stairs to the edge of the lake, where the population of the Sunken Quarter procured fresh water. And since the lake sat beyond the city walls, a small checkpoint had also been erected to make sure no one slipped inside.

Niena kept her distance from everyone once she got through the checkpoint, and wandered down the edge of the lake a little farther to where the towering tor above cast its shadow on the water. She sat down and reached inside her blouse—the same one she had worn traveling, but with a good wash—to make sure she still had the crude diagram she had drawn. It had taken all the previous day meandering up and down Main Street to get an idea of the patrol schedule and the shift changes. That wasn't much, but she figured that would be far better information to pass on than nothing at all.

Despite being early, Niena didn't have long to wait.

"Further this way," Silmon's voice whispered to her from behind an outcropping. "Out of the light."

Niena complied, and noted that the D'harn was dressed not in a blue cloak but rather standard clothes and a leather jerkin. Apart from the paleness and the ears, he would have fit in on the streets with no problem. "New wardrobe?"

"Gilbrannen's idea," Silmon confirmed with a hint of annoyance. "He seems to think it will help with getting past the city defenses once we get to that step. Speaking of which, what do you have for us?"

Niena swallowed. Either they would keep her in place until Tollan returned, or they would do away with the whole operation and her father along with it. "Would you like the bad news first?"

INTERLUDE III

The Rift

ONCE THERE WAS OPEN fighting in the streets, sanctioned by the regime, my father could do nothing to repair relations with the D'harnir, but that never kept him from trying. He made plenty of enemies speaking out against the Macula Society, which had torn down democracy to install a monarch from within their own ranks who would be able to unilaterally outlaw dealing with elves. But my father was suspected of aiding and abetting the elves as they fled persecution, and when no evidence could be found, his house was instead vandalized. Of course, there was no evidence because my father had left that aspect of his work to me.

Under the cover of night, my father bade me to get as many D'harnir out of the cities as I could, and find them a place where they could live in peace. When there was nothing else to be done, and when the zealots tired of their narrow focus on the elves and turned their attention instead to the halfbloods and sympathizers, my family elected to join us and the others to build a new life away from the influence of men. Perhaps we could start again, and live as our forefathers once did. What a naive idea.

We may have escaped from civilization, but we continued to lose good people—even my halfblood cousin—to the untamed wilds and vicious predators of the north. If we weren't being hunted by the prejudice of men, it was by the hunger of manticores. We would later find out that such was happening to elven refugees everywhere, as creatures which used magic to hunt began to prey upon the elves as in the days of old. The deep places of the world were filled to overflowing, and without the tacit protection of stronger men their numbers dwindled. The strength of my father and I could not keep the dangers of the world at bay.

Even worse, it did not take long until those with a thirst for D'harnin blood pursued us into the wilderness. It did not matter that we had retreated to a new home where we lived according to the Mishenna; humanity had grown in ambition and was beginning to expand its borders once again.

— Haron Geled, Last Scribe of the Union
26th of Hollyn, in the 48th year after the Rift

NINETEEN

Like a belvint that abandons its nest and
young to the jaws of a snake is one who
willing leaves another in danger.

— Codes of Entreaty 4.23

"INTO THE TREES!" TOLLAN shouted frantically, still staring in horror at the impervious creature that had swallowed Thaxon whole. "Find cover!"

He forced himself to take his own advice, jumping down from the driver's seat of the covered wagon and scrambling to get off the road. Tollan wasn't a military strategist, but he knew the only way they could live long enough to form a counterattack was to get out of their enemies' sights.

The soldiers inside the wagon had piled out with their weapons at the ready, fanning out to divide targets before hearing Tollan's order to take cover. Three men had gone down in the initial assault, counting Thaxon and the driver, meaning that they had ten left. Another almost died as he dived into the swamp for cover, but the incoming arrow ricocheted off his plate armor with a loud *twang*.

The volleys kept coming. Tollan ducked behind a tree trunk as another arrow screamed past his head, nearly grazing him. The shot came from above and to the left, and Tollan could barely make anything out in the swampy mist. Maybe some kind of hunters' platform, mounted in the crook of a tree?

Tollan threw his empty rifle down and waved his sword, hoping others would see him even if they couldn't hear him. "Keep going! They're above us, in the branches!"

A free-for-all ensued as the soldiers churned their feet through the pools of water and dense foliage. Tollan forged ahead, making sure to step where root systems would make the ground more stable, and kept up with the others a little easier. He had never been more glad of Corporal Crandas' morning exercises, as painful as they were.

Up ahead, Tollan thought he saw shapes in the fog: angular constructs that looked artificial rather than natural. In fact, they reminded him of battlements, crisscrossing the tree branches. Tollan's heart pounded with the realization.

More mossy, warty mounds raised up out of the swamp in front of them, but it was already too late. The trancheons moved in tandem to box his soldiers in, advancing in eerie unison against the human intruders.

Tollan didn't even have time to call out a warning before two more of his men were drawn off their feet toward the gaping maws. Instead, he leapt from his perch on a gnarly root and brought his sword down hard on an outstretched tongue. It severed clean through, and the trancheon writhed in pain as the soldier it had ensnared threw off the rest of the sticky flesh.

It was Ruger.

Tollan helped him up, and they both ran. What was left of the team scattered in all directions. They weren't listening to any of his orders, instead fleeing any way they could in abject terror. Tollan picked up one of the rifles the others had dropped, and decided that the mission was now up to him. Down to half their number already, with no enemy casualties to show for it, and no way to call for help . . .

Ruger and Tollan panted desperately for air as they took cover against another tree. "Thanks, Lieutenant. Thought I was done for," Ruger said.

"We might still be," Tollan said, sheathing his sword and checking the rifle. It was still loaded, so all he had to do was cock and fire it. Perfect. "There's only one way out of this."

"What are your orders, sir?" Not a trace of the old Ruger. This one simply wanted to make it back to Celwaith Tor in one piece.

"Just a second. Stay put," Tollan said, leaning carefully around the trunk. Another aggressive *hiss* of an arrow, and bark exploded next to Tollan's face. He pulled back into cover, rattled—that could have been his face. But he had seen exactly where it came from. "I have one. Ruger, I need you to run as fast as you can back to the road."

"Back?" Ruger repeated. "I thought you said that was a bad place to be."

"Yes, back." Tollan took his helmet off and swiped a forearm across his sweaty forehead. "I need you to draw fire. Stick to the roots, and you won't fall as much. If you make it through, wait for me."

Ruger gripped his rifle, took a deep breath, and then he was gone.

Tollan cocked the hammer of his own weapon, and as soon as he heard an arrow fire from the same place as before, he leaned back around and braced his arm against the tree for a steady shot.

The undefined, foggy silhouette of an adversary had moved to another branch to get a better shot at Ruger, but he was still in Tollan's view. He didn't hesitate like he might have once; he lined up the shot and fired.

The figure fell out of the tree with a *whump* and a splash. Tollan threw down the rifle and bolted for the impact site. This was his only chance.

A body lay there, unmoving, in its own blood and wearing a gray cloak that blended with the color of the swamp mist, but he didn't have time to examine anything or rejoice in his fortunate marksmanship. The figure was surprisingly light for being so tall, and Tollan heaved it over his shoulders for additional cover while he ran.

More arrows whizzed past. He pushed his legs harder, ignoring the burn in his calves, and burst out of the trees to scramble up the embankment. Out on the road there was no cover save for the corpse on his back, so he needed to move even faster.

The ruined wagon beckoned ahead, riddled through with holes and arrow shafts. One living horse whinnied in fear and pain, still attached to the wagon alongside its dead kin. Tollan wasted no time and threw the body over the horse's back.

Ruger limped up behind him, kneeling for cover behind the rear wheels. Blood trickled down his calf. "Is that one of them?"

Tollan confirmed with a quick motion, throwing back the gray hood to reveal an angular face and pointed ears.

"What the hell is that?" Ruger exclaimed, staring at the impossibility.

There was no time to discuss—real or not, Tollan had to get this body back to Celwaith Tor. He urgently pulled himself up on the horse, drawing his sword to cut the straps binding it to the cart.

"What about me?" Ruger called, his rifle propped up on the wagon chassis and aimed back at the trees. "I can't get out of here on foot!"

A twinge of guilt crossed Tollan's mind, but he quickly buried it. If he didn't make it back, Thaxon had died for nothing. He would not allow that to happen, and there was nothing else he could do. He was about to cut the horse's bonds anyway when he noticed in shock that Ruger's firearm had been raised to point at him.

Another figure in a misty gray cloak stood behind Ruger, an outstretched arm positioned at the base of his skull. Tollan's eyes widened in realization of the power that these enemies wielded. Without another hesitation, he loosed the horse.

Tollan hung on with his knees for dear life as the horse bolted. Searing pain shot up his arm as Ruger's bullet grazed him, but he kept going. He glanced back only once, to see more shadowy figures rushing out of the trees while Ruger slumped to the ground, unconscious or dead. "I'm sorry," Tollan whispered in remorse.

He urged the horse to greater speed back along the road to Celwaith Tor. He tried to apply pressure to his wound, but that was difficult while keeping his prize from slipping off the back of the horse. His single best hope was to put enough distance between himself and the swamps before nightfall.

TOLLAN PRESSED ON THROUGH the night, stopping only at the Outpost Heron reconstruction site to stitch and bandage his arm and exchange his wounded horse for another that could go the distance. He didn't think he could sleep even if he tried, with the deaths of his men, of Thaxon, weighing on him. He felt sick to his stomach, and wondered what he could bring himself to tell the Denvalds.

When he couldn't bear the guilt anymore, he tried to think about the mysterious body he carried bundled with him. It had to be an elf like in the old stories, he reasoned, but that was impossible. The skin and cartilage of the dead creature's ears felt as real as any man's, and there would be no reason for the Crownless to perpetrate a hoax of this kind.

It was little wonder the army hadn't been able to trace down the cause or reason behind the attacks. They hadn't even considered the supernatural or magical as an option. The lack of memory in the hijacked shipment guards had been a hint in the right direction, and the pale-skinned enemy that day at the gate had been whispering unintelligible words under his breath.

Tollan realized with a shiver that the elf had attempted to bewitch him. If these creatures were capable of such power, that made everything more complicated.

No one could be trusted.

Tollan finally saw the welcoming towers of Celwaith Tor the next day at quarter until noon. He had made good time without needing to haul anything but himself and the elven corpse, though he was liable to fall off the saddle from exhaustion any moment now. He snapped the reins and picked up the pace to cover the last few miles.

There was no time to wait in line at the gates. He made sure the elf was covered so as not to draw unnecessary attention, and shouted for everyone to move. "King's business!" he called hoarsely. "Make way!"

The sea of people parted slowly, and those who wouldn't move on account of his orders moved to avoid being trampled. The guards inspected his seal and let him pass with little delay but a handful of questions. He didn't have time to answer them truthfully or thoroughly, so he merely repeated that he was on the king's business, classified until further notice. He repeated the process at the next three checkpoints, spurring the horse across what was left of Wraelian Square to the keep. It was a blessed relief to finally dismount, but there was far more to be done before he dared sit or close his eyes.

"Halt!" one of the royal guards said unnecessarily. "What is your business in the palace?"

Tollan showed them his lieutenant's pass, and his orders. "This is extremely urgent. I need to speak with someone of rank or close to the king."

"What's that on your horse? A body?"

"That's correct. This is one of the culprits responsible for the recent attacks. I recommend you inform someone immediately."

"Right away," the guard replied, ushering Tollan and the horse past the open portcullis to wait in the small courtyard. The guard made a hasty exit into the castle, carrying Tollan's papers with him, and leaving the other to watch the entrance.

Tollan led the horse over to a small fountain in the middle of the courtyard and slumped to sit along the edge. He wanted so badly to lie down and fall asleep . . . He didn't think he had ever stayed up so long in his life. The next few minutes of waiting were interminable and a constant battle to keep his eyes open, but finally his patience was rewarded.

A man with dark hair and a silver circlet on his brow stepped out from the large wooden doors. He was dressed in fine clothes, mostly showing Drüstanian yellow but accented with deep red. "Lieutenant Cresthaven?" the man inquired. "You're alone?"

It could only be the crown prince, Tollan realized. He remembered to bow just in time. "Yes. Do I have the honor of addressing Prince Anseldr?"

"You do," the man said, studying Tollan with a cautious eye. "Are you well? You appear ill."

"I'm sorry, sir," Tollan said, standing a little straighter. "I rode all through the night to get here. I could not afford to lose the information I bring to you now." He gestured to the cloaked body still sprawled across the horse's back.

One of the guards helped him lower the bundle to the ground, and Tollan uncovered the face.

Anseldr placed a hand over his mouth, paling in disbelief. He reached out and touched the pointed ears. "Is . . . is that real? Not . . . some kind of decoration or prosthetic or . . . something else?"

"I shot him out of a tree myself, sir," Tollan answered briefly. "I barely escaped with my life."

"What of the rest of your men?" Anseldr asked. "And the weapons shipment?"

"My men are dead or captured, sir, and the attackers saw right through our feint—they took everything. They attacked without warning, deep in the swamps, and they used trancheons against us . . . It was utter chaos," Tollan said, suddenly conscious of his heavy breathing and run-on sentence. His eyes welled with tears. "I'm sorry, sir, I did all that I could."

Anseldr nodded, still staring at the corpse. It looked even paler now that the better part of twenty-four hours had passed since the fatal shot. "I believe you, Lieutenant. It begs more questions about our adversaries than it answers, but it does explain our past difficulties. Well done, in spite of the losses. This knowledge is worth it." He looked around, as if suddenly realizing they were still in public. "We should get this . . . thing . . . up to somewhere more private. Guard, help the lieutenant carry it up to the library study—and not a word to anyone."

The guard bowed, then bent down to pick up the corpse by the armpits.

Tollan swallowed and grabbed the ankles. He was actually being taken inside the palace's private residences. He wasn't sure whether to blame his exhaustion, the smell of the dead body, or the enormity of what he was doing, but he felt faint.

They stuck to back stairwells and corridors, and Anseldr went in front of them to clear the way and ensure no one caught sight of the covered body. They arrived at a suite of rooms filled floor-to-ceiling with books, followed by a back room with a heavy wooden desk.

Another man with darker skin and a well-tailored black suit sat behind the desk, reading. He looked up to see who was coming and nearly dropped his book. "What is the meaning of this, Anseldr?"

Anseldr held up a hand to wait for introductions. "Lieutenant, this is Darakh Shi'ev, Kiramet scientist and inventor of the rifle you used. Darakh, meet Lieutenant Tollan Cresthaven, the soldier who put your weapon to good use and procured us the first hard evidence of our enemy."

Shi'ev frowned. "A little young, isn't he? No offense, Lieutenant."

"None taken," Tollan said, shifting his grip on the corpse's ankles. His upper arm ached where the bullet had grazed him, and he hoped the stitches weren't splitting. "Is there somewhere you'd like us to set this down?"

Anseldr gestured to the desk, and Shi'ev reluctantly gathered his papers and all but one of the books. Tollan and the other guard slid the corpse across the desk, face up, and Tollan removed the mist-gray cloak obscuring much of the figure.

Shi'ev's eyes widened, but his disbelief was almost immediately replaced by curiosity. "Fascinating," Shi'ev said after bidding the guard to go back to his post. He rubbed the cloth between his fingers, considering. "It appears to be water-repellent, and the color is the perfect gray-green shade to go unseen amidst the swamps. How did you manage to spot him?"

Tollan gave as much detail as he could remember, making sure to mention the platforms and battlements he thought he saw scattered throughout the trees and further back into the swamp. He tried to keep his voice even and steady, even as Thaxon's death and his choice to leave Ruger behind flashed in his mind. He elected not to recount those specific events for his own sake. "I came straight here," Tollan said, feeling overcome once again by exhaustion.

"You were very right to," Anseldr reassured, watching as Shi'ev turned the dead elf's head this way and that while taking down the last notes of Tollan's report. "This could be the turning point for us. I believe the king will give Mr. Shi'ev the authority to examine the body more thoroughly, at which point we may be able to determine how they continue to bewitch our men."

"I would not go that far. I would be lucky to emerge with a hypothesis," Shi'ev corrected. Turning to Tollan, he proffered a question. "Did you feel anything odd during the encounter, like before?"

Tollan raised an eyebrow, wondering how Shi'ev could have known about that.

"Anseldr allowed me to read your report from the gate," Shi'ev explained as simply as possible. "Did you feel that same 'pressure' on your mind that you did then?"

"Now that you mention it, yes," Tollan said. "I didn't pay much attention to it while I was running for my life, and it wasn't as sharp, but I did feel a slight ache in my forehead."

Shi'ev grunted. "The debilitating terror your men experienced may have been another form of entrancement. Not only did the elves coordinate the trancheons against you, but they may have instilled fear into the minds of your men. The winds have blessed you in that you seem to be more resistant, or else you might not have made it out alive."

The thought hadn't occurred to Tollan, but looking back at what happened, he couldn't deny the logic. The image of Ruger's rifle, pointed straight at him as he sped away, flashed into his mind. "What would you like me to do now, sirs?"

Anseldr nodded expectantly. "I imagine you are aching for a bed right about now, but allow me to bring all of this to King Pelendion and inquire if there is anything else he needs to know directly from you.

Please, sit down and relax for a few moments." He gestured to a leather-upholstered chair in the corner. "Shi'ev, leave that for now and come with me."

Shi'ev hurriedly measured something across the dead elf's forehead with a pair of calipers, and jotted down another note before setting his ink and quill aside. "Coming," he said, and the two men left Tollan alone with the body.

With an exclamation of pain and relief that echoed his muscles' sentiments, Tollan sank into the soft cushions. Next to the chair sat a globe of the world. He absently turned it and watched the continents spin past as he waited. The sheer number of books in the royal library astounded him—what he wouldn't give to spend days in here. He scanned the shelves for anything concerning military history, thought maybe he would go pick one out. At least, if the chair wasn't so comfortable . . .

The next thing he knew, he felt a hand shaking him, and over the scientist's shoulder he saw a face that everyone in the city knew well, framed by a large golden crown.

Tollan shot out of his seat and down to his knees, worried he had offended the king by drowsing off. "Y-Your Majesty," he stammered at first. "F-forgive me, I had closed my eyes for a moment and—"

King Pelendion laughed warmly. "No, Lieutenant Cresthaven, I should be thanking you for doing Drüstania such a service. Your country owes you and your men a great debt. Stand up, soldier."

"Yes, my liege." Tollan got to his feet and stood at full attention, any fatigue now scared out of him.

Now that Tollan could see the king properly, rather than from afar, he noted that Pelendion was a stern-looking man, but laugh lines and crow's feet suggested he had not always been so. Now, he presented a grim smile that was equal parts pride and worry.

"Anseldr and his Kiramet friend here have filled me in on your story, but I wasn't sure I believed it until I saw the body you brought back," Pelendion said, looking with trepidation and disgust at the corpse on the desk. Shi'ev had returned to his measurements and notes, making observations presumably about the minor physical differences to human anatomy. "To think that these creatures have lived at the edges of our society for so long that there had been no trace save for myths and legends ... It makes the occasional manticore in the wild seem almost tame by comparison."

"Yes, my liege," Tollan repeated, unsure of what else he should say to his king.

"Rest assured that we will be needing your experience more in the coming days as we prepare a counter-attack. We must take the fight to them before the cunning fiends have a chance to regroup in the shadows." Pelendion clenched a fist, still looking at the corpse, then turned his gaze back to Tollan. "They will not cause me to lose faith in the Drüstanian people again. But for now, what amenities we have here in the palace are yours. What reward may I offer you for such splendid service to the crown?"

Reward? Tollan wondered at the concept. All he could even wish for right now was a bath and a bed. "I'm sorry, Your Majesty? I was just doing my duty as your officer."

Pelendion smiled genuinely and laid a hand on Tollan's shoulder-plate. "Ridiculous. You deserve far more in putting so much on the line for the security of the kingdom. Normally I would promote you, but you're already a lieutenant and far too young to be a captain."

Tollan's mind went blank for a moment before a vision of Thaxon's last moments intervened. He tried to get past the lump in his throat, but it was there to stay. "I simply wish for the families of my men to know that their sons had not died in vain, especially my friend, Thaxon Denvald. They are the true heroes, not me."

Pelendion nodded, seeming proud of the answer. "Well said. I will certainly make provisions for their posthumous honors. But is there anything for you personally? Or your family?"

The smithy, Tollan realized. There was little to no chance they would get it back after the occupation, not with his father's treason on record. They had worked hard to own the building outright, and Tollan could not allow that to go to waste. "Your Majesty, if I may. My father ran a small blacksmith forge in the Barren Quarter for most of my life. It would be nice to live there again, once it was no longer needed for the war effort," he clarified. "My father abandoned it and skipped town—I think there's still a bounty out on him for that. But I've never known any other business, sire."

Anseldr stepped forward to interject, his gray eyes kindling with recognition of the story. "That much is true, my liege. A blacksmith named Voster Cresthaven left town immediately after receiving a notice regarding the use of his smithy to supply the militia. The captain of the guard believed he may have had something to do with the Wraelian Square bombing, so I put out an arrest warrant and bounty for him."

Pelendion tilted his head, considering the request for a moment. Tollan had worried that his father's rash decision might reflect poorly on himself, but Pelendion clapped him on the shoulder again cheerfully. "Very well. I daresay your service today has canceled out your father's debt, though should he ever return I still want you to bring him in for questioning. The bounty shall be removed at once. My scribe will call on you in the morning, to make sure the smithy's deed of ownership is written up in your name."

Tollan blinked. That wasn't exactly what he had asked for, but the king was evidently more than willing to order it. His tired mind couldn't keep up. "Um, uh, thank you, my liege," he fumbled, bowing at the waist.

"Also, you and any family you still have in the city shall be my guests at a banquet in your honor, tomorrow evening," Pelendion said almost as an afterthought. It probably was, knowing how many banquets were served to guests in the palace. "For now, Lieutenant, one of my personal servants is waiting in the hall to take you to a spare room and draw you a bath. Shi'ev, my brother, and I have much to discuss."

Anseldr clasped his hands together in gratitude. "Sleep well, Lieutenant. You've earned it."

Tollan bowed again and left the office, finding the servant standing in the corridor as promised. As he was leaving, he thought he heard Shi'ev mention something about dissecting the corpse, but Pelendion refused vehemently, saying that the people needed to see the body first —to put a face to the terrorism.

Tollan didn't know what would happen once the public found out. It could either cause mass panic of the unknown, or unify and galvanize the people with a defined enemy rather than the divisive assumption that anti-monarchist protesters were responsible. The king was likely banking on the latter, and maybe by lifting the checkpoint requirements he could reclaim some public goodwill.

The attendant brought a plate of fruits and cheese, prepared a bed that looked more comfortable than a cloud, and drew a steaming bath before leaving Tollan to his own devices. He fell fast asleep after a minute lying back in the warm water, without even touching the other luxuries.

TWENTY

*Reunions can be more difficult than
farewells, for it is then that one realizes
what has truly been lost to time.*

— Codes of Binding 1.35

NIENA HADN'T SLEPT WELL or enough, for reasons obvious only to herself. Even after oversleeping by an hour, she was yawning. She thought maybe some tea would help, so she dressed and went down to the kitchen to make some. She refused to ask the Denvalds' servants to do it for her, even if Letaccia had insisted and allowed her to borrow some of the late Serenia's clothes.

She had spent most of her night up on the rooftops of the nearby neighborhoods, out of the street patrols' way but still close enough to take notes on their patterns. Fewer soldiers walked the streets at night and the checkpoints were shut during curfew, but that was only useful if one knew the patrol routes and guard changes. She knew of no other way to appease Gilbrannen, however, since Tollan still hadn't returned.

Niena greeted the staff in the kitchen, starting to prepare Lady Denvald's breakfast. She had considered applying to work in the palace as a maid or kitchen servant, but if the Denvald house was any example, the odds of her overhearing strategically valuable information would be almost zero.

At any rate, she couldn't keep up this charade. She needed something more interesting to pass back to Gilbrannen, or there would be little reason for him to keep her father alive.

The bell at the front door rang just as Niena removed the whistling kettle from the stove. She hurried to the dining room where she would be able to see the visitor from the window. Although one of the valets always answered the door, she never knew what sort of useful information might waft through a prominent house like the Denvalds'.

The door creaked open, and the valet didn't greet the expected courier or peddler. It was Tollan himself, dressed in the finest, brightest yellow soldier's livery and carrying a wooden box under his right arm. Niena's mouth dropped open, and she rushed out from her vantage point to wrap him in the biggest hug she could manage.

He spluttered, at least as shocked as she was. "Niena!" he exclaimed, half-returning the hug with one arm while struggling to hang on to the wooden box with the other. "What—when did you get back? Is Dad here, too?"

The question drove a stake through Niena's heart. She hadn't considered where all these lies and double-crossings would take her, but she couldn't tell her brother the truth in full view of the house staff. "I, uh, got in four days ago, and Papa is still up north getting a few things sorted. He hopes to be back soon, but wanted me to come ahead and make sure you got back from training all right." That was true enough, she supposed, but her voice would have easily betrayed that she was hiding something. "I'll tell you more about all that later." That was also true.

Tollan released her from the embrace, and looked her up and down on the threshold. "I daresay you fit in with the Gilded Quarter better than Aunt Anise! Where did you get the dress?"

Niena laughed, a little awkwardly. She still felt self-conscious, wearing a dead woman's dress so much more extravagant than her old threadbare green one. "Don't let her hear you say that. I guess your friend Thaxon's sister had some clothes just a little short for my size, and Lady Denvald said it would be good for someone to wear them. Speaking of Thaxon, where is he? I've been looking forward to meeting him."

Tollan looked uncomfortable. "There's a lot that I have to tell you, Niena."

Niena paused. If only he knew how much she needed to tell him. "Come in, then, and sit down. I'll fetch Anise."

Tollan stepped inside and thanked the valet, who closed the door behind him. "Hold up, Niena," he said, halting her halfway up the stairs. "I don't think I have time to fill you all in at the moment. Things are moving too quickly. I'm here to speak with Lady Denvald."

"What's wrong, Tollan?" Niena asked, seeing the melancholy in her brother's eyes. "What things?"

"Thaxon is dead."

The household staff collectively took in a stunned breath.

"We had reason to believe that the ... terrorists ... had an encampment along the East Road, through the swamps," Tollan said. "It turns out they did. Who we're up against, Niena ... They're more powerful and dangerous than we can even imagine."

Niena stood on the stairs, a sick feeling in her gut. She had so many questions, but it sounded like her brother knew about the D'harnir, or at least what they could do. That would make things easier when she was able to tell him the full truth.

"Okay," she said. "Come with me." She led the way upstairs to the landing, then down the hall to Lady Denvald's room. Anise was there already, and she lit up like a firework when they walked in.

"Oh! Tollan! Thank goodness you've returned!" Anise bubbled, seeming not to notice their somber mood.

"Where's Thaxon?" Letaccia sat up in her bed, looking past Niena and Tollan and expecting the red-haired lad to follow them. "Where's my son?"

Niena and Anise stood back in quiet shame as Tollan told her of Thaxon's death during the ambush on the road. He didn't go into much detail other than to say he wouldn't have completed his mission without Thaxon, and that his friend had faced his death with courage. Letaccia sat and listened with an empty expression on her face, shaking her head in disbelief and sorrow. Niena couldn't imagine what the woman was going through, having lost her only two children in the span of little more than a month.

Tollan finished by offering her the wooden box he carried with him. His voice grew hoarse. "Jarl Anseldr asked me to present this to you in Thaxon's remembrance. He served Drüstania with honor, and his name will be written in the king's book of heroes."

Letaccia opened the box, and as she held up the contents—a golden medal emblazoned with the Drüstanian crest—the tears began to flow. When Tollan came closer to console her, she became angry. "No! You . . . you were supposed to protect him! I told you to protect him!"

Tollan backed away, his own eyes wet with grief. "There was nothing I could do. He was taken so quickly—"

"Get out! All of you!" Letaccia shouted, and broke down sobbing.

Anise herded the two of them out into the hallway and gently shut the door behind her. "She needs some space for now."

Tollan wiped his eyes, and Niena touched his arm in sympathy.

"Thaxon was such a nice boy," Anise said. "I'm glad you were with him there, at the end."

Niena's eyes drifted back to the closed door and wondered when Lord Denvald might return. They needed to be together to make it through this. Letaccia needed him now, and he was still away on business. Niena felt an immense sorrow and sympathy for the woman despite never meeting her son.

This was what Niena was helping Gilbrannen accomplish, she thought with guilt—the destruction of families. The Denvalds may have been wealthy, but they had opened their home to the Cresthavens without so much as a question, simply because their son had said they should. They didn't deserve this tragedy. The Cresthavens at least had a chance to be together again, but the Denvalds never would.

"Let's go down to the dining room and talk," Anise continued. "Can I get you anything to drink, Tollan?"

Tollan sighed. "I can't stay," he clarified, apologetically meeting Niena's concerned gaze. "The king has called another mandatory address this afternoon in the square, and he wants me to join him in front of all of Celwaith Tor."

"Oh, heavens, you've met the king?" Anise exclaimed. "He must have been impressed with you."

"He shouldn't be," Tollan said. "Let's just say that I was able to bring something back that has allowed us to turn the corner in this fight. It will all make sense at the address, but until then, it's all classified."

"When will we see you again?" Niena asked, frustrated that he was leaving so soon.

Tollan reached inside a pocket and pulled out two envelopes, sealed and stamped with wax, one of which he handed to Niena. "This is for you both. All the details are inside, just make sure you present it at the palace after the address. It's an invitation to a royal banquet in my honor."

"Banquet?" Niena and Anise said in unison.

"I didn't much care for the idea, but Jarl Anseldr claims it's all part of the routine," Tollan continued, then handed the other envelope to Anise.

"And what, pray tell, is this?" Anise inquired suspiciously. "I hope it's a promissory note for the rest of your wages."

"Even better," Tollan said. "Open it."

Niena watched as Anise used her fingernail to pry up the edge of the seal, trying not to damage or tear the wax. She pulled out a slip of paper and unfolded it. "Redaction of bounty," she read aloud. "And . . . deed of possession?"

"Dad's no longer a wanted man," Tollan said, smiling. "And the king has signed the smithy and the land it sits on over to me in perpetuity, with the condition that the forge will still be under military use until it is no longer needed."

"My, but this is exciting!" Anise said. "Your father will be so pleased."

"If he ever comes home. The city guard will still need to question him, but he is no longer suspected of treason." Tollan looked at Niena questioningly, and his thoughts were obvious.

There was nothing she could say to him. It would have to wait until after the banquet, when she could tell Tollan everything—or at least as much as he could stand to know. She and Anise walked Tollan to the door and said their farewells, then began their preparations for that evening. They wouldn't have time after the proclamation to return and dress before the banquet, so they needed to leave the Denvald house in full formal regalia.

Niena had never worn a corset before in her life, and not only because of the prohibitive price. Although the constriction she felt around her midriff couldn't come close to matching the anxiety she felt on the inside.

NIENA FELT THE COBBLE of Wraelian Square under her shoes, the place where this nightmare had begun for her. Though many differences stood out compared to the day Tollan had departed for training: her father wasn't here, Niena and Anise were both dressed in finery that neither would have been able to afford, and overlooking the crowd was a burlap sack, bound to a pole installed above the remains of Wraelian's crumbled statue.

"What do you suppose that is?" Anise asked, indicating the roughly human-sized bundle. "The burning of Berelda's effigy isn't for another three months."

It did rather resemble the festival held in Celwaith Tor every winter, commemorating the death of the evil soothsayer that had ruled Drüstania before the Arvad dynasty overthrew her. However, this time Niena suspected the figure was made of more than straw.

She shivered and tugged at the small sleeves of the deep green dress she had borrowed from the Denvalds. It was too short at the hem and left more exposed than she liked, but it fit her well otherwise. "It might be a prisoner, judging by the four guards posted around it," she answered.

Niena glanced around the crowd, checking to see if Lady Denvald had made it down from her room. Anise had offered to help, but Letaccia refused to even speak to her now, and instead ordered her servants to roll her down themselves on a makeshift wheelchair. Niena spied the contraption and its owner's black veil toward the edge of the square, near where hundreds of conscripted soldiers had begun to cordon off the exits.

Niena truly felt bad for her and knew Anise did as well. She hoped the woman didn't begrudge their family for . . . well, for surviving when her own children had not. But that couldn't be helped at this point.

At least Lady Denvald hadn't thrown them out of her house entirely, as was her right to do.

A hush fell over the crowd as the king strode out onto the balcony high above, preceded by the herald's script as before. "People of Celwaith Tor and citizens of Drüstania, I bring you news of our struggle with the terrorists and warmongers that have been hampering our trade and your livelihoods.

"If you had not already heard, our valiant army managed to halt another attempt on our fair city at the gates less than a week ago. The attack consisted of replacing vital militia supplies with copious amounts of black powder, no doubt intended for detonation in the keep's armory where it would cause the most harm. But when we imprisoned and questioned the soldiers responsible for the incursion, they had no memory of their own treachery."

Niena's heart sank lower. Based on what she had overheard from Gilbrannen and Silmon, her brother had been right in the thick of that encounter. His inability to be affected by D'harnin magic had both halted the infiltration and revealed how the elves did it. All of those facts pointed to there only being one thing so important for Tollan to bring back from the swamp.

Proof.

Pelendion continued. "We suspected our men had been drugged or hypnotized. A dozen of our finest new recruits, led by Lieutenant Tollan Cresthaven of the Barren Quarter, set out along the East Road to spring a trap, dangling another shipment of supplies as bait. And despite incurring heavy losses, Cresthaven succeeded in bringing back proof of our attackers' identity."

On cue, one of the four guards surrounding the figure in the center of the square ripped off the burlap sack. The tall, pale body underneath was naked save for a loincloth, both like a human and yet unlike.

The parts of the crowd close enough to get a good look gave a collective gasp, and Anise placed a hand over her heart. "Winds take us! What is that?" she asked, and similar murmurs could be heard rippling across the square.

But Niena stood there emotionless, knowing precisely what everyone would see. The truth of the elves' existence was public.

The world could never again go back to ignorance, not after today.

"Your eyes do not deceive you," Pelendion proclaimed. "That is no human, but rather something that had been lost to fairy tales and legends of our forebears. My stalwart people, we are not at war with ourselves and never have been. These creatures have used their magic to deceive us."

The nervous murmurs grew to a fever pitch, beginning to drown out Pelendion's words.

"Stay calm!" Pelendion called down from on high. "Yes, these elves —or so they appear—are a grave threat. Yes, they can infiltrate our cities, steal our hard-earned goods, and kill our loved ones. But Drüstania will not be so easily defeated, or it is not the country I love and lead."

The agitated crowd calmed down, their king's words stirring faith and camaraderie in his plan of action. Niena had to respect the man's oration skills, painting a picture of unknown malice to draw the people together against it. Two more men now appeared on the balcony behind Pelendion, and one was a foreigner dressed in black. The other, Niena realized with a start, was Tollan.

The king continued. "It was through the bravery of Lieutenant Tollan Cresthaven and the ingenuity of the Kiramet inventor Darakh Shi'ev that this lone elf was brought to justice. He will be the first of many, as we now know their tactics, and we have a lead to their stronghold. The strength and science of men will prevail over their sorcery, again and again until they are gone or have given up."

"What is that cryptic nonsense supposed to mean?" a particularly cantankerous older man muttered to Niena's left. She might have chuckled if her father's life wasn't on the line.

"Two thousand of our militia will set out fully armed from Celwaith Tor on the morrow, leaving the rest to maintain the city's checkpoints and security," Pelendion said, presenting his plan of action to discourage any further naysayers. "Lieutenant Cresthaven will lead our forces through the eastern lowlands right to the enemy's doorstep. We shall reap one hundred fold in them what they sowed here among us in Wraelian Square!"

Tollan took a step forward, raising his fist. "Justice and vengeance!" he shouted. All the soldiers, standing in ranks at the outermost edges of the square, repeated the words in unison. The people quickly followed suit, until voices twenty thousand strong chanted the call to war.

TWENTY-ONE

The knowledge and skills learned in youth persist until the end of one's days. So, too, does the memory and disappointment of not being enough.

— Codes of Binding 1.09-10

NIENA AND ANISE WAITED in expectant silence as the chants died down and the exits opened. The people gradually streamed away once they had passed by to see the face of their new enemy up close. Niena could smell more of the dead D'harnin body than she wanted to from where she stood, and didn't much care to get any closer.

Once there was a clear path to the palace gates, the two of them made their way through the dwindling crowd. Anise was especially careful not to let the hem of her dress drag in the street—it would simply not do to appear as a guest of the king with a soiled hem.

Anise ran a hand through her hair, making sure all her artificial curls and pins stayed in place, then turned to Niena. "Oh, dear, I wish you would have settled on something a little less . . . simple for your hairstyle."

Niena shook her head adamantly. "Anise, I'm not from the Gilded Quarter. I'm all for dressing up in respect of our host, but one doesn't have to be elaborate to be elegant."

"I suppose," Anise said, though she clearly didn't agree. "Do you think there will be any fashionable single officers my age?"

Niena sighed, her aunt's materialistic concerns the last thing on her mind. It was patently ridiculous compared to what she worried about. "We're going to war, and you're thinking of courtship. I'm sure the king's entourage will find you delightful."

"Well, I'm certainly not going to mention my intentions inside!" Anise exclaimed in mock indignation as they approached the gate. "That's why I'm asking you out here."

Niena smiled at the guards as they approached and offered them the invitation. They moved aside, and a valet came forward to tend to them and show them the way indoors. Niena attempted to memorize the various corridors they passed, but all she could remember was the order of turns and the flights of stairs. There were so many rooms—and she had thought the Denvald residence was overly extravagant.

The valet showed them to a sitting room on the third floor with a bay window, looking out toward the east. The vertical rocky bluffs fell away below them to the lake, with the edge of the city barely visible on the window's right side. Far ahead, the East Road diminished toward the darkening horizon.

"A lovely view," Anise observed, but Niena couldn't agree.

Tollan would be leaving on that road tomorrow, followed by two thousand men as they sought out the D'harnin enclave in the swamps. Niena had to keep him from going—it was a wonder that he had returned alive from the last mission, but now he would be a primary target.

Maybe she could convince Gilbrannen to do something to extract her brother, or else he would lose his potential source of information.

Why was she kidding herself? The elf probably wouldn't even care beyond writing the entire operation off as a loss, leaving no hope for her father.

The door behind them clicked, and Niena turned to see Tollan swing it open and step inside. This time he was in far fancier clothes than his livery; although Drüstanian yellow still featured prominently in his outfit, he appeared much statelier and more refined in his doublet and frilly collar. His hair had been trimmed since that morning, and his rank and honors were pinned to his breast.

"Well," Anise said appreciatively. "Look at you! I always said you would clean up nicely, if you ever cared to. Didn't I, Niena?"

Niena swallowed her unease. "Yes. You look handsome, Tollan."

She couldn't keep her internal tension from her brother's observant eyes, however. "I know you must have a lot of questions, but I can't answer them yet," he said. "The king is expecting us in the reception hall, and we'll be going straight on to dinner. He is very busy, as you can imagine. Once he leaves to consult with his officers, we should have some time to talk."

Niena wanted to pull her hair out. She would have to sit through a bunch of dry and frumpy court traditions before addressing the only item of any importance. She had hoped to halfway enjoy the banquet with her brother, but she doubted she would be able to eat much now.

"How delightful," Anise said. Of course, she would have no problem melting into the mess of etiquette and highbrow snobbery. "Who all will be present at dinner tonight?"

"To be honest, I'm not sure." Tollan shrugged. "Other than the king himself, Jarl Anseldr, and the Kiramet inventor, I don't know anyone here. I'm as new to this as you are."

Niena nodded in understanding. She offered her arm for Tollan to lead. "Well, let's not keep His Highness waiting, shall we?" She might as well have said that she wanted to get the whole thing over and done, but that kind of attitude would not do. She reminded herself to keep her own ears peeled—there was no telling what sorts of information Gilbrannen might find valuable enough to let her father keep on living.

Although the D'harnir being publicly revealed would be of interest to Gilbrannen, it would be news to no one by the time she was able to get it to Silmon that night. She needed something more, something interesting enough to take the heat off for a little longer, so that Tollan could help her come up with a plan.

The attendants opened the decorated double doors into the reception hall, and Tollan led Niena and Anise past a dozen soldiers at attention in full armor. Niena had heard that the throne room was far larger than this, but all the same it was extravagantly furnished and no less imposing for it.

King Pelendion looked on at the far end of the chamber, flanked on his left by Queen Coranna in a shining white dress. The king's beard was neatly shaped and trimmed while his golden hair fell past his ears to give him a charmingly rakish look. The queen's hair was tied back into a tight bun, from which her locks spilled out in a fan shape down to her shoulders. They sat on twin thrones, radiant and regal, waiting for the guests to make their way down the red carpet.

Tollan stopped approximately ten paces from the king and gave a stiff bow from the waist. Niena and Anise performed a deep curtsy as was tradition.

"My liege," Tollan said steadily. "I would like to introduce you to my aunt, Anise Cresthaven, and my sister, Niena."

"We are honored, Your Majesties," Anise assured.

Pelendion nodded at each of them in welcome, his smile turning downward almost immediately. "I realize that this is a stressful time for all of you, given what the young lieutenant has discovered, but his service to the kingdom is to be both admired and rewarded. We must take our moments of pleasure when they come, for tomorrow may bring darker things to us."

The king paused, and Niena felt uncomfortable with the pressure. If she opened her mouth to say the wrong thing, she might reveal her ignorance of tradition or etiquette. Not that she was normally concerned with those kinds of things, but she needed to fit in if she was to learn anything of value tonight.

When no one spoke in kind, Queen Coranna interjected. "Indeed. Let us focus on celebrating our victories rather than worrying about future losses. You are all most welcome in our palace this evening. Please, enjoy the food and music and make yourselves at home."

"I regret that I will not be present at the banquet for much of the evening," Pelendion said as an afterthought. "There are a great many preparations that must be made before the morrow. Still, you will be in the capable hands of my brother, Anseldr, and his wife, Emeline, for the remainder of the evening. If you require anything, you need only ask."

Tollan bowed again. "As you wish, Your Majesty. We are grateful that you have shown us this much favor at a time of crisis for the nation."

Niena had never seen her brother so formal and composed. It was strange to say the least—his training had changed him, whether for better or worse she didn't know.

The king and queen stood from their thrones and bade them to follow. "Come, all of you," he said, as two armed guards fell in behind them. They exited the reception hall through a side door and proceeded down a corridor that opened out into a large dining and performance chamber. "The table is already set for us."

And what a table it was, welcoming them with a myriad of pleasant smells. Carved of red oak wood and stained to a deep burgundy, it was draped with handwoven lace cloths and littered with floral arrangements and the largest platters of assorted fruit and cheeses

Niena had ever seen. Despite the length of the table, she noted that there was no meat or vegetables, implying that this was merely the first course of many.

The room was already filled to the brim with other people, most of them dressed in even more gaudy finery than Niena and Anise's own. They all fell quiet now that the king had entered, including the string quartet on the stage, and bowed or curtsied accordingly in respect. Niena felt self-conscious from all the eyes staring as she took her seat next to Tollan's place of honor, and wondered if she should have taken Anise's advice about pinning her hair back.

No. Niena wasn't beholden to all these pretenders. She would mind her manners, and mind them well, but a little ruffling of all the posh feathers in the room would do them good.

The dinner passed slowly, filled with surface-level small talk that quickly tapered off when the person became reminded that the Cresthavens did not frequent their usual social circles. The only exception was, remarkably, the jarl's dark-haired wife, Emeline. She sat on Niena's left and proved to be genuinely personable, not only asking with curiosity about life in the Barren Quarter but filling Niena in on the gossip and inside jokes around them.

"The performers are simply splendid," Guildmistress Farthing was saying about the quartet, further down the table. Niena used to work with Anise at the weavers', but hadn't recognized the head of the textile guild until overhearing her name. "But I say that every time they play for us. Isn't this the second movement from Roristern's *Promises of Penance?*"

"Indeed, it is," Emeline replied with a polite smile, glancing over at Anseldr who was enraptured by the cellist's quick fingers. "One of my husband's favorites for being so technically impressive to play. They've been practicing it for months, or so I understand."

"They have," the scientist Darakh Shi'ev chimed in wryly. "It is impossible not to hear their sessions from the library every day during my studies. I much prefer Kiramet music; the accidentals and dissonant chords are more unpredictable and mentally stimulating."

Niena cleared her throat, seeing an opportunity in the awkward moment to turn the conversation in her favor. "What kinds of studies, if I might ask, Mr. Shi'ev? Does it have anything to do with how my brother was able to kill that . . . creature?" She had almost said *D'harn*, but caught herself just in time with how disastrous that might be.

Shi'ev pursed his lips, and gave her an appreciative nod. "An astute question for one so young, Miss Cresthaven. No, the handheld firearm your brother used is a fully functional design. That doesn't mean I can't improve it, but I need to turn my creative energies in a different direction or else I become restless."

Niena got excited for a moment, but such a weapon would be old news to Gilbrannen by the time Niena got it to him. Especially since other elves had already seen it in action. She needed something more, and perhaps information about Shi'ev's next project would prove more fruitful.

But King Pelendion chose that moment to retire from the banquet. His military generals awaited him in private to plan the next day's offensive. Unfortunately, while farewells were made to the king, it kept Niena from asking Shi'ev any further questions about his studies.

Luckily, once the room had settled down and the quartet had gone on to the third movement, Shi'ev was the one to ask Niena a question. "What do you think of the quartet, Miss Cresthaven? Is it to your liking?"

"It is beautiful," Niena said, not untruthfully. Her mind had been in a dozen other places until now, so she took a moment to let her mind drift on the melodies and harmonies. "Different than what I am used to hearing in the markets, sir, but smooth and more pleasing to the ear. I can't say I've heard music from your country before, but if you prefer it to this it must be something to behold."

"Quite." Shi'ev chuckled, and Niena wasn't sure what amused him about her answer. "Music is fascinating, isn't it? That mere sounds can make us feel so many different things—from the heights of pleasure and ecstasy to the depths of sorrow and dread."

Niena frowned in confusion, sensing that his statements led somewhere specific. "I'm not sure I follow you, Mr. Shi'ev."

The corner of the man's mouth turned upwards. "Don't you wonder how it is that these so-called elves are able to bewitch people? To cause men to do their bidding and remember nothing when they wake again?"

Guildmistress Farthing swallowed her dainty bite of roast duck and dabbed at her mouth with a silk napkin. "His Majesty said today that the elves deceived us with their magic. Are you proposing that is not accurate?"

"Perhaps," Shi'ev replied, evading the question. "Or perhaps we only interpret their enchantments as magic."

Niena spoke up, not wanting the conversation to be derailed into semantics. She thanked the winds that Anise was caught up in flirting conversation with a nobleman, or else she never would have gotten this far. "Hold on. If I understand you correctly, you believe that people can be influenced or controlled by sound? And the elves have learned how to exploit that?"

Shi'ev shrugged, washing down his meal with a swig of red wine and retrieving the napkin from his lap. "Let me put it this way. If I ever tried to manipulate someone without their knowledge, it would be through sound. Thankfully, your brother has provided the perfect experimental subject to see if that would even be possible, but it could be a long time until I have anything more concrete than that."

Niena nodded excitedly. It surprised her that Shi'ev was willing to talk about his work so openly—but she supposed there was little reason to keep secrets from humans when elves were the enemy. All the better for her father's sake. This was precisely the sort of information Gilbrannen might find useful, and she felt her anxiety start to ease as the banquet wound down.

But if anything, the hardest part was still ahead of her.

Niena excused herself from the table, giving Emeline and the others pretenses of visiting the privy, and covertly tapped Tollan on the shoulder as she passed. Hopefully, he would take that as a sign to follow her, but she continued on her way as if nothing had passed between them.

As she left the room, she could hear him wrapping up his conversations and reassuring Anise that he would be back in a few minutes. Relieved, Niena shut the door behind her and walked slowly enough down the corridor so that her brother would catch sight of her.

"Hey," Tollan called as he fell into step beside her. "You needed something?"

"Not here," Niena said, her voice lowered. "Is there anywhere we can talk privately?"

Tollan nodded hesitantly, and led her around the corner. She recognized the corridor, as they had completed a circuit all the way back to the sitting room where she and Anise had first waited for him. The layout of the palace started to make a little more sense, at least on this level.

Tollan lit a few candles on a center table to brighten the room and gestured to the long, cushioned seat behind it. "All right, we're alone," he said, latching the door. "What's the matter? Did one of those pompous oafs make a remark about you?"

Niena half-smiled, happy to know Tollan hadn't lost his general distaste of upper society in his time with the Denvalds. "No, I just couldn't stand waiting any longer to hear your story. Tollan, we hadn't ever gone more than a few days without seeing each other until now."

Tollan reached out and folded her into a hug, and even though she melted into it, she still felt distant from him. "I know, and I'm sorry," he said. "It couldn't be helped. When the king says to go, you go."

Niena released the embrace. They sat on the cushioned furniture, opposite each other with the candles burning hot between them. Niena could see the first stars peeping through the eastern sky outside the bay window. "So, tell me all of it," she prompted, thinking it would be better to end with her side of recent events.

"That ... would take a while," Tollan said, rubbing his forehead. "And you already know most of it. Training got cut short by an attack on Outpost Heron, Thaxon and I stopped another attempt on Celwaith Tor at the gate, and we attempted to spring the attackers' trap along the road to catch them in the act. We were woefully unprepared for their strength and numbers."

Niena nodded sympathetically, but she couldn't know what that had been like for him. "And you were the only one to make it out."

"As far as I know," Tollan said, staring into the candle flames. "These creatures are beyond reason, Niena, and they have deadly capabilities we can't even imagine. They are brutal, remorseless killers, nothing like the fairy tales we used to read about them."

Niena took a deep breath to calm her nerves. She remembered how difficult it had been to come around to elves being real, but she couldn't imagine having to do it while her friends died around her. "It's ... almost like we've been at war for years and never known it," she said.

"Exactly," Tollan agreed. He sat up straighter and narrowed his eyes at her. "Now, it's your turn. Fill me in—what possessed Dad to take you up north on such short notice? Leaving Anise with nothing but a note while the smithy was seized?" He threw up a hand in exasperation. "Why?"

Niena needed to get him on her side before telling him the whole truth, and she had no problem admitting fault for that. "You're right.

We shouldn't have left the way we did, but Papa believed it wouldn't be possible if he waited any longer—and I didn't want to let him go alone. I'm sorry." She didn't know where to go from there. It occurred to her that her father must have been at a similar loss for words the night he had told her. "Kasdan told me he delivered your birthday gift?" she asked, changing the subject.

Tollan dangled it out of his pocket, the etching shining in the candlelight. "Runs perfectly, as long as I wind it. I don't know how you ever afforded it, but I use it every day. Best gift I've ever had."

"I'm glad," she said, her tone neutral. She needed to quit stalling and tell him. It was now or never. "Why . . . do you think it is that you made it out of the swamp and not any of the rest of your men?"

Tollan sat up in alarm, hurt by the question. "What do you mean? They were all better soldiers than I was—I almost got drummed out of the service because I couldn't keep up. I barely made it back through the swamp to the horses."

Niena shook her head. "No, Tollan. If it is so easy for these elves to control people, why didn't it happen to you? Why didn't they hold you back, or drive you away in terror?"

There was a dreadful silence, as Tollan didn't have an answer. Niena waited for him to reason it through. "I don't know," he said finally.

"Because . . ." She almost couldn't bring herself to say it around the lump in her throat. "Because our mother was one of them. One of the elves."

Tollan stared at her, unblinking. "That's impossible," he whispered. "How do you know this?"

Niena reached up and untied the dark leather cord around her neck, and showed the necklace to him. "This was Mama's. Papa took me to see our old farm, and where he buried her. He gave me an old journal that explains how men and elves came to live separately ages ago, and . . ."

"Wait, stop," Tollan said, and held his hand up. He stood and paced along the edge of the room, and reached up to touch his jagged ear.

Niena of all people knew how difficult this news would be to believe, but her brother seemed to be accepting it. She tried to step closer, but he turned away.

"I wouldn't lie to you," she said gently.

"But Dad would," Tollan said with a measure of scorn in his voice. "He either lied to us our entire lives, or he lied to you about this. And I don't know which one would be worse."

Niena hadn't expected this reaction from her brother. "No, you don't understand. It was to protect us . . ."

"I don't care what the reason was, Niena. It's not good enough." He pointed to the necklace still dangling from her hand. "Tell me where Dad is, right now. No lies, I know he's not 'hunting' or whatever story the two of you decided to pass around."

Niena's face went pale as a sheet. This wasn't how their talk was supposed to go. She knew the relationship between Tollan and their father had been strained lately, but she had no idea it was this bad. She wasn't even sure anymore that Tollan would help her feed information to Gilbrannen if she told him the truth, but there was no way around it. "Tollan, I—"

A heavy knock at the door cut her off.

"Lieutenant Cresthaven?" a gruff male voice called through the heavy oak. "Are you there?"

"Come," Tollan said, giving Niena a look that said their conversation wasn't over.

Niena saw in the light from the corridor that the man who had interrupted them was an officer, with more decorations on his dress uniform than seemed logical to wear. Tollan bowed, and she hurriedly curtsied to follow.

"Sergeant Major Senn, sir," Tollan addressed him, coming to full attention. "To what do I owe the pleasure? I was taking a moment to catch up with my sister before we march in the morning."

"It is Colonel Senn now, Lieutenant," the man said, his close-cropped gray hair and beard giving the impression that he was no-nonsense. "It seems we have both fallen on the king's favor. His Majesty requires your presence at his special military session. A few questions have come up about your experiences in the swamp which should aid in planning our counterattack."

Tollan nodded. "Thank you, sir. I will be right there."

"The orders were that you should come at once, Lieutenant," Senn instructed, a little harsher this time.

"Understood." Tollan turned back to Niena. "I will be heading out in the morning with the rest of the army, and staying here in the palace until then. There is no use upsetting Lady Denvald more than necessary. Tell Anise that I regret departing again so soon."

"I will," Niena said, breathing hard. She didn't want to leave their conversation like that, but Senn's presence made any continuation impossible. Maybe she would have another opportunity once the army returned, but it crossed her mind that Tollan might not come back. He had narrowly escaped death once, but that was no guarantee of the future. "Stay safe, Tollan. Please."

Tollan locked eyes with her one last time as he stood in the doorway, and she saw something cold there that stabbed an icicle through her soul. During all those years of pointless sibling fights and petty disagreements, she had never felt so far removed from him. Even that fateful day when Tollan had been drafted was only a physical separation, but this . . .

Tollan left with his commanding officer, and didn't offer another word to her. And only when the door had closed behind him did she let the tears she had withheld for so long fall from her eyes.

TWENTY-TWO

Never settle for half-measures when building a life, a family, or a home. The endeavor you fail to see finished may see fit to collapse on you.

— Codes of Binding 7.14-15

TOLLAN HAD TO WALK quickly to keep up with the colonel as they climbed a flight of stairs, but his mind churned even faster. He wished he had a moment to sort through what Niena had told him, but it was her most unbelievable assertion that kept ringing in his head.

How could their mother have been an elf? It made a meager amount of sense, since both she and her family had never been a common topic of conversation. Tollan and Niena had learned not to ask after their father had given a myriad of short, closed answers growing up. They had assumed that his grief was so deep that he didn't want to dwell on it, but now . . .

Tollan had never questioned the story of his scar. He had just accepted that he was too young to remember the accident with an exposed nail that had torn out a piece of his ear.

Another lie, if any of what Niena had said was true.

But there was another possibility, one that had sent a chill down Tollan's spine when he thought of it. Niena and his father had been out in the wilds for almost a month, and both the northern watchtower and Outpost Heron had been burned to the ground during that time. Whatever reason they had to leave Celwaith Tor, it was highly plausible —even probable—that his family had run into a party of the elven terrorists. And now that Tollan knew firsthand the magical power that the elves wielded . . .

Niena had been bewitched like the others, enchanted into believing that she was one of them. For what purpose, Tollan didn't know, but she hadn't been herself either that morning or over dinner.

Of course, that left the question of what had happened to Tollan's father, but he knew from experience that Voster Cresthaven was one of the most bullheaded men in the Barren Quarter. Perhaps the elves couldn't break him, and they sent Niena back alone with implanted memories.

He had no way to prove it, but he was sure that was what happened.

Colonel Senn preceded him into the strategy conference, holding the door open for him.

Tollan took a deep breath and mentally washed his hands of whatever might happen to his family while he was away. His foremost duty now was to his king, and anything else would have to be a secondary concern.

He stepped into a wide room with a semicircular table facing the king on a small but still elaborate wooden throne. Every officer at the table wore their military finery, and spread out on the table was a map of Drüstania and the outlying lands and seas.

After the introductions and pleasantries, Senn took the empty seat at the table and King Pelendion ushered Tollan over to take a closer look at the map. "Lieutenant, if you would be so kind as to point out precisely where your group was ambushed, and any other relevant locations."

"Yes, Your Majesty." Tollan followed the line indicating the East Road with his eyes and rested a finger on the location. "Right here, only a few miles before we would have reached the remains of Outpost Heron. We were attacked from both sides of the road, but we broke formation northward and glimpsed more structures in that direction through the mists."

"Right into the heart of the swamp," said one of the generals with a thick, drooping mustache. Tollan thought he was named Verune, but couldn't remember for sure. "That's where they would have to be hiding, if they've been on our doorstep for so long. No one has dared set foot in there for decades, because so few came out again."

"And now we know why," Colonel Senn acknowledged. "Even if someone was to try to map that part of Eastmarsh, the magic of these creatures could have diverted anyone around their strongholds without knowing it. The question is, why would they start to attack us now, when we've done nothing to provoke them?"

"Point taken," Pelendion said, cutting off a question that would merit nothing but speculation. Tollan assumed that such things had already been argued about past their reasonable time. "Lieutenant Cresthaven, based on your experience, what sorts of abilities would you say these elves have?"

Tollan tried to remember anything additional that had stood out to him, but most of that mist-shrouded day had become difficult to recall in detail. "All I can say for sure, my liege, is what Mr. Shi'ev took down in my report. They have an extraordinary talent for blending in, as the color of their cloaks matched the swamp and mist precisely. That may be supplemented by some innate ability, like what I saw at the gate, or it could be extraordinary craftsmanship and optical illusions.

"Otherwise, the only expressly supernatural ability that I've seen firsthand is their mental influence, including over beasts like the trancheons," Tollan finished, not sure what else to say. He noticed a court stenographer in the corner taking down his words for the record.

Another voice spoke up, from the end of the table, one that Tollan was not familiar with. "Is it possible, then, that all of this magic—or whatever it is—has facilitated their hiding all these years? It may be entirely defensive in nature, though they've adapted to use illusions of the mind against us in battle."

General Verune nodded. "An adaptation to their circumstances. Astute observation, Colonel Reeds. Your Majesty, were we able to uncover anything about these elves in the archives? Even old wives' tales and folklore would be better than no knowledge of them at all."

King Pelendion stroked his neatly-trimmed beard in thought. "No. My library overseer says there isn't enough congruity between such legends to merit placing strategic weight on them. We must work with what we know, and attempt to anticipate the unexpected."

Tollan cleared his throat when it became obvious that the king was done speaking. "Might I make an observation, Your Majesty?"

"Of course, lad," Pelendion raised a hand to welcome his opinion. "That's why you're here. What do you see?"

All eyes looked again to Tollan, and he balked at the pressure of all these powerful men expecting him to be worth their time. He tentatively expressed his thoughts. "I don't believe the elves have much strength beyond traditional weaponry. If they had attacks of physical sorcery to use against us, instead of illusions and mind control, why would they be so keen to steal other weapons from us?"

Colonel Senn apparently agreed, as he clapped his hands together once in excitement. "A better point has not been made, Lieutenant. That brings with it a lot of good news."

"Not necessarily, Colonel," General Verune objected with a note of warning in his voice. "They may be reluctant to reveal their true strength, only to turn the tables at our most vulnerable moment. We already know they are adept at hiding themselves. That may also apply to their strategy."

"Regardless," King Pelendion interrupted, "we must proceed before they have the chance to follow up or fade back into the shadows. We have the advantage in numbers, and we may have an advantage in weaponry as well. A courier has informed us that the Kiramet ambassador, Le'shom, returned to port with several ships full of their rifles—the first installment of our order. They are being delivered to the capital the long way, going south around the swamp; however, enough will be held back to arm your columns before you proceed into battle."

Tollan wasn't familiar with how long it took to travel by ship to Ash'kiram and back again, but less than a week was impressively fast. Not that anyone complained, since they needed the firearms as soon as possible, but it seemed odd.

"They will be put to good use, my liege," General Verune said reassuringly. "Though the enemy will have the two hundred rifles they managed to steal from Cresthaven's operation. That will merely put us on an even playing field. In case there are any unforeseen complications, will you authorize the use of fire mortars?"

"Fire mortars? On land? You can't be serious, sir!" Colonel Reeds spoke up. "Our men would be placed in considerable danger."

Tollan was familiar with the term, but had never personally seen them in action. They were petroleum-based quicklime explosives, particularly useful in siege scenarios. Light a single fuse, lob the ceramic container up over the target with a trebuchet or catapult, and watch burning oil rain down on the enemy. But with such formidable and imprecise weapons, there was a heightened chance of collateral damage.

"My liege," Tollan spoke up once more. "There could still be a few of my men being held captive there, or other soldiers that have gone missing. If we use fire mortars . . ." He trailed off when Pelendion held up a hand, his meaning obvious.

"Yes, it is dangerous," the king said firmly, but not without compassion. "And I agree, we should do anything in our power to rescue anyone these knaves have taken alive. However, I do not know if we can guarantee victory without such measures. If the militia gets within range of the stronghold but encounters stiff resistance, they will be able to firebomb it with minimal losses. But that should be only a last resort. Is that clear?"

The officers all nodded in agreement.

Pelendion stood, bringing the meeting to a swift end. "Officers, I leave the rest of the preparations to you. I have distributed orders to the corporals and commissioners that your men, all two thousand strong, will report for duty east of the city by dawn tomorrow. General Verune is in command of this operation, so you will all report to him for the duration of the campaign. Lieutenant, that goes the same for you, but you will be assisting the general directly. That may entail leading men as you already have, or merely accompanying the general and providing insight."

Tollan hoped it was the latter and not the former. He didn't think he could bear to be responsible for the deaths of any more of his countrymen. But regardless, he would still have his chance to avenge Thaxon, and that was more than all right with him.

All the officers bowed low as Pelendion left, and the stenographer gathered his papers to presumably compile the minutes for the archive. Tollan soberly recognized that this meeting had been history in the making, and it was good to have someone recording it. Perhaps children would one day read books on his contributions to Drüstania against the elves, just as he had once read about Wraelian's war against the barbarian incursion from the southern seas.

Unlike that long and arduous campaign though, this one would be over almost as soon as it began. At least, Tollan hoped so.

NIENA CAREFULLY SHIMMIED ONTO the slanted ledge outside her bedroom window, clutching onto the rough shingles with her bare feet. The city street sparkled almost three stories below, dark save for the moonlight on the remnants of the evening rain. The clouds had opened as she and Anise were escorted back to the Denvald residence, the weather turning sour in conjunction with Niena's mood.

It was just as well that she was supposed to meet with Silmon tonight. She wouldn't have been able to sleep anyway, playing her talk with Tollan over and over in her head.

She wished it was easier to sneak out of the Denvald house in the middle of the night. There was always someone awake, between all the maids, servants, and Lady Denvald's phantom pains in her severed leg. Or maybe the cries were sobs of grief for her son—Niena couldn't tell which.

She tried not to look down, not until she had shut the window behind her and climbed up to a more secure vantage point. She had done this before to monitor the night patrols, but the roof had been dry and not so precarious then. At least the occasional guards passing below never thought anyone was crazy enough to leap across alleyways and risk plummeting to a gruesome death.

But Niena wasn't crazy. She preferred the word "determined."

Silmon had said to meet him on the western roof overlooking Wraelian Square, opposite the palace keep. Gilbrannen had apparently regained some faith in his fellow elf to send him this far into the city alone.

She ran across the adjacent roof and thought the gap looked narrow enough to make it. But in midair, she realized she hadn't factored in the uphill elevation. Her lower body smacked against the brick wall, and she scrabbled for a handhold on the slanted roof. Everything below her waist dangled over a three-story drop, and she continued to slip downwards.

A gloved hand reached out from the shadows and snatched her own.

"You are late," Gilbrannen said, covered in the same drab color of cloak that Silmon had worn down by the lake. He pulled, giving her enough leverage to get a bare foot over the ledge. "Nice shoes."

"Gilbrannen," she said, breathing hard as she heaved herself onto the rooftop. Her arm muscles screamed at her for the stunt she had just pulled. "Doing your own dirty work for a change?"

The D'harn raised an eyebrow, smiling. "It is only dirty work if you choose to make it so, Niena. I was getting impatient holed up in the outpost, so I thought I would come check on you in Silmon's stead. It was easy enough with fewer checkpoints and patrols tonight than usual. You appear to be finding your way around the city as fleet of foot as we do—well, almost."

Niena ignored his jab at her misjudged jump and pulled a set of hand-drawn diagrams of city intersections from her waistband. The motion made the hem of her nightgown come untucked from her breeches, and she hastily righted herself. "I've been practicing. Routes and times for all the Gilded Quarter night patrols."

"Yes, yes," the D'harn said, stuffing them dismissively in a satchel. "I mean, yes, they are useful to us, but given today's developments I should think they are the last thing on your mind."

"I suppose so," Niena said, miffed that her hard work had been dismissed. "How did you know?"

Gilbrannen stood to his full height, looking toward Wraelian Square and beyond it to the palace. "Silmon overheard talk near the water gate, and so he sneaked into the city for Pelendion's address. The king had the corpse from Neraliel displayed like a trophy. And I take it that was your brother standing next to him?"

Niena blanched. She had hoped to ease into her explanation of the whole situation, but much like speaking to Tollan, she hadn't been given the chance to frame it all in the best light. "I had no idea he came home until a few hours before the address. And I've only had a few minutes to talk with him since—he ships out at dawn with two thousand men behind him."

"Yes," Gilbrannen said quietly, drawing out the final consonant like the warning of a snake. "They have already begun gathering outside the city, to the east. With your brother's help, they will be able to find and destroy Neraliel in short order. The D'harnir of the swamp are neither as well defended nor as carefully hidden as those of us in the north."

Niena looked at Gilbrannen, his emotionless voice making her nervous. "You sound like you don't care," she said.

"You heard correctly," Gilbrannen said coldly. "It was the sloppy handiwork of Neraliel's warriors which exposed us, so they will shoulder the risk. They must either stand against the Drüstanian troops and be wiped out, or evacuate and find a new home. Every enclave has been forced to do that numerous times throughout the years, including ours."

The callous perspective took Niena by surprise. "And if the hammer falls on them, Por'monir may go unnoticed?"

"You catch on quickly." Gilbrannen paced, and threw back the hood of his cloak. The moonlight caught his stony face, and his eyes betrayed an anger hiding beneath the surface. "When Neraliel is wiped out,

Pelendion will believe that is the end of the matter. Por'monir may have to wait another few generations for our goals, but we can begin again."

Niena frowned. That was it? The war was over? "Does that mean you'll let Papa go?"

Gilbrannen sighed, and drew a dagger from his belt. "I truly am sorry, but no. Both of you have seen far too much for that to ever be an option."

"What?" Niena exclaimed in horror. "But he lived here for two decades, and never even told his own children!" She backed up and glanced behind her, wondering how far she could run before Gilbrannen caught her, and now hoping that there was a patrol within earshot. "You could have trusted him."

It was too late to run. Gilbrannen lunged forward with the blade, and she slipped on the roof as she tried to dodge. She went down, coming to rest in the valley between two peaks of the roof. He caught her and held her down, cold steel on her neck.

"Wait!" she choked out, desperate. "I—I haven't told you everything."

Gilbrannen stopped, his weight on her easing but still allowing her no room to move. "You have one minute. What else do you have for me?"

Niena wasted no more time. "I attended a banquet at the palace, in my brother's honor. I spoke with a scientist and inventor from Ash'kiram, a close friend of the jarl named Shi'ev. He said he is working on something to counter your magic spells."

Gilbrannen's eyes widened. "How is that possible?"

"I don't know," Niena said, her words tumbling over themselves. "He said that sounds were the only thing capable of affecting the human mind that way, to control their thoughts. Or something like that—I can't remember precisely." Niena felt the dampness of the rooftop seeping through her clothes and tried to keep her fear from showing in her face. Surely that had to be good information. "Is he right?"

Gilbrannen was silent, his eyes darting this way and that. He got up, sheathed his blade, and looked up at the palace across the square again. "We cannot take the chance that he is," he said, more to himself than her. "This can work to our advantage, if we move fast."

Niena stood up and wiped herself off, unsure if she should run or let things play out. "What are you talking about?"

"I believed that our plan to fracture the country and foment insurrection had become impossible, but there may still be a way forward. Can you remember the layout of the palace?"

Niena frowned, not seeing his angle. "Generally, but why?"

"In sending two thousand troops to Neraliel, Pelendion has left the front door wide open," Gilbrannen reasoned with a small laugh. "Celwaith Tor stands more vulnerable than even before all of this started. A coordinated incursion into the palace to assassinate the king and plant evidence of the Crownless could topple the kingdom into anarchy, and if we manage to steal or destroy these experiments you mentioned, all the better."

It all made sense now, Niena saw. The resulting power vacuum would completely take pressure off the D'harnir and allow them to continue this war of attrition a little longer without starting from scratch. With a citizen militia this strong, and Pelendion having no son, there was a heavy chance of a coup wresting power away from the king's two younger brothers, or even a total breakdown into regional factions vying for supremacy.

"Meet me on this spot in another two days, at midnight," Gilbrannen instructed as he raised his hood and turned to leave. "The army will be occupied with Neraliel at least that long."

"Wait," Niena called after him. "You almost kill me and expect me to keep helping you with your—crusade? I'm not doing a thing for you until I know that Papa is still alive!"

"You hear that?" a muffled voice came from the streets below. "There's someone skulking about, up in the square."

Gilbrannen dropped into a crouch and motioned for Niena to do the same. She obliged, peeking cautiously over the edge. Two guards circled the corner of the building and examined the alleyway directly below.

"I coulda sworn there was someone here," the first said.

"I didn't hear anything." The second shrugged, then continued on. The first reluctantly followed. "All these night shifts are turning you loopy."

"Loopy? Why I oughta … My mum always said I had ears like a Mersien shale-hawk …"

When they had passed by, Gilbrannen turned back to her with a tense smile. "All right," he whispered, sarcasm bleeding into his voice. "Not that it should matter, but I give you my word that your father is still alive. Is that good enough for you?"

Niena realized how stupid she must have sounded. There was no way to prove anything all this way from Por'monir in two days. She sighed in resignation. "It will have to be."

"Two days," Gilbrannen reminded her. "Until then, what is it you humans say? May the winds keep you aloft."

"No one says that anymore," Niena corrected him, but he had already vanished.

TWENTY-THREE

Whenever guilt lingers, and regret seizes
the soul, remember: it is never too late to
make the next right choice.
— Codes of Binding 2.18

IT'S ALMOST LIKE A *reunion*, Tollan thought with a heaviness in his chest. The vast majority of the two thousand men they led into the marshes were fellow recruits from their days together in the western foothills. Many familiar faces surrounded him, or else faces that merely seemed familiar from waiting in line at the mess tent. But two faces that should have been present were not.

Tollan crested the last rise before they entered the lowlands and looked back from his horse to see how far the trail of armed and armored men extended behind him. It stretched out until he couldn't see where it stopped, with the columns covering the road like flies on carrion. Even with how endless the procession seemed, it was small compared to when he had stood before the entire population of Celwaith Tor with the king.

That moment had been one of immense guilt for Tollan. The people now saw him as the hero, the one to unmask their true enemies. And maybe he was, but he shouldn't be honored for it. He had just been lucky enough to survive, while leaving his men behind.

If he hadn't been so single-minded of the mission, or if he had acted faster or with more surety, maybe Thaxon would still be with them today to bring down fire and brimstone on the elves. And if not Thaxon, then Ruger.

No, Tollan reminded himself. They all would have died if he stayed, and there would have been no traces left to report. The elves were simply too powerful for his small group of soldiers to fight off.

They would pay for what they had done.

He would make them pay.

"Lieutenant," the general said, shaking him from his reverie.

"Yes, sir?" Tollan asked.

"The vegetation is quite thick in the deep marsh. It will be difficult for us to keep formation as we proceed. Once we reach Outpost Heron, I will be sending a whole column forward to Cape Vrosingr to retrieve our firearms. I'd like you to take a few men to scout ahead and confirm our entry point for when they return."

Tollan frowned. If the elves had snipers in the trees like last time, they could all lose their horses if not their lives by the time they even saw them. For that matter, this entire operation was a gamble based more in holding sway over the public opinion than sound military strategy, so it would be better to continue marching the army toward the objective rather than waiting. The rifles didn't provide that much more of an edge over crossbows, especially in the swamp's close quarters. But Tollan didn't dare ask any questions of that sort. "Aye, General, you can count on me. If we encounter resistance, should we turn back immediately?"

Verune set his jaw. "Yes, there's no need to be heroic this time, Cresthaven. Come back with word as soon as you see signs of the enemy."

"Sir, yes, sir," Tollan said, secretly resenting the reference to his heroism. He hadn't been a hero—he had been scared.

A few hours later, the frame of Outpost Heron's rebuilt watchtower came into view, and there was enough solid ground for the militia to set up camp. The lead column pressed on in hopes to reach Cape Vrosingr shortly after dark if they kept up a steady marching pace.

Tollan rounded up a few other men on horseback and set off ahead as ordered, quickly outpacing the column. It was late afternoon and the sun had burned through more of the humid mist thickening the air, so visibility would be more improved than if they waited until morning.

The covered wagon, or what was left of it, had been shifted off into the ditch at the side of the road. There was no sign of the second horse carcass, so Tollan assumed predators had dragged it into the murky depths of the trees. Tollan pulled the group up short and proceeded slowly, scanning the branches for any sign of movement. Nothing.

"What, eh, exactly are we lookin' for, Lieutenant?" one of the scouts under his command asked through his missing teeth. His name was Marlaph Stemson, and Tollan had actually met the man before when he was driving Tollan's wagon of recruits to training. Marlaph found it knee-slapping hilarious that such a young boy was already promoted to lieutenant when he had been a scout in the army since before the Pamarthen raids.

"We should have been attacked by now," Tollan said suspiciously, hopping down from his horse and looking deeper into the trees on the north side of the road. "Unless they have multiple ambush points set up."

"Or, beggin' yer pardon, sir, maybe we don't have anythin' they want," Marlaph said.

"Possibly," Tollan said, circling a few of the closest trees and staring up into the branches, searching for the platforms he had seen before. Dread walked an involuntary shiver up his back, but he chalked it up to standing in the place where his best friend died. "They have nothing to gain from killing us now. We're not worth the effort."

He strayed a little further back in the treeline, being careful to avoid the pools of standing water and swatting at flies that came too close to his face. He didn't see anything out of the ordinary, even after he spotted one of the elven platforms affixed to the side of a trunk. It was cleverly camouflaged, but now that he had seen one, he could follow the network of hand and footholds that crisscrossed the canopy. Still no trace of movement.

"Let's keep going for another mile or so, then head back," Tollan ordered, checking his pocket watch for the time. He pulled a busted wheel from the wagon and leaned it against the tree to mark the entry point. "We ought to be able to trace a path to their stronghold and return by dark."

They couldn't take their horses into the swamp, so they tied the halters to trees and continued on foot. As Tollan and the others weaved back and forth through the trees, traversing the roots and portions of solid ground, his sense of dread grew. It was too quiet, even with all the noises of the swamp around them. He expected an attack at any moment, the crack of a stolen rifle from each successive platform they found.

The trail ran cold for a moment, and Tollan searched around for another tree with suspiciously-shaped branches or platforms, and saw none. His heart sank, worrying that there might not be a larger stronghold here, and rubbed his aching neck as he peered upwards.

Marlaph coughed surreptitiously from beside him. "Might wanna be lookin' at the ground now, Lieutenant."

Tollan examined the swamp beneath their feet. It was still the same sporadic pools of standing water, the same buzzing flies and knobby tree roots, with even the most solid ground causing the scouts to sink to their ankles in mud. But then he saw it, and smacked himself in the forehead.

There was an oddly paved path, winding away like a massive snake among the trees to the northeast. It looked so natural that only someone searching for irregularities would have spotted it, because it was land left entirely unbroken by pools or obstacles. He tested his weight, and it held.

"This way, men," Tollan called, and they proceeded at a much faster pace along the path.

We're walking straight into a trap, Tollan thought after more than a mile, but they continued forward. He checked his watch again, knowing they would be stuck out here after dark if they didn't turn back in another half hour at most.

Not five hundred yards later, the path ended at a large body of water, maybe thirty yards across at the narrowest point, with the only way across being a thick wooden bridge.

Tollan squinted into the mist, and saw what he could only describe as walls and battlements grown out of tightly-knit trees and vines. They were of similar construction to the sniper platforms back near the main road, but much, much larger. That's when Tollan realized: the structures hadn't been built and hidden, they had been *grown* perfectly for such use, perhaps over hundreds of years.

But of course, Tollan thought wryly. *The elves can control animals—why not plants, as well?*

Where the bridge ended, the large structure was split down the middle by the huge, arching bows of two sycamore trees, larger than any he had ever seen. The gap between them yawned open like a mouth, welcoming any visitors inward to their fates.

But still there was no whistle of arrows, no crack of rifles, and no trancheons rising to drag them below the still waters.

"This is where we stop for today," Tollan told the others. "It'll be dark soon. Let's report back to the general."

The group turned and retraced their steps toward the main road. More than once, Tollan thought the path had changed, but they returned without incident. The horses seemed as relieved to see the outpost as the men riding them.

"That would be the place we're looking for," General Verune said when Tollan and the other scouts had described it in detail. "Strange that you didn't meet any resistance. I'm starting to think this was a wild felinx chase after all, Lieutenant."

Tollan raised an eyebrow. "You mean we're too late? They've already packed up and left?"

Verune's mustache shifted one way, then the other. "Possibly. I don't think they would have let you come so close to their stronghold if they hadn't, but perhaps they are luring in more of our troops before they spring the trap. At any rate, find yourself a place to sleep. We march tomorrow, as soon as Column Eight returns with our weapons."

Tollan tossed and turned that night, and it wasn't because of Marlaph's snoring. His unease from earlier had never lessened, and the sounds of the swamp ensured that he was tormented by fitful dreams of trancheons rising from the mud around him. Lying on the mushy ground around Outpost Heron gave him a physical chill he hadn't felt since the first few nights of basic training, but this time he didn't have Thaxon's company and fire-making skills to help. The next day would bring relief to both discomforts in one way or another, but the only way through was pain.

THE ARMY ROSE AROUND dawn from their precarious sleeping positions around the outpost and along the road. They eventually fell into a casual formation, waiting for the command to march or for rifles to be distributed. No one had any food or drink beyond what they had the foresight to bring with them, but Tollan did. Remembering what Thaxon had once done for him, Tollan had pilfered a bagful of dried meat from the palace pantry. He subtly slipped a couple pieces to men who he thought might need it, on the condition they didn't let word get out.

It was almost 10-o-clock by Tollan's watch when Column Eight returned with their firearms, enough to arm about a quarter of the present soldiers. By noon, the first ranks of men had left the road and begun cautiously circumventing the trees and dank muddy pools, with Tollan leading the way.

The lead column's corporal was a man of about thirty, who insisted that he be present in the first rank. If they were going to be ambushed, Corporal Taftley Pindarson wanted to be in the thick of it with everyone. General Verune, by contrast, traveled several columns back in the formation among the horses and artillery, as a more navigable path through the swamp was cleared by felling trees.

It proved to be a warm and dry day, which made visibility much better than the previous evening but still limited to less than fifty feet. But it was now possible for even the least observant soldier to follow the elven trails among the huge tree branches. There was no sign of movement, but that didn't mean the elves weren't lurking nearby.

The men stayed on alert for trancheons, checking each step to make sure they weren't about to disturb a giant man-eating toad, but again, there was nothing. Hundreds followed in Tollan's footsteps, attempting to retain their formation as best as possible amid the trees and uneven ground.

At last, they reached the elven sycamore gate, and the column of soldiers under Pindarson's command lined up in front of the wooden bridge, waiting for the rest of the columns to catch up. Once Verune arrived with the artillery, he ordered the advance but held Tollan back to observe.

"Be on your guard," Tollan warned Pindarson's men as they proceeded out across the still water. The swamp was eerily quiet, apart from peepers and bugs. A second column of soldiers lined the bank, rifles pointing across the water to cover Pindarson if necessary. Who knew what lurked in the water on either side of the bridge . . .

Tollan was still staring at the lack of ripples below when the first explosion hit, sending up a fireball just as the first ranks reached the midway point of the bridge. Soldiers flew into the air, and parts of the bridge began to crumble into the water underneath the others.

"Back to the shore!" Marlaph called, his voice cracking, but they had already begun to flee without his exclamation.

Tollan expected a full-on defensive volley of bullets and arrows from behind the walls, but none came. The surviving men that had fallen into the water climbed back up on the splintered bridge rather than being sucked to the depths by the tongues of a horde of trancheons. It seemed the elves had left their abundant supply of black powder to defend their stronghold on their behalf.

What remained of Corporal Pindarson's corpse was fished out of the water, and Tollan felt sick to his stomach. He performed a head count once ranks had been closed back on solid ground, and found the column had lost eight men to the explosion, putting their column's number at sixty-four. Once that was done, he hurried back to the senior officers.

"What was that?" Verune barked.

"The place appears to be set with traps, sir," Tollan said. "The bridge is out, and we've lost Corporal Pindarson. I still have not seen any movement inside the walls either—my gut tells me they're gone, and they want us to lose a lot of men picking through whatever they left behind."

"Understood, Lieutenant," Verune said. "Unfortunately, we still need to press on. They must have left some trace behind of where they fled."

Colonel Raulin Reeds spoke up from behind Verune. "I will send a few men around the perimeter of this lake. Perhaps there's another safer way in."

"What do you want me to do, sirs?" Tollan asked.

"Finish what we came for, Cresthaven," Verune said as if it was obvious. He handed Tollan a whalebone whistle, like the one Corporal Crandas had used during training to issue quick orders. "Take command of the column and forge ahead. Find a way to cross that bridge and watch your step from here on out. Bring back anything of value, and if there's anyone left inside, kill or gag them. No more enchantments."

"Sir, yes, sir," Tollan said, in awe that he was being given command of a whole column, even temporarily. He didn't deserve to lead after what happened to his men last time, but he was not about to protest the general's orders. Before returning to the front, he asked a few of the rear columns to cut down trees and bring them up to cross the gap in the bridge.

It wasn't long until the column was on the move again. Tollan winced with each new plank they trod upon, expecting another bomb to go off at any moment. But they arrived on the other shore safely.

The sycamore gates offered little resistance to their battering ram, and Tollan's column fanned out across the settlement. Tollan looked around with suspicion, rifle at the ready, trying to keep the majority of his men in view at all times. The place was smaller than he had expected, but death could be waiting around any corner.

Most of the interior of the stronghold was not military in function. The buildings mostly appeared to be simple and functional domiciles, though Tollan had never seen anything like them before. Built on stilts about a foot off the soft ground, their roofs curved inwards to slough all the water off and through a gutter into rain barrels on each side. In a climate this dense it could efficiently supply all of a family's clean water needs.

Tollan noted that the barrels next to the smaller houses approached full, and those next to the larger buildings were full to overflowing, suggesting none of them had been used in several days at the least.

Another explosion rocked the ground, and a soldier tumbled out the door of a small house before the whole thing collapsed. Tollan rushed to his side, checking for injuries as others gathered around. "Are you all right? What's your name?"

The man coughed and groaned, and Tollan could see the man was almost as young as he was despite being covered in soot. "I think so, just dazed. I'm Yodric. Yodric Kjorfalk, sir."

Tollan was relieved. "What happened in there?"

"The charge was delayed and went off in the rafters—there was a tripwire on the ground when I went in."

"Was there anything inside that looked important?" Tollan asked.

"No, only furniture."

Tollan helped Yodric to his feet in the muck before turning to address the rest of his company. "You hear that? No one takes a step inside one of these structures without assuming it's rigged to blow."

"Lieutenant!" Marlaph shouted from up ahead. "You'd better come take a look at this."

Tollan's stomach dropped into his boots when he came around the corner. There, in front of a large building in the center of the enclave, five stakes stuck into the ground, and atop those stakes were impaled five decomposing bodies wearing Drüstanian garb. A single word was painted on each of their yellow tunics in blood, spelling out the phrase "and so to all men."

The highest and middle corpse bore the gaunt, slack-jawed face of Ruger.

Tollan turned away and retched.

"Aye, 'tis not a pretty sight," Marlaph said with reverence, coming closer. "Were these yours, from the last time you came out here?"

Tollan nodded, but his throat seized up with another bout of bile.

"No worries, lad. All of yous are too young to be goin' through this sort of thing." Marlaph offered his water skin. "Fer that matter, so am I."

With a grateful nod, Tollan accepted the water and quieted his upset stomach. "Take them down and make sure they're buried in honor," he said when he could bring himself to speak again.

There was no sign of the other seven members of his team, Thaxon, or the others that had been devoured by trancheons. He wasn't sure whether Ruger and the others had been dragged to this place alive and then killed, or if their bodies had been brought here merely to taunt the army when it arrived. Either way, it didn't matter. These men had been entrusted to him, and he had abandoned them to rot in the hands of their enemies.

He swallowed back another wave of nausea.

If the Drüstanians had been alive when brought to the elven settlement, and if they still had their wits about them, they might have left some sort of sign or message where their captors were headed.

However, Tollan realized with a chill, any race of people who could bewitch others and steal their will might not have any use for detaining their prisoners. They might simply put the soldiers to work, and they would never be able to fight back or escape their mental shackles until they had outlived their usefulness.

He enlisted the aid of Yodric and Marlaph to help him check out the larger, stockier building behind the gruesome display. Tollan suspected any sort of brig or prison might logically sit in the center of the settlement, to make escape less of a possibility.

Tollan unlatched the door and carefully pushed it open with his sword, staying as far away from the structure as possible to dive out of the way should an explosion collapse part of the building. Nothing happened, and he motioned for the two men to follow him inside. The interior was divided up into three main rooms and a corridor which ran the width of all of them.

"Split up," Tollan ordered, assigning them each a room. "I'll take the one on the end. Be careful."

The chamber he stepped into had the distinct smell of rotten eggs, signifying sulfur. A long table filled the bulk of the room, and a barrel near the door had traces of saltpeter. *This must be where they mix their black powder,* Tollan thought. He knew saltpeter could be distilled from urine from a book he had read on the discovery of black powder, but where could swamp-bound elves get their hands on an element like sulfur? A nearby hot spring?

He never had the chance to answer the question, as the entire structure shook with a series of loud bangs starting from the opposite end of the building. Another trap had been triggered.

"Get out now!" Tollan called to Yodric and Marlaph. The walls groaned around him, and he didn't think he could make it to the door.

He fumbled at the window latch, unhooking it from the wall as he felt the floor start to give way beneath him. He dove through the opening and tucked under into a roll as he hit the marshy ground. The whole structure fell in his direction and would have crushed him if he had tarried a second longer.

The building was on fire, engulfed from the opposite end by black smoke and the scent of powder. Tollan stumbled to his feet and saw Yodric on his knees and covered in mud, staring at the blaze.

"He was still in there," Yodric said in horror.

Tollan felt a surge of energy course through him. He would not let his men down, not this time. He waded into the flames, reaching down with his gloves to shift burning pieces of rubble aside. His father's forge had been hotter, he thought with a grin.

Tollan saw some rubble shift in front of him, and a hand poked out. Now Yodric was with him, and they lifted the piece of roof and pulled Marlaph out from under it. The older man yelped due to his blackened burns and a clearly broken leg, but he was alive.

They set the old tracker down several yards away. "I was thinkin' it was all over fer me," Marlaph huffed out. "Couldn't breathe, so hot . . ."

"Hush now," Tollan ordered. "You'll be all right." He reached around his neck for the tiny whalebone whistle, and blew three long notes to recall the others.

"What are you doing?" Yodric asked.

"There's nothing here," Tollan said in annoyance. "There's no point in risking all our lives over this. The elves left nothing behind for us." It was true, after all. If every building had been picked as clean as these, there was no reason to assume they would find anything.

Tollan wouldn't have been surprised if the elves had cleared out immediately after attacking his decoy supply shipment. The elves had seen him escape with one of their own, and must have known that he would report straight back and bring the hammer down on them.

Marlaph coughed, and the spit from his mouth was black. "The general's not goin' to like that. We haven't found anythin' useful."

Tollan narrowed his eyes. He recalled the lesson Corporal Crandas had once taught him, and decided that sometimes it was better to refuse carrying the pail of water, as long as it saved lives. "Who says we haven't?"

In a few minutes, after the column had gathered and a stretcher had been fashioned for Marlaph, they shipped out and crossed the bridge to rejoin the rest of the army. The bodies of Ruger and the others were gathered along the bank of the lake to give them a proper burial, along with Corporal Pindarson and the others lost that day.

"What have you found?" General Verune asked, watching as the last few trees were chopped down to make way for the fire mortars.

Tollan saluted, trying his best not to do so halfheartedly. "Nothing here, sir. Found some evidence that the elves assemble their own black powder, but an explosive trap destroyed all of it."

"Any evidence of where they could have gone?" Verune asked.

Tollan shook his head. "Every building was picked clean. These creatures could not have remained hidden from us for hundreds of years if they weren't thorough. But logically, they could only have gone one direction: north." He had made up that last part, but they couldn't prove him wrong.

"Impossible," Colonel Reeds said harshly. "My men have circled the lake twice and found no trace of a trail northward. Besides, there is nothing in that direction except for Spinewood Forest—and that place is thick with manticores."

Verune pursed his lips, nodding gravely. "These swamps were once thick with trancheons, but we haven't seen even one today. A little odd, don't you think?"

Tollan smiled. The general bought it.

"No, Colonel," Verune said. "They would have had to go north as the lieutenant said, because to the east, west, and south is human civilization. But for us to proceed north without a trail would be foolhardy. What were your losses, Lieutenant?" he asked Tollan.

"Nine, sir, counting Corporal Pindarson," Tollan answered. "The other bodies were from my prior mission. The elves had propped them up as a warning."

"Regrettable," Verune said, scowling at the sycamore gates across the water. "I dislike bringing the king bad news. However, if our enemies return here, we can ensure they think twice about attacking us."

Tollan didn't want to mention that the elves likely didn't intend to return here, or else they wouldn't have made the place a death trap. He might be willing to lie to General Verune, but making the man look stupid would not do him any favors.

"Are the mortars in position?" Verune turned to ask Colonel Senn.

"They are, and awaiting your order," Senn said.

"Good. Melt that island into the lake."

Tollan watched as the mortars exploded in the air over the settlement, raining down liquid fire that would keep burning hot for days even in the wet conditions. Occasional violent explosions sounded across the marsh as the oil came into contact with unexploded traps. There would be nothing left but mud and ash when they were through.

When Tollan finally turned homeward, the army was several souls larger than if he had elected to scour the village as thoroughly as he was ordered. And he knew that Thaxon would have approved of his choice, slightly dishonest though it was.

He might have even offered to steal a bottle of wine to celebrate.

TWENTY-FOUR

Bloodshed rips open the heart of one enemy but hardens all others against you. Do not seek out violence, but work instead for the common defense of the innocent.

— *Codes of Entreaty 4.13-14*

NIENA COULD NOT BELIEVE what she was about to do. Two months ago, it would have been utterly unthinkable. But there had been many impossible things crammed into those two months, so what was one more? Better to wind up branded a traitor to the crown and a terrorist than live with the thought of her father dying in a D'harnin prison due to her actions.

She hiked up the intentionally dirtied skirts on the dress that she had worn to the banquet, and mentally crossed her fingers. This time she had done up her hair, so she looked properly posh, but she had refrained from wearing the constricting corset. If it was the same pair of guards that had been at the palace doors two nights ago, and they recognized her, the charade would all be over quickly anyway.

A quick, deep exhale to steel herself, and the performance was on.

Niena screamed and rushed across the square, throwing in a stumble here and there for good measure. "Help! Guards! You have to help me," she begged, landing in a pitiful heap a few paces in front of them.

The two guards had already drawn their weapons. One of them carefully approached her with an outstretched hand but his sword still at the ready. "What's the trouble, miss? It's after curfew."

Okay, so they were cautious, but willing to give Niena the benefit of the doubt. She could work with that.

"I've been attacked," she gasped, pointing back the way she had come in her best imitation of a traumatized but spoiled rich girl. "Someone broke into my room and tried to have his way with me!" She conjured a few tears, doing her best to look helpless in her sodden dress that had fallen off one shoulder.

The guards bought it. "Now, now, you're all right with us, miss," the second one said, lowering his blade and reaching for his keys. "Bloody army had to go off and leave us understaffed again. This is patrol's work," he muttered under his breath as he locked the palace gate.

The first guard offered his hand again to help her up, and she took it. "I'm Distern, and that's Burtram. Why don't you take us back that way, and we'll see if we can spot him?" he asked, letting her lean on him for support.

Niena clutched at his arm, then worried that she was being a little too dramatic. But she was committed to the role. "No, no . . . I can't go back there!"

"Not to worry, miss," Distern said. "We'll protect you."

"That's right." Burtram nodded, an obviously fake smile plastered on his face. "Now, give us a few more details while we walk back to your place, anything you can remember of him."

Niena made up things as she went, knowing they wouldn't make it much farther than the edge of the square. As she described the crooked nose of her fictitious assailant, half a dozen cloaked figures dropped out of the shadows and mobbed the guards from behind.

Distern and Burtram never had a chance. The elves slit their throats and dragged them aside before the blood could pool in the middle of the street.

Her mouth agape, Niena was livid. She yanked the shoulder of her dress back up and almost tripped on her hem going after them. "Gilbrannen," she hissed. "You didn't say you would kill them!"

The elven terrorist's voice came not from any of the six looting the bodies, but rather from right behind her. "No, I did not."

She whirled, and saw another six cloaked forms behind Gilbrannen's own extremely tall stature. All of them dressed in dingy blacks and browns, meant to blend in with the shadows or appear as vagabonds in the streets if they did happen to be spotted.

"What did you think we were doing to do?" Gilbrannen asked, a hard edge to his voice. "Serve them tea and ask nicely to see the king?"

Niena looked at him for a moment in disgust. "I thought you would put them to sleep, or bewitch them, or whatever it is you do."

Gilbrannen smirked, and raised a hand to catch the keys to the palace gates tossed to him by one of the assassins. "That does not always work as well as you might think, and it would require someone to stay behind to maintain control over them. It would be a distraction and a liability to this mission, not an asset."

"But you—"

"This is what warfare looks like," Gilbrannen said with a careless shrug. "Get used to it."

Niena watched as the elves tossed the dead guards over the courtyard battlements. The bodies tumbled down the steeper side of the tor and landed on an outcropping with the faraway clatter of armor.

A sickening thought crossed her mind. If she succeeded in saving her father from the clutches of the D'harnir, how many others would have died in his stead because she had lied to them? "I'm so sorry," she whispered after the guards, knowing they could no longer hear her.

"Time to move," Gilbrannen said to her as the others started across the courtyard toward the palace.

Niena swallowed. "You wanted into the keep. I got you in. You know the basic layout and where to go—you don't need me."

"False. You know I trust you implicitly," Gilbrannen said with a note of sarcasm, "but if I did not know better, I might suspect you of arranging a trap for us. You will take us straight to the king, and whatever happens to us along the way will happen to you, as well."

Niena sighed. She wished she could have planned out something as elaborate as Gilbrannen implied, but again, she was reminded of how much she was out of her depth.

Glancing between Gilbrannen's companions, she realized abruptly that one was missing. "Where's Silmon?" she asked.

"I sent him back to Por'monir to report on recent developments," Gilbrannen said dismissively. "Shilvand will want to know."

Niena almost tripped on her hem again as they entered the palace grounds, and she decided that there was no point anymore. Hoping the Denvalds never missed the dress, she took hold of one of the green seams below her waist and ripped. She had worn her brown breeches underneath, and they contrasted starkly with the remnants of the elegant dress around her upper arms and middle.

"Functional. I like it," Gilbrannen observed, and she refused to answer out of spite. He offered a spare cloak he must have brought for her to better conceal her identity. "Lead the way."

Niena snatched it from him and threw the scratchy cloth around her shoulders. She took her coiffed hair down and pulled up the hood, hoping she would visibly blend in with the others. She toyed with the idea of doing something that would get the whole group captured, but realized that her only alibi would depend on Pelendion's guards believing she was under the elves' magical influence. There was also no guarantee that one of the D'harnir wouldn't escape back to Por'monir with word of her betrayal.

No. For her, the only way out was in.

"Not the main doors. Too many guards, and eyes," Niena said, guiding them along the shadows at the edge of the courtyard. She pointed at the smaller, less ornate door off to the side, hidden among the arches. "Servants' entrance," she elaborated.

"Where is the armory from here?" Gilbrannen asked before they proceeded.

"No idea," Niena replied. "They didn't exactly give us a tour of the place. Likely ground floor, close to wherever the royal garrison is."

Gilbrannen motioned for one of the others to split off and look for it. "See if you can make trouble. Find something to blow up as a distraction for our escape."

He turned back, and led the remaining eleven elves up to the door, with Niena in the middle of them. On a three-count after listening at the keyhole, Gilbrannen lifted the latch and shoved the door open, startling a pair of guards who had just passed. The group of terrorists engulfed them before they could react, and another pair of bodies stained the ground.

Niena's conscience ached as she looked on in horror. What if one of these men had been Kasdan? All of them had lives of their own, dreams to chase, families to provide for, people that they loved and who loved them. And now that was all gone, in the swipe of a D'harnin blade.

But Gilbrannen wasn't slowing down, and he jerked his head in a prompting fashion to ask her for directions. Now that they had breached the palace, the hardest part of the plan began, and speed was of the essence. The faster they accomplished their deed, the easier it would be—at least for the elves, Niena thought with guilt.

Niena peeked around another corner, and found the servants' staircase. A lucky guess on her part, thinking logically about where the attendants might travel from the kitchens up to the dining halls and bedchambers. They went straight to the fourth and final landing, where the king's personal suite and presumably any executive offices might be.

This was uncharted territory now. Niena had no idea where anything else in the palace was or what they might find around the next corner. For all she knew, the king might sleep elsewhere and merely maintain the illusion of residence on the top floor.

But as soon as Gilbrannen cracked open the stairwell door, there was no going back.

Four of the elite kingsguard attacked immediately, having been far enough away from the door to get their weapons at the ready and charge. Though four on twelve was nowhere near a fair fight, the bottleneck of the corridor would be enough to keep things at a standoff in terms of strength.

One of the elves went down to a mean swipe of a battleaxe, and at that point Gilbrannen was done with the charade. Niena watched as he reached out with his free hand, whispered a few mysterious words in the ancient D'harna tongue, and cut down the guard as he stood there, dumbstruck by the spell. She backed into the stairwell and stayed out of the fray, eyes wide at the carnage.

The kingsguard saw the loss of their comrade and regrouped so as not to be divided and picked off. Before the elves could advance again, two of the knights had formed a blockade at the next junction with large ovoid shields they pulled from the wall that had appeared decorative until that moment. The other guard kept going, clearly intending to alert the rest of the palace to the incursion.

It was never going to happen. Two of the leading D'harnir cast spells of their own, stopping the defenders cold. It gave Gilbrannen the opportunity he needed to take out his bow—her father's bow, Niena now saw—and fire a shot through the center of the runner's back. The man crumpled to the richly-carpeted floor with a thud.

The elves were about to finish off the last two kingsguard, staring blankly back at them, when Gilbrannen held up a hand. "No."

Niena raised an eyebrow. There was not a chance Gilbrannen had decided to spare them without an ulterior motive.

"Someone must have heard us by now," the elven terrorist leader said in a harsh whisper. "Keep the guards on a tight leash—make our enemies kill them to get to us."

A strategically diabolical choice, Niena had to admit. Gilbrannen called for her, and she regretfully left her hiding place in the stairwell.

"Which way to the king's quarters?" he asked.

"You're asking me? All I knew was the stairs and the third floor, not the fourth." Niena stopped talking when she heard a sound from up ahead. A door had crashed shut, which meant they were about to have more company.

"What is the meaning of all this?" A man dressed primarily in a fluffy bathrobe came around the corner, cursing and rubbing his eyes at the end of the hall.

It was the jarl, Prince Anseldr, Niena realized in horror. "Some of us are ..." He broke off from his intended diatribe, and awoke instantly once he noted the elves and the dead body at his feet. With fear in his eyes, he bolted back the way he'd come.

Gilbrannen's aim proved to be just a hair off, and the jarl escaped around a corner, unharmed.

The entire party gave chase, the two enchanted kingsguard leading the way with their weapons drawn and their two magical handlers following behind to whisper spells into their mind. Judging purely by the guards' movements and expressions, Niena never would have suspected they were under a spell if she hadn't known—it was like they had switched sides without a second thought.

"Search the rooms, and cover the exits," Gilbrannen called, and a few D'harnir broke off to comply with the order. "No one gets off this floor alive. Especially Pelendion."

Their quarry was crafty, and had knocked down many end tables and armor stands in an attempt to slow down the pursuit. It puzzled Niena that Anseldr was running away from the stairs, clearly with a destination in mind.

Niena had a dreadful feeling in her gut that said this chase wasn't going to end well. Least of all for her.

Anseldr burst through a pair of double doors at the end of the last hallway, leading into a large room on the other side. Gilbrannen rushed the others, but the bewitched kingsguard failed to reach the doors before they closed. With a boom, they heard something large fall in front of the doors as a barricade.

"Bash it in," Gilbrannen ordered, and the elves and enchanted humans alike began hacking at the thick door. Two archers stood aside and covered the group, taking down another two kingsguard that had heard the commotion.

The wood was soft, meant for decoration, and splintered inward easily. The group of assassins rushed through the hole they had made and climbed over the toppled bookshelf Anseldr had left in the way.

Moonlight streamed in from the windows around the royal library's ceiling, the only light inside save for a scattering of candles that had burned low. But the illuminated scene proved to be so disturbing that Niena had to turn away.

On an operating table in the center of the room lay a single D'harnin body, splayed and tucked open with pins and pincers alongside all manner of cutting tools. The body was sapped of moisture from days of decay, but that didn't make it any less gruesome as every organ and orifice was open or plucked out. Anseldr stood on the other side of the table, behind Darakh Shi'ev, whose hand was poised over a strange clockwork contraption in a box.

"What … kind of … sick experiment is this?" Gilbrannen said, unable to restrain the rage that Niena could sense boiling off of him.

Shi'ev's eyes found Niena briefly as he scanned the group, and she thought for a terrible moment he might have recognized her even under the brown hood she wore.

Anseldr spoke up. "You kill our mothers and children," he said, "possess our soldiers to do your bidding, and you call *this* a sick experiment?"

"Kill them," Gilbrannen ordered through clenched teeth.

The two kingsguard, still under the sway of the trance, moved forward along either side of the operating table, about to hack the jarl and scientist into at least as many pieces as the dissected elven corpse. But Shi'ev had one last card to play, and in an instant, the knights had halted their advance.

Shi'ev turned a tiny lever on his invention, and a gear with rounded teeth came into contact with a tiny string that ran the length of the box. As it spun, the string vibrated against a drum skin and produced an unsettling rumble. It was loud and yet so low that Niena felt it more than heard it, and the sound throbbed rhythmically in time with the gear.

Niena felt a familiar sharp pain in her head, like something burrowing into her brain through her ear. She winced and pressed on her temple, a subdued reaction compared to the D'harnir writhing in agony beside her, almost unable to remain standing.

Niena looked again at the corpse on the operating table. Something moved inside it. Even the week-old dead flesh was responding to this … noise.

The two kingsguard shook themselves free from their magical bonds, looked around in confusion, and at once cut down the elves while they squirmed, defenseless against the sound. The screams piled on top of the low frequency rumble in a cacophony of horrors.

Niena frantically grabbed for Gilbrannen's arm and dragged him out the door, hoping no soldiers were coming up behind them. She didn't have a weapon, and Gilbrannen was in no condition to fight anyone off.

The D'harn stumbled, and she hauled him back to his feet. They retreated to the servants' stairwell, and the kingsguard took up the pursuit after dealing with the other elves. "Move!" she barked, and Gilbrannen regained strength the further they ran from Shi'ev's machine.

She wondered if the other elves had managed to kill the king, or if the horrible sound had carried far enough to stop the assassins as well.

Niena and Gilbrannen started down the staircase only to realize more soldiers were coming from below. Someone had raised the alarm.

She dragged Gilbrannen down to the third-floor landing and entered the main hall again, knowing it was better to be on familiar ground. If she was correct, after another couple turns, they would enter the reception hall and dining room from the other night.

Gilbrannen, now seeming to have his wits back, closed the door to the stairwell behind them and tipped over a strong oak storage cabinet to bar the way. "Worked well enough for them, ought to buy us some time."

"What was that thing?" Niena asked, even though she knew it had to be the result of Shi'ev's cryptic conversation with her during the banquet two days ago. He had done quick work.

Gilbrannen reclaimed the lead, brandishing Niena's father's bow in one hand and a throwing knife in the other. "Whatever it is, it's too powerful for us to fight against. We have to leave, now."

The main staircase, which Niena had climbed with Anise before meeting the king, was swarming with yet another group of soldiers coming from below. "Not that way," she said, pushing him on toward the other rooms. They had no way out and precious few places to hide.

A muted explosion shook the palace, hard, followed by a series of other smaller detonations.

"Hah," Gilbrannen said, trailing behind Niena. "The black powder stores in the armory—we were able to do what Silmon could not. That should keep them occupied."

Niena doubted there would be much structural damage. The stores would have been depleted by Tollan's militia on their way to engage Neraliel's defenses any day now. But if the charges started a fire, the palace could be engulfed in flames in short order, and the kingsguard would soon have more important concerns than chasing them.

Their hopes for a distraction were dashed when the kingsguard mounted the stairs and spotted them. Calling out for surrender, they drew swords and charged down the landing toward the two fugitives.

Niena huffed, and spat her disheveled hair out of her mouth. There was one last door before they would be caught, and she knew what was behind it. "In here," she called, and ducked into the familiar sitting room with the bay window. Gilbrannen followed, then helped her wedge a table and the couch against the door.

"What now?" Gilbrannen asked. "We are trapped."

"How quickly power can change hands," Niena retorted, thinking how ironic it was that they had put Anseldr in a similar position only minutes before. "At least we have a window."

Gilbrannen went over and looked down, seeing the abyss-like drop all the way to the lake at the base of the tor. "You can't be serious."

"Well . . ." Niena started to panic. "I had hoped there might be a ledge outside or something we could use."

The soldiers rattled the door from outside, and when it wouldn't budge they immediately went to work on breaking it down.

Gilbrannen eyed the window again, and the empty air beyond it. "Yeah, that would have been helpful. That is five hundred feet at best. We would die as soon as we hit the water. Unless . . ." He trailed off, throwing aside his dark cloak and rifling through a small pouch at his side.

"Unless what?" Niena prompted, throwing whatever decorative detritus she could find against the door. It wouldn't do much to stop them, but anything was better than nothing at this point. "What?"

"Got it," Gilbrannen said, and pulled out a small spool wrapped in something as fine as fishing line. "Spider silk rope."

There wasn't time to ask how the D'harnir had managed to harvest and weave spider silk into a rope, but the innate strength and elasticity of such a material would be useful. "You're sure that thread can hold both of us?"

"This could hold a full-grown female manticore, provided the strands do not fray as they stretch," he replied, quickly unwrapping the knotted end of the sticky cord. He took out his throwing knife and cut off a length of it before anchoring the rest to a shelf that could hold their combined weight.

An axe blade busted through the top of the door. "We're out of time," Niena said, backing away from the stack of furniture.

"Not yet," Gilbrannen said, and broke through the window's thick glass. A cold wind blew in, underscoring how much empty air lay below them. He knocked out the remaining pieces from the bottom of the frame and handed her the loose end of the rope. "Wrap this eight times around your arm and make sure you hang on to the end of it."

"Wait, I'm going first? I've never done this before," Niena protested.

"We are not climbing," he said.

"We're jumping? I thought you said that was a bad idea!"

"We were never *not* jumping, once you led us in here."

The door continued to splinter, torchlight spilling in through the holes. They had moments until capture if they didn't leave now.

Niena stood on the precipice, shivering as she clung tightly to the sticky string wrapped around her forearm. "I don't think I can do this," she murmured, her heart fluttering in fear.

"Fortunate you have me, then," Gilbrannen said, and grabbed the line right above her own hand. Just as the barricade they had constructed finally gave way, he shoved her off the ledge and dove out the window beside her.

INTERLUDE IV

Finding New Homes

c. 0 – 15 years after the Rift

WITH THE PASSING OF *time, more and more of the smaller D'harnin villages were discovered and wiped out, or forced to flee to other enclaves. Within five years of the Macula Society uprising, we heard stories of six other enclaves of the D'harnir scattered across the continent, ironically gathered in the most inhospitable of places for their own safety. Inhospitable, because despite the vicious predators and hard landscapes, it was preferable to going up against the armies of the king.*

Our own sanctuary, situated on the northern edge of the brooding Spinewood Forest, continued to grow. We called it Por'monir, combining the surnames of the first two families I was able to rescue from the clutches of the Macula Society. After the deaths of my cousin and a few others, the magic-wielders of the village came together and imbued aspects of their power in a totem that would irritate the manticores and keep them at a safe distance. I have no idea how it worked, and they refused to tell me, but all that mattered was the extraordinary results. Por'monir was safe, for a time.

When my father Ervan and the rest of the family arrived, we were all provided for and treated extraordinarily well; we had decided to give up all that we had to protect them, and they were grateful. But some D'harnir in the village attributed their newfound poverty to the faults of mankind as a whole rather than those of specific men. They mistrusted my father and me and gave us little charity in their hearts despite our attempts to live by their ways and follow the Mishenna.

It had been just over a decade of harvests when a trio of hunters stumbled across our perimeter. After so long in hiding, Por'monir's lookouts and wardcasters had become careless, and as a result the hunters came in full view of the village inhabitants. My father went out to meet them and convince them to stay as guests, but they refused him, knowing that there was still a large bounty for D'harnir posted by the king.

My father did not stop the hunters, but instead, he let them leave peaceably. He hoped that his actions might cause them to reconsider and not mention what they had seen, but many in Por'monir took it as a betrayal of the trustworthiness he had always shown to them. The king's warriors would not be long in coming once word of the hunters' story got out.

— Haron Geled, Last Scribe of the Union
27th of Hollyn, in the 48th year after the Rift

TWENTY-FIVE

*And from among the largest clan is
chosen an arbiter for the mediation of
disputes, one who is in honored standing.
This one must swear to impartiality, and
only a united Council has the power to
declare a violation.*

— *Codes of Binding 9.09-10*

"THE CRAFTSMANSHIP IS EXQUISITE, Temelia."

"Thank you, Arbiter, but the accolades should go to my mother," the D'harnin woman said graciously, but in a reserved manner befitting her respect of his station. "As you know, the Monir family has been weaving silk garments since the enclave was first founded. Our spiders spin only the finest threads, and my mother has guided them in the ancient fashion since she was a small girl."

Shilvand turned this way and that opposite the mirror, admiring the way the tunic shimmered in the morning light. It complemented his stark white hair precisely, and the cut was more than flattering. "Yes, but this time she has outdone herself. Why, it fits so well I barely feel as though I am wearing anything at all."

Temelia did not react to the comment beyond a slight tinge of color coming to her pale cheeks. He wondered if she fancied him, and wondered how he would feel if she did. His first wife had died from an incurable wasting disease, despite all the enclave's healers taking shifts for weeks, and he had never re-bonded after. Not because he didn't want to, but because balancing a life such as his was hard enough without worrying if a wife would discover sensitive information or reveal it to his enemies.

No, if he was ever to bond again, he would need a woman who he could trust implicitly not to betray the cause, and Temelia was a little too easy to read.

"I will tell my mother that you are pleased," Temelia said as her surreptitious blush faded away.

"Please do," Shilvand encouraged, then abandoned his reflection and turned back toward her. "What do I owe for such a stunning addition to my wardrobe? It must have taken weeks for the spiders to complete it."

Temelia waved in dismissal. "Not a thing, Arbiter. Consider it our thanks for leading our people so well these past ten years."

Shilvand found the gesture charming, but he wouldn't hear of it. "Oh, come now, surely I owe you something. Not everyone would agree that I have been a great judge of Por'monir."

Before she could reply, a series of shouts came from outside. Shilvand excused himself and rushed out to see the reason for the commotion. A member of his own Falir clan aggressively poked a finger in the chest of the tanner across the street. "Calm down, the both of you. What seems to be the trouble? You know the Codes of Entreaty say to work out your disagreements with understanding and quietness of voice."

Shilvand's kinsman, the young Hemilhet, smiled with relief at his presence. "Arbiter! Thank the Mishenna you are here. This man promised to sell me a goat skin for a quarter bushel of wheat not two days ago!"

"What an unashamed lie!" the tanner exclaimed, subduing his voice in volume but more than making up for it with his angry tone. "I promised no such thing. I said that I had sold one for that amount last week."

Shilvand held up a hand, silencing both of them. Instead of wading into the mess of accusations, he cut to the quick with two questions. "Have any goods changed hands yet?"

The two D'harnir failed to answer.

"Do you have any witnesses, or a written promise that he would sell you the skin for that amount?" Shilvand asked his kinsman.

Hemilhet reluctantly shook his head.

Shilvand pursed his lips. "Then as far as business is concerned, it is one's word against the other, and the negotiations have not been concluded. Hemilhet, you must accept the tanner's current price or make him a better offer, though I would not blame him for refusing your business at this point."

"Yes, Arbiter," Hemilhet said, respectfully but with some amount of anger still simmering beneath the surface.

The tanner nodded his thanks.

"Remember," Shilvand said in parting. "We are not like the humans and their need for conflict. They revere the wind, the most unpredictable of all things, while we found our lives on the Mishenna which never changes. We are capable of solving our problems in a way that is mutually beneficial, without being slaves to our base passions." He knew Hemilhet, as a member of his secret police, would understand far better than the tanner the truth of that statement. Hemilhet was still young, though, and burned with the spritely nature of youth.

The business transaction resumed with cooler heads, and Shilvand returned across the street to where Temelia stood watching him.

"You see?" she said, gesturing to the results of his intervention. "You show no favoritism, even to your own kinsman. You mediate fairly and see things clearly. Anyone who claims you are not a decent arbiter of Por'monir is jealous of you."

Shilvand sighed. His enemies were suspicious of his special division of the Protectors, the Dast'rel, and their activity around the lower levels of the Hall of Meeting. But as long as there were enough people like Temelia who trusted his vision for Por'monir, there was still hope. "I appreciate that, but as our enclave continues to grow and prosper, I am afraid that conflicts will also become more and more common."

Temelia shrugged. "More people, more opportunities to aggravate each other's nerves. But we are prospering, and all thanks to you."

Shilvand smiled at her. She saw things precisely as he wanted her to see them, without the ugliness strewn throughout the rest of the world. It was the innocence of his people that he wanted to protect most of all. "I will make sure to bring a few quail hens by here tomorrow, as thanks for your family's time and this wonderful tunic."

"That is not necessary," Temelia reassured him. "Just keep doing what you do best—making peace."

A D'harn in a dark blue cloak rushed up, and Shilvand recognized him as one of his own Dast'rel. He should have been posted in the underground caverns, not above in the streets. "Arbiter, please come with me," the soldier said. "An urgent matter requires your attention."

Shilvand met Temelia's eyes with a strained smile. "As you say, an arbiter's work is never done. Be well."

He followed the blue-cloaked figure up the hill toward the Hall of Meeting, and once they were out of earshot, the soldier gave him more details. Shilvand picked up the pace with renewed vigor, incensed at such an untoward development in his plans.

Silmon had returned from the forward outpost.

SHILVAND'S MOOD CLOUDED OVER in moments. Silmon tried, diplomatically, to relate the events that had led to Gilbrannen's decision to storm the palace, but there was no escaping the fact that the D'harnin plot to collapse human society had been disastrously bungled.

Setbacks were to be expected, but in this case, desperation had caused the worst kind of incompetence.

"So, let me see if I can wrap my mind around how your 'simple mistake,' as you call it, has affected us," Shilvand said with a malicious sarcasm coating his voice. "Instead of abandoning your infiltration plan once one of your targets died, you allowed one of the gatehouse guards to see through your disguise and trace the wagon back to where it was attacked.

"Instead of fading back into the swamps as would have been prudent, Neraliel's warriors forced a pitched battle where the enemy escaped with a D'harnin body as proof of our existence.

"Instead of cutting our losses and biding our time once more until a better opportunity in the future, Gilbrannen has now gone into the lion's den on the dishonorable word of Voster's daughter.

"And finally, instead of waiting a day or two to report the outcome of this careless assault, you travel almost a week just to stand here and tell me that if Gilbrannen has been lost, it is far too late to do anything about it?"

Silmon stared blankly, his lack of reaction showing either that he was too stupid to understand what had happened or that he had already resigned himself to his fate. "As succinct a summary as could be given, Arbiter, with one small change. Gilbrannen demoted me upon his arrival, so I did not have the authority to defy his orders and wait. He said that, regardless of the outcome, he would be returning home as quickly as possible."

Shilvand sighed. He understood Gilbrannen's thinking; an assassination attempt on the king was perhaps the only way to salvage the dire situation. But despite his fondness for the lad, such brashness had the possibility to doom them all. "You attempt to shirk blame. Unfortunately, you are still the only one within reach of my disappointment. His demotion stands. You will be relegated back within the walls of Por'monir until such time as you prove yourself worthy again. I only hope to be so lenient with Gilbrannen when he returns. Report to the Dast'rel overseers for your duties."

"Yes, Arbiter." Silmon bowed. He turned and fled out the door of the private chambers.

Shilvand watched him go, unsure of the enclave's next move.

There was one saving grace. Most of the enclave knew nothing of the larger picture. He shouldered the responsibility for the conflict so that most of his people could live in peaceful ignorance. But now, unless Gilbrannen succeeded in doing away with King Pelendion, all that the Dast'rel had been working toward for the past decade could be erased.

He was the arbiter of Por'monir. It was his job to think of alternatives.

Pushing down on the ornate armrests of his chair, Shilvand stood. He needed to work out his frustrations by finally paying his brother-in-law a visit. And after that, he would consider ways to turn these failures to the enclave's benefit.

He rarely descended into the caverns anymore. There usually wasn't a need, and being publicly active in the community proved more beneficial to his plans anyway. If he was seen doing good and interacting with the many people of the enclave, his rulings would be more respected for it. In addition, his actions provided the perfect cover for the Dast'rel to carry out their duties without too many questions from the populace.

After following the curving stairs deeper underground, the Dast'rel agents on duty offered to escort him, but he waved them back to their positions. He could find his own way, even though it was an annoying number of turns in the dim light of the blue lanterns before he finally arrived outside of the prisoner's cell.

"Hello, Voster."

The man inside, who had been leaning against the rough stone wall with his eyes closed, jerked awake. His eyes were wild, his beard unkempt, his body gaunt and malnourished instead of strong and full. After long weeks of eating and drinking nothing but the minimum a human could endure, Voster's physical strength had waned to where Shilvand had nothing to fear.

But the human had clung to his wits and his hope with the stubborn persistence of a manticore. "I wondered ..." Voster said, his voice creaking out alongside a sickly cough, "... when you would show up. Where is Niena? Is she safe?"

Shilvand refused to answer the question, unlocking and entering the cell instead. The smell of sweat and excrement that assailed him was more that of a caged animal than a sentient being.

"I wish that Tynathria were here today," he said, "so that she could see you as you really are: a weak, worthless man, without connection to nature, living in his own filth and masking his inadequacy by tearing down others' happiness. Such has been the lot of all men since the beginning of time."

Voster nodded, his bloodshot eyes narrowing. "Would she see me as I am? Or would she see the fruits of her brother's lust for power?"

"Perhaps you are right," Shilvand said begrudgingly. "I was never able to see the extent to which you poisoned her mind before she died."

Voster charged him, using what little of his strength he had left to swing at Shilvand's jaw. But with a whisper and a thought, a ward materialized and halted Voster's arm, bouncing the attack off thin air mere inches from impact. Before the surprise could even register on the man's face, Shilvand spoke into being another spell that wormed its way inside Voster's mind and lodged there.

"No, no!" Voster said, swiping at his eyes, but the images clouded his mind and not his vision. Tears tried to form at the corners of his eyes, but he was too dehydrated to cry. "Athria . . ."

Shilvand spoke through the image he had generated of his younger sister, berating Voster and watching as despair bloomed on Voster's face. The Dast'rel wardcasters had discovered how to use magic to produce physical pain, but he doubted that any amount of torture could hurt Voster in his very soul like this.

Shilvand knew that such malicious uses of magic went against the traditional interpretations of Mishenna. Magic was for giving and building up, not taking and tearing down—or so the D'harnir had once believed, receiving the consequences of such a weak perspective. Power was the only way to protect his people.

Besides, he was owed this. Voster had stolen Shilvand's sister away from a good life among her own people. The suffering of Tynathria's wayward husband alone justified the entire campaign against Drüstania.

Voster came back to himself for just a moment, long enough to realize that what he was seeing could not be happening. Just the possibility was potent enough to get a rise out of him. "What . . . have you done . . . with my daughter?" he panted out, the anguish in his heart replaced by fury.

Shilvand eased back out of the spell, knowing he could just as easily plant nightmares with words. And Voster could conjure those images up on his own without magic, long after Shilvand had left. "Oh, I have sent her back out into the world. She believes in the cause now."

Voster slumped back to the bench in the corner, drained of all his energy. His voice came out a raspy whisper. "She would never help the likes of you. I know your spells don't work on her."

"Good guess, but no," Shilvand said, standing in his shimmering white tunic amidst the darkness. "One does not need spells to turn the simple-minded. When someone only cares about one thing, they will do anything when it is threatened."

Understanding and dread became visible across Voster's face. "You can't use me forever," he said. "She will outsmart you."

"Perhaps, if you have raised her well enough," Shilvand said, leaving one last parting thought as he locked the cell. "But the world out there is full of dangers and dangerous men, as my sister would now attest if she still could. I wonder how Niena and her brother will fare against the chaos of war without you to protect them."

Voster sat up again with effort, his face in shadow from the nearby oil lamp. His eyes widened, then dulled in despair from the knowledge Shilvand had revealed—Voster had not once let slip the existence of his son, even in his thoughts, while under the spell. *Quite impressive for a human*, Shilvand mused.

Voster said nothing more, so Shilvand left him alone to ponder whether Niena had told of her brother willingly or had succumbed to similar tortures of mind and body. The arbiter returned to the main cavern, marveling at how his mood had suddenly improved.

Rather than immediately mounting the long stairs back up to his more mundane duties and keeping up appearances, Shilvand took a different passage. Given Silmon's recounting of recent events, he thought he should check in on another of his projects and urge it along if necessary. Even within the Dast'rel, only a handful of people knew about these experiments.

He banged twice with the knocker on the stone door, the sound reverberating back through the corridor. "The cold of night is kept at bay by the corpses of the fallen." The password alluded to the wood fires that kept Por'monir thriving through the harsh winter months, a reminder that nothing in this life could ever be kept without being willing to sacrifice for it.

A moment passed, and the bolt drew aside. "Enter," a muffled elderly voice said through the cracks.

Shilvand heaved against the door which had been cut from the rock on either side. The seam split, and the light nearly blinded him compared to the dimness of the corridor outside. Lamps lined the upper walls of the chamber, illuminating cages stacked against one wall. About half of them were filled with small creatures like rats, birds, and the like, and the others contained only trace amounts of blood.

Wirvanen, the true patriarch of the Falir clan, stood in front of a desk strewn with papers in the center of the room. He was old and withered, but still very much alive. "Ah, my son. It is good you have come earlier than I expected. Come in, before someone sees."

"I have harrowing news, Father," Shilvand said, closing the doors behind him. Most of Por'monir believed his father to be interred in a mausoleum near the base of the mountain, so it was ironic after a fashion that the elder D'harn now lived surrounded by stone. "Our plans are coming to fruition more quickly than we prepared for."

"Hold that thought for a moment longer," Wirvanen interrupted, turning back to the wall of animals scratching about their cages. "I believe I am about to make a breakthrough."

Shilvand fought the urge to protest. Ever since they had faked his father's death a decade ago to focus on researching lost magical arts, it seemed he was always on the verge of a breakthrough but never breaking through. Wirvanen rarely divined anything revolutionary anymore, instead only finding alterations on familiar spells. "What is it this time? Another illusion ward?"

Wirvanen picked up a cage from the end of the stacks and moved it to a stained, empty table away from the rest. It contained a rat, well-fed and healthy—and sure enough, the Falir patriarch produced a few seeds from his pocket and fed them to the creature. "I think you will be more than pleased, Shilvand. This could be what I have been looking for all these years."

"You mean ... the Goreweaver?" Shilvand asked, recalling the legends of dark magic in the early eons of the world. The fabled spell had proved so violent and volatile that the D'harnir of that age had banished the sorcerer who discovered it. It was the first time in recorded history that a D'harn's ears had been publicly shorn, and the particulars of the spell had been lost to history ever since.

"Or something quite like it," Wirvanen said, hedging his claim. "Would you care to watch?"

Shilvand crossed his arms, skeptical after so many failures, and waited. His father picked up a book in which he had scrawled characters in the ancient D'harna script, then outstretched a shaky hand toward the cage with the rat inside it.

Wirvanen's voice began low and guttural, speaking the same tongue as for the spells of healing but forcing the words to scrape through his throat. The rat writhed, flipping over on its back, and clawed at the air.

All the other animals in the chamber went berserk as the curse grew louder, slamming themselves against their cage doors in desperation. They could sense the destructive energy being channeled into the rat's squirming body, which now leaked blood onto the table beneath.

The hairs stood up on Shilvand's neck as his father spoke the final words of the incantation. The rat spasmed and lay still, dead.

Wirvanen staggered, and Shilvand moved quickly to keep his father from falling. The elderly D'harn settled into his chair, breathing deep, frail but invigorated by his success. "Go on, take a look," he encouraged Shilvand.

Shilvand moved closer to the cage, peering at the tiny creature's body. Fissures had opened across the rat's skin, showing the flesh and sinew underneath in places and causing immense bleeding. The similarities to the old Goreweaver spell were undeniable—and yet, they were not nearly enough.

"It still needs work," Wirvanen said, regaining his strength. "But I daresay that I may finally be close to the answer."

Shilvand's mind spun with the possibilities. With this powerful spell, it didn't matter what firepower the human king could bring to bear against them. The strength and industry of men would be as trees before the woodcutter's axe of sorcery and vengeance.

At last, the two races would be on an even playing field.

"Well done, Father," he replied. "Make refining this spell your highest priority. We may soon have need for it."

TWENTY-SIX

*Many strive after freedom and trip on
their own arrogant boots; for the flowers
of opportunity are crushed by the heel of
consequence.*

— Codes of Entreaty 3.31

NIENA'S HEART LEAPED INTO her throat as she went over the edge,
propelled by Gilbrannen's unforeseen push. The scream lodged in her
throat from the shock, and mere seconds stretched into infinity. She
watched figures moving in the shrinking window above as the stone of
the castle walls and then the bluff underneath cascaded upwards past
her in slow motion. She fell backward, unable to see the ground below,
and she thought that might be for the best.

Gilbrannen clung to the line above her, trying desperately to twist
the spider silk around his forearm and secure himself. His dark cloak
streamed off his shoulders, dragging him backwards, and Niena realized
that her own had been whipped off by the wind of their exit. Her hand
protectively clutched her mother's pendant to prevent losing it, too.

The castle above grew small in Niena's vision, which meant they
were approaching ground level. But she also noticed their fall slowing

as the spider silk stretched to accommodate their weight. The horrific thought flitted into Niena's mind: what would happen when it needed to spring back? Would it snap? Would it fling them into the cliff a hundred feet off the ground?

The line stretched to its full length, wrenching Niena's shoulder and knocking her and Gilbrannen together with the sudden deceleration. For an instant, she could see the surface of the water maybe thirty feet below, rippling in the moonlight, before the rebound began to pull them back up. If not for the terror of imminent death, she would have thought the view pretty.

And then, suddenly, nothing suspended them any longer. Their pursuers had cut the line. Niena finally let out a scream as she plunged feet-first into the water.

The freezing water forced her arms above her head, invading her mouth and nose with a force that threatened to render her unconscious. Her arm and wrist cramped, still tangled in the silk rope as she thrashed to return to the surface. She couldn't see, she couldn't breathe, and for an instant, it reminded her of hiding from the clawcrens in the wilderness. Finally, she burst from the surface and gulped in fresh air.

"Gilbrannen!" Niena called. "Gilbrannen!"

She didn't hear anything. That wasn't a good sign.

Treading water and trying to get to shore, she desperately looked around for any sign of the D'harn. A pale hand raised out of the water a few yards away then sank back down, and she kicked her feet to swim toward him. Reaching the spot, she saw Gilbrannen floating under the water's surface, unmoving.

Niena panicked. She couldn't lose him—there was no hope of getting her father back without him. She tugged at Gilbrannen's arms, attempting to raise him out of the water enough to breathe. Even though he was far lighter than a man of the same size, it took an immense amount of effort to hold him up with her wrenched shoulder while swimming to shore. She unclasped his cloak to keep it from dragging them down, grabbed the handle of her father's bow still hanging from his shoulders, and kicked with all her might.

Her calves burned by the time she finally got to the rocky edge of the water, and Gilbrannen still hadn't moved.

Niena had no idea what to do—she had never learned any sort of drowning prevention methods, and even if she did, there was no guarantee it would work on a D'harn. But she had to try something to get the water out of him. She rolled Gilbrannen over so any water in his chest wouldn't stay there, and smacked him across the back a few times.

At first, she thought nothing had happened, but after a few moments, water bubbled out of his mouth. He coughed violently. Niena rolled him back over and propped his head up on her lap.

"Ow," was all he had to say.

Niena looked up at the keep of Celwaith Tor, far above them at the top of the cliff. They were lucky the guards hadn't cut the line any sooner, or else they might not have survived the landing.

She looked back at Gilbrannen and noticed his right hand clenched around something small. She turned it over and saw his knife, remnants of the spider-silk rope on the blade. He had cut the line, at the apex of their fall.

Niena rubbed her sore shoulder and realized they needed to move now. The city guard would need time to descend the Tor through the city, exit through the water gate, and circle the lake to where she and Gilbrannen had washed up, but that was no time to waste.

"Hey, you alive?" she said, poking Gilbrannen in the chest.

"Ah!" he exclaimed, before coughing again several times. "Easy. I think I broke some ribs on the way down."

"Sorry," Niena said, and surprised herself by meaning it. "They'll be coming after us soon. Can you move?"

Gilbrannen puffed air through his cheeks, steeling himself. "I guess I will have to. Help me up."

Niena did so, prompting a labored yelp from his lips that sounded more undignified than she expected. She squinted at him. "Don't you have some kind of magic healing powers or something?"

Gilbrannen clutched his chest and frowned in annoyance at her flippant remark. "There is precious little I can do myself without the aid of another D'harn. I can speed up my natural healing processes somewhat, but anything else is out of the question."

"Lean on me, then," Niena offered, knowing she might be on thin ice with him as it was. At least he had to know she didn't set a trap for them; it had just been . . . bad luck. She picked up her father's bow from where it lay on the shore, slung it across her own back, and motioned Gilbrannen to come closer. "Where can we go?"

Gilbrannen took her up on it, draping an arm around her and gingerly finding a pace that got them moving without hurting his ribs too much. He pointed north, into the woods. "Back to the outpost. There is no one there now, but it is hidden, and we can stock up for the journey north."

"We're going back to Por'monir?" Niena asked hopefully, helping Gilbrannen up an embankment on the edge of the treeline. It would be difficult for one person to navigate the hills in the dark alone, but she had to do so for two.

He groaned and powered through, wincing from the strain on his chest. "I know I sent Silmon back yesterday, but we must follow him as quickly as we can—that Shi'ev fellow's invention could mean the death of us all."

Niena wondered if the worst case had occurred to Gilbrannen. "What's more, they've captured at least some of your team alive. I imagine it will not be long until one of them cracks under interrogation."

He stubbornly refused to take another step, holding her back, stricken by the full weight of his failure.

"Are you all right?" she asked.

Gilbrannen looked back, past the first few trees in the direction of the city, where a trail of lanterns sprouted from the closest gate. The glittering lights moved quickly in their direction. "I think I will be, but Por'monir may not. Most of the scouts were from Neraliel and would not know enough to reveal us, but two of them ... I hope they have enough sense to kill themselves rather than submit."

They picked up the pace, matching strides while Gilbrannen held a hand over his aching chest and whispered incantations to dull the pain. Well over a mile of rough terrain separated them from the hideout, and if they didn't make it by morning, the king's trackers would surely find them.

IT WAS ALMOST DAWN by the time they reached the natural bridge, having taken hours to traverse the few hilly miles with Gilbrannen's injuries. No hidden assassins waited in the trees for whistle signals this time. Both Niena and Gilbrannen, drained from their feats of escape and lack of sleep, stumbled up along the bed of the spring and under the outcropping.

"We ... we have to keep going," Gilbrannen said, taking deep drinks of the clear spring water and wincing every time he pushed his face up. "Get one of the horses ready."

Niena gave him a stern look. "We're not going anywhere right now. You're hurt, and you're going to need your strength if we're riding the whole way back to Por'monir."

Gilbrannen rolled over and slumped against the cave wall, pointing at the entrance. "No. The sun is coming up, and they will be able to track your heavy footfalls and my limp without trouble. We have an hour at most before they get here."

Niena sighed. Her own body longed to lie down and pass out, and she hated admitting when he was right. "Then you keep resting and don't move. I'll take care of the rest."

"I could not move even if I wanted to," Gilbrannen said, lying back and closing his eyes.

Niena took one last drink from the cool, clear water, and set about packing saddlebags. Provisions were lacking, but she wolfed down a piece of gamy venison and stuffed the rest in a pair of saddlebags. A few of the scouts had left behind their cloaks, so she grabbed two to replace the ones lost in the escape from the palace—a blue one for Gilbrannen and a leafy green one for herself. And while going through the rest of the encampment, she found her father's leather-bound book and reclaimed it.

When Niena left the cave, it was significantly brighter outside, and she dreaded that they had taken too long. She opened a makeshift gate, releasing the elves' horses to roam wild. She held back the coal-black mare named Evwoin that had carried her from Por'monir. Gilbrannen told her then that the mare was the most even-tempered and reliable of any of their horses. "Well, Evwoin," Niena remarked as she heaved the saddlebags over her back, "if we ever needed your endurance, it's now."

"Up here! They came this way!" a voice shouted from outside and down the hill.

Niena blanched, hoping she had secured their possessions well enough. She led Evwoin over to Gilbrannen and shook him. "Wake up," she whispered. "They've found us!"

Gilbrannen didn't respond for a moment, but he came to himself all at once and the adrenaline was enough to get him on his feet. Getting into the saddle on such a large, hearty breed of horse was another thing altogether, and he couldn't stop himself from yelping in pain when heaving himself over the top with Niena's help.

Evwoin whinnied, and the Drüstanian soldiers came into view outside the opening to the natural bridge. Even worse, they carried crossbows. "There they are! Fire!"

Niena threw herself up onto Evwoin behind Gilbrannen. "Go, go!"

Gilbrannen kicked his boots against the horse's sides, hard, and they jolted into motion.

Niena glanced toward the other exit and saw they had been cut off in that direction too. "They're everywhere!" she called, but Gilbrannen galloped straight toward the enemy soldiers. Niena held on for dear life, hoping that the bold move would startle them enough to miss their shots.

The crossbow bolts whizzed by in narrow margins, just before Evwoin bowled over two of the armored men coming up the hill. Gilbrannen tugged on the reins, but the enemy soldiers had spooked Evwoin. The two fugitives were at the mare's mercy.

The horse took off west through the trees, with Pelendion's men firing after them. Niena yanked Gilbrannen down to duck under a low-hanging branch and heard the thud of another bolt bury itself in the bark as they passed. They made enough distance from the soldiers to breathe easy. After another few minutes, there would be no catching up unless the soldiers had cavalry backup on the way.

"There wasn't any important information back at the hideout, I hope," Niena asked, being careful not to place any pressure on Gilbrannen's chest as she held on.

"None they can read," Gilbrannen said. "Why do you care?"

Niena mentally checked herself. She didn't know why she had asked that. She had been playing along with the D'harnin terrorists for so long, was she even starting to think like them? "I don't, but I know you would," she said, fudging her answer.

Gilbrannen groaned again as he tried to slow Evwoin and bring her back on course again. She responded well to his guidance, but the pain of such a small movement betrayed the seriousness of his wounds. "Niena, I cannot keep doing this. You are going to have to take over for me."

"Me?" Niena balked at the idea. "But I've never ridden a horse except when it was guided!"

There was nothing else for it. They swapped places on Evwoin's back, allowing Gilbrannen to relax a little more and rest his injuries. As they traveled north, he gave her the most rudimentary of lessons in aligning the mare's speed and direction. She caught on quickly and surprised herself how easy it was to learn.

"Must be your D'harnin half," he mumbled and shut his eyes as he leaned against her shoulder.

As the day wore on, Niena worried that Gilbrannen had been hurt far worse than he let on. His condition wasn't improving, even though he kept whispering in the ancient elven tongue to himself. Whenever she pressed him, he told her he would be fine.

I guess he knows the limitations of elves better, she thought cautiously as they continued through woods and the back side of farming country. Now her third time passing through the region, she began to understand the lay of the land pretty well.

They stopped at sunset, an hour or so outside the Mersien Wold. Niena didn't dare keep pushing on through the night, as she remembered the wild dogs. She didn't have any vinegar to spread to mask their scent either. With any luck, the danger was distant enough for the two of them to finally sleep a full night because they couldn't stop anywhere else.

"How are you feeling?" she asked Gilbrannen before they dismounted.

"Like I was on the receiving end of an avalanche," he replied, moving as little as he possibly could. The last few miles had been the most difficult for him, with a lot of ups and downs across creek beds and rock outcroppings. "This is where you want to sleep tonight? Out in the open?"

It wasn't exactly out in the open, as the thicket was enclosed by trees and bushes, but it would be cold—especially if it rained. "Best I can do."

"All right," Gilbrannen said, bracing himself for the pain and the long step down to the forest floor. "Help me down."

She offered him her hand, and he gingerly lowered himself off the horse's back. Before his foot touched the dry leaves below, he yelped and fell the rest of the way to the ground where he lay in a heap, quivering.

Niena stared in shock before leaping down and going to his side. "Gilbrannen!"

He raised a hand to ward her off. "I am fine . . ."

"No, you're not!" she insisted, kneeling next to him and reaching for his tunic. "Let me see."

"No," Gilbrannen said, but he had no strength to stop her.

Niena sucked in a breath through her teeth as she could see more and more of his chest. His skin showed a mottled purple, the bruises and hemorrhaging from his broken ribs inflamed from continuing to ride all day. "Oh," she said, pity evident in her voice. "I knew you were hurting, but . . ."

"Just leave me alone," Gilbrannen said, his voice tight and cracked. "I will feel better after a night of sleep."

Niena shook her head adamantly. "I don't think you will. It looks bad, Gilbrannen. We can't keep going all the way to Por'monir with you in this shape."

"Well, we cannot stay here."

"True enough," Niena said, trying to remember the distance to Ensdale on the other side of the Wold. "But I know a place where we could."

TWENTY-SEVEN

"YOU HAVE YET TO tell me how it works," Anseldr pressed his old friend, gesturing to the strange device that had saved their lives the previous night. Events fit together a little too conveniently for his taste. "And more importantly, tell me how you knew it would work. After mere days of study, you knew how to counter the elves' magic spells. Your dissection of the elven corpse could not have been that fruitful."

"You might be surprised," Shi'ev said, one side of his mouth twisting upward. "But you are right, the instrument's construction involved more than guesswork."

Anseldr rubbed his sleep-deprived eyes impatiently. With the help of Shi'ev's device, the elven intruders had been apprehended easily before being bound and gagged to prevent any verbal use of magic. Two had been caught in the royal suite surrounded by dead guards, but it seemed that they had not yet breached the king's bedchamber.

A narrow escape, indeed, Anseldr thought with a shiver. Pelendion might have died, or worse—he might have become a bewitched puppet of the creatures himself if it hadn't been for Shi'ev's contraption. He prompted the scientist to continue. "Enlighten me."

Shi'ev appeared reluctant to divulge his secrets. After a moment, he pointed to the machine as it sat on the library table, singling out the primary components in turn. "This string is made of manticore gut—quite rare, but necessary for the proper resonance. It vibrates through this bridge against the drum membrane beneath to create a low-frequency sound that is below the range of human hearing, for the most part. As for precisely why it affects the elven brain the way it does, that is a much longer story."

Anseldr did not care for the attempted deflection. "I have the time today, old friend. How could you have known to seek out such a sound?"

Silence stretched out for several moments, to the point that Anseldr wondered if Shi'ev would refuse to answer. But he finally spoke, low enough that he couldn't be overheard. "There are precious few of us left in the Macula Society, but we keep the flame of knowledge alive. Our surviving archives date back to before the dark ages."

That was not an admission Anseldr expected to hear. He had heard of the Macula Society, a secretive group of scientists in Ash'kiram that supposedly had their hands in every business coffer from here to where the winds met, but he had mostly dismissed them as conspiracy theory or rumor. Now, to find out that his childhood friend was among them . . .

That intrigued him.

"The records claim that manticores hunt using magic," Shi'ev continued. "They could sense an elf's presence, and also release a roaring call that paralyzed the elf in pain and confusion long enough to go in for the kill."

Anseldr took a step back, the implications running through his mind. His face grew hot. "You knew that the elves existed? And you never saw fit to tell me, let alone the king?"

Shi'ev held up a hand to calm the conversation. "I know what it sounds like, but our last encounter with them was over six centuries ago. A few of us presumed they had gone extinct, but most, including myself, had begun to doubt they even existed. As I told you before, however, the discovery of the drakaina preserved in the desert has . . . renewed interest in the old accounts."

Anseldr supposed that could be an accurate version of events. It explained why Shi'ev had been more excited than surprised when Lieutenant Cresthaven had returned with the elven corpse. But Shi'ev had refrained from the truth until now, and the reason remained both a mystery and a problem. Perhaps he had trusted the scientist farther than was wise.

Anseldr unclenched his hands at his side and controlled his breathing. "Do you have any other information to share that may benefit the kingdom of Drüstania at this time?"

Shi'ev raised an eyebrow. "Are you asking in an official capacity?"

Anseldr narrowed his eyes. "No."

"There is no further information at the moment, but I will make sure to inform you if anything arises." Shi'ev's tone had become more clipped and professional, and Anseldr sensed that a measure of their friendship had been lost.

At that moment, Emeline burst through the door into the library, her face distraught. "Anseldr! Come quickly!"

He turned to face his wife, bewildered by her sudden entrance. "Emeline? What is it?" he asked, taking her hands in his. It wasn't like her to rush through the palace like this.

"It's Pelendion," she said, out of breath. "He's taken ill."

Anseldr glanced at Shi'ev, who seemed just as surprised by the news as he was. "How ill?"

"I don't know," Emeline replied, her eyes pleading with him to come away. "Coranna said that he complained of a headache this morning, but he collapsed during luncheon. The guards placed him in bed, and we sent for the physician."

There can be only one explanation, Anseldr mused with a heavy feeling in his stomach.

"Perhaps the elves breached the bedchamber after all," Shi'ev said, stating the obvious. "May I accompany you? There are a few Kiramet remedies which may help."

"By all means," Anseldr said, then squeezed his wife's trembling shoulder. "Lead the way, love."

The next few hours slowed to a crawl. Pelendion continued to burn with an infernal fever and did not wake from his bed, despite the ministrations of both Shi'ev and the royal physician. They exchanged cool washcloths across the king's forehead every few minutes, dripped herbal tinctures into his mouth, and waited on him hand and foot while Coranna and Emeline paced the corners of the chamber.

Anseldr did not move to help unless asked, unsure of how best to assist and not wanting to fret like the women. Instead, he remained standing and watching at the foot of the bed, willing his brother's eyes to open with each new treatment.

The physician came to him multiple times and proclaimed he could do nothing more until Pelendion awoke, but Anseldr demanded more. Best case, they fought only against a type of poison they had never encountered before; worst case, they fought against magic, cursing the very life force of the king. Resorting to the usual medical methods would not suffice.

They finally drew blood to test for contaminants, but by evening, the tests still had found nothing. The physician likened the illness to tuberculosis, but the onset of symptoms was so sudden that Pelendion could not have contracted it normally.

Just before the clock struck seven, a bout of coughing shook Pelendion so violently that Shi'ev and the physician had to hold him down. The blankets by his mouth became stained with blood. As the fit subsided, Pelendion's eyes finally opened, and he squinted in the candlelight.

"I . . . cannot see," Pelendion said, his voice thick and hoarse. "There are only shadows."

Anseldr came alongside the bed and grasped Pelendion's forearm. "I am here, brother," he spoke gently.

Coranna instantly rushed to his other side. "So am I, Pel," she said, trying and failing to make her voice cheery. "How are you feeling?"

"Not . . . well, my queen," Pelendion choked out. His bearded face had gone pale and his blue eyes, once filled with vitality, were sunken and weak. He coughed again but swallowed back whatever came up. "I don't know . . . how long I have."

"Don't talk like that, Pel," Coranna protested, tears welling in her eyes. "We've been looking after you for hours. You'll get better."

Shi'ev brought over a small cup filled with hot broth and crumbled a cube of dried herbs into it. "Here, Your Majesty, drink this if you are able. If nothing else, it will aid with the pain, but Kiramet doctors swear by it."

The physician helped Pelendion sit up straighter, despite his dizziness and inability to see clearly. He sputtered a little with the first sip but continued to drink. "Drink all of it," Shi'ev said. "Your throat should feel better almost immediately."

The king did as instructed, stopping for breath only once. When he had finished, Anseldr could have sworn a small amount of color came back into his cheeks. Pelendion lay back and reached for his wife's hand.

"Anseldr? Are you still here?" His voice sounded encouragingly stronger too.

"I am, sire," Anseldr replied, feeling Emeline close behind his shoulder. "What do you need?"

Pelendion took in a ragged breath before speaking in a halting fashion. "You continue to prove your loyalty to Drüstania and to me, and I am ashamed of how little I have listened to you these past weeks and months. If it had not been for your plans, Celwaith Tor might be in ruins now."

Anseldr swallowed, humbled by the admiration he had never received. Everything he had done, he had done for the good of the nation. Emeline rested a supportive hand on his back.

"I am trusting you now," Pelendion continued, pausing to cough again. "You must end this threat to our people swiftly. Do as you deem necessary. You shall have the authority of my crown until I am well or until you inherit the throne yourself."

Anseldr drew himself up, then bowed from the waist. "I will see to it, my brother, I swear. Do not concern yourself with anything but your recovery."

"I must . . . sleep," Pelendion said, his eyes darting this way and that in an attempt to focus his vision. The physician agreed and bade them all to leave the room for a short time. But Pelendion protested. "No, stay with me, Cor. Your company is soothing."

An expression of relief crossed the queen's face, and she returned to her husband's side.

"Shi'ev," Anseldr called. "With me. We have much work to do."

"What can I do to help?" Emeline asked.

Anseldr drew her into a hug, knowing what he was about to do would not be worthy of a lady's eyes. "You should stay nearby to help Coranna, love. She needs someone to encourage her through all this."

Coranna overheard, smiling at Anseldr in thanks.

Anseldr and Shi'ev walked back to the library, together but otherwise alone. The Kiramet scientist turned to him along the way with a raised eyebrow. "What is your next move?"

Anseldr's stony gray eyes narrowed, and he marched faster, his fur-lined boots clicking on the floor. If he had the authority of the king, he would use it before news of the elven infiltration became public knowledge. "We retrieve your machine, and then we discover what prolonged exposure does to the elven mind. The information our captives hold is the key, and we will wring it out of them at any cost."

ANISE HELD HER HEAD in her hands, elbows on the dining room table despite the lack of propriety. She really ought to have turned in, since even the servants had gone to bed, but it would be an exercise in futility with the roiling thunder and rain outside. She had hardly slept a wink last night anyway out of worry for Niena, who had been missing again for almost two days. The girl hadn't even left a note this time. Perhaps she hadn't meant to leave—perhaps someone had taken her away?

Far worse things had happened to people in the city of Celwaith Tor, after all.

"Ms. Cresthaven?" a deep voice said next to her. "What is the matter?"

Anise straightened up, attempting to blink away the few tears that had welled up in her eyes. "Lord Denvald! I thought you were upstairs."

The heavyset man pulled out the chair next to hers and settled into it, though he appeared to have lost weight. He had returned from his lengthy business trip to Cape Vrosingr several hours ago, having learned the news about Thaxon by express courier. "I was, but Letaccia wanted me to leave her for the night."

Anise looked at him with concern. "That seems strange of her."

Lord Denvald grunted. "Does it? She blames me."

"For what, my lord?"

Denvald sighed and reached for a cigar in his vest pocket, then tossed it on the table dejectedly. The flash of lightning outside preceded the distant rumble of thunder a few moments later. "The worst part is, she's not wrong. I'm the king's second cousin—I could easily have asked him to overlook Thaxon in the draft, and he would still be with us now. But he was so determined to join up after . . ." He trailed off.

Anise sat with her hands in her lap, not sure if it was her place to say anything about the man's loss. But it was clear that he wanted, or perhaps needed, to hear some encouragement.

"Oh, my lovely Serenia," Denvald said, his voice cracking in grief though he managed to hold his countenance together. "Thaxon took after his mother, but she took after me. We always thought she might marry Jarl Stenden's son and solidify our ties to the royal family one day, but—"

Anise reached out instinctively and touched his hand. "No parent should have to lose their child, much less both of them. None of what happened could be your fault."

"No?"

"No. Thaxon was the type of young man who loved his sister enough to lay down his own life in pursuit of justice. If you ask me, that sounds like he was raised rather well."

Lord Denvald nodded somberly, taking her hand in his and briefly squeezing it. "It is little comfort when I cannot even give my son a proper burial, but thank you, Ms. Cresthaven. Sometimes the pain is so great that little comfort is all that can be given."

"Well." Anise let go of his hand and stood, gesturing to the kitchen. "Shall I brew a cup of tea for you, my lord? Always helps the spirits on a stormy night like tonight."

"Please, call me Marton," he said with an embarrassed half-smile. "No, don't go to any effort this late on my account. I apologize, I came in here looking for someone to listen to my problems when you were in the middle of your own."

Anise had hoped that Marton would forget how she had been leaning on the dining table. She headed for the kitchen despite his protest. "Well, Marton, I intended to make some for myself anyway."

He rose from his chair and followed. "In that case, I should be delighted."

Anise set about stoking the fire in the stove, keenly aware that Marton was watching her.

"You know, the number of times I have set foot in this kitchen must be less than a dozen," he said. "Normally, the servants bring me everything, and I never lift a finger."

Anise poured the water from a tank that was filled daily by servants carrying pails up from the lake. "You may continue sitting at the table if you wish," she said. "It will be a few minutes."

"Oh, no, I did not mean to suggest you were a servant," Marton replied in concern. "Besides, I would rather not be alone."

Anise could relate to that sentiment.

He cleared his throat. "If I may ask, what were you thinking about when I came downstairs just now? You seemed distraught."

Anise carefully placed the kettle on the heated stove top, not meeting the man's eyes. Straying this far from the etiquette of their respective stations was uncomfortable, but it excited her to have a lord take interest in her affairs. "It's my niece, Niena," she said. "You might remember that she and my brother had skipped town around the time of the draft?"

"Yes," Marton said with a frown. "I saw the wanted posters out for him. Why, have you heard from her?"

"She returned to the city the same day you left, without my brother Voster," she explained, a lump constricting her throat. "She was able to find me here and stayed for a few days, but two nights ago she disappeared again without even as much as a note." She held a hand to her mouth, stifling a sob that threatened to escape.

Marton stepped closer and put an arm around her shoulders. "There now," he said softly. "Have you spoken to the authorities yet?"

"Today," Anise sniffed, leaning into the embrace. "No one matching her description had been incarcerated or counted among the dead."

"Well, that is something to be thankful for, at least," he said, perhaps wishing that his children were only missing and not deceased. "She came back to you the first time. Trust that she will again."

"That is the trouble," Anise protested. "I don't even know if I should be worried about her, whether she is in danger, or if she up and left without a care for the aunt who raised her." She stared at the floor, trying to smooth out the wrinkles in her dress, borrowed from Lady Denvald's expansive closets. "I have always been the last to know anything in my family, the last priority for any of them."

"Impossible," Marton said, taking her hand again. "Why, if anything, you must be the glue that has held the family together for years, if your brother is so irresponsible as to run off unannounced."

Anise blinked. "You think so?"

"I cannot say for sure, but from what I have seen of you and your talents in this house . . ." He raised her fingers to his lips and kissed them. "No one could ask for a more loyal or dutiful woman."

Anise took in a short breath, understanding now that Marton was propositioning her. She knew she ought to snatch her hand away, but she felt an invisible pull toward him. She found that she wanted to hear him out. "What are you saying?" she asked in a whisper.

Marton's other hand found her waist and pressed her close, the colors of his doublet and her dress clashing, but none of that mattered.

"That I would like you to stay on here at the estate as long as you like, so we can, shall we say, get to know one another better."

Anise froze in his large arms as he leaned in to kiss her, and she nearly shuddered with desire. It had been so long since anyone wanted her in this way. She had thought it wasn't possible anymore.

The tea kettle sang just as Lord Denvald's lips grazed hers, and she came back to her senses to push him away. Taking several deep breaths to calm herself, she hurried to take the water from the stove. "My lord. You are married, we cannot possibly—"

"I know," he said, looking even more drained and haggard than he had mere minutes ago. "But it would not have to be that way."

Anise stared at him in disbelief. "What way would you have it?"

"My wife hates me," he said, his voice weary and broken. "Even before our children's deaths, she despised me for my long business trips and attending to my courtly duties when they did not involve her. I have not held her in my arms for at least a year, and I cannot bear the loneliness anymore."

Anise poured the water into an elaborate pot already filled with dried tea leaves while she waited for the other shoe to drop. If Lord Marton Denvald wanted a tryst, he could have one with far younger and more attractive women than herself. But she sensed he wanted something more.

"I would pay you well to continue attending to my wife during the day," Denvald said, as he set a tea strainer across the top of a teacup. "And then, at night, you might . . . consider my needs." His tired eyes met hers, and the implication was obvious.

Anise placed a hand over her chest, looking away from the man and back again several times. A vision sprouted in her mind of everything she had ever wanted—a life among the elite, with dinner parties and fashionable gowns and more money than you could shake a stick at. That and more was being offered to her right now if she only said yes.

But she didn't want it like this, laced with infidelity.

"I'm sorry, Lord Denvald," Anise said, gathering herself up with as much dignity as she could muster after such a suggestion. "I'm afraid you will have to serve your own tea after all."

She skirted past him and left the kitchen, intending to go upstairs to her bedroom and pack up what few things she had with her. She would tender her resignation as Lady Denvald's caretaker in the morning, as she couldn't rightly live under the same roof with the poor woman's husband.

Marton followed close behind, pleading with her to reconsider. "I'm sorry, I thought you would be open to the idea after—"

Anise whirled, now furious that he would not let it go. "No! I cannot believe you would even think of that while your wife is grieving upstairs. I will be leaving in the morning."

"Where will you go? Listen—"

"You listen!" she hissed at him, keeping her voice down now that they stood in the grand entrance hall where sound could carry. "I take back everything I said earlier—it's a wonder Thaxon turned out as well as he did with someone like you for a father."

She could tell that the remark had struck true, as Lord Denvald fell silent and did not say anything more. Instead, he pulled a pad of paper from his waistcoat and went over to the side table to fetch a quill. Anise almost left him there while she went up to her bedroom, but she wondered at his abrupt change in manner.

She didn't have to wait long. Lord Denvald signed his name, tore out a slip, and handed it to her. It was a bank promissory note for seven hundred and fifty measures of silver, more than twice the savings Voster had left for her. "Your dues, then, since I cannot convince you to stay," he said in explanation.

Anise was not dumb enough to miss what the exorbitant amount meant. She was supposed to stay quiet about what happened—that was how these things worked. Well, she hadn't intended to go blathering all over town about Lord Denvald anyway. She accepted the signed check gingerly and nodded in thanks.

A knock came at the door, startling the both of them.

"What the devil? At this hour of night?" Denvald said, moving to answer it himself.

To Anise's surprise, outside in the street stood a bedraggled Tollan. The rain dripped off his armor in unbroken streams of water. The militia must have returned from Eastmarsh early, Anise reasoned.

"Good heavens lad, come inside! Let me find you some dry clothes," Lord Denvald said, bustling off to page his valet to do it for him.

Anise didn't care that her nephew was soaking wet. She fell on him in a tight embrace which he returned wholeheartedly.

TWENTY-EIGHT

*Even the power to do good is useless
without a principled heart, for many seek
to twist the needs and desires of others to
their own advantage.*

— *Codes of Entreaty 3.15*

GILBRANNEN LOOKED A LITTLE better the next morning, but as they crossed the shale deserts of the Mersien Wold, his condition continued to deteriorate throughout the day. They weren't able to move as quickly without using magic to rejuvenate the horse, and he had to direct every spare amount of concentration inward. It was almost evening by the time they skirted the town of Ensdale and reached the old homestead, and by then Gilbrannen looked as pale as the linen sheets on the Denvalds' bedding.

The ramshackle farmhouse looked the same as when Niena had been there last, though the forest leaves had begun to change color into a deep orange. She tied Evwoin to the remains of an old fence post and helped Gilbrannen down as carefully as possible. She had worried that they wouldn't make it before he gave out, but they were cutting it close.

He seemed light and frail to Niena as she did her best to carry him inside. She cleared a small area and spread out the horse blanket for him to lie on, with the saddlebags as a pillow. He refused to eat at first, but she finally coaxed him to take a few bites of dried venison.

"How did it go so wrong?" Gilbrannen asked, looking up at Niena with sunken eyes. His words wheezed like his raspy breaths. "I should have listened to your warnings about Shi'ev. My parents know nothing about where I have gone or what I have done. We were supposed to take back our land, and now I am going to die far from home."

"Maybe it was never your land," Niena objected, not willing to hear Gilbrannen turn himself into the victim. "It used to belong to everyone, but compromise was impossible because neither side could see past their own self-interest. Your feud was with my ancestors, not me, and if you die here now, my papa may never come home again."

She paused to tuck in her cloak around him for extra warmth. "So don't you dare die on me."

Gilbrannen remained silent for a while after that, either lost in thought or simply struggling to breathe. "There is . . . one thing we have yet to try," he whispered at last.

Niena waited expectantly, hoping he had taken her words to heart.

"You and your brother both are . . . unaffected by illusion spells because of your elven blood," Gilbrannen explained. "You might be able to . . . harness the ancient tongue yourself."

Niena pondered that. "You mean I could heal you?"

"I cannot fully . . . heal myself because the process requires a . . . transfer of energy, but I will teach you a simple spell, and if it works . . ."

"Yes?"

Gilbrannen looked at her with a serious gaze, and she knew he meant what he was about to say. "Your father will be free when we return. I swear it."

Niena supposed that was as close to an apology as she was likely to get, but she would take it. For Gilbrannen to trust her with magic was a monumental step, but if it didn't work, all she had done would be for nothing. "All right. What do I need to do?"

The next hour became a process of trial and error, first learning the proper words in the old D'harna. They were utterly alien to her, and the process felt like trying to pronounce the most difficult of tongue-twisting limericks, but it became easier as she practiced. What came next, though, was even harder.

"Remember what it felt like when we were attempting to influence you? Did you feel any pressure or pain?" Gilbrannen asked.

"Like a manticore's roar, or when Shi'ev turned on his machine," Niena suggested.

Gilbrannen coughed several times but nodded through it in excitement. "Yes! Think of that place in your mind, and go there." He looked around and pointed toward a small leafy plant that grew up out of the derelict floorboards. "Use it to concentrate on that plant, feed it with your essence."

Niena took a deep breath, and one of her oldest memories came unbidden to her mind. When she was young, a bird, a robin, had come close and taken a seed from her hand. Her mother also had a connection with nature, Papa once told her, and now Niena needed to believe that was hereditary. She stared at the tiny plant, focusing a part of her mind that she scarcely knew existed, and spoke the incantation slowly and deliberately.

Nothing happened.

"It is okay," Gilbrannen rasped, his breathing even more shallow. The longer they worked at this, the less his internal wounds could be held back with his own concentration and magic. "Try again. Close your eyes if you need to, or touch the plant. Increase your connection with it."

Niena did both, and as she spoke the ancient words again, she felt a tiny spark in her mind. She seized at it, feeling the presence of the plant in her hand as she said the incantation a second time. It was almost like she had become the plant for a moment, desiring sunlight, earth, and water more than anything else in the world.

When she opened her eyes, the tiny plant had nearly doubled in size, the pointy leaves opening outward toward her like she was the sun.

"Very . . . good," Gilbrannen said, smiling through his evident pain. "You . . . can do . . . it."

He looked far worse than he had a moment ago, Niena realized with a shock, and she felt drained, but also invigorated. The room was brighter, she realized—the sun was starting to come up. How long had she been in a trance?

"Now . . ." Gilbrannen paused to whisper his own incantation, keeping himself from slipping away. "You have to . . . try it . . . on me. On my . . . ribs." His eyes closed as he kept repeating the mantra.

Niena repositioned herself, nervous and tired but understanding what she had to do. The stakes were so high, and she barely knew anything about magic, let alone how to do it correctly. But she shoved her questions and uncertainty out of her mind and reached out a hand to rest it gingerly on Gilbrannen's horribly bruised chest.

As she uttered the spell once again, what had been a spark with the tiny plant now became a roaring fire. Either because Niena had opened herself more to the mystical power, or because the D'harn as an organism was so much more complex than a plant. Perhaps it was both, but the sensation swept her along in a whirlwind of thoughts and feelings, not all of them her own.

She felt Gilbrannen's regrets of a love lost, his loneliness without siblings, his longing for the approval of his parents, his internalized hate—no, not hate, but fear—for all the things of mankind. Niena recoiled from him, scared that by feeling his pain she might become more like him. But when she pressed deeper, she saw that the fear had become inexplicably softened. There was a chink in his armor, and Niena utilized it to go deeper still.

All of Gilbrannen's aches and pains now called out to her, begging for an ounce of her attention and energy, but if she paid attention to them all she would have nothing left to heal his largest, most serious wounds: his broken ribs and the inflamed flesh around them. She focused her energies there and allowed herself to relax into the trance. Time ceased to have meaning between Gilbrannen and herself, minds entwined while they teetered on the edge of oblivion, the eternal night.

Something abruptly shook her free of the trance, and Niena had no choice but to stop. She worried that she had said a word incorrectly as she came back to herself, and noted that her whole body ached, down to the bones. She opened her eyes and saw Gilbrannen still lying there in front of her, unmoving and still in the heat of the afternoon.

"No," Niena refused to accept it. He couldn't be dead. Not after all that she had given him. "Gilbrannen!"

His body twitched violently, and he coughed heavily before gasping in a full breath of air.

Niena sighed in relief. "Are you all right?"

Gilbrannen held up a hand, still in a coughing fit. With his other hand, he pressed gently on his chest and began to breathe more evenly. "I . . . I think I will be," he said. "It still hurts, but the internal bleeding has stopped."

She had done it. He would survive, though he needed rest. And that meant, as long as he hadn't lied to her again, her father would be released from captivity when they reached Por'monir.

"I intend to keep my word," Gilbrannen said, guessing her thoughts. "There are some of us who take promises lightly, but I do not."

"I know," Niena said, realizing that the connection had gone both ways and Gilbrannen had seen inside her mind as well. Her fears were laid bare for him to know . . . and exploit. "But you could always change your mind."

"I am not going to," Gilbrannen said, his voice a little stronger. "You could have let me die, both now and back in Celwaith Tor. I would not blame you after all that we—I—did to you."

"Well, maybe killing people isn't the best way to solve your problems," Niena said with a tired smirk. "Try to remember that next time you have an urge to storm the keep."

She forced him to lie back on the saddlebags. The sooner he recovered, the sooner they could be off for Por'monir and end this whole debacle. She ached all over, more physically drained than even after their escape. It had taken all of her strength to heal Gilbrannen, and as she leaned against the stone wall of her parents' homestead, every thought of the future gave way to sleep.

AT LAST, NIENA OPENED her eyes, after dawn the next morning by the look of it, though it was hard to tell through the trees. But the time didn't concern her—it was a nearby sound that had woken her.

She looked around. Gilbrannen slept next to her, gently snoring but without the fits and starts of labored breathing as before. The room around them hadn't changed, with one side fallen in and all the foliage outside peering in through the holes.

Niena heard the rustle of leaves nearby, sounding oddly like when the wind blows through the upper branches of a great tree, but there wasn't any breeze. She whipped her head around to find the source, fast enough to see a figure dart past the back window—like the last time she had been here, but closer to the house.

She snatched up the bow and quiver she had reclaimed from Gilbrannen, settling into her firing stance. It felt a little alien to her after so long, but she remembered her father's lessons. Gilbrannen stayed motionless, so she nudged him with her leg a few times. When he still didn't respond, she crept toward the back of the house to investigate it alone.

The door stood open, fallen off its hinges to welcome the cool morning air and the last sounds of nocturnal crickets mingled with early birdsong. Niena eased into the opening, careful of her footing so as not to make noise, and whipped her nocked arrow around the corner.

There was nothing. Nothing but the motionless trees and yet, strangely, still the sound of wind-tossed leaves.

Niena, a voice whispered simultaneously in her ears and her mind. She jumped, and the hairs at the back of her neck raised in alarm when she glanced around and still saw no one.

The windless rustle sounded again, this time from around the side of the house, and the mysterious voice called again. *Over here, child.*

Niena kept her mental guard up and followed the call. This was unlike anything she had ever heard or read about. Holding her breath, she turned the corner of the house and was greeted only by the sight of her mother's cairn and epitaph.

Niena's eyes widened. Could her mother reach out to her from beyond the grave—was that even possible? She had no reason to think that was the case, but she *had* seen the dead D'harn's body respond to Shi'ev's sound machine . . .

"Is anyone there?" Niena called out in a whisper. Only silence answered at first. "Mama? Is it you?"

The voice came from behind her, echoing in her mind. *No, child, I am not Tynathria, but I knew her once.*

Niena turned and saw an ethereal figure constructed of ghostly branches and leaves, floating above the ground. She took a step back in fright, still clutching her bowstring. "I'm not a child. What are you?"

Peace, Niena. You were a child when last I saw you, the visage said, holding the palms of her hands outward in a non-threatening manner. *You have nothing to fear from me. I was once called Omeira, but it has been many summers since then; I am a dryad of the wood.*

Niena frowned. "You mean like a spirit?"

Not as you would define them, but rather a manifestation of nature, Omeira corrected gently. *There are few of us elementals left these days, and only those of D'harnin blood can see or speak to us.*

Niena lowered her bow but kept her arrow nocked. She was wary of letting her guard down with an unknown being—especially one that hadn't featured in any fairy tales she had ever read. "How do you know my name? You said you knew my mother, but I've never heard of a dryad before."

Tynathria chose not to see me, though I often watched her go about her days here, Omeira said wistfully. *I could tell that she had a good heart, but every attempt I made to connect with her was met with silence.*

"What do you mean, she chose not to see you?" Niena asked.

She thought shutting herself off from her birthright would protect you and your unborn brother, and it did for a time. But I was there the day the manticore attacked the farm, when she opened herself to magic once again. She drove it away . . . but not before she paid the most terrible of prices.

Niena stared down at the cairn, gaining a new perspective on the strength of both her parents to abandon all they knew for love—and for her mother, that had meant giving up the core of who she had been. Niena had not heard this part of the story and realized perhaps even her father hadn't known how much his wife had sacrificed to be with him. "What was she like? I don't remember."

The apparition floated closer, seeming to examine Niena's entire being with her unblinking leafy eyes, and smiled. *You look much like Tynathria apart from your hair, but your heart resembles hers more than any I have ever seen in my thousand years tending this forest. She had the same tempestuous spirit, the same tenacity, and the same love for her family that could never be held back.*

Niena felt a lump in her throat and tears well up in the corners of her eyes. It was one thing to hear such a thing from her father, but quite another to see that recognized by someone else who had been around her mother. She wiped at the tears and offered her thanks to the dryad. "I've always wondered what she would think of me. I'm grateful for your words, Omeira. But you didn't reveal yourself just to reminisce about my mother."

You are correct, the specter said, more gravely. *I bear a warning, to anyone who will hear it. My kind can feel all the currents and eddies in the magic of this world, and all the more strongly since there are few magical beings left. The laws of nature have been twisted against themselves, by something so dark that I cannot fathom how it first came about.*

Niena swallowed, her mind racing. She suspected Omeira meant the awful invention that Shi'ev had constructed. Although there didn't seem to be anything inherently magical about the device, there was no denying its awful effect on magic-wielders. "I think I know what you mean," she said, hoping the dryad would elaborate further.

No, that is impossible, Omeira continued. *This perversion of magic has lain hidden for so long and is only now becoming known again. You must hurry on your way, or the whole world may collapse into ruin once more.*

Niena knew what Omeira referred to. Sometime after the D'harnir had faded into obscurity, men warred against each other until just a few scattered villages were left to fend for themselves. Much knowledge had been lost, and the period was commonly referred to as the dark ages before a civilized society could be cobbled back together.

"What can *I* do to stop it?" Niena asked. "I'm nobody."

Omeira appeared to be in anguish as if she was looking beyond the mortal realm and seeing the unspeakable. *All the winds are gathering into a storm cloud, striving against each other but conspiring to cover the lands in darkness. Your family lies at the center of this conflict—I can sense it. You must find them and bring peace.*

Niena's mind reeled. "How? Papa is locked away in Por'monir, and my brother, Tollan, thinks I've lost my mind."

The Cresthavens must stand together against these forces, Niena. If not, the world will be consumed in fire and black magic.

"Who are you talking to?" Gilbrannen's voice called from close by, and Niena flinched. When she looked back again the dryad had vanished in a rustle of ethereal leaves. Gilbrannen passed the corner of the house and looked around her in puzzlement. "Is there anyone else here?" he asked.

Niena ducked the question. If Omeira had wanted to be seen by Gilbrannen, she would have stayed. "No, I—uh, you're feeling better?"

The D'harn rolled his shoulders and cracked his neck. "Much better after that rest, though everything still aches. I can move without my ribs grating now, thanks to you."

"You taught me well, I suppose." Niena smiled, then frowned as her stomach growled audibly. "By the winds, I'm hungry. Do you think you're ready to press on? I don't even know what day it is after sleeping that long."

"Neither do I," Gilbrannen said, squinting at the sky. "Keep in mind that manticores are nocturnal, so if we leave, we should do it soon. I do not think we will find a better shelter north of here, so we need to keep moving until we are out of the forest." He looked around again. "What were you doing out here, anyway?"

Niena looked down at her mother's grave, and back out into the motionless trees. Omeira's warning hung over her like the figurative storm cloud she had mentioned. "Just . . . reconnecting with my mother, you might say. Let's eat and keep moving—something tells me we don't have as much time as we think."

TWENTY-NINE

But be wary, for if your leaders possess reason without conscience, they may become arrogant and believe they can elude the truth whenever convenient.

    — Codes of Entreaty 3.03

TOLLAN PULLED HIS SWORD blade out of the coals for the umpteenth time. He set the glowing metal on the anvil and reached for the hammer he had once used to make horseshoes.

It felt strange working at the forge without his father there looking over his shoulder. He and Anise had returned to the smithy the previous morning, leaving the Denvald house as soon as could be arranged. The army had mostly wrapped up its use of the premises, so there hadn't been any problem reclaiming it. A few supplies had been left behind by the armor-smiths, so Tollan decided to avail himself of them and finally give his gear the Cresthaven treatment.

The armor had been easy, a simple job of reshaping to fit his thin shoulders more closely before reinforcing it. The blade, however, was another animal. After applying the proper amount of carbon, he needed to fold the metal over itself several times to mix it evenly throughout. The next part was his favorite: shaping.

"I heard that you and Anise had moved back in," a voice interrupted before Tollan could bring his hammer down. He frowned and looked up to see who had addressed him. His sister's best friend, Keordi, stared back.

"Hello, Keordi," he said simply.

"Is Niena here?" Keordi asked, skipping right past pleasantries as she often did. He found her annoying at times. "We didn't part ways on the best terms before, but now . . . Well, I came to apologize."

Tollan winced. He wondered what could have come between them. "Sorry, she's left again, as far as I can tell. Probably went back up north, but she didn't check with any of us first."

Keordi nodded sadly, as if she had expected it. "That used to be so unlike her, but I suppose it's no surprise now. Thank you, Tollan." She trudged back up the street.

"Wait!" he said, desperate for answers. "What happened? Did she tell you anything about where she went?"

Keordi laughed without mirth as she continued walking. "Nothing at all. I should have believed her."

Believed her about what? Tollan wanted to call out, but his metal was cooling quickly and if he didn't shape it now, he risked starting over. He had never seen Keordi so quiet and vague before, and it frustrated him even more than when she talked too much.

He swung the hammer time after time, flattening the steel into a thin but durable beveled line. With each hit, he remembered another moment that had brought him to this point: the draft, the war games, the wine. He stopped to heat the metal again before returning to the anvil. The confrontation at the gate, the road to Cape Vrosingr, his last sight of Thaxon's hand. The blade gradually appeared before him, a flared base tapering to a rounded point, and finally a double fuller running the length to meet two-thirds of the way down.

Tollan stood back and stared at it, the product of two days' leave upon returning from the swamps. He still needed to attach the grip and pommel and sharpen it at the grindstone, but at long last, he felt like he had what he wanted. After heating it one final time, he relished the hiss and steam as he quenched it in oil.

He wondered what his father would think of him now, if he would be proud of the life he had forged for himself. Or would he chide Tollan for the choices made along the way? Tollan felt empty as he considered his father's absence from all the recent changes in his life. He knew deep down that it was not supposed to be like this.

He took out his pocket watch and opened it. Forty-seven minutes after three in the afternoon, if it was still accurate. He had forgotten to wind it one morning for an extra hour while returning from Eastmarsh. Even Niena, his sister and his closest friend growing up, had decided to abandon him when he needed her most—and now, the elves had bewitched her to do who knew what. If only neither of them had ever left Celwaith Tor . . .

The front door opened, and Anise stepped out. The rest of the day she had been hard at work unpacking the attic and trying to bring things back to a sense of normalcy, but it seemed the time had come for a break.

"What's all this?" Tollan asked, indicating her clothes.

Anise wore a plain dress and apron, with her hair in a simple bun. Lord Denvald's advances must have truly shaken her for her to dress like a completely different person, Tollan thought.

"Just figured while I was getting the house in order, I should wear a few things I could afford to get dirty," she said, embarrassed. "Why, don't you like it?"

Tollan shook his head, backtracking when he realized he had stepped in it. "No, that's not it! It, uh ... suits you." He winced and realized that might sound even worse to her.

Anise smiled. "Well, thank you, Tollan. I think maybe it does at that."

He removed the sword from the oil and set it on the workbench where he would let it rest before attaching the pommel. Anise came over next to him to admire it. "That looks wonderful, Tollan! Much more befitting one of His Majesty's lieutenants."

"You think so? It might be off-balance now ... I've never made a blade this large before."

Anise nodded. "I think you have Voster's skill."

Tollan shrugged, not sure if that was a compliment or not. "I guess he is the only one I ever learned from."

Anise tilted her head and appraised him instead of the blade, her eyebrows bunched together in concern. "What is it?"

He sighed, knowing that she would never let it go if he didn't tell her. Probably where he had learned to ask so many questions, at least before he became a soldier. "Anise, do you know if Dad ever ... loved me?" he asked, staring down at the sword. "Truly?"

"Oh, Tollan. What makes you ask that?"

Tollan ran through all the things in his head that weighed on him. His father had always gravitated more toward Niena, spending more time with her after work, keeping secrets from Tollan, and even running off to the northern wastes together. But there were other reasons, too. "He never let me try to make things like this," he said, indicating his sword. "I was always short on friends, but working here, I never had the chance to meet any." His eyes burned, but he blinked the tears away. "And he never even left me a note on my birthday. Niena did, but he didn't."

Anise gathered him into her arms, showing no small measure of empathy. "Your father has an odd way of showing his love, that's for sure," she said, rubbing his back. "Trust me, even when we were younger, he darted into and out of my life unexpectedly more times than I can count. But Voster always came back, eventually."

Tollan hugged her back, not sure how that made things any better. "And what if he doesn't, this time?"

"You only have to believe what he told me—he left to try to protect you."

"But why? From what? It doesn't make any sense."

"I don't know, Tollan. I think a lot of the decisions he made for you, he made to protect you, but he seldom gave his reasons for anything."

Tollan thought about that. The world was a scarier place than he ever could have imagined while making horseshoes, so perhaps he could forgive his father for being overly cautious. But it still hurt how he had gone about it.

"Sometimes, being part of a family means choosing to believe the best of people who don't deserve it," Anise said, letting the embrace linger. A commotion came from up the hill, and she released Tollan. "What is this, now?"

A heavyset yellow-clad Drüstanian guard rode on horseback through the dusty streets, nearly bowling a few unwary pedestrians over, and stopped at the smithy fence. "Lieutenant Tollan Cresthaven?" the rider called.

"That's me," Tollan replied, taking off his forge gloves and wiping his hands with a rag. "What do you need?"

The guard dismounted and let himself into the yard. Whatever he needed to say, he did not want it overheard. Anise strolled away a few paces, though Tollan could tell she angled her ear to catch what details she could.

"Come on, out with it," Tollan said. He was supposed to report to the palace the next morning for a new assignment, more specifically to Jarl Anseldr since the king had taken ill before the army's return from Eastmarsh. Perhaps this had something to do with his new orders. "Do I need to report in early?"

The guard met his gaze with a sobering expression. "The king is dead."

TOLLAN TRIED TO REMEMBER the last time he had set foot in the Cathedral of the Winds. He knew he had come a few times with Anise as a child during one of her charity functions, but not since he had been old enough to help his father around the forge.

The building was every bit as impressive as he remembered. The vaulted ceilings and angular pillars directed all attention upwards to where open windows allowed the wind to blow through chimes and across pipes to create a natural chorus of sounds. But today, as the body of King Pelendion rested in state at the front of the cathedral, the windsong took on a sadder and more foreboding tune.

Tollan stood at attention with the other officers of much higher rank, flanking the podium where Friar Empton continued his eulogy and blessing. Queen Coranna stood nearby, handkerchief in hand. The king's youngest brother, Jarl Stenden, had arrived from Cape Vrosingr when he heard that Pelendion had taken ill, and he was seated next to Jarl Anseldr and Emeline in the front. The Kiramet ambassador Le'shom and Darakh Shi'ev were in the second row, given positions of honor alongside the extended royal family. Lord Denvald refused to look in Tollan's direction, absent his wife and characteristic cigar. In the back, Tollan could just make out Anise's face, whose presence in the crowded cathedral was only allowed due to Tollan's minor part in the ceremony.

"The nation of Drüstania has suffered a grievous loss," Friar Empton continued, the elderly man's quiet halting speech still carrying to the furthest corners of the room. "Pelendion I of House Arvad always placed the needs and desires of his people ahead of his own. Even when the unity of Drüstania was shaken by terrorism, his efforts showed us that mistrusting our countrymen is never the answer when outside threats abound. But like his father, Wraelian, he was taken before his time by illness."

Empton's thin white hair glowed in the sunlight filtering down through the windows overhead. "The winds blow where they will: they bring us rain and good things, and also bring drought and pestilence. But there is one thing that the wind cannot take from us: the memories of those we loved, and our dreams for the future of Drüstania. Now, let us remember our King Pelendion in silence and think of how we shall honor him tomorrow."

Tollan and the officers fell to one knee and bowed their heads. The chimes above and a stray cough or two stressed the weight of the moment. Instead of following the friar's prompt, he found his mind straying once again to Thaxon. He still rose from sleep each morning to think his friend might be close by, and he imagined that this funeral was Thaxon's instead. Tollan's eyes welled up, and he seized on the opportunity for closure to bid his close friend a final farewell.

On cue, Queen Coranna moved to the front of the casket to look on her husband's uncovered form one last time. Streams of tears marred her veiled face as Anseldr and Stenden came alongside to close the lid, shutting the king's body in darkness. It reminded Tollan of the trancheon's maw. He exhaled the breath he had been unconsciously holding, and the dark memories with it.

Friar Empton spoke again once Tollan and the officers had risen to their feet. "In the next few minutes, the procession to the royal tombs outside the city will begin. But I have been informed that Pelendion's brother, the crown prince Anseldr, would like to say a few words."

A wave of whispers rippled through the crowd, wondering at the lack of propriety. As Tollan understood it, the heir would not speak publicly until their coronation a week after the prior king's funeral. But given his few interactions with the man, he did not believe Anseldr would break from tradition like this without good reason.

Anseldr stepped up to the podium, thanking Friar Empton briefly, then turning to address the gathering. The cathedral returned to a hush. "People of Celwaith Tor, I stand before you today because you must understand something about the passing of my brother. His illness was not like that of our father. This was not a natural death."

Tollan's eyes widened, but he did not break attention. He had heard rumors of dead guards found on the side of the tor, of a break-in at the palace. But no one had been able to tell him anything concrete.

"Four nights ago," Anseldr said over the disquieted crowd, "a band of elven assassins infiltrated the palace to kill the royal family. Thanks to the quick thinking of visiting Kiramet scientist, Darakh Shi'ev, we thwarted the incursion and captured many of the terrorists alive, but we were not quick enough to prevent a deadly spell from being placed over my brother."

Of course, Tollan realized. Once the elves had made their blunder and given up one of their forward strongholds, they simply waited for the militia to leave for the swamp before making an even bolder move. *Wait . . . wasn't that the same night that Niena went missing?* That could not be a coincidence.

Anseldr continued, his voice lacking the firm projection of Pelendion's addresses but possessing a calming quality over the attendees. "After thoroughly interrogating the elves separately, not only have each of them admitted to the assassination, but they have given up the location of their home, known to them as Por'monir, hidden deep in the northern mountains.

"We now have a unique opportunity to strike at the heart of our opposition," Anseldr continued, raising his gloved hand and making a fist. "The elven stronghold we raided in Eastmarsh was little more than a village, a false front that they quickly abandoned."

Calling it a village was an exaggeration, Tollan thought, as it had been large enough to house more than a thousand individuals comfortably. But in terms of construction, it had all been fairly fragile; none of it would stand the test of time in such a wet climate. Perhaps that had been the point—a people group that had gone undiscovered for centuries, magic or not, would have needed to live hand-to-mouth.

Anseldr scanned the cathedral, giving the impression of looking at every person in turn. "Pelendion's last directions to me were to end the elven threat swiftly. I have already issued assembly orders to all detachments of our armies and militias from Cape Vrosingr, Helsfen Hold, and Stilbry and Güthanas in the south. In two days' time, I will personally lead the largest Drüstanian assault force in history to march on Por'monir, more than ten thousand strong.

"We shall besiege the enemy's gates, we shall prevail, and we shall avenge the deaths of our king and our people."

The sound of applause eclipsed the cathedral's windsong, an unheard-of occurrence at a Drüstanian funeral. The procession began shortly after, and four decorated kingsguard bore Pelendion's casket out through the cathedral doors where the rest of the population waited to bid their farewells. The rest of the royal family filtered in behind the casket, followed by Tollan and the rest of the officers.

As Tollan passed Anise on his way out of the cathedral, he could plainly see the worry in her eyes. She would be left alone at home once more, and he felt for her. But Tollan had a duty to the king—well, he supposed that duty was to Anseldr now that command had passed to him.

As if Tollan's thoughts had manifested it, Anseldr himself appeared beside him, having drifted back in the procession. Another departure from protocol and tradition, Tollan observed. He sensed that Anseldr only cared for such things when it suited him, which was not necessarily a bad thing.

"Lieutenant," Anseldr said under his breath, body language still pointed outwards at the crowd watching them pass by. "I have not had the chance to speak with you directly since you returned."

"Yes, sire," Tollan said, unsure of what honorific to give the man before his coronation. "I have submitted my report of our findings in Eastmarsh, however."

"Oh, this isn't about that," Anseldr assured. "Shi'ev noted something the night of the incursion that you may be able to clear up. He claims that he saw your sister Niena with the party of elven assassins."

Tollan mirrored the other man's posture, careful not to let his surprise show. So, Niena had been present, no doubt prompted by magical influence to lead the terrorists through the halls of the palace. He dared not tell Anseldr about his and Niena's last conversation, or it might implicate him as well. "She ... has been missing since we returned from Eastmarsh," he said haltingly. "How did he know it was her?"

"They had spoken at some length during your honorary banquet, and she wore part of the same green dress from that evening," Anseldr said, tilting his head to study Tollan's reactions. "Once the tide had turned against the infiltrators, the elven leader slipped away with her and jumped out a window into the lake below the tor. Patrols the next morning saw two figures on horseback fleeing from a bandit den a few miles north of here."

An uneasy feeling grew in Tollan's gut. If the bodies hadn't been recovered after such a long fall, they must have survived and escaped. "Am I being held for questioning, Your Majesty?"

"Relax, Lieutenant Cresthaven," Anseldr said. "You have more than proven your loyalty to Drüstania, as we would have no knowledge of the elves without your heroics. It is possible these saboteurs were watching for someone they could use, and picked out your sister from the banquet as a target."

Tollan allowed himself to breathe easy. That did seem plausible, though he knew Niena would have been compromised since before the night of the banquet. "Yes, that's true. May I ask, how was Mr. Shi'ev able to turn the tide against the elves that night?"

"That is an explanation for a different time and place," Anseldr said, gesturing to their surroundings and the many listening ears. "But suffice it to say for now that those methods have already decided our victory over Por'monir."

Tollan thought the declaration was either incredibly optimistic or the unashamed truth. "Understood, sire. I will look forward to hearing more—and I will bring my sister in for questioning if she should return before we leave."

"Good man," Anseldr said. He picked up the pace to return to his place next to the king's casket but thought better of it for a moment. "One last thing: the incursion left the kingsguard a few members light. I want you to be one of them, and accompany me during the assault on Por'monir."

Tollan was sure he heard wrong. "I don't believe I'm worthy of such an honor, sire."

Anseldr nodded, a proud but solemn smile breaking his melancholy. "Of course you are," he said. "You are the only known soldier who has been able to see through the enemy's illusions from the start, and I want you by my side should the worst happen."

"I am at your service," Tollan said.

"I know you are," Anseldr said, clapping him on the shoulder. "Report to the palace tonight to assist in planning our assault." The prince moved back to his position behind his brother's casket, his velvet cloak billowing behind him.

A million thoughts ran through his mind, but his sister occupied most of them. He assumed that she had been captured and bewitched, but knowing she accompanied the assassins into the palace . . . What if she hadn't been? What if everything she had told him about their mother that night was true, and she had been helping the elves of her own accord?

No. Tollan refused to think the worst of her, even now. Anise had been right earlier when she had said to believe the best of his family.

He followed the funeral procession onto the field where the army would assemble in two days, and out into the hills where the royal tomb of House Arvad had been prepared to receive its newest occupant. Tollan hoped he had the skill to protect Anseldr from following his brother's fate.

THIRTY

Although a manticore on the wing is relentless in its pursuit, the sins of the past will catch up to you even more surely.

— *Codes of Binding 2.17*

THE TREES WHIPPED BY in a blur, leaves and thorns grasping at their clothes as they passed. The scratches hurt where they connected with bare skin, but they were nothing compared to the fate that awaited them if the coal-black mare beneath them slowed down.

Niena sat on Evwoin's back, hanging onto Gilbrannen for dear life. "Can't she go any faster?" she asked nervously.

"She is built for endurance, not speed!" Gilbrannen said as he snapped the reins again anyway, urging the horse to a breakneck pace.

"Why did you bring us this way anyway?" Niena accused.

"It is the fastest route back to Por'monir without retracing steps—we've wasted too much time as it is!"

"Only if we wind up dead," Niena spat, glancing behind them into the shadows of the changing leaves.

"Where are they now?" Gilbrannen called.

"I can't see them! They must have gone around," Niena shouted, then ate her words as a bloodcurdling roar sounded above them, echoed by a second creature a little farther off. The sound hurt her ears and made it hard to think straight. And, like with Shi'ev's noise machine, Gilbrannen reacted far more acutely to it.

"I . . . *arrgh* . . . think you mean above," Gilbrannen grunted. "They are . . . trying to cut us off." A darker shadow fell on them, and he yanked the reins hard to the right.

Behind them, the massive chimeric form of a manticore crashed down through the forest canopy, reaching out with sharp claws and an even sharper tail to sweep them to the ground. The beast was four yards long from human-like nose to scorpion-like stinger, only a little smaller than the one Niena and her father had encountered. She looked straight into its glowing red eyes for an instant and her blood ran cold.

"I thought manticores were solitary hunters," Niena complained through gritted teeth, gripping the saddlebags harder between her legs as they tried to outmaneuver the beasts. She had tried using her bow, but there was no way she could aim while moving like this. "And you said they were nocturnal!"

The other manticore, about half the size of the first but still large enough to take a chunk out of a shoulder or a horse haunch, chose that moment to drop in front of them. Gilbrannen veered off again, but he was rapidly running out of places to go. "That one is a juvenile," he shouted back. "The male parent hatches the egg and teaches it to hunt!"

"Lucky us!" Niena said, gasping. "Look out!"

The larger manticore had used the distraction of its child to gain on them through the trees on their left, and it pounced.

Gilbrannen shouted a spell she had never heard before and raised his fist. A near-invisible ovoid barrier spread from his clenched hand, which temporarily stopped the manticore in its tracks. It roared, causing Gilbrannen to clutch his head and drop the barrier. Niena held on to the saddlebags and reached frantically for one of his throwing knives—but didn't get the chance.

The adolescent manticore caught up with them and attacked the horse's right flank. Evwoin fell first with a pained whinny, the saddle straps snapped, and Niena and Gilbrannen went tumbling down a steep embankment through stray roots and thorn bushes.

They landed in a heap at the bottom, bruised and bleeding. Niena pushed herself up and spat dirt out of her mouth. She hoped Gilbrannen hadn't torn open any of his recently healed wounds, but she realized it barely mattered. They could not outrun the manticores now.

Evwoin's plaintive horse calls ended in a sickening crunch as the adult manticore broke her neck. The creature turned to roar at the two escaped pieces of prey. It stalked down the hill between the trees, its offspring following close behind in eerie mimicry.

Niena hauled Gilbrannen back to his feet and waited for the end, standing over their badly damaged saddlebags. If she was going to die today it would be with courage, the same way her mother Tynathria faced down a manticore to save her.

I'm sorry, Papa, she thought desperately as the two predators cleared the last tree and readied to strike. *I tried.*

"Get down!" a voice called from behind them.

Niena and Gilbrannen fell to their knees as a group of green and gray-robed D'harnir brandishing rifles surrounded them and faced the manticores. The predators arched their backs, antagonized by all the new enemies, but they did not flee.

Gilbrannen pointed out a movement to their right, and the bat-like wings of a third manticore flashed out from behind a thicket. "We have even more company."

"On the left, too," Niena said. "They're closing in."

"Get ready to move," the leader of the D'harnir said gruffly and sighted down his weapon's barrel alongside the other five members of his party.

"You're going to fight them?" Niena asked. She didn't get an answer.

The four manticores charged, and the six D'harnir let their bullets fly. None of the shots proved fatal, but the manticores pulled up short and clawed at themselves in pain. "Now," the leader said, making no move to reload.

They ran from the beasts, which gathered their wits and began again to stalk and surround their prey. They lunged closer, wary of more rifle shots coming their direction. When they found none to challenge them, they swooped in for the kill.

"Wards up!" the leader shouted, and the D'harnir stretched out their hands and formed a combined protective shell to keep the teeth, claws, and stingers at bay. The manticores continued to circle and test their defenses, but they could find no exploitable gaps.

Shouldering the saddlebags and moving as fast as she could, Niena could see the creatures getting more and more agitated with this game, and their growling intensified. Finally, two let out a roar in unison, and the resolve of the D'harnir broke with the awful sound. "Run!" the leader said, and they abandoned all defense to turn and cross a shallow river with a clearing on the other side.

The manticores inexplicably halted their pursuit at the water's edge. A couple of them tried to fly over, but they didn't go far until turning back. With their prey out of reach, the territorial beasts now realized that others of their kind lurked nearby. Hissing and posturing commenced until the largest, a female, asserted her dominance and forced the others to go their separate ways.

"What ... happened?" Gilbrannen said, holding his head and shaking the fog of the manticore roars from his mind. "Why did they stop?"

The leader of the group lowered his gray hood and offered him a hand up. "We only know that they stay away from this part of the forest. You got lucky coming close enough that we could help—the beasts have us surrounded in every direction."

"Never seen anything like that," Gilbrannen said, still in shock as he stumbled back to his feet. "Let alone manticores working together."

"Yes ..." the leader said, trailing off as he looked suspiciously at Niena. She stared back at him, not willing to trust the newcomers despite their timely rescue. "Who is this? Why are you traveling the Spinewood with a human girl?"

Gilbrannen held his hands up in placation, then had them examine Niena's scars along the top of her ears. "No need to worry. She is one of us, at least partly."

Niena wanted to take offense at that statement, but she figured they weren't in a position to quibble over semantics. Instead, she jerked her head away from the leader's dirty hands and got up of her own volition. Her cuts and bruises stung, but she presumed healing magic would tend to the worst of it.

"Ah, a half-blood," the leader said in understanding. "I thought the last of those had died out, oh, a few hundred years ago. Where did you come across her?"

"Sorry." Niena stopped him to clarify, sick of being referred to like she wasn't there. "Who are you all? Seems a dangerous place for D'harnir to congregate."

"If it could have been avoided, we would have done so," the leader said, now eyeing the saddlebags at Niena's feet. "I am called Fendaral, and we are what remains of the wardcasters of Neraliel."

"Fendaral, of course," Gilbrannen said, putting the pieces together. "I am relieved that you made it out. I suppose that explains where you obtained the rifles. We knew the humans were coming to finish you off after what happened on the East Road, but . . ."

"You thought we would not be smart enough to have contingency plans in place," Fendaral accused. "That we would be the perfect scapegoat for your plans."

Niena fought to hide a smile. It was about time that Gilbrannen saw the consequences of his actions.

"No," Gilbrannen denied, even though he had once told Niena differently. "Silmon's failure is on his shoulders alone. We would never intentionally betray our kind. How many are you? Did everyone escape Neraliel in time?"

Fendaral paced. "For the most part, though we suffered casualties along the way, mostly the perimeter guard and foragers. Our camp is among the ruins through that line of trees, but supplies are running low. We had intended to take refuge in Por'monir, but every time we try to leave this area, the manticores converge to pick us off. We are trapped, and now, so are you."

Ruins? Niena thought. Now that sounded interesting and familiar.

"If you do not mind," Fendaral continued, "all of your questions have been answered. You owe us a few words in return, or I have half a mind to throw you back outside with the winged menaces."

"This is Niena, and I am Gilbrannen," he replied. "We are making for Por'monir in the north as well, with urgent news. I am sure that Shilvand will offer refuge to all of you there."

"Were you not listening?" Fendaral asked irritably. "No one can leave this place. The manticores are circling just beyond the edge of whatever barrier is holding them back. We so much as set one foot out of here, they start swarming for a chance at a fresh meal."

Niena asked the first question that came to her mind. "You have those handy weapons though—why not use them to clear out the manticores?"

"Because, young one, it took us twenty shots to fell just one of them," Fendaral said. "We have a scarce supply of ammunition. I have no doubt we would run out before they would."

Gilbrannen cleared his throat, looking down. Niena thought she detected a trace of remorse or guilt, but that couldn't be the case. "Thank you for thinking us worth your ammunition. We would not have survived without your help."

Fendaral grunted and gathered the saddlebags from where Niena had left them. "Though your enclave may be different, we are not in the habit of condemning people to certain death by inaction. There is no point in killing you when time will come for us all. The provisions you have with you will be divided into our rations."

Niena followed close behind. Por'monir, and her father who still languished in a cell there, were more out of reach than ever. "What are we supposed to do? We can't stay here!"

"Get used to the idea, unless you would rather face down another group of manticores," Fendaral said and led them back to the camp.

Niena locked eyes with Gilbrannen and saw the same desperation staring back at her but for different reasons.

NIENA WATCHED AS GILBRANNEN spent the next day and a half restlessly probing the perimeter, despite being warned otherwise. Fendaral had been truthful in his estimations of the manticores surrounding them, but that hadn't stopped him from continuing to find a way out.

The Neraliel refugees had largely shunned him for his part in losing their homes, and Niena could tell that Gilbrannen at least regretted his callous heart toward them in the past. His plan to assassinate the king had been reckless, and these D'harnir were out in the cold because of Silmon's similar mistake.

The refugees had already been trapped in the ruins for nigh on a week before Niena and Gilbrannen arrived, and rations were limited to a few scraps of dried meat a day. At that rate, they would only be able to survive for another two weeks until they starved. Even when Fendaral took down a large elk that had slipped through the wall of stalking predators, it was minuscule split up into nine hundred portions.

Living conditions were not any better, as few fortunate D'harnir found shelter in the ruins, and the others had to make do with lean-to coverings or nothing at all. Niena and Gilbrannen, being latecomers and now apparent outcasts, were in the latter group and had to sleep against the trees to keep the rain off.

After resigning herself to the less-than-ideal situation, Niena spent most of her time practicing her newfound affinity for healing magic and getting to know the less stand-offish refugees. Unlike the secrecy of Por'monir, she found that most of Neraliel's people had known and approved of the sporadic attacks perpetrated against humans. Because the village was so small, transparency had been a necessity. They all had known they would need to abandon their homes should they be discovered—but none of them had believed it would come so soon.

On the third day after their arrival, Niena went to Fendaral and asked him to return their saddlebags, less the rations which had already been contributed to the collective. He had refused the last time she brought it up, but he seemed a little more charitable this time. "Is there something specific you need from them?" he asked.

"A leather-bound book," she said. "My father gave it to me, and it might have the key to escaping these ruins. But first I need to confirm that these ruins are from Por'monir's first settlement."

"I can tell you that," Fendaral scoffed. "There are no hints of D'harna language or decoration anywhere in this old village."

"Can I please just have the book?"

"I suppose there is no harm in it." Fendaral relented and produced the tome from the saddlebags. "The people like you, if not your incessant questions. Keep me informed of anything useful you find."

Niena offered him her thanks and took the book. She flipped through it, looking for the right page as she searched the perimeter for Gilbrannen. She found him to the north, being eyed down by a manticore not twenty yards away.

"It does not matter where I go," he said in frustration when Niena ran up to him. "As soon as I get close, another waits for me to set foot outside the barrier. There has to be at least a dozen of them out there."

"Never mind that," Niena said and handed him the book, pointing to one of the handwritten paragraphs. "I knew this place sounded familiar when we arrived. I read about it."

Gilbrannen examined the passage, a few different emotions flickering across his face as he did so. "This would be in the right vicinity of our first settlement about six or seven centuries ago. But I know nothing of a magical totem that could hold back so many manticores."

"You've never heard of anything like it?"

"No. But according to our histories, much of what our elders knew about magic was lost in the subsequent attack," Gilbrannen explained. His eyes lit up as he realized how it could help their plight. "If it is here, and it is small enough to take with us, it could protect the entire enclave while we kept moving north."

Niena smiled, glad to see Gilbrannen getting on board with her plan. But the smile evaporated when something else occurred to her. "Would the manticores follow us, even with the barrier?"

Gilbrannen considered that while watching the nearby creature stalk back and forth beyond the perimeter. "Difficult to say. They naturally prey on D'harnir and other creatures that have a magical resonance. But I do not believe they would pursue us far beyond their nesting grounds here in the forest."

That was good enough for Niena. "Right. Well, the totem has to be buried somewhere around here. Maybe in one of the collapsed buildings?"

"This has promise, Niena," he said and pointed back through the trees in the direction of the ruins. "Start walking that way, and count your paces. When you get to the opposite side and see a manticore, stop and retrace exactly half your steps. I will do the same perpendicular to you, and hopefully the result will give us an approximate location of the totem."

Niena agreed, honestly surprised that he had devised such an elegant solution so quickly. She figured they would start by removing stone and dirt from the collapsed buildings, but this method cut out most of the guesswork.

She cut back through the ruins, carefully counting her steps and staying in as straight a line as she possibly could. She could feel the eyes of the D'harnin families on her back, no doubt wondering what in all the nine seas she was doing.

At almost a thousand paces, Niena winced at the sound of a manticore roar. A large female swooped down through the trees and landed right in front of her, swiping with her tail. Niena scrambled back and felt the wind off the poison stinger tip. *That was lucky,* she thought to herself. *Another few steps and I'd have gone too far.*

She counted back the way she came and found Gilbrannen waiting for her maybe ten yards from her estimated midpoint.

There was nothing: no buildings, no remains, just dirt and grass in the center of the ruined village. And a bunch of D'harnir standing around staring at them. "I guess we start digging," Gilbrannen said awkwardly, looking around at the nearest structures.

Niena took out her book again to review for clues, then stopped. She had an idea. "Gilbrannen, do you think there might be tunnels under here? You know, like—" She almost said *like you have in Por'monir*, but he cut her off with a snap of his fingers.

"Right! One of the ruined structures might have a cellar entrance. Maybe Fendaral knows."

As it turned out, one of the crumbled structures near the outskirts led into what appeared to be an underground corridor that had long since collapsed. But once they showed Fendaral their evidence, he brought the matter to the arbiter of the enclave and they both agreed it was worth an attempt.

The next week and a half consisted of an abundance of hard labor on nearly empty stomachs. Busting up the larger stones and supporting the roof with fresh-cut trees was grueling work, but all the able-bodied members of the enclave pitched in to make it happen.

The dangerous part, Niena found, was the shifting dirt and stone that collapsed before they could brace it, undoing hours of work in moments.

A falling stone slab almost crushed Gilbrannen on one of those occasions, and he barely managed to deflect it with his warding spell. It was the same one he had used against the manticore when they had been riding on horseback.

Niena rushed over to confirm he was okay. "You have to teach me that," she said, not expecting him to take her seriously.

"Of course," he replied, coughing through the cloud of dust hanging in the air. He reached for her hand. "Now help me up."

They began practicing that night. The ward was a short and simple spell—it had to be, since it was often used on reflex. But it took a lot of energy out of the caster, increasing exponentially with the amount of force it resisted.

"It is not like an illusion ward," Gilbrannen explained. "An illusion can be maintained with little effort and concentration, but things that affect physical reality? You might collapse from the strain if you use the spell for too long or frequently."

"Understood." Niena hoped she wouldn't need to use it at all. But if the dryad Omeira's warning had told her anything, she needed every tool at her disposal to protect her family. Despite being exhausted every day from the excavation, she made sure to practice casting her spells every morning and evening, until they were almost second nature.

Finally, a long two weeks after she and Gilbrannen first arrived, as the enclave's rations were on the verge of running out, the passageway was clear. Fendaral insisted that Gilbrannen be the one to venture down into the tunnels; since his ally, Silmon, was the one to get them into this mess, Gilbrannen would be the one to get them out.

Gilbrannen offered no dispute, and Niena volunteered to go with him. She led the way with a torch fashioned from dry wood and bitumen, and they passed under several stone arches carved with the image of a winged bird, not unlike the decoration on Por'monir's Hall of Meeting. A faint runic language could be seen scribbled on sections of the walls between engraved murals. "What are these?" she asked.

He stared at a few of them, his eyes darting back and forth across the images. "These are very old, very powerful runes. An even older script of D'harna, if I'm not mistaken." He paused and waved at Niena excitedly to bring her torch closer. "Impossible."

"What?" She handed him the light.

"I think these passages might be from the Codes of Nature."

"A third set of codes?" Niena asked. Her father's book had only quoted from two, Binding and Entreaty.

"Por'monir and Neraliel had lost them to time—only fragments survived orally," Gilbrannen said, his fingers moving over the script to the next section. The first carving was simple, just geometric shapes, but as he moved down the hall more features and details filled each successive image. "They record the beginning of time and the spells that set the world in motion."

Niena was shocked. "Your magic is that old?"

"Why does that surprise you?" Gilbrannen asked as if it was obvious. "The D'harnir did not discover magic. It was designed for our people at the dawn of time."

The corridor opened outwards down a set of wide stairs, and the murals on both sides culminated on the opposite wall: a large, engraved relief that the shadows from Niena's torch illuminated in stark contrast. On one side, it depicted a man and woman holding tools, and on the other, a pair of elves with beams of light emanating from their hands. The figures gathered around a great tree in the center—and its branches were covered in what looked like wicks of flame rather than leaves.

Extruding from the tree, placed in a stone sconce that held it upright, stood a bronze staff with a dark, smooth stone mounted at its top. "That must be the totem," Niena said with excitement. She hurried down the stairs and wrapped a hand around the staff. It was cool and heavy to the touch, but it lifted out of the sconce without difficulty.

The torchlight dimmed, and Niena turned to see Gilbrannen still caught up in his reading of the runes. "Come on, Gilbrannen. We don't have time to read everything. We have what we came for."

He reluctantly pulled himself away from the walls. Niena suspected that his yearning had been tempered by the crowd of almost a thousand D'harnir waiting to be led to food and shelter. But they had no time to lose, and Niena's other concerns weighed heavier on her as they traversed back through the underground passage to the surface.

Omeira's warning still echoed in her mind: *The world will be consumed in fire and black magic.* After two weeks with the survivors of Neraliel, Niena may have been delayed too long to prevent the dryad's warning.

She crawled out of the tunnel's narrow opening and into the sunlight.

INTERLUDE V

Last Contact

c. 15 – 20 years after the Rift

ON THE EVE OF *the arrival of the king's men, bound to destroy the sanctuary we had worked so hard to build, the D'harnir decided among themselves that my family should depart from them. The council of elders thanked my father for our family's part in helping them escape from the Macula Society, but in their pride, they believed the rift between our peoples could no longer be healed.*

My father tried to convince the elders to reconsider, even using passages from the Codes of Entreaty to make his point, but their hearts had hardened now that they were forced to flee their homes once again. They believed my father's mercy was a two-edged sword; on the one hand, it was his mercy that had allowed them to escape all those years ago, but on the other, it was his mercy that now delivered them into harm's way.

My father agreed with a heavy heart and asked me to look after the rest of the family. He was getting old in years and still had one last stand to make. The king's army arrived before the D'harnir were ready to flee, and he went out to them as he had to the hunters. He offered peace between men and elves, and my mother and I watched as arrows pierced his chest in reply. We rode away as the army advanced on Por'monir.

I returned to the site of the battle some weeks later and found the village had been utterly destroyed. Uncounted, unburied bodies remained in burned-out homes, and I did my best to lay them to rest in my approximation of D'harnin custom. I had hoped that in so doing, I might find some sign of survivors and where they might have fled, but I could only determine that they followed the Plindre River northward into the most inhospitable part of the mountains. I tried for years to search them out, to rekindle some trust between us like my father wanted, but I could not afford the time until the trail ran cold. My elderly mother took ill, and so my nephews and I built a watchtower between the lands of men and the remnants of Por'monir.

One thing I know for certain, having witnessed the once-great Union of man and elf, of D'salnir and D'harnir: the fates of all rest entirely on whether we can learn to forgive each other and make the right choices for our descendants. For if men succeed in their ambitions, the world will one day be subdued into a charnel house, and all that is good will go with them into the night. But if the elves returned to prominence now, so set against coexisting with men that they abandon their faith and principles for the sake of fear or vengeance, the harsher aspects of nature will overtake all that has been made to survive the winter.

— Haron Geled, Last Scribe of the Union
28th of Hollyn, in the 48th year after the Rift

THIRTY-ONE

As for matters of repayment: he who holds back the jaws of the eternal night shall be treated as a kinsman in all but name.

— *Codes of Binding 3.06*

VOSTER SAT IN HIS cell, staring at marks he had made on the cave wall, lit only by the solitary blue flame of one of the elves' odd oil lamps. Without daylight, it was impossible to know how long he had truly been imprisoned under the city of Por'monir. He instead marked how many times he slept and hoped that was enough to keep track of the days for him. According to his count, he had been here over two months, and he hadn't seen Niena since being separated that first day.

No one had spoken to him in weeks, not since Shilvand had come to taunt him. Even the guards merely dropped off his moldy food and musty water, with nary an acknowledgment of his pleas for communication. He refused to believe what his brother-in-law had said about Niena, but the possibility had continued to gnaw at him. And he hated that Shilvand had intended him to have these feelings so that he would be in pain even while alone.

He stood, distracting himself with his basic strength exercises against the wall and the floor. The lack of good food had caused him to start shedding weight drastically, and he knew that if he didn't keep up his exercises, he would waste away to nothing. His broad shoulders were not so broad anymore, and he could see his ribs for the first time since his teens, but he thought he might be able to fight and run if necessary.

Panting, he returned to his bench and lay down. It had only been a momentary distraction, and now his mind turned to Tollan instead. The boy had always been impressionable, and Voster knew from his own father's war stories how being in the army could change a man. But, regardless of what had happened to Niena, maybe Anise would be enough of a good influence to keep Tollan grounded in what mattered.

There was so much he didn't know from being locked up. The world could be an entirely different place by the time Shilvand decided to let him go, and he wondered if that would ever happen. The elf was obsessed, nothing like Tynathria's brother he had met long ago. Something had broken inside Shilvand when his sister chose to be with Voster over family.

Tynathria, or as he knew her, just Athria. He wondered if she would have revealed her lineage to the children in time rather than kept it a secret. Maybe he should have done so sooner, or not at all. But even now, sixteen years after her death, there was still a gaping hole in his heart. Those few years building a farm together and raising little Niena had been the happiest of his life, and returning to the homestead had reopened all those griefs that had festered beneath the surface.

And so, the cycle continued in his mind—from worry, to questioning, to doubt, to regret, and back again. He longed to see his children again, but he had to come to terms with the fact that he might not. Whatever happened now would not be his fault. It would be Shilvand's.

A clatter came from the outer hall, but it was too early for another meal. An unfamiliar D'harn in guard attire appeared in the latticed door alongside the urgent jangling of a key in the lock. Voster sat up, wondering what bad news the winds had brought him this time.

The figure turned and dragged a body inside the cell, also wearing a blue cloak. Another D'harn followed him in, dressed in rags and just as emaciated as Voster. But this D'harn's ears were shorn.

"Tolvanen!" Voster exclaimed in a whisper. "What's going on? Where's Niena?"

"No time," Tolvanen said hastily, his voice straining as he pulled another guard's body in from the corridor and left it at Voster's feet. Based on his appearance, it looked like Shilvand had treated him much the same. "I do not know where your daughter is, but she is not in any of the other cells. Help us disrobe these guards—the disguises will help us escape unnoticed."

Voster didn't know if his daughter's fate was for better or worse— and if she had decided to serve Shilvand's plans.

"Who's your friend?" Voster asked as he stripped one of the bodies and threw on the clothes. As it turned out, the guards weren't dead— just completely limp and sleeping *hard*.

"Tolvanen's nephew, Arondin," the unknown D'harn said, handing Voster a small square of spongy cake-like bread. "Eat this, it will help you to recover your strength."

Voster abandoned his attempt to get dressed and swallowed whatever it was, not even registering the taste in his mouth. It instantly eased the hunger in his stomach, and he felt some energy begin to seep through him. "How did you find us?"

"The Junir clan has suspected for a long time that Shilvand is not the honorable arbiter he seems to be," Arondin answered, gesturing for Voster to continue putting on the guard's clothes. "I was working in our fields on the other side of the mountain to bring in our last harvest, when I happened to see some of our grain get siphoned off by workers from the Falir clan. I followed them here, had a look around, and came upon Tolvanen. Are you done yet? We have to go."

Voster unlatched the D'harnin guard's belt and slid the breeches off. They were far too long for him, but he rolled up the cuffs and made do. "Ready. What's the plan?"

Tolvanen shrugged into the cloak, then helped Voster into his. "We might have a problem, Arondin. He is too short to pass as a D'harn."

Voster grimaced. It wasn't often he was called the short one. "Why does it matter? These tunnels run for miles in several directions away from Por'monir—let's just get away from here."

"Not in your condition," Arondin said, giving them each a dagger from the downed guards. "There is nothing but wilderness for almost a hundred miles, and the first snow came yesterday. There is no way back into the enclave without going through the main gate. I now have proof that the Falir clan has conspired to attack humans and stockpile goods against the other clans' well-being. We are directly under Por'monir right now—if I can get you both to our clan's matriarch, Molenia, she will protect you until we can convene the Council and depose Shilvand as arbiter."

Voster realized that the burgeoning conflict could be stopped right then. Niena and Tollan would both be safe from the prolonged war that Shilvand wanted to bring. "All right, I'm with you. Tell me what to do."

Arondin applied his sleeping potion a second time to the nostrils of Shilvand's secret police, ensuring they would continue to doze for a good long while. "Follow me. Do as I do, and make no sound. It may take trial and error to find the right passage."

The three of them ventured out through the network of corridors and chambers, following the sparsely placed oil lamps. Occasionally, they came to a dead end, but Arondin had a sense of the direction they needed to travel. They crept from shadow to shadow, listening at every intersection, but the place was completely deserted.

"I don't like this," Voster said. "It's too quiet."

Arondin and Tolvanen made no reply and instead kept moving, making the most of their good fortune.

The corridors opened out into a large natural cavern, with a staircase spiraling around a massive stalagmite up into the pointy ceiling. Still, no one stopped them, and they moved as quickly as they could up the stairs toward the promise of freedom. Voster's calves hated him for the climb, but he would not allow himself to give out now.

The stone gave way to wood, and they exited from the underground into a storeroom, which Arondin quickly surmised was in the basement of Por'monir's Hall of Meeting. Again, no guards materialized to stop them, so they made their way upstairs into Shilvand's family quarters. One of the rooms had a window that led out onto the sloped roof, and Arondin explained the plan from there. Once on the back side of the longhouse, they would be able to jump a couple of yards to an outcropping that jutted out of the mountainside, a remnant of when the settlement's foundations had been carved from stone. Then the hill would provide cover as they climbed down into the Junir clan neighborhood to find refuge in Molenia's home.

Voster followed Tolvanen and their unexpected savior out the window, but that was as far as the plan went without a hitch.

Before his eyes could fully adjust to the bright outdoors, a shout from below caused them all to flinch, and Voster almost lost his footing on the steep roof. The soldier that had spotted them from the courtyard blew a syncopated four blasts on a small horn, alerting at least two dozen others standing at attention on the carved promontory courtyard overlooking the rest of Por'monir.

"So close," Arondin said through clenched teeth. "Run for it."

They climbed like madmen, vaulting over the peak of the roof and heading for the back corner. Arrowheads thudded into the rafters right after they ducked below the peak. Voster blanched when he saw the length of the jump they would need to clear the gap to the outcropping, but the alternative was a more immediate threat.

Arondin went first, sliding down the roof to gain momentum and then kicking off. He sailed over the opening, catching the ledge and rolling out of the way. Tolvanen went next, replicating the move with slightly less dexterity. They waited for Voster on the other side.

He didn't care for these acrobatics, but the elven archers provided all the encouragement he needed. His feet scraped down the side of the icy roof, moving faster and faster until he was airborne.

Voster knew he wouldn't clear the gap almost as soon as he pushed off. He panicked, kicking his legs and flailing, and managed to catch Tolvanen's outstretched hand. Voster dangled there, breathing hard, and realized his situation had not improved.

"I ... cannot ... pull him up," Tolvanen said, straining and beginning to slip.

Voster made the mistake of looking down and seeing the almost twenty-foot drop onto hard stone and the icy remnants of recent snow that had thawed and re-frozen. He scrabbled at the side of the outcropping with his free hand and feet, but he couldn't get a grip.

Arondin tried to reach down to him as well, but they had already slid too far downward. He held onto Tolvanen's other arm, but that threatened to pull him over.

"Go!" Voster shouted before he fully realized the words in his mouth. "Tell your clan. They have to know."

Arondin seemed torn until Tolvanen nodded in confirmation. "Do it," the older D'harn said and released his hold on the ledge.

Voster fell, tumbling away from the mountainside, certain that he would strike his head and all would go dark. His knees absorbed the shock of the blow, and he crumpled forward into the crusty ice and snow, covering his head. Tolvanen landed behind him an instant later.

He breathed hard, not feeling the pain at first that he knew he should. He opened his eyes and looked down, taking stock of his body. Blood leaked from a serious scrape along his elbow and forearm, but the aches only started when he was violently yanked to his feet.

Shilvand's secret police surrounded them. Voster listened for any sign of Arondin, but it seemed as though he had escaped, at least for now. Tolvanen yelped when his hands were jerked behind him—a bulge in his forearm told Voster the bone had broken from their fall.

The soldiers dragged Voster and Tolvanen to the front of the Hall of Meeting, where they would presumably be taken back underground to their cells. But as they rounded the corner of the building, Voster saw the pious shimmering white robes of the enclave's arbiter standing at the end of the promontory.

Voster remembered this place well and had on occasion returned here in his dreams. The view across the frozen wasteland was stunning beyond compare, even though the morning was overcast.

Shilvand turned away from presiding over his sanctuary and looked on as Voster and Tolvanen were brought before him. The guards did not bind them, but instead held them both at spear-point. "I am almost surprised that it has taken you this long to find your way out of your cells," he said. "Whoever aided you will be caught before he can do any harm, I assure you."

Voster looked around below the edge of the courtyard, expecting to see the bustle of business and the thousands of elves that lived in Por'monir going about their daily lives. But the enclave was silent, save for clusters of soldiers dotting the ramparts at regular intervals. "No one allowed in the streets? Are you afraid your people would pity an old man who once saved one of their own from certain death?"

"You make me sound so conniving," Shilvand said, shaking his head in amusement. "If I was afraid of my people seeing humans, you and your daughter never would have reached our gates in the first place. My Dast'rel guard would have killed you both."

"Fascinating," Voster said, glaring at the ones who held his arms behind his back. He might have been able to take them once, but not in his current state. "This is not the average day then, I take it."

Shilvand exhaled through his nose and crossed his arms. "We received word from our perimeter guard two days ago that a large army of men crossed the Plindre River moving north. The wardcasters will protect the city from view, but the mere threat your kind poses is more than enough to cause the people of Por'monir to shut their doors in fear."

Voster recalled when he and Niena had walked the streets of Por'monir before. All the families immediately gathered their children and went inside. Shilvand's version of history had long since won out in the hearts of his people.

Tolvanen straightened his back in defiance. "And now everyone will associate this intended attack with the faces of Voster and Niena. You want your people to think of humans as nothing more than barbarians, so you provoked them to act like it."

Shilvand took two steps closer and looked Tolvanen in the eyes. "I regret that things have come to this. I truly do. It was supposed to be so simple, but the carelessness of our southern brethren has required a change in our timetable. So, yes, if my people learn to associate any human contact with the threat of destruction, it will be better for them."

"And what then?" Voster asked, goading his brother-in-law. "What if the army comes and finds Por'monir, as I did, and your wardcasters can't keep them away? Hiding indoors will not be enough."

Shilvand's eyes flashed with hatred. "If that happens, King Pelendion will receive far more than he bargained for in waging war with us."

"I think you've been in hiding for so long that you've forgotten what war means," Voster said, recalling again his father's stories. "It is destruction and death until one side or the other runs out of blood to give."

"How eloquent," Shilvand replied, his white hair blowing in the morning breeze. "That is an apt description—and here I thought the race of men were not natural poets.

"As it turns out, the D'harnir are prepared to take plenty of blood."

Voster recalled his brief time in Por'monir, all those years ago. Shilvand had struck him as a decent person, certainly protective of his younger sister, but that was to be expected in a world that had proven so harsh to elven kind. He had even stood up to their overbearing and legalistic father, Wirvanen, at times.

But little remained of that person. The protective had turned into the possessive, and his noble, thin face had become harsh and angular. He resembled his father Wirvanen more now than he ever had in his youth.

Voster knew in his heart that he could never convince his brother-in-law to pursue peace. The whole journey had been for nothing. His imprisonment had been for nothing. But there was no one else to defy Shilvand's power. "The Codes demand that you stop this," he said.

Shilvand struck Voster across the face. "Do not speak to me of a way of life you know so little about!" he hissed. "The Codes became outdated the moment the D'salnir drove us out of our land. They forfeited any part of fellowship with us for their own gain."

"Does that mean the Mishenna no longer applies to them?" Tolvanen asked, nursing his arm which had swelled with a purple bruise. Voster marveled at the D'harn's composure and compassion despite his injury. "The Codes of Entreaty say to never answer wrongdoing with vengeance."

Shilvand stared, his jaw clenching and unclenching. "I suppose you would have it apply to manticores as well as men? Enough."

Tolvanen fell silent, realizing the futility as Voster had. His eyes drifted to the horizon in disappointment, then stopped. He pointed with his uninjured hand, past Shilvand's glowering face, beyond the walls of Por'monir, and across the dead grass and snow to the far end of the valley.

Voster spotted it instantly, and his heart sank.

The sun had come out from behind the clouds, and it glinted off line after line of armored men and polished weapons as they crested the far rise and marched inexorably toward Por'monir. Their columns stretched from one side of the valley to the other, and still they kept coming.

Voster swallowed back a bit of bile that had crept up his throat with the realization that his son would be somewhere on that battlefield. He desperately hoped that Niena, wherever she was and whatever she was doing, had fled as far away from here as her legs could carry her.

The state of unresolved cold war that had existed between the two peoples for more than six hundred years was about to erupt in flames.

THIRTY-TWO

*But should your enemy not turn away in
peace, let them fall upon your prepared
defenses like unto their own swords.*
— Codes of Entreaty 4.15

THE WEATHER IS PERFECT for a siege, Tollan thought with an amused expression on his face. The first snowstorm of the year began as the army had crossed the Plindre, making the last leg of their journey that much more difficult. However, the morning had proved to be warm enough that the newly revealed sun would melt the ice from the plain in short order.

Prince Anseldr stood next to him, a bear pelt wrapped around his shoulders for warmth. The acting king raised a spyglass to his eye and aimed across the valley to target the hidden city of Por'monir at the far end. "All I see is shale and ice above the treeline," he said, frowning and squinting. "Are you sure this is the place?"

Tollan leaned and pointed toward the geographical features the captive elves had described under interrogation. "Right between those two ridges, jutting out of the mountainside maybe two or three hundred feet in elevation from the valley floor. It's large, maybe one-third the size of Celwaith Tor."

"Impossible," General Verune spoke up from their left. "There's nothing there. We had no such problems seeing the elven structures in Eastmarsh. Why can you see it when we can't?"

Tollan shivered in the wind, recalling his sister's words. The only explanation for his sight was the one he wanted least to consider: elven blood. "Perhaps I have some kind of natural immunity, I don't know," he offered with a shrug. "The structures in the swamp were deserted, so there wouldn't have been spells actively protecting them."

Anseldr took down the spyglass, giving up on trying to see the enclave by conventional means. "Regardless of the reason, your service record speaks for itself, Lieutenant. If you claim the elves' hidden city is there, then it is." He turned to the general. "Give the order to keep marching. We stop mid-field, inside artillery range, and send a messenger forward with terms of surrender."

"Hold on, Your Majesty," Shi'ev called, poking his head out of a misshapen covered wagon on their right. He had brought his strange noisemaker along with a large assortment of tools and materials, to amplify the output from his contraption to cover the whole battlefield. "It might be prudent to use this as an opportunity for a field test. If the machine works, we should be able to cut straight through any illusions for all to see."

"Prudent in one manner of speaking, but letting our enemy in on the secret might prove fatal," Anseldr said in dismissal. "Let us first see their capabilities. Besides, we already know your machine works as intended."

That much at least was true. Every short test Shi'ev had run on the journey here had invariably given Tollan a splitting headache. If the elves had even that much sensitivity to the sound, Tollan reasoned, whatever concentration they required to summon spells would be shaken. He just hoped that the noise would not additionally distract any of the human soldiers at a crucial moment.

Shi'ev protested. "Sire, we still do not know the machine's effective range. I have amplified the sound as best I can, but—"

"That is all we can expect from you at this late hour," Anseldr interrupted, his ire becoming visible. "Leave the military strategy to the officers, and have the machine ready for my signal."

Stunned silence replied first, but Shi'ev recovered quickly. "Of course, sire," he said curtly, taking heed that his suggestions weren't wanted. He retreated inside the covered wagon, closing the flap a little too violently in frustration. Tollan almost felt sorry for him; Anseldr had been the one to insist that the Kiramet scientist come along, but it seemed the long journey north had gotten to everyone's nerves.

Anseldr turned back to the general. "Proceed with my orders."

Verune saluted and clicked his horse's reins to sweep around the massive formation and lead the advance. Within minutes, the whalebone whistles blew, and the entire army moved in unison across the field.

The pipers reminded Tollan of his training, blowing the same marching trills he had so naively learned months ago. The army coordinated in a sight of wonder: ten thousand men arrayed in perfect rows, only interrupted by the towering siege engines, cannons, and catapults necessary to batter down Por'monir's defenses. From what Tollan could see of the city from here, though, the army wouldn't need half of the firepower they had brought.

But it was impossible to know what magical tricks the elves might have at their disposal, and overconfidence often preceded defeat. That must have been why Anseldr decided to conceal their secret weapon until a pivotal moment, Tollan realized. Any earlier and Shi'ev's contraption would become an obvious target to the enemy.

One of Anseldr's decisions didn't make sense to him, however. "Sire," Tollan said tentatively, guiding his horse closer alongside the acting king. "May I ask why we are not simply burning the city to the ground like we did in Eastmarsh? It strikes me that our artillery would have no trouble destroying Por'monir at a distance."

"That is our last resort if this siege becomes a standoff," Anseldr explained, appearing to relish the opportunity to teach his youngest guard a thing or two. "However, the royal treasury has become rather depleted after paying the militia's wartime salaries for two months—Pelendion made it a point to live within our means and minimal taxation. If we do not return with some measure of spoil, I may soon need to raise taxes or else ask Ash'kiram to supply a loan—and neither option is appealing."

Most likely because neither option aided the public perception of a new king, Tollan reasoned. He could not ingratiate himself with the people by demanding more tax money or making Drüstania dependent on a foreign government.

Before Tollan could reply, the whistles blew once more. The army came to a near-simultaneous halt, having crossed half of the distance to the hidden city. Anseldr pulled out his spyglass and examined the mountainside from their closer vantage point.

"Anything, my liege?" Tollan asked in desperation. He hoped that something, anything, would be visible to assuage any doubts about Por'monir's presence. The army would be getting restless by now. If Tollan was any other soldier in attendance, let alone the king, it would be unheard of to trust the word of one man's sight against ten thousand.

"Nothing," Anseldr replied, handing over the glass. "Describe what you see for me."

With magnification, Tollan could now make out much more, down to the tiny blue-clad figures that dotted the walls. Many of the buildings appeared to be carved out of the mountain face itself, though there were still wooden components that would burn well. Tollan related every detail. "The strength of their construction could make bombardment less deadly," Tollan concluded, "but thinking positively, fewer valuables would be damaged by our fire mortars if it comes to that."

"Some good news, at least," Anseldr said. He redirected Tollan's gaze toward a white speck moving at a steady pace across the field. "Now, what happens to our messenger should be most enlightening."

Tollan trained his sights on the speck, which resolved into a lone rider on a pale horse. The rider carried high the yellow banner of Drüstania, the dove and snake crest fluttering in the cold wind. The horse reached the end of the plain and began to weave back and forth up the rocky path at the base of the mountain which culminated at the city's entrance.

Every soldier with a clear view sucked in a horrified breath, except for Tollan. He looked around in confusion, then back at the rider climbing the mountain, the banner still streaming behind him. "What? What is it?"

Anseldr's eyes darted across the mountainside, searching. "The messenger's vanished. Horse, banner, everything."

Tollan frowned, squinting through the spyglass. "He's right there, though. Almost to the main gates."

"I suppose we know where the perimeter of their illusion ends," Anseldr said with satisfaction. "Go on, tell me what's happening."

Tollan obliged. The rider had reached a stretch of flat ground in front of the gate and urged the horse into a steady canter. Tollan winced as the horse ran headlong into the wooden barrier and went down hard, followed by the messenger tumbling out of the saddle. "The horse collided with the gate," he called to Anseldr. "The rider didn't even try to stop or turn aside—the illusion must still hold up at close range."

The messenger crawled back to his feet and hurriedly snatched the once-pristine banner off the ground. Tollan watched him reach out and feel the wood of the gate which likely resembled thin air to him. Bewildered, the messenger finally pulled a scroll from his satchel and recited the prince's warning to surrender.

In response, more than a dozen arrows arced from alcoves above the gate and hit the man straight in the chest. He fell backward, his limbs splayed to either side, and this time, he did not rise.

Tollan lowered the spyglass and described what had happened, his heart heavy as the only witness to the battle's first casualty. He couldn't help but feel responsible for it, as well; the army might have walked right past Por'monir if it hadn't been for his ability to see through the magic curtain.

"That is as clear an answer as we could expect to receive," Verune said, who had returned from the front lines. It gratified Tollan to see the general gain sudden faith in his abilities once the presence of an illusion spell had been indisputably proven. "Shall we prepare the first charge, my prince?"

Anseldr spoke carefully and with purpose. "No. Not a charge, a march. These spells can affect more than a small area or a few individuals at a time. We will stagger our forces across the field to prevent being overtaken by a strategically-placed illusion or weapon of some kind."

Verune nodded. "Wise."

Anseldr wasn't finished and gestured to one of the siege engines on their right. "Move a battering ram and four thousand of our troops under Colonel Senn right up the center until they encounter resistance. You will lead another four thousand to back up Senn, but stop short and spread out by column with cannons to cover the advance. Shi'ev and his invention will accompany the second group."

Shi'ev, who had disembarked from his wagon to listen, spoke up once again in protest. "That might be too close—we don't know what sorts of larger ranged weapons the elves may have."

Anseldr's expression grew colder as he raised an eyebrow. "As you so wisely pointed out, my friend, we do not know the range of your noisemaker, so having it closer to the city is the wiser strategic decision. Colonel Senn will no doubt encounter more hostile spells as his men batter down the gates, at which point your machine will be needed to take the pressure off."

Shi'ev climbed back up on the cart, after which the driver clicked the reins. "Understood, sire."

Tollan's gaze followed the cart as it rolled away. He wondered about the mild hostility that had sprouted between Anseldr and his supposed friend. He had first chalked it up to tension from the impending battle and the cold journey here, but he sensed something else beneath the surface. Then again, enough loyalty existed between the two men that Shi'ev, a foreigner, had put his life on the line for Drüstania.

"What of the remaining two thousand men?" Verune asked.

"Keep them back with me in reserve, to guard the heavier artillery," Anseldr said. "With any luck, we won't need to send a third wave. If it comes to that, I will lead them in myself."

"I will see your orders done, my liege," Verune said crisply. With a salute, he followed Shi'ev's cart and began disseminating orders to the colonels and corporals under him.

Tollan and Anseldr remained on horseback, watching all the pieces on the chessboard take their positions around them. Each column of seventy-two soldiers posted themselves a small distance offset from the others, to prevent as much magical interference as possible. At least, that was the unfounded theory.

"Sire?" Tollan spoke up as the last troops moved into place.

"Yes, Lieutenant," Anseldr acknowledged. "What do you see? Any change to Por'monir?"

"No," he replied. "And that's what worries me. They've prepared for this. That lone saboteur that escaped Celwaith Tor with my sister in tow—they could have easily reached Por'monir ahead of us."

Anseldr regarded Tollan with a cold stare. "These elves have shown no care for innocent human lives. Each time they have attacked us, it has been from the shadows. If they could take us in a battle of sheer numbers, they would have done so. Our victory today will be total and overwhelming, though I doubt it will be bloodless."

Tollan winced. It did make sense from that perspective, even if it was callous of the men's lives they risked. Or his sister's life, possibly inside those enemy walls. "Yes, sire. Forgive me."

Anseldr's face softened a little. "If your sister is here, or anyone else these savages have mentally enslaved, we will find them and free them if we can. You have my word."

Tollan bowed his head. "Thank you, Your Maj—um, Prince."

Anseldr straightened on his tall horse, taking a deep breath. "All right. Let's see what they have for us." He drew his sword and held it aloft, the decorative tassel on his pommel blowing in the stiff northern wind.

The pipers sounded the order to advance once more, and the synchronized *thump* of thousands of footfalls resumed. Moments later, the rhythm was punctuated by the concussive cracks of cannon fire, the shells soaring high overhead toward the hidden city.

Tollan took out his pocket watch and noted the time at a quarter after nine in the morning. *The hour of justice has come to the elves,* Tollan thought as a satisfied grin spread across his face.

For Thaxon.

THE EXPLOSIVE THUNDER ECHOED throughout the valley as the deadly projectiles touched down inside Por'monir. Some struck the walls, others missed entirely and churned up the mountainside, and still others tore through the roofs of buildings that contained innocents. D'harnin citizens who had no idea of their leader's culpability.

"Looks like your magic wards can't protect you anymore, Shilvand," Voster said. "None of them can see you, but they know you're here. The illusion of safety can't produce the real thing."

Shilvand's long white hair blew in the wind, a serene image of someone broken and angry on the inside. "Ironic, considering it was your son who led them here. We have long expected this day would come."

Tollan, Voster thought with a guilty twinge. It had to explain how the cannons could aim at Por'monir without seeing the target—Tollan was down there advising them. His elven blood had drawn him right into the center of all this, just as Voster had worried.

Shilvand summoned one of his men, standing at the head of his secret police. "Silmon, get word to the wardcasters and tell them to drop the illusion. Instead, have them focus on the incoming fire, and deflect as many of the shells as they can."

"They cannot defend against this barrage for long, Arbiter," Silmon cautioned. "Perhaps—"

Shilvand cut him off with a harsh chop of his hand. "Gather as many of the Dast'rel as you can, the ones we have trained in the hidden knowledge, and distribute them along the parapets. Make sure they remain attentive for my signal once that first line of humans comes close enough."

Voster was not encouraged by what those orders seemed to suggest. Tolvanen must have had a better idea of what they meant, because he immediately spoke up. "No, Shilvand," he whispered, clutching his broken arm. "Do not say that your family has turned to the dark arts."

"There is nothing dark about them. They are merely a tool of nature we have long forbidden ourselves from using." Shilvand turned back to Voster and drew his hand up in front of the man's chest. He undulated his fingers and whispered rhythmic words in the ancient D'harna tongue.

Voster felt something move inside him, as what remained of his muscles and flesh rippled unnaturally to the magical call. It started as discomfort but grew quickly to pain. He fell to his knees on the cold stone, feeling as though his skin might burst. He tried with all his strength to escape the grip of the guards holding him fast on either side —only to realize that he was no longer restrained. The guards had backed away.

Shilvand stopped short of reciting the full incantation, and the internal pressure and pain ebbed away. But he dragged Voster to the edge of the promontory and knelt next to him, pointing out at the oncoming troops. "No, I will not kill you yet. You should see our victory firsthand."

Voster pushed himself up to where he could look Shilvand in the eye. The D'harn had a crazed, manic expression on his face, drunk with the impossible power he had tapped into. It went against all that Tynathria had told Voster about her people's gift: magic was for creation and healing, but Shilvand had twisted it to do the opposite.

The soldiers below marched closer, unaware of what horrors awaited them.

KASDAN MARCHED DOWN THE field with the rest of his column, escorting some crazy-looking covered wagon toward what looked like absolutely nothing. To his eyes, the cannons fired at bare ice and rocks, but as they got closer and closer he could see that the shells were fading out of existence when they neared the point of impact. And even more strangely, those impacts could still be heard despite no visible change to the mountainside.

He had not bought into the narrative like the rest of the city when King Pelendion had unveiled the elven corpse in the square. It didn't make sense for these creatures to have existed without any human contact at all for so long. He even wondered if the body was a hoax perpetrated to justify the extreme measures Anseldr took to lock down Celwaith Tor.

But the city checkpoints had subsided, the king had died unexpectedly, and the army was ordered to march out into the northern wastes in pursuit of the creatures—in late fall no less, led by the crown prince. None of those things were congruent with a power-hungry monarchy, and logic told him that the elves had to be real.

But the linchpin in his internal debate had been his sister, Keordi. She came to him in the wee hours of the night before the army left Celwaith Tor, and she told him the most outlandish story about Niena Cresthaven. The girl had apparently tried to convince Keordi that she was half-elven of all things, and that she and Voster had left town originally to investigate the attack on Wraelian Square.

Kasdan's sister had always been one for sarcasm, but never for telling tall tales. He wasn't sure how his feelings for Niena would fare now if it turned out she really was related to these vengeful magic fairy people. But, he realized, if today turned sour, he may never see her again anyway.

He watched as another cannonball whizzed past overhead, destined to vanish midair. Except this time, it didn't.

Like a stiff wind blowing away the mist, but instead blowing away the visage of an empty mountainside, the curtain of illusion peeled back. Instead, there stood a huge city with towering stone walls and an enormous reinforced wooden gate. Any assault on the gate would mean hauling a battering ram up a three-hundred-foot switchback slope in full view of enemy archers the entire way.

Kasdan's jaw dropped open along with the other men in his company. Their target was now unveiled, and it appeared more than formidable.

The column came to a halt as General Verune ordered, allowing the first wave to continue forward and upward. Kasdan, thankfully, would be hanging back with the second group of four thousand to protect Verune and whatever weirdly-shaped invention the Kiramet scientist had dragged into battle.

If Kasdan's column was ordered to advance as a second wave, they would be armed with much more knowledge than the first few ranks. Kasdan thanked the winds that he wasn't up in front, likely to be obliterated by magic or at least a hail of arrows. Some overly patriotic kids thought dying for their country was a noble cause, but Kasdan had decided long ago it was better to live and earn a wage to support his family if he could.

Still, Kasdan thought, the artillery would provide the advancing troops decent cover. The cannon fire became more focused, now able to select specific targets within the city. A well-aimed barrage arced through the cold northern skies, bound to crash down near the peak of the elven city.

"LOOK OUT!" VOSTER SHOUTED hoarsely, staring up at the sky. A cannon shot barreled straight toward them, but Shilvand and a couple of his Dast'rel police conjured a shield that stopped the shell in midair. It fell to the ground, harmless, and many others did the same across the city.

"You see?" Shilvand growled at Voster, breathing hard. The strain of the ward spell had taken a toll on him. "We will prevail over your kind. There is nothing your king can do to stop us."

"What ... happened to you, Shilvand?" Voster asked, his insides still queasy. "Tynathria would never have wanted—"

"My sister was weak. She was an easily manipulated fool to fall in love with the likes of you," Shilvand interrupted, gesturing for his police to drag Voster back to his feet. "My father should have killed you that day, on this very spot. That is the job of an arbiter under the Mishenna—to issue justice."

"What justice?" Tolvanen exclaimed. "This man saved my life once, you remember that?"

"Yes, everyone in the enclave remembers given how often you remind us," Shilvand snapped as his secret police deflected another barrage of cannon shots. "That alone is the whole reason I have had to pursue this cause in secret rather than with the approval of the whole enclave. Thankfully, now that a hostile army has turned up on our doorstep, I shall not have any problems convincing the rest of Por'monir that we must aggressively defend ourselves against the human scourge."

The sound of cannon fire abruptly stopped. A strange hush passed over the valley, the only noises now the settling of rubble and the whisper of the winds. Even the Drüstanian soldiers far below had stopped marching.

After a moment of looking down on the now motionless battlefield, Shilvand raised an eyebrow. "What is it? Why have they stopped?"

Tolvanen squinted off into the distance. "The ridge to the southeast, behind Pelendion's forces. Something is coming."

Shilvand looked closer, and Voster spied it at the same time: a small mass of figures, dressed in gray and green. "I ... cannot believe it," the D'harn said in shock. "The survivors of Neraliel have come to our aid!"

A cheer went up among the Dast'rel, and Voster's heart sank. The Drüstanian army had numbers and firepower on their side, true, but the D'harnir had the advantage of the high ground as well as preparation. The newcomers could tip the balance of the battle irrevocably into the elves' favor.

Voster had no doubts that Shilvand's forces would kill every last human soldier if given the chance, and each successive death might be Tollan's. Voster wanted nothing more at that moment than to hold his boy in his arms, but he knew time was running out.

"I have proclaimed all mankind guilty of their crimes against the D'harnir," Shilvand said, a dark smile passing across his face. "That is my right as arbiter. And you, Voster, will stand as witness to the great trial, as those who would malign us pass into the eternal night!"

THIRTY-THREE

*Sometimes, if an escalating disagreement
does not involve you, the best thing you
can do for either person is to get in their
way.*

— Codes of Entreaty 4.22

NIENA AND GILBRANNEN CRESTED the ridge across from Por'monir, followed by the entire company of refugees from Neraliel. They had heard the echoes of cannon fire from a mile off and Niena had feared the worst, but this had surpassed her fears. Tollan had to be somewhere among the thousands of troops scattered across the field, and her father was still trapped beneath the city. The two people she loved most were caught on opposing sides of the battlefield. She remembered Omeira's prophecy, and her heart constricted with the weight of her obligation.

She had to go down there.

"Well," Gilbrannen said to break the tension, as the artillery cannons stopped firing. The newcomers had been noticed. "Looks like we arrived just in time to save the day."

Niena opened her mouth to reply, but no sound came out. Gilbrannen's dry, biting humor aggravated her, but she was too tired to correct him. She couldn't care less which side won the battle as long as her family made it out alive.

Fendaral stood at Gilbrannen's other side, holding the staff which had been the source of their protection from the manticores. None of the Neraliel elders had been able to divine how the totem had been made, but it had worked. All nine hundred of their enclave had been able to travel northward unmolested by the beasts. "This is your home, Gilbrannen," he said. "How do you want to proceed?"

Niena studied the field, noting that all the catapults and a few of the cannons remained further back, protected by a group of soldiers much smaller than those attacking Por'monir directly. The siege engines had been left practically unprotected by comparison.

Gilbrannen spotted the same thing and pointed it out. "We have to take down their ranged weapons," he said. "Por'monir may not be standing at the end of the day otherwise. How many people do you have trained or capable of fighting?"

"Less than four hundred," Fendaral said. "Perhaps five if we include everyone strong enough to wield a blade."

"That will not be necessary," Gilbrannen said. "Just as long as the ones who go know how to wield magic and how to harness a hostile mind."

Niena balked at the word *harness*. She supposed the outnumbered elves had no other option, but discussing mind control in such a cavalier manner still bothered her.

Fendaral considered it for a moment. "Most of them know the spell but have never used it in combat. Several have used it on a trancheon which, if you don't know, is *very* different."

"It will have to do," Gilbrannen said, pausing to listen to the distant trill of the enemy's whistles. "The enemy is repositioning. This is our best opportunity."

The troop movement was almost hypnotic at this distance, Niena realized as she stared. The yellow-gilded columns from all across Drüstania reoriented themselves in formation, facing backward. A few from the much larger group closer to Por'monir drifted back up the field to provide support to the rear guard, but the ones nearest Por'monir made ready to advance again once the artillery barrage resumed.

Fendaral gave up the totem staff and sent it away with the other five hundred women, children, and elderly. If the manticores had managed to follow them all the way from the edge of Spinewood Forest, they would at least not be able to touch the most vulnerable.

Gilbrannen touched Niena's shoulder to get her attention. "You should stay back and help protect the others if necessary."

"Why? Because I'm a lady?" Niena scoffed, finally finding her voice. "You didn't think of that when you dragged me into the royal palace. Not a chance that I would stay back now—my brother is down there, and I intend to find him before any of you have a chance to kill him."

Gilbrannen fell silent, and his arm dropped back to his side. "You are right to blame me," he said. "And if you want to go down there, I will not stand in your way. But you need more than a bow to defend yourself."

He unbuckled a scabbard from around his waist, housing a sword that Fendaral had loaned him, and held it out. "Take this. Be sure that you are not throwing your life away on a blind chance."

"If I was, I wouldn't regret it. A blind chance is far better than none," Niena said, more certain of herself than she had ever been. She would either find her brother on this field, or she would die. There was no third option. She slid the light but strong sword free and tossed the scabbard aside, knowing it would only trip her up.

Gilbrannen nodded. "The blade suits you. I will get you as far as I can if you stay close, but otherwise, you will be on your own."

Good, Niena thought. She now had plenty of experience being on her own against the world, so she could handle that. But all the enemy swords—those intimidated her.

The refugees faded back into the treeline, leaving four hundred warriors: Fendaral's forces, and any other young elves willing to fight. They were horrendously ill-prepared for battle, without so much as a full meal in weeks. Niena doubted that a single stomach among them was not growling fiercely. But even if Fendaral's army was at full strength, they would still have been outnumbered at least four-to-one by the Drüstanian soldiers protecting the artillery.

Fendaral paced in front of the haphazard attack line, then shouted to the assembly. "D'harnir! Are your weapons loaded?"

Each elven soldier who carried a rifle raised it high in unison. Niena spotted a grim smile on Gilbrannen's face, and she assumed he enjoyed the irony of the two hundred stolen weapons being used against their makers.

"That is well!" Fendaral called. "We are vastly outnumbered, but though we do not have the advantage of strength, the magic of the ancients is ever on our side! Spread out in two lines. First line, use your wards of force to absorb the first enemy attack, then stand aside and let the second line advance past you and fire. Discard the expended weapons and cover the next group until they can fire.

"After that, rush in as close as you can and make mental contact! Turn them against each other, become chaos, use any methods necessary to force your way through to the siege machines and take them down!" Fendaral worked up to a fever pitch, and Niena braced herself to start running. The distant cannons behind the elf leader fired again, underscoring the need to stop them before Por'monir could be rendered into dust.

"Today, we fight not just for the abandoned beauty of Neraliel, but for our future home in Por'monir! For the safety of our children, for the memories of our elders, and for all D'harnir!" And with that final word, Fendaral raised his firearm and led the advance.

The D'harnir on either side of Niena cheered. Though she didn't join them in spirit, she charged down the hillside beside them all the same. Fendaral formed the point of a D'harnin spearhead formation, the elves preparing to breach the Drüstanian rear lines in perfect unison. Niena allowed herself to fall backward in the pack so that she wouldn't be among the first to clash with the enemy soldiers. But she made sure to stay close to Gilbrannen, just in case.

The uneven, rocky ground passed by underneath her, and they closed the distance with their opponents. Niena reminded herself of her warding spell, her mind echoing the strange syllables in time with her churning legs. The Drüstanian soldiers stood their ground three hundred yards away, then one hundred, then fifty paces.

That was when the enemy rifles let loose.

A handful of D'harnir could not bring their wards up fast enough and went down, but those who had survived faded back behind the second line. The group advanced to a stop, aimed their firearms, and pulled the trigger, and a hundred enemy soldiers toppled as the bullets tore through their chain mail. The used rifles were tossed aside, and the formation advanced to twenty-five paces, where it played out a second time except that now the D'harnir lost no one.

Niena pulled up short as the enemy lines met. It was like an invisible force parting the sea of enemies with Fendaral as the focal point. Their forward momentum slowed immediately, and the counterattack became fierce. But the D'harnir who had cast their protection wards held the line, leaving Gilbrannen and the second line with enough cover to sow confusion among the human forces.

The enemy soldiers began to turn on each other with reckless abandon, leaving many unsure of themselves and who they were fighting. Most were unwilling to kill their own countrymen, even bewitched, so the first three columns fell back in the face of the elven onslaught. The enchanted men chased the defenders back to the next set of columns, and the vicious cycle repeated, this time with living shields instead of magical wards protecting the attacking D'harnir.

The bloodbath sickened Niena to watch, but she had to focus on what lay beyond it. Near the closest cannons, some of which were being realigned to fire at the new threat, a group of soldiers sat higher than the rest, on horseback. That would be the officers, and with any luck, Tollan would be accompanying them.

She followed Gilbrannen's blue cloak further onto the field, wading through dead bodies and refusing to look down. She held her sword at the ready and hoped to all the winds that she wouldn't have to use it.

TOLLAN WATCHED IN HORROR as the elves carved a path straight through their rear guard. It was unthinkable, and yet men fell like wheat before a scythe. Their forces were being callously turned against them.

Anseldr was furious, and perhaps beginning to lose his confidence in their easy victory. "Hold formation, blast it!" he called, half to the piper and half to the soldiers who couldn't hear him over the noise of the battle. "It doesn't matter, push through that formation and crush them."

The shrill whistle went out, repeating the signal to hold at all costs, to almost no discernible effect. More and more men turned and fled from their enchanted compatriots.

Tollan swallowed, second-guessing Anseldr's strategy. The acting king still refused to call Shi'ev's magic-annulling contraption into action. "My Prince," Tollan spoke up, needing to suggest an alternative but refraining from questioning the current orders. "Should I lead a few columns around behind and box them in?"

"A grand idea, Lieutenant—but I shall have one of the corporals take care of that. I want you here," Anseldr said, then issued the order. Tollan watched as his old mentor, Corporal Crandas, peeled a hundred and forty-four soldiers off each side of their formation. They would encircle the elven fighters, leaving them no path to escape.

"That should finish them off," Anseldr growled. "This is merely a distraction from our goal."

As Anseldr finished speaking, the defensive formation crumbled inward further. The elves inexorably continued to push their way through, almost reaching the first of the Drüstanian catapults. The center of the fighting came close enough that Tollan could almost make out the faces of the bewitched, emotionless soldiers, and the determined elves at their backs.

"How? How are they doing this?" Anseldr fumed.

"Sire," Tollan urged. "You're in danger. You should move forward and tell Shi'ev to start his machine. It's the only way."

Anseldr nodded, coming back to himself. "You're right, Cresthaven. I've been a fool to wait this long. Get down there with the rest of the kingsguard and hold the elves off, at least until I can get new orders to Shi'ev and General Verune."

Tollan remembered the chaos of battle the night Thaxon had died. This time, he would subject himself willingly to that chaos. "Yes, my liege." He dismounted and made sure he had his reinforced sword. It would not be in danger of shattering this time.

The kingsguard formed up behind him. Tollan prepared to lead the charge and saw that the elves had advanced to a hundred yards. They had set to work dismantling the first catapult while still guarded by human thralls.

Tollan spotted an elf with a cloak of a different shade than all the others: blue, instead of green. The figure stood at the forefront of the attacking line, alternating between parrying blows with his dagger and reaching out with his hand to cast spells on another human mind. The different color had to mean something, perhaps rank.

"That's our target," Tollan ordered. He went to draw his sword but thought better about it and took his loaded rifle from where it hung over his shoulder. "We break their leadership, their resolve will follow. Let's go."

The kingsguard charged forward, with Tollan in the lead. As they ran, he cocked the hammer back on his rifle. The enemy objective was clear, and he knew just how to tear the elven offensive wide open.

VIOLENCE SURROUNDED NIENA. THE blood of man and elf alike spattered across her clothes. The D'harnir suffered losses but held their own with the unwilling aid of their mental slaves. They managed to overtake one of the siege machines, a trebuchet poised to hurl large ceramic vessels with fuses sticking out over the walls of Por'monir. Explosives.

She yelped and raised her sword to block an incoming blow. It became hard to stay out of the fray, now that the elves had been outflanked by at least two columns that had circled behind them. She scrambled toward the catapult, following Gilbrannen's blue cloak as best she could.

Gilbrannen led a few D'harnin soldiers around in front of the catapult, creating a living shield of human soldiers to give the others time to tear down or hack apart the giant war machine. Gilbrannen seemed sluggish whenever she caught a glimpse of him through the melee. He would soon tire out—the effort of continuous enchanting could not be maintained.

Niena looked ahead and saw a group of elite soldiers in brilliant yellow charging forward to save the catapult. And Gilbrannen stood right in their path.

Niena scrambled forward, past the large wheels of the siege engine. She ducked the haphazard parries of desperate D'harnir, and blocked the sweeping blows of human soldiers neither enchanted nor scared enough to abandon their cause. "Gilbrannen! Look out!" she called, and couldn't tell whether he heard her. She pushed forward, away from the catapult, looking everywhere for the signature blue cloak.

A sudden flash of fire from behind Niena knocked her to the muddy ground, and the roar of an explosion washed over her. Her ears rang fiercely, so much worse than that day in Wraelian Square that she thought she might have gone deaf. She gripped her sword and got her feet under her, only then spotting the source of the blast.

The catapult went up in flames and the men and elves in direct proximity were burned alive, covered in some kind of liquid fuel. Around the space the D'harnir had cleared, human soldiers fell to the ground as the holds on their minds were released. Niena held a hand to her mouth, knowing Fendaral's forces would not last after that blow.

She sensed movement behind her and ducked aside before a broadsword bisected the space she had vacated. Niena raised her blade as another blow came down, and her elbows creaked with the strain of knocking it aside.

"No, stop!" Niena cried out. "I'm human! I'm one of you!"

But the man either did not believe her or was so filled with bloodlust that he could not stop. Their blades met again and again, with Niena being forced to backpedal at every swing. It took all her effort to keep the broadsword from striking her. She couldn't even think straight to conjure a defensive ward.

She tripped and fell backward to the cold ground. It was unavoidable now; she had to kill or be killed.

Completely on survival instinct, she rolled out of the way of his next attack and tangled her feet up in his. He fell forward . . . right onto the sword which she had unwittingly pointed upwards toward him.

The light and thin D'harnin blade slipped through the chain mail and into the man's chest. Niena watched in disbelief as the wide-eyed man crumpled to the ground next to her, sputtering for air.

"No, no, no," she said, getting to her knees and trying to remove the sword, to take back what she had done, but it wouldn't budge. "I didn't mean to!"

Niena hyperventilated in the cold air, letting out a scream of sadness and anger as the man breathed his last. The man's one mistake had been to confuse her for an elf. And she had killed him for that. She tore the green cloak from her shoulders and chucked it into the flames of the burning oil on the ground.

I'm no better than any of Gilbrannen's assassins, she thought bitterly. What if that had been Tollan attacking her?

She saw a flash of blue out of the corner of her eye and whirled.

Gilbrannen was locked in a furious duel with two of the kingsguard. They pressed him back toward the burning trebuchet and the liquid fire covering the ground. He managed to dispatch one with a slice to the neck and parried the other's attack with his dagger.

Niena ran, stumbling over the uneven ground of corpses, watching as Gilbrannen's desperate attack glanced off the side of his opponent's head. The metal helm that had saved the man's life fell and bounced along the ground as he lost the grip on his weapon, now at the full mercy of Gilbrannen's blade. His face caught the light of the fire, and Niena's heart stopped in terror.

It was Tollan.

THE WORLD SPUN AROUND him, and Tollan knew he was alone. His rifle shot at the catapult's explosive shells had worked well, but not well enough. The elves that had swarmed the construct had burned, but the Drüstanian troops had already begun to flee from the magical onslaught. The other royal guards had either perished or gone, and even Anseldr had retreated to a more defensible position.

He would die at the hands of a cursed elf, never to see his family again. He raised his head, wishing to stare his skilled opponent in the face, but the dizziness threatened to overwhelm him.

The pointed-eared leader in the blue cloak drew his dagger back, about to deliver the killing blow. Tollan didn't have time to move out of the way, and even if he did, his strength was all but sapped.

It didn't matter. He had done his duty.

"Noooo!" a strained, female voice cried out from his left as the blade thrust toward his chest. There came a flicker of recognition with it, but he didn't have time to wonder about it.

Just before the dagger's tip would pierce Tollan through, a hand slipped between them and miraculously halted the blow. The elf strained harder for a moment, but the blade was held tight in an invisible vise.

The enemy pulled the serrated blade away and leveled it at the young woman who had reached out. "Niena," the D'harn said in frustration. "Step aside."

Tollan looked again, and to his surprise and awe, his blonde-haired older sister had been the one to save his life. He blinked in dizziness, thinking he must be hallucinating from getting cracked in the head. But no, she was real, and not at all like he remembered her.

Niena pushed herself back to her feet, covered in mud and blood and whispering strange words that Tollan didn't know. She held her hands out, palms outward, ready to perform again whatever impossible magic she had conjured. She carried their father's bow across her back. "No, Gilbrannen," she said, panting. "You have spilled so much blood, some of which is my responsibility. But I will not let you kill my brother."

The elf that Niena had called Gilbrannen took a step back, almost slipping in the mud and ice. He stared again at Tollan, without the rage of battle, and found what he was looking for. "Yes. I can see the resemblance between you. The same eyes, but a different color."

Niena didn't relax her guarding stance, not even after Gilbrannen had sheathed his dagger. She pointed back across the field at the columns of human soldiers that were forming new battle lines to advance and retake the artillery. "You had better regroup with the others," she suggested. "Divided, you don't stand a chance against that many."

Gilbrannen looked to see the situation for himself and nodded solemnly to Niena. "You would be wise to take him and leave now," he said before hurrying away and leaving brother and sister alone together.

Tollan relaxed onto his back, allowing himself to breathe now that the immediate threat had passed. His sister watched the elf go for a moment longer, then knelt to tend to him.

"Tollan," she said urgently, cupping his face in her hand and looking him over for serious wounds. "Are you alright? Can you hear me?"

"Yes," he wheezed. "I'm . . . dizzy, and everything hurts. What are you . . . How are you here?"

Niena hushed him, placing a hand on his head. "Stay still for a moment," she ordered and closed her eyes. She chanted a few more of her strange whispers, and Tollan felt the spinning partially ease, along with his splitting headache.

"You ... you can use their magic," he said rather obviously, but realizing what that meant for the first time. "All of it was true. I worried you had been enchanted."

Niena shook her head, smiling as she came out of her trance. "No, just coerced. But we can't talk about all that now. Your friends are coming, and we have to move. Can you walk?"

Tollan raised his gloved hand to his head. He felt fine now. "Yeah, I think so. I don't know what exactly you did to me, but it worked."

"I'll tell you all about it later," Niena said, extending an arm to help him up.

Tollan grasped it, and wrapped his arms around her once he had stumbled to his feet. "You had better. Thanks for the save."

Another fireball erupted as the remaining elves stole a trick from Tollan and tried to destroy the artillery as they fled. As Niena had warned, the Drüstanian troops began to retake their lost ground. One column broke off from the others and started toward Tollan and Niena's position, presumably to see what could be salvaged of the burning catapult.

"What do we tell them? About you?" Tollan asked. A young woman on the battlefield would not be easy to explain.

"Just say that I had been taken prisoner or enchanted, and freed by the explosion," Niena said, shifting impatiently from one foot to the other. "Anything that will let us leave. We have to get inside Por'monir right away."

"Into the city? Whatever for?"

"Because Papa is still in there," Niena said. "It's what I tried to tell you before, it's why I helped them. They took him hostage."

The pieces fell into perfect clarity in Tollan's mind, and he understood all at once what was at stake here. If the Drüstanian army succeeded in sacking the city, their father might die with insurgents and innocents alike.

Whether his father loved him or not, Tollan could not let that happen. At least for his sister's sake.

He would neglect to report back right away. The acting king had told him that rescuing prisoners was a priority, and he would give that excuse if questioned. He bent to pick up his sword and saw a uniform that might work for Niena with a closed-faced helmet. He waved her closer and began pulling the gauntlets off the previous owner. "Sorry, you're going to have to wear this. It's the only way we'll get through without being questioned or held up."

His sister eyed the corpse squeamishly, but she moved to help before the approaching column arrived.

THIRTY-FOUR

"ARE THE HUMAN SOLDIERS close enough to our Dast'rel wardcasters?" Shilvand inquired, clenching his fists in impatience.

"Not yet, Arbiter," Silmon reported. "The mountain incline has slowed their siege tower considerably, but they have resumed their advance."

Voster and Tolvanen watched in mute silence with the rest of the D'harnin secret police as the skirmish played out on the far side of the icy battlefield. But that died down after a few of the catapults went up in blazes of fire, implying they were loaded with explosive ammunition that hadn't been unleashed on Por'monir yet.

Voster realized King Pelendion or whoever else in charge must have believed victory to be so assured that there was no need to burn the city to the ground. Otherwise, he would have already sacked the city. No, the Drüstanians were out for vengeance, and that meant claiming every last part of Por'monir for themselves.

Now that the small counter-offensive along the Drüstanian flank had mostly fizzled out, that left Pelendion's primary force to batter down the main gate. That is, if Shilvand's dark arts would allow them.

"In range!" Silmon called. "The Dast'rel are ready!"

Shilvand drew himself up to his full height, procuring the best view as he looked down from the promontory. Below, four thousand tiny men approached, and the first of their ranks were walled in on two sides by mountain stone. They were now less than a hundred paces from the city gates. "Perfect," Shilvand said eagerly. "Decimate them."

Silmon stepped to the side of the courtyard and spoke a brief spell into existence. The elite officer's hand emitted a bright red light into the sky that almost blinded Voster when it flashed twice before flickering out.

The arbiter of Por'monir beckoned for Voster's and Tolvanen's captors to bring them to the cliff's edge alongside him. "Now you will know the true strength of the D'harnir," he said and gestured to the advancing yellow-clad soldiers.

Roughly a third of the human warriors stumbled and fell as they marched up the mountain. They writhed on the ground, the other soldiers halting their march to reach down and help them. Voster recognized the effects as the same that Shilvand had perpetrated on him earlier, but that time the D'harn had halted the spell before its conclusion.

The affected men began to peel apart from the inside, their skin flaying open on its own and releasing torrents of blood. It was like their bodies twisted and turned inside out while still alive to feel it. The remaining soldiers looked around in panic and horror before the Por'monir archers released volley after volley of arrows from their windows above.

More than a hundred men had been killed, in mere moments. Voster was thankful he could not see the details from afar, but still, he dry heaved. The only thing in his stomach had been that small nutrient cake Arondin had given him. He could not believe that so many D'harnir had abandoned or reinterpreted their values to call this violence necessary or justified.

He looked at Tolvanen and saw his own horrified expression mirrored back at him. Even an army this large couldn't stand against power like this.

GENERAL ANTON VERUNE'S STOMACH twisted as he stared through the spyglass at the causeless carnage being inflicted on his men. "Fall back!" he called desperately to the piper. "Tell them to fall back one hundred yards—they can't be able to keep that up across long distances!"

"I wouldn't be too sure, General," Darakh Shi'ev cautioned, uncovering the oddly shaped wagon that carried his invention. "They may have chosen to wait until we were in a bottleneck. We must activate my device and retake the upper hand."

Verune held up a hand, watching as his men regressed down the mountain away from the front lines that had exploded into piles of flesh. The magical attacks lessened and dissipated, and the men held back as ordered. "Mr. Shi'ev, Prince Anseldr is still in command of this battle, and I will not usurp his authority even to the last man."

A messenger rode up, bearing a folded piece of paper. "Orders from the prince, sir."

"And not a moment too soon," Verune said, snatching the parchment from the soldier's hands and rapidly scanning over it. He frowned.

"What does it say?" Shi'ev asked.

"Prince Anseldr has retreated to a secure vantage point, and placed me in sole command for the rest of the battle," Verune said, irritated but understanding the prince's unwillingness to remain on the field. They had expected a much easier victory. The message also said to firebomb the city regardless of spoils if Drüstania continued to incur heavy losses, but most importantly the use of Shi'ev's noisemaker was finally authorized.

He looked back toward the rear, where the foot battle raged on. Corporal Crandas' reinforcement columns had surrounded the fifty or so that remained of the elven attackers, cutting off any escape. Still, the enemy continued to hold their own and would do so as long as they had their cursed spells. Verune would put a stop to that, now.

"What are your orders, sir?" the messenger pleaded. "We've lost two trebuchets already, and the enemy is working their way toward a third."

Verune gestured to Colonel Reeds, who drew near. "Take five hundred men and ensure they get no further—that should overwhelm them completely once they lose their magical crutch." As the corporal and messenger rode away to muster the troops, he turned back to Shi'ev. "I hope your device works as well as you think. The battle depends on it."

Shi'ev clapped his hands twice and got to work alongside his assigned guards. They drove stakes through the spokes of the wagon's wheels to keep it from rolling, and unhitched the horses.

"General," Shi'ev called once he had double-checked his machine. "I suggest you move away with the rest of your men to a safe distance. Most of the sound my machine generates is too low to hear, but that doesn't mean it isn't loud enough to puncture your eardrums if you stand next to it."

Verune looked at Shi'ev in concern, wondering exactly how far would be far enough. "What will you do?"

The Kiramet genius fished a couple of small pieces of rag from a pocket and packed them into his ears. Verune chuckled and began to lead the others away. Sometimes over-engineering was unnecessary when the simplest solution would do.

GILBRANNEN KNEW THAT THE last fighters from Neraliel were doomed, but it didn't matter. They had to take out as many of the fire-throwing catapults as possible before their destructive payloads were hurled over Por'monir's walls. Their combined force could kill hundreds if not thousands of innocent D'harnir who knew nothing about the war he had helped orchestrate.

Any one of the mortars could strike his parents' home, and it would be his fault.

Mistakes had been made, he admitted to himself as he fought on and enchanted man after man to take the brunt of his opponents' force. They had pushed too far and too fast, beyond their readiness—and now, Gilbrannen wasn't even sure that fighting and violence were the ways to accomplish what was best for his people. It hadn't done Neraliel any favors, and now Por'monir was at risk as well.

If they had reintroduced themselves to humans on equal terms, how well would they have been received? They couldn't all have Niena's upstanding character, but if even half of them did . . .

The soldier he had enchanted fell to the ground, stabbed by one of his comrades. Gilbrannen shifted focus and harnessed that man's mind with another spell, but it took a few seconds longer than the last. He had to block another blow, making it harder to concentrate. Either these men weren't as pliable as the others, or Gilbrannen was fading fast. Neither option appealed to him.

"Push forward!" he called over his shoulder to the dwindling D'harnin attackers. "Clear a path to the next catapult! We are almost through!"

Fendaral moved up alongside him, blocking a mace blow with a twist that knocked the weapon free of the assailant's grip. He caught the mace handle in his off hand and brought it around with a crash against the man's head. "We cannot take much more of this, Gilbrannen! We have been outflanked!"

Gilbrannen growled in frustration, having repeated another circuit of the enchanting spell. "No! We can do this! Keep going!"

At that moment, a deep rumbling shook the battlefield, a noise that struck fear into Gilbrannen's heart and pain into his mind. He released his mental grip on the soldier in front of him and clutched at his ears, recognizing with dread the same fearsome weapon he had seen in the palace of Celwaith Tor. The noise had been amplified a hundred-fold.

There would be no standing against the Drüstanian army now.

Gilbrannen was far enough removed from the source of the infernal noise that he could at least think and speak. He tugged at Fendaral, who had frozen stiff in his tracks, and shouted for him to move. "Retreat! Fall back to the ridge!"

But the wall of yellow-armored enemy soldiers surged. The initial shock of their fellow soldiers being freed from the magical spells wore off, and the men were hungry to avenge their fallen brethren. Gilbrannen's reflexes slowed, and each parry sapped him of more strength as he ran.

Fendaral followed close behind him as they made for open ground, but most of the other D'harnir had not been able to counter the distraction and immediate loss of their powers. The Drüstanian soldiers closed in, and it was all Gilbrannen and Fendaral could do to place one foot in front of another and block or dodge incoming attacks.

They and a handful of others at last breached the edge of the battle, and though more soldiers were in hot pursuit, the elves would not be caught. The D'harnir were lighter, more agile, and not encumbered by fifty pounds of chain mail and plate armor.

Fendaral stumbled and fell, and Gilbrannen rushed to help him up. But a bullet wound marred the center of the D'harn's back, and other projectiles thudded into the ground around them. If they had been in Por'monir with access to healers, there might have been hope, but the men chasing them would not wait. Fendaral would not move again.

You were right, Gilbrannen thought in sorrow and pushed himself back into a run. The infernal sound grew fainter with each step, and he felt his faculties coming back to him.

He had made the same mistake a second time. *We should have retreated sooner.*

This war will be the end of us all.

NIENA WINCED, THAT ALL-TOO-FAMILIAR sound chilling her to the bone. "Oh no," she murmured through the ache in her skull.

Tollan gasped, halting in his steps. He held a hand up to cover his jagged ear. "It's Shi'ev's machine! I have no idea how he managed to make that thing so loud!"

Niena didn't respond at first, her mind dedicated to the now-herculean task of moving closer to the noise that made her want to crawl out of her skin. "It only affects people with magic capabilities . . . or elven blood . . . or something," she finally managed to say. "Some sort of vibrating resonance. It hurts the elves even worse than us and keeps them from using their spells."

"I guess what you said about our mother was true," Tollan admitted with a touch of irony, still holding the side of his head. He seemed to have an easier time focusing or blocking out the sound than she did. "I'm sorry I didn't believe you, Niena."

Niena offered him a smile that probably looked more like a wince and readjusted the yellow livery around her shoulders. She was tall enough to pass for a man, but she worried her profile would be too thin. "It was hard for me to swallow too, believe me." It pained her that they couldn't afford to sort out the whole story now. "Where is Shi'ev's device?"

Tollan gathered himself and pointed. "It's there, on a wagon in the center formation. Looks like everyone else has cleared away from that area. We should go around, too; if this is how it feels at this distance, I would rather not get closer than we have to."

Niena agreed, and they set off to circumvent the Drüstanian forces. She looked back to check on Gilbrannen's group of fighters, but no sign of them could be seen. They had fled or been overwhelmed, and she surprised herself by hoping for the former. Gilbrannen might have come to see his pride more clearly, but that mattered little if he didn't survive long enough to make it right.

"Looks like we've begun our assault on the gate," Tollan said, tilting his head to indicate Por'monir.

Niena looked up to see the huge siege tower rolled right up against the stone arch. She remembered the design of the gate from when she had entered, and even the most well-equipped battering ram would have a hard time getting through the reinforced wood. Especially while D'harnin archers continued to pelt down arrows.

She looked again, wondering if her eyes had deceived her. The path leading up to the gate was bathed in the deep red of blood, far too much blood to have been spilled by arrowheads alone. It could only have been magic, Niena realized. Shi'ev's device had been activated to stop it and place the forces on more or less equal ground.

Niena turned to stare behind her at the burning remains of the catapults. *Fire and black magic*, she recalled, and her spine tingled with dread. Omeira's words had come alive, and they were running out of time. This standoff would not hold for long.

"What is it?" Tollan asked when he realized she had stopped walking.

"Nothing," Niena replied. She wrapped a hand around her mother's necklace and pressed on. "Let's go."

VOSTER KNEW AN OPPORTUNITY when he saw one. All the D'harnir standing in front of the Hall of Meeting doubled over and grabbed at their heads in pain at the low rumble coming from the battlefield. Even Tolvanen was affected, but Voster couldn't worry about him until he saved himself.

Voster reached for the Dast'rel guard that had released him and withdrew a long, curved dagger from his belt. He didn't know if the miraculous distraction would last, so he leapt forward without hesitation and placed Shilvand in a choke-hold, resting the point of the dagger below the D'harn's rib cage.

Severe pain racked Por'monir's arbiter, but he had enough of his wits about him to understand what had happened. "You . . . stop . . ."

Voster dragged Shilvand back across the courtyard and shook Tolvanen. "Come on—we have to get out of here."

Tolvanen groaned weakly in acknowledgment but still shuffled with Voster away from the promontory's edge.

The guards stirred, still holding their heads and trying to block their ears to no avail. But a few gathered themselves together enough to see what Voster had done.

Voster continued to move away from them slowly. He called out in as calming and strong a voice as he could muster. "If you want your arbiter to live, you will let us go. I don't want to kill him out of respect for my wife, his sister, but don't make me reconsider."

"Do not worry about me, kill him!" Shilvand choked out from behind Voster's elbow. "All of this is his fault!"

The guards tried first to use their magic, but quickly found they couldn't. Two of them were fast enough on the uptake to nock arrows on their bows instead. Voster urged Tolvanen and Shilvand to move faster, being careful of his friend's broken arm. But cover proved elusive, and even through the pain of the mysterious rumbling sound, the elves' training held true. They loosed their bowstrings.

Voster's survival reflexes kicked in, and he shoved Shilvand aside to dive out of the way. An arrow nicked the back of his pilfered Dast'rel uniform and bounced off the stone wall behind him.

Shilvand had escaped unscathed as well, and he scrambled out of the line of fire. "Stop them!" he ordered, rubbing his throat, and pointed after Voster and Tolvanen.

Voster hurried his old friend down the hill and around the corner, out of the immediate danger of the archers. The D'harn stumbled, and Voster clutched his good arm to keep him from falling.

"No time to waste," Voster said, glancing behind them. The Protectors had begun to give chase. "Where do we go?"

Tolvanen nodded toward a covered alleyway. "Through there! It's the fastest route to the Junir clan dwellings, and we can stay below cover."

"Good thinking," Voster said, thankful his friend was still present with that oppressive noise permeating everything.

If Arondin had found the Junir matriarch and convinced her of the truth, they could evacuate the entire family out of Por'monir before the

Drüstanian forces destroyed it. Along with any others who would not mind trusting a human with their lives.

They ran through the doomed city, Shilvand's murderous disciples following close behind.

"TOLLAN—I MEAN, LIEUTENANT! Over here!" a voice called from their left, and Tollan was startled to see Kasdan Harroway amid the crowd of soldiers giving Shi'ev's machine a wide berth.

"Kasdan," Tollan said, grinning awkwardly and stepping in front of Niena before he got a good look at her. That was all they needed, a familiar face to create a scene and cause someone to realize there wasn't anything official about their business. He tried to tune out the horrible soul-piercing hum in the air and put on a believable performance. "I didn't know you were here with us!"

Kasdan stepped out of his rank and came closer, so he didn't need to shout over the deep rumbling of the noise machine. Beads of sweat could be seen on his dark forehead despite the cold wind once he removed his helmet. "I tried to keep my post at Celwaith Tor, you know, to protect the family if anything else happened, but it was all hands on deck to end the elven threat. Just got lucky my column was in the middle and not on either end, I suppose."

Niena ignored Tollan's attempt to protect her and leaned around him to say hello. "Chilly weather we're having, isn't it?" she said coyly, flipping up the visor on her borrowed helmet.

Kasdan did a double-take, unable to believe his eyes at first. "Niena! What—how did you get here? Keordi told me some pretty strange things and said your aunt's been worried sick about you!"

Tollan winced. "Keep it down, will you? We're in something of a bind here—"

Niena placed a hand on his shoulder, silencing him. She leaned closer to Kasdan to keep her voice low. "What did she tell you? Who else did she tell?"

"No one," Kasdan said defensively, looking at her with bewilderment. "She said that . . . you know . . . you're one of them."

Tollan looked at Niena in alarm, wondering how many other people she might have told. He supposed that if anyone should have believed Niena, it was her best friend, but he remembered when Keordi stopped by the smithy. He took it things had not gone so well between them.

"Let me get one thing straight," Niena said, her face turning red. "I am *not* one of them. It may be in my blood, but I am not a D'harn."

"Then what are we?" Tollan asked, knowing now beyond doubt that he possessed that same blood—if not from Niena's use of magic, then from how Shi'ev's invention continued to grate on his nerves.

Niena drew herself up. "We are the Cresthaven family, and that's the end of it," she replied. "Is that clear, Kasdan?"

He nodded once. "I never doubted that. Keordi said she had tried to find you after the king's proclamation, but you weren't at the Denvalds'. A few days later she went to the smithy—"

"And Niena had already disappeared, yes," Tollan finished for him, knowing the rest of the story. "We can't waste any more time. We have to go," he said, pointing at the gates of the elven city. The battering ram was almost through.

"Go? Go where?" Kasdan asked.

Niena scrunched up the corner of her mouth, and shared a look with Tollan. At least she had checked with him first this time. He sighed and shrugged. "I suppose we could use the help. But it's going to be dangerous."

Kasdan glanced back and forth between the two of them. "What do you need from me? Anything."

Tollan felt his sister squeeze his hand in solidarity. "Our father is being held somewhere in that city, and we need to get to him before the army levels the place." The words sounded just as preposterous coming from his lips as they had in his head.

A light clicked on in Kasdan's eyes. "Ah, so that's where he's been the last couple of months? He was captured trying to gather information on the elves?"

"That's close enough to the truth," Niena said, though Tollan suspected it was a lot more complicated than that. "It's a really long story. I promise to tell you in full once we make it out. But we have to go now."

Kasdan glanced around, thinking. "There's little I can do while we're still in formation—I can't just leave. We're drawing too many eyes as it is, and desertion would draw more."

"It's not desertion," Tollan said, rationalizing how they might justify their mission. "You're following an officer who has selected you for a special assignment from Prince Anseldr himself. It's the Drüstanian oath, after all."

"What?" Kasdan asked, confused.

"We have sworn to protect the people of Drüstania, right? Well, an upstanding citizen is being held against his will inside Por'monir, and it is our duty to break him out."

Kasdan smirked. "Never mind that this upstanding citizen is a relative of yours. I hope no one asks Prince Anseldr about those orders."

Tollan's eyes roamed over the battlefield, searching for the acting king's decorated stallion. He became concerned when he couldn't spot it above the ranks. "I don't know if they can anymore. Wait—can either of you hear that?"

The sound of rhythmic flapping became discernible on the wind. It was distinct enough from the clash of battle and the noise machine, but it blended in enough that he couldn't tell the direction it came from. Tollan's stomach clenched in dread, though he had no idea why.

"Oh no," Niena said, staring at the southern sky. "Manticores."

"You're kidding . . ." Kasdan trailed off once he saw them. "I guess that tracks with how today is going."

Almost two dozen of the hideous creatures swooped past overhead on huge leathery wings. The soldiers all cowered in fear, but the hairy beasts paid them no mind. They made beelines straight for the center of the army formation—and the wagon that housed Shi'ev's contraption.

THIRTY-FIVE

Whether by sword, magic, or influence, wielding power incorrectly often brings terrible consequences—not all of them physical.

— Codes of Entreaty 3.12

ANTON VERUNE STARED THROUGH his spyglass, transfixed by the creatures falling from the sky into the midst of his perfectly ordered battlefield. There were at least twenty of them, and although Verune had never seen a manticore in person before, the bodies of lions, tails of scorpions, and fanged humanoid faces gave it away. The winged beasts swarmed around Shi'ev's strange noisemaker, using their claws and tails to batter it. The stakes held, but the wagon would not.

Verune wasn't sure whether the manticores had come specifically to aid the elves like the trancheons in Eastmarsh or not, but whatever the reason, the sound of Shi'ev's machine was driving them insane. The creatures were supposed to be territorial, but they had inexplicably put away all their rivalries just to ruin his day.

The machine would not last long under the assault, and without it, Verune would not be able to pull a victory from this debacle. Perhaps

Shi'ev would be able to figure out some other way to protect the troops, but the Kiramet scientist hadn't been seen since he had switched on the blasted thing. Why Anseldr had taken up with a foreigner, he would never know.

The Drüstanian troops closest to the machine broke ranks and fled, fearing that once the machine was dismantled the creatures would come for them. Verune cursed. In a matter of minutes, the entire battle had turned to sheer chaos. The first ranks were having difficulty with the city gate's defenses, the middle ranks were fleeing from creatures that had no business being there, and their rear guard had taken severe losses.

The amplified low rumble of the noisemaker finally ground to a halt, and Verune knew he had no other choice. Anseldr might have his head for this, but they were now past any hope of taking the city intact, and it was now his call to make.

He shouted for a messenger and ordered the surviving catapults to ready the first volley of fire mortars. It was time to end all this.

"AT LEAST WE HAVE our distraction!" Kasdan shouted over the chaos.

Niena churned her legs harder and hoped she didn't slip on a patch of ice as they ran. "That's not what I had in mind!" Niena fired back, before noticing the low rumble and mental pressure of Shi'ev's invention had faded away, replaced by the occasional stabbing pain of manticore roars.

She yanked the helmet off that Tollan had scavenged for her disguise and threw it aside to glance behind her. The manticores had torn the device, as well as the wagon it had rested on, into a plethora of unusable pieces. Now the horde turned its attention to the Drüstanian soldiers on the battlefield, though a few fought among themselves to assert dominance.

Tollan pointed ahead, up the rocky slope to the gates of Por'monir. "They're through! The battering ram broke through!"

But the victory was short-lived. Without the protection of Shi'ev's low-frequency sound waves, the elven wardcasters were free to resume their magical onslaught on the men below. Only a few soldiers made it inside before the ground once again became flooded with crimson.

"Are you sure there's no other way into the city?" Kasdan shouted, clearly rethinking his decision to go with them. "We can't get past that!"

Niena tried to keep her breathing steady as they huffed and puffed their way up the switchback path. She didn't know how Tollan and Kasdan managed it in full armor. "None that I know how to find!" she called back. The underground tunnels might have been an option, but they didn't have time to search for the passage Gilbrannen had once led her through. It might make for a decent escape route if they could find a way down.

The incline leveled out as they approached the gates. Terrified soldiers streamed past on every side, running in the opposite direction. Some of them stopped in their tracks and writhed on the ground before peeling apart. Niena refused to look, but the coppery stench of blood became unbearable.

A handful of arrows peppered the ground at their feet.

"Take off your armor!" Tollan shouted as he ducked behind an outcropping and tugged at his fasteners. "Anything that would mark you as Drüstanian!"

Niena blanched, realizing that Shilvand's wardcasters wouldn't know how to distinguish them from their true enemies. She yanked off the oversized armor pieces, livery, and chain mail, then helped Kasdan extricate himself from his. It felt a lot colder in just her breeches and the remains of Serenia's green dress that she had borrowed so long ago.

She slung her father's bow and quiver over her shoulders. It was her only weapon, since the man she killed earlier still bore Gilbrannen's sword through his chest.

They were about to rush the last few hundred yards to the gate when an explosion shook the ground and lit up the sky. The battering ram crumpled from the impact of an impossibly well-aimed fire mortar. With no soldiers to brace the rear, it started a precarious roll back down the mountainside.

"Stay back!" Niena said, and they all hugged the outcropping again as the siege engine slid past, gaining speed and covered in flaming oil.

The catapults were unleashing their deadly payload on the city.

"General Verune thinks the battle is lost," Tollan reasoned, watching as more of the ceramic mortars were lobbed toward the city walls. "He's ensuring that if Drüstania can't win, then Por'monir can't, either."

Niena swallowed and watched as one of the firebombs exploded over the city, spewing liquid fire over the gates and onto the roofs of several buildings. Any wardcasters or archers guarding the entrance could not have survived that. It wouldn't take long to smother the entire city in flames.

Fire and black magic.

"It doesn't matter," she said, gritting her teeth. "We're finding Papa. You can leave if you want to, Kasdan."

"Not happening," he replied, gesturing to the ongoing chaos on the battlefield. "I think my chances inside are about as good as they are out here. We'll just have to keep under awnings and stone archways."

Niena looked to her brother for confirmation. He nodded resolutely and led the way forward, brandishing his sword. They avoided puddles of inferno to slip inside through the narrow, splintered, and burning wooden gate.

No resistance challenged them, and no one could be found in the streets. It was even more empty than the first time Niena had visited. It astonished her—if projectiles and fire ever rained from the sky over Celwaith Tor, the way would be flooded with all manner of panicked people, clutching whatever meant most to them and hoping not to be trampled underfoot. Had Por'monir been abandoned by everyone save Shilvand's forces? Like Neraliel?

A firebomb exploded overhead, the superheated liquid threatening to scorch them to crisps. Niena stood transfixed at the sight a moment too long, but Kasdan grabbed her hand and pulled her to safety in a sheltered alleyway alongside Tollan.

"Thanks," she told him, sweat starting to drip into her eyes from the heat. He squeezed her hand once in acknowledgment, and let go without lingering.

"Look! There's someone." Tollan pointed, and Niena's mental question of whether the city might be occupied was answered.

A D'harnin family pushed their way out of a building in the center of the blaze, spilling pails of water in front of them to clear a path through the flames. The water had little effect against the burning petroleum, so the adults carried the children who couldn't run and sprinted up the street to where the oil hadn't reached. The flames licked at their shoes, but they stamped them out and ducked inside another structure that hadn't caught fire.

All of these people had such faith in their leaders and the magic that previously protected them for centuries. They didn't believe it was necessary to escape, even with the city burning around them. They would continue to hunker down in their places of shelter until the storm passed, or as was more likely, they all burned to death.

"Come on, Niena!" Tollan called from the other end of the alley. "It's clear. How can we find Dad?"

Niena caught up with her brother and Kasdan, not sure what they needed to look for. "I have no idea," she said reluctantly. "Papa is being held in a network of caves and tunnels under the city—but we didn't enter through the streets last time."

"You don't even know if there's a way down from here?" Tollan asked, his voice squeaking a bit in disbelief.

Niena didn't answer. There had to be a way. Maybe the Hall of Meeting, she thought—Shilvand's living quarters might have a clue if not a direct route. "Just come on!"

They ran, sticking as close as possible to stone walls and arches to shelter from the sky. The further they got from the gates, however, the less carved stone stood tall to protect them. A cannonball crashed down twenty yards away, causing a small one-story wooden hovel to collapse in on itself.

Niena spotted a flash of yellow on the ground up ahead. "Careful," she said as they approached. "Looks like some of the Drüstanians made it at least this far."

Kasdan recovered the man's shield, while Tollan checked the man's neck for a pulse. There was none, and he shook his head. The fletching of an arrow peeked out from underneath the body. "He wasn't pulled apart by those spells."

"Halt, outsiders!" a gruff voice called, vaguely familiar. "Stay right where you are."

All three of them looked up to the rooftops and saw they had been cut off on both sides by D'harnin archers dressed in familiar blue. Tollan glanced at Niena, and she shook her head. There wasn't much they could do in such tight spaces against so many foes.

Niena raised her hands in surrender. At least the D'harnir didn't appear to be wardcasters, so they were on more even terms. "I am a friend of Gilbrannen's," she said cautiously. "I am a half-blood, not your enemy."

"That is not how I remember things," the voice called out, and Niena recognized at last who spoke to them. Silmon stood above them amid the secret police, the same D'harn who she had witnessed blow up Wraelian Square that fateful day. "We never heard from him after the night he intended to assassinate King Pelendion," Silmon said with suspicion. "It is not hard to presume that you betrayed him and led the army right to us."

"I swear it didn't happen like that, Silmon," Niena protested, but she knew it was useless. The D'harnir believed only what they wanted, and she had to admit that the situation looked incriminating without Gilbrannen there to vouch for her. "Gilbrannen and I came with the survivors of Neraliel, the enclave condemned by your mistake."

Silmon's face boiled with hatred at the reminder. "Kill them," Silmon ordered. There was a momentary hesitation before the arrows flew.

Kasdan raised the fallen Drüstanian's shield and fell to one knee, making himself as small a target as possible. The shafts thudded into the reinforced wood.

Niena immediately cast her magical ward to protect herself and Tollan, but she could only do so much on short notice. After only the first few impacts against the invisible barrier, she could feel the strain it put on her mind to keep it up.

Tollan charged from behind her, wearing none of his armor but determined to do more than stand there. "Tollan, no!" Niena called after him, but he was already sprinting.

"Kasdan, give me a boost!" Tollan yelled, and Kasdan barely had time to glance over and raise his shield. Tollan used it to vault upward, scrambling onto the roof where several elven archers perched. It divided their attention and took the pressure off Niena and Kasdan for a moment.

Niena sucked air through her teeth as an arrow slipped through her distracted defenses, ripping a gash along her exposed arm. Kasdan moved to stand in front of her protectively, drawing his sword and raising his shield to compensate for her weakening protection spell. She dropped the ward and reached instead for her father's bow and nocked an arrow.

She ignored her injury and fired off two arrows as quickly as she could, causing the D'harnir archers above to take cover. Both of her shots missed, but her attention had drifted to the other rooftop. Her baby brother acquitted himself incredibly well against three D'harnin warriors simultaneously, but they had him cornered. The sky behind them was dark with fire and smoke—it would only take a well-placed explosion to kill them all, friends and enemies alike.

Niena saw her opening and loosed another arrow. It flew straight between the shoulder blades of Tollan's nearest attacker, giving him the opportunity he needed to reposition and go on the offensive.

Kasdan stiffened in front of her, and she feared he had been struck by an arrow while she was distracted. "Kasdan!" she called to him. "What's wrong?"

Niena recast the defensive ward around them. Kasdan didn't reply to her, his eyes glazing over. Her heart skipped a beat as she recognized what that meant. *No, no,* she thought in desperation, frantically searching for the D'harn attempting to control Kasdan from within.

She slung the bow again across her shoulders and instead wrenched the shield from his hand. She forced him back against one of the building's walls, eliminating the need to watch their backs. Two arrows plowed into the shield and split the wood, poking out the rear side.

Kasdan would turn against her at any moment. In desperation, Niena changed to the only other D'harna spell she knew: the one for healing. She could feel Kasdan next to her, could feel his mind straining to fight against the elven influence but failing faster and faster—until she supported his fight. The magic would not claim Kasdan. She would not allow him to be enchanted against her.

She heard the clash of metal and glanced up to see Tollan backpedaling. Arrows from multiple directions whistled past him, and the threatening form of Silmon leaped across from the adjacent roof.

Niena's heart ached. She had allowed the two of them to be separated once more, and this time, there would be no second chances.

TOLLAN PARRIED THE ELF'S next blow more successfully, but he could not find the right footing to gain any leverage. He backed up again, doing his best to put his adversary between himself and the archers across the way. Something about him seemed familiar, but he couldn't put his finger on why.

The elf Niena had called Silmon stalked closer, locking eyes with him. "You stopped us at the gates of Celwaith Tor that day."

Tollan gritted his teeth. "You got me." This time, though, Tollan's sword would not break as they fought. He charged across the rooftop at Silmon, suddenly sure of his footwork as he recalled his training.

They locked swords, the metal grating as they pushed against each other. Amazingly, Tollan had the greater strength, or perhaps weight, and his adversary slipped back a pace toward the edge of the roof.

"Give it up," the elf snarled, breaking contact and twirling out of reach. One of the distant archers loosed another shot, and Tollan barely managed to deflect it with the blade of his sword.

The distraction proved vital. Silmon advanced again, hand outstretched, speaking one of the strange incantations Tollan had heard a few times now. This one was more guttural, and the effects began almost instantaneously.

If Niena had used magic to heal him before down on the battlefield, this was that spell's opposite.

Tollan fell to his knees, his sword clattering down next to him and sliding off into the street below. His abdominal muscles spasmed in pain. He clutched at his middle before the rest of his body joined in the same pain, like ripples throughout his entire body.

He saw Niena and Kasdan down below, huddled against the wall of an alley on the far side. He could do nothing to assist them. Another wave of pain inundated him, feeling like his skin would burst open.

The elf proclaiming his death leaned down close to him, whispering the final words of the spell.

It never came. Another group of elves clambered up from the streets below, dressed in drab colors like the family Tollan had seen running from the burning house. They attacked the ones dressed in blue with blunt weapons, knocking some from their sniper perches.

One of the newcomers tackled Silmon to the rooftop, interrupting the incantation beyond recovery. Tollan's heart skipped when he saw that his miraculous defender was shorter and stockier than any of the other elves, and his bedraggled hair and beard were gray, flecked with blond.

"Stay away from my son," Voster said, straddling Silmon. He wheeled back his fist and clocked Silmon square in the jaw.

The elf struggled, trying to pull a knife from his belt, and they rolled several times as they fought. Tollan panicked. "You're on the edge of the—"

His father and Silmon fell ten feet to the ground, and Tollan raced to the edge to see. The elf had taken the brunt of the impact, and when they came up, Voster wrenched the knife from Silmon's side and held the cold edge to his throat.

"Listen to me," Voster said to him. "You can still walk away."

Silmon looked around, seeing his fellow soldiers had been dispatched by a large number of civilians. He nodded silently, and Voster allowed him to stand. With not a word and a spiteful glance over his shoulder, Silmon fled down the hill between a pair of burning buildings.

Tollan rolled to his feet, still queasy from the effects of Silmon's spell, and lowered himself down to the street corner. His father was already there, waiting for him.

"Tollan, my son," he said, looking the young man up and down in disbelief. "Is it you?"

"Yeah, Dad," Tollan replied. A handful of emotions flickered across his face. "I'm here."

Tollan's father came and wrapped his son in a tight embrace, clutching at his shoulders in disbelief. His father smelled awful, and he had lost so much weight, but none of that mattered. A few tears welled up in Tollan's eyes, and he started to believe that his father had never stopped caring for him.

"Papa," Niena's tired voice cut in, and he welcomed her into the embrace without letting go of Tollan.

All three of them rested in each others arms for a moment, happy amid all the destruction to be together again at last.

Kasdan spoke up. "I hate to break up such a touching reunion, but we don't have much time." To accentuate his unclear estimate, another mortar exploded and rained down a few blocks away. "The catapults are advancing."

"Right," Voster said, breaking the embrace to greet the young man. "Kasdan, lad—thank you for your help."

"It's been mostly these two, I'm afraid," Kasdan said. "I've just been along for the ride."

"I believe it," Voster said with a smile, his gaunt face regaining some of its familiar color. "They can be quite determined."

Without warning, Niena stumbled and almost fell. She looked faint now that her adrenaline had begun to wear off.

"Niena!" Tollan exclaimed, helping her shakily regain her balance. He wondered if her constant use of magic was to blame, its effects leaving her weak with exhaustion. "Niena! Are you all right? Talk to us."

Niena took a few deep breaths and leaned on him for support. "I will be. I just . . . don't have much energy left."

"Kasdan and I will help you," Tollan said, beckoning their friend over to support her other side. "Where are we going, Dad?"

His father turned and called up to one of the elves. "Arondin, is everyone on the way to the Hall of Meeting?"

The elf in question, perched on the edge of the roof overhead, looked out to the horizon and upward to the large building at the peak of the city. "I believe so. Tolvanen is leading the way into the caves, with about eighty members of the Junir clan and a few others. But if we don't leave now, we may not have a chance. Those catapults show no signs of stopping their advance, and the fires are spreading."

Tollan cut in, giving his father a quizzical look. "Wait, you're helping them? After all they've done to us?"

The reply came with a disarming pat on the shoulder. "Patience, son—these people have committed no crimes. Most had no idea that Shilvand was waging a war with Drüstania until today."

Tollan supposed he could understand, though he would continue to be wary of the elves. At least these few had proven not to be a threat, and that would have to be enough for now. He reclaimed his sword from the ground where it had fallen and followed the train of people.

The weight of his sister pressed on his shoulder, and his father was a welcome presence at his back.

NIENA BREATHED HEAVILY AND closed her eyes for a moment, savoring the brief respite as they waited for the last stragglers of Tolvanen's clan to get inside the Hall of Meeting. She leaned against one of the carved wooden support pillars while her brother and Kasdan helped carry precious belongings or young children across the threshold.

She was reminded of the few remaining people of Neraliel, no doubt still waiting past the far edge of the valley for their warriors who would not return. She hoped Tolvanen or someone might be able to find them once the battle had passed and give them a home beyond this conflict.

Almost a hundred of the Junir clan along with a few other stragglers had managed to outpace the fire mortars. Each new explosion rang out closer and closer to the Hall until one of the mortars rained down burning oil not sixty yards away.

Voster looked on in worry, propping the double doors open with benches from around the fire pits. "Hurry!" he called, waving the group indoors. "We're out of time!"

Finally, it appeared that the last D'harn had entered out of the rain of fire. Arondin came up from the storeroom, looking for anyone else to guide down into the catacombs. "Is that all of them?"

Kasdan shook his head as he passed, carrying a small D'harn child. "There's an elderly woman still coming up the stairs—I think she's the leader."

Niena remembered the friendly Junir matriarch from their brief time speaking with the council. Molenia, she thought her name was.

"I've got her," Voster said, rushing to the door.

"Dad, we have to go!" Tollan shouted, having returned to help Niena down into the catacombs. He had his pocket watch out, and it warmed Niena's heart for a moment to see him using it. "The artillery will be in range any second! We can't save her!"

Just as Tollan finished, a well-aimed cannon shot blew out a chunk of wall close to the dais at the end of the room. Their father paid it no heed and quickly ventured outside to help Molenia.

Tollan and Niena watched with nervous breath. Their father lifted the last presumably surviving member of Por'monir's Council of Elders into his arms, and he began running back toward them.

But she was not the last.

A D'harn in shimmering silk robes stepped out from the shadows at the side of the stone promontory, brandishing one of the ornate daggers used for shearing. Niena recognized the white hair instantly, but Shilvand came upon her father too quickly for anyone to stop him.

"Papa! Behind you!"

Voster had almost reached the double doors when he spun around in alarm. Shilvand's dagger instead plunged deep into the chest of the Junir matriarch, and a stain of red spread from the wound. The D'harn drew back his weapon in shock at what he had done, and Voster let Molenia fall to the ground as she gave up her last breath.

Before Shilvand could strike again, Voster went for the dagger. They grappled in the doorway of the Hall of Meeting, Voster's bony hand clutching the D'harn's wrist in an attempt to wrench the blade away.

Tollan drew his sword and stepped forward from Niena's side to help their father finish the fight, but he stopped in his tracks and stared at the sky. Niena followed his gaze, and a chill went through her. A single firebomb had been flung higher and further than all the others. The Hall of Meeting was now in range, and the ceramic shell would burst right above them, on the roof of the Hall.

"Everyone, get back!" Tollan shouted, dragging Niena away from the open door and toward the back of the hall. She heard Arondin hurrying the last of his kin down the hidden stairwell in the storeroom. If she wanted to live, she knew in her heart she should do the same.

But Niena wouldn't give up, not now that they had been reunited. "Papa!" she called, weakly struggling against her brother.

Shilvand strained against Voster, trying to spit out a spell between his clenched teeth. He never had the opportunity to finish it.

The projectile struck the roof above them and exploded, the force of the blast ripping through at least two support beams and lighting everyone in fiery orange. The burning oil spread, and the front of the Hall of Meeting could no longer hold its own weight. Niena looked on in horror, unable to prevent what happened next.

Voster let go of his opponent and dove inside the doors at the last moment, letting the oil fall squarely on Shilvand. But even as flames consumed the Arbiter of Por'monir amid screams of pain, the roof of the Hall of Meeting buckled and fell. Voster collapsed under the deluge of burning debris.

"No!" Niena cried, shaking herself free of Tollan's grasp. She rushed to the settling pile of dust and rubble and desperately moved pieces aside. She paid no attention to the smoke in her eyes and the creaking of the structure around them.

Tollan came to her side again, urging her away. "The whole place is coming down! He's gone, Niena!"

"I won't leave him!" Niena choked, hoarse from the smoke and her tears. Her fingers blistered from the heat, but still she pushed on. "I know he's alive!"

Tollan looked down at the sword in his hand. He had left so many men behind on the battlefield when there was a chance they could have lived. And this was his own father. He clenched the hilt tighter and nodded to her. "Whatever you need."

A hand lifted weakly out of the rubble, from underneath one of the huge collapsed supports. "There!" Niena said, pointing.

Tollan tried to go closer, but the flames intensified. "It's too hot!"

Niena took a deep breath and readied herself. Although she was drained, she needed to coax out one last use of magic. "It's all right. We'll go in together, and my warding spell will keep the fire at bay."

Tollan frowned. "No, you've been weakened too much already. I'll get one of the elves to help us."

Niena's green eyes flashed in defiance. "We don't have time, Tollan. Move now." She centered herself by touching her mother's necklace, imagining the elf woman was alongside them to impart the desperately needed strength. When she began speaking the incantation, she fell faster and deeper into the magical trance than she ever had before.

She could feel Tollan's presence at her side as she moved forward. The fiery heat peeled back like a curtain before her outstretched hands. The two siblings advanced, and the flames retreated from around their father's buried form.

Their father's labored coughs could be heard now, intermingled with Tollan's frantic strikes as he hacked through the heavy wooden beam holding his father down. The burning building creaked again, threatening another collapse that would end it for all of them. Niena almost lost her concentration, but centered her mind again and gave herself over to the D'harna words leaving her mouth.

Tollan broke through the charred wood, and he wedged his sturdy iron blade under what remained of the beam. He leaned on it with all his might, and Niena could feel that effort as though it was her own. "Push, Dad!" Tollan shouted.

Voster stirred, but though his atrophied muscles flexed, he could not escape the crushing weight of the beam.

Niena reached the last reserve of her energy. Her consciousness dwindled to a pinprick, and the heat of the flames began to lick around the edges of her shrinking magical ward. "Now, Tollan ..." she whispered, more a prayer than anything he could hear.

Tollan screamed in exertion, and the beam budged enough to one side. Voster rolled out and got a knee under him.

Niena couldn't hold it back any longer. Her mind gave way under the strain, and the flames roared in around them. The last thing she felt was her brother's arm around her shoulder, dragging her across the ground.

But then, there was nothing.

ANSELDR WATCHED THE LAST of the battle unfold through his spyglass, having found an overlook peeking out from the trees on the western ridge. The city of Por'monir burned, most of the buildings a charred husk of what they had been. On the other side, the army of ten thousand he had assembled was now a fraction of that former strength, having been decimated by a surprise attack, magic, and finally a horde of creatures that by all accounts should have been lone hunters. He couldn't blame his soldiers for running in terror of their enemies' capabilities.

He pulled down his spyglass in disgust and stuffed it in the saddlebag next to him. He prepared to return to the field and confer with the remaining officers about what else could be done to salvage any expenses from the ruins. Verune deserved a commendation for keeping his cool in such a volatile situation, but Shi'ev's invention had proved immensely less helpful than advertised. If Anseldr was lucky, perhaps the scientist himself had been carried off by one of the manticores.

"Ah, there you are!" a familiar voice called from behind him, and Anseldr sighed audibly. Luck was hard to come by, it seemed.

"I thought you might have chosen this cliff for a vantage point," Shi'ev said, approaching on his own steed. "Verune appeared frustrated that you left without speaking to him."

"You saw what happened down there," Anseldr said, keeping his voice neutral. He tugged on his horse's reins to turn and face Shi'ev, who rode bareback on one of the horses that had previously pulled his covered wagon. "Nowhere in the valley was safe."

Shi'ev looked around, confused. "But you brought none of your kingsguard to protect you? That seems foolhardy."

"My kingsguard were the last hope to protect our flank," Anseldr explained. "Without Lieutenant Cresthaven's quick thinking or Verune launching the fire mortars when he did, this might not have been a victory. I suppose it was inevitable that we would suffer losses, but neither of us expected such a close call."

"Indeed," Shi'ev said, looking over Anseldr's shoulder to the battlefield below. The manticores had finally thinned out, either threatened to leave by the larger, stronger females or content to carry off a few soldiers to feast upon later. Only two had been taken down by the combined efforts of rifles and crossbows. "My invention worked precisely as intended, at least for a time. It is most curious why the manticores were drawn to it—perhaps they correlated the sound to a youngling in distress."

"Worse, how did so many wild manticores come to be in one place since they are known to be territorial except while in heat?" Anseldr grumbled, though he had a hunch about that. "Were they led here? Captured and released by the elves that attacked our flank?"

Shi'ev shook his head slowly. "Speculation will not change the outcome of this battle. Por'monir may be destroyed, but it would not surprise me if a significant number of survivors are hiding in cellars or caves."

"They will be dealt with," Anseldr assured. They still had more than enough men to search the ruins for survivors and valuables. "We are not leaving until the last coal has been raked over."

"That would be unwise," Shi'ev said, surprising the prince. "You saw how a small group of elves was able to hold their own against our trained soldiers. Inside the city, the quarters will be tighter, and they will be able to use the full strength of their spells without my invention. It would be a death trap for your men."

Anseldr could not deny that. But if he did not stamp out the elven threat now, they would only come back with a harder resolve in the future. And that didn't even address the dwindling royal treasury coffers, especially if they could not salvage any valuables from the ruins of Por'monir.

Responsibility for Drüstania had fallen to him in the wake of his brother's death, and his choices could affect the lives of a hundred thousand people. The thought both sobered and exhilarated him.

But he chiefly needed to show that he could acquit himself well as a new king, so that his people would accept him. It would be far easier to cast the army's slim victory in a positive light if he returned with almost half of his forces rather than a quarter or less.

"You are correct," Anseldr answered at last. "Our work is done today. The elves will not soon forget our strength, and your scientific breakthroughs will help us fight back should they ever return. We should find General Verune and sound the retreat—it will be a long journey home."

Anseldr clicked his reins, and his horse started carefully down the slope. Shi'ev followed close behind. "I think you will find Ash'kiram to be a powerful ally to Drüstania in the coming days as well," the Kiramet scientist pointed out. "We could be more than trading partners."

Anseldr frowned, keeping his eyes on their snowy descent through the evergreen trees. "How do you mean?"

"I and the ambassador would have to put in a good word, so do not take this as a guarantee. We may be able to provide you a loan—enough gold to satisfy Drüstania's financial needs in the short term without raising taxes on your citizens."

The offer was tempting, an easy way to avoid the costliest consequences of Anseldr's choice. But such a generous offer rarely came without strings. "What assurance would your prime minister require to approve such a loan?"

Shi'ev chuckled as if the question amused him. "Apart from signing on to the customary interest rate, there is nothing needed but Ambassador Le'shom's recommendation. However . . ." He trailed off.

"What?" Anseldr asked.

"If word ever reaches the public of how your brother was poisoned, I cannot promise that Ash'kiram will stand with you in solidarity," Shi'ev said in a low voice. "In order to maintain good business with the Drüstanian people, we will publicly disavow and dethrone you."

Anseldr pulled his horse up short. There it was: the other shoe had dropped. Even though Shi'ev had been the one to supply him with the untraceable disease that had ravaged Pelendion's body, Anseldr would bear all of the risk. Even if he now killed Shi'ev, no doubt Ambassador Le'shom had taken details of the plot back with her to Ash'kiram. He could no longer escape the web of deception he had constructed for his own gain, not for many years to come.

But eventually, he would find a way.

"I understand, old friend," Anseldr said calmly. "You have nothing to fear from me. Kiramet trade will always be welcome on Drüstanian shores."

"In that case," Shi'ev said with a cheery smile, "long live the king."

As the two men continued toward the remnants of the Drüstanian army, there was no doubt in Anseldr's mind. Even shackled to the Kiramet business oligarchy, he knew his people would come to thrive under his kingship. Unlike Pelendion, who could only dream of a better, more prosperous Drüstania, Anseldr had the resolve to make those dreams happen.

Their horses cleared the trees, and the tattered Drüstanian battle standard could be seen flying over the blood-soaked battlefield. Or rather, just a piece of it. A manticore had swiped its claws at the bright yellow banner and torn away the half that featured the white dove.

Only the serpent remained.

THIRTY-SIX

The whole of civilization is built on this: that a father protects, that a mother nurtures, and that their children learn the same. For a family united can withstand any hardship.

     — *Codes of Binding 1.04-05*

GILBRANNEN TRUDGED THROUGH THE city, his boots leaving perfect indentations in the wet ash. Por'monir had burned all through the night, stopping once a torrential freezing rain had blown through in the morning once the oil from the fire mortars had been consumed.

He looked back over his shoulder at the battlefield, now empty save for bodies and carrion-eaters. The horrid smell from below mixed with the scent of char, and reminded him how many had lost their lives on both sides.

And for what? Gilbrannen mused, kicking at a now-exposed fireplace in his parents' house, mostly a pile of ash and rubble. He had already come to terms with the likelihood of their death, but he had still held out a sliver of hope until now, days later.

"Find anything?" called Silmon from the street, aiding in the search for survivors and supplies. The people of Neraliel had waited patiently outside the city for the fires to die down, and shared what they could with anyone they found. But since the refugees had little before, there was a lot of nothing to go around now.

At least the manticores had left to pursue other prey, and the survivors would be safe if the creatures did come back. The totem staff would see to that.

Gilbrannen shook his head. "No. There is nothing left here."

Most of the bodies inside the city either couldn't be identified or had burned away completely, leaving the lucky survivors in root cellars and the handful of dwellings and shops made entirely of stone. Shilvand's body had not been recognized among the dead either, but survivors had already taken up the call to arms against humanity just as the patriarch had hoped. Not many able-bodied fighters still lived though.

Silmon stepped inside what used to be the house, looking around. He moved gingerly, a bandage wrapped several times around his midriff. "I am sorry about your family, Gilbrannen. This part of town was gutted by the fire. It will take some time to rebuild."

"Rebuilding is a lost cause," Gilbrannen said, cutting him off with a vehemence that welled up out of nowhere. "If we stay here, the humans will come back later and finish the job." He sighed, rubbing his eyes in tired resignation to the truth. "We brought this on ourselves, Silmon."

The other D'harn said nothing, either because he didn't want to agree outwardly or because he was considering the idea. It surprised Gilbrannen that Silmon had not yet pointed out his hypocrisy, demoting Silmon for a mistake that Gilbrannen himself went on to make.

"Maybe . . ." Gilbrannen started, trailing off.

"What?" Silmon prompted.

"Maybe the reason the D'harnir never reconciled with humans in all these years is because we never tried," Gilbrannen said, remembering the carved murals of the Codes of Nature he and Niena had found. "Maybe it is time to turn over a new leaf, or rather an old one."

"What are you saying?" Silmon said, sounding enraged by the idea. Gilbrannen couldn't blame him for feeling that way. "You know the histories better than anyone. We were driven out of their communities —men despised us and our ways. You just said why we cannot stay here."

"But they had forgotten us before all this," Gilbrannen protested. He remembered his arguments with Niena, having found no trace of her or her brother anywhere in the vicinity. Not only was the blood of his own family on his hands, but her family's, as well. "We were myths to them, neither good nor evil. Now when they think of the D'harnir they will only remember how we hurt them."

"That is a good thing," Silmon said impatiently, his hand drifting to the bandage at his side. "Maybe now the D'salnir will feel some measure of our pain."

"No one should have to experience what our people went through," Gilbrannen replied. "And if Niena Cresthaven has shown me anything, it is that there are those who want to live at peace with us. Men may have started the last war, but we started this one."

Silmon scoffed, turning to leave. "It has always been the same war, Gilbrannen. It always will be until we return to Celwaith Tor as inheritors instead of infiltrators. Your time with that human girl has changed you—not for the better."

Gilbrannen watched sadly as Silmon crossed the scorched street to another group of collapsed houses. The D'harn called out for a few hands to grab tools and follow him to the Hall of Meeting. It had collapsed under the deluge of fire, cutting off the hidden entrance to the caverns below. Gilbrannen wondered how the others would react once it was uncovered, but realized they would likely praise Shilvand for his wonderful foresight in stashing away enough grain for them to last the winter. There was no telling what other interesting things they might find down there in addition.

He considered what might happen if he tried to explain Shilvand's plan and how the arbiter was the one truly responsible for this destruction. Few would believe him, even if the remaining militant members of the Dast'rel didn't shut him up first.

I have changed, Gilbrannen admitted to himself. Knowing Niena had changed him, somehow.

He reached into his satchel and pulled out the green leather-bound book that Niena had given him the day before the battle. *You need it more than I do*, she had told him. He remembered when he returned it to her in her cell as a ploy, so she would let her guard down. He regretted everything he had done to her, though he never questioned it at the time.

Gilbrannen had been taught the Mishenna as a boy like every other D'harnin youth, had memorized the Codes at night in this very house. His parents and teachers had interpreted the Codes as laws that only applied to those practicing them, but now he wasn't so sure. Niena hadn't ever learned the Mishenna except for reading the scattered proverbs in this book, and yet she had always seemed to abide by it in her words and deeds. She cared about people—cared enough to save him, even though he had imprisoned and blackmailed her to further Shilvand's secret war.

He placed the book back in his pack and followed Silmon. Gilbrannen resolved to tell his people the entire truth of what had happened. He needed to take responsibility for his part in this destruction, no matter how difficult that may be for his people to hear. The consequences of that choice were irrelevant—it was simply the right thing to do.

It was time to begin mending the rift.

"THIS SWORD IS WELL made, Tollan," Voster said, turning the blade over again and running his fingers down the double fuller. "Thin but not brittle, pliable but sturdy—if I didn't know better, I would say a far more experienced blacksmith made this."

Tollan shuffled his feet in the sand, unsure how to accept the praise. "Thanks. I—uh, I learned from watching you."

"That you did." His father slid the blade back into its scabbard, producing a satisfying clink before handing it back. He had washed and tied his scraggly hair back, so he looked more like the man Tollan knew. His burns had all but healed by the use of elven magic, but he remained dreadfully thin from lack of nourishment. "I guess we have a lot to talk about, don't we?"

Tollan strapped the sword back on his belt, a small measure of pride swelling up inside him. The sword was a twofold accomplishment: it showed his prowess as a soldier of Drüstania, and his talent as a blacksmith.

He looked out over the beach where the elves were hard at work lashing together logs to build a ferry. Past them, the cold waters of the northern seas roiled, and in the distance an island rose up as a dimple on the horizon. The last two days had been a whirlwind, helping the Junir clan collect supplies and ready themselves for a life away from the mainland. Tollan glanced back at the tent they had set up out of the wind and below the cliff face, where Niena continued to rest. She had collapsed into a coma during their escape and hadn't stirred since.

"Shouldn't Niena be here for this?" Tollan asked, playing absently with the chain of his pocket watch. For the first time in his life, he felt that he didn't want to know the answers to his questions.

"Only if you want her to be. She already knows everything I'm about to tell you," his father said.

That hit a nerve, bringing up feelings of jealousy. He wrapped his cloak tighter around him at a chill wind off the sea, avoiding his father's gaze. "How long has she known?"

"She saw a D'harn at the bombing of the square and didn't know what it meant," his father answered. "I told her to keep it to herself because I hadn't seen one since your mother died. I told her the full truth about your heritage the night after the draft took you away."

Tollan bit his lip, listening to the rhythm of the waves change as the tide came in. "Why didn't you ever tell us before?"

Voster sighed, taking a seat on the nearest stone jutting out of the sand. "Not an hour went by in that wretched cell without wishing I had," he said, staring vacantly. "It was fear that always held me back. Not knowing what might happen, or how you would react. I always wondered how your mother would have handled it."

Tollan nodded slowly. As explanations went, it was weak, but at least it was honest. And he knew beyond doubt that Anise hadn't held back the truth, as she couldn't keep a secret to save her life. "Then who was my mother, really? I mean, not that you ever talked about her much, but . . ."

"Tollan," he said, his tone serious. "I never lied to you about the kind of person she was, or even how we met. I don't think I could bear to tell you anything but the truth, except for what I thought necessary to protect you."

To protect me, Tollan echoed in his mind. It reminded him of the odd wording in Anise's note. "So, you and Niena thought that the best way to protect me was to confront our attackers and what, ask them to stop?"

Voster spread his hands apologetically, a pained smile crossing his face. "I'm not saying it was a good plan. But we weren't even sure Por'monir was involved at the time—who knows how many other hidden D'harnin enclaves are scattered about."

"Dad, that was . . . idiotic."

Voster chuckled. "I see you learned sound tactics at training camp. Let's just say . . . things could have turned out much differently."

"Perhaps," Tolvanen called to them, taking a break from supervising progress on the raft. "But as you in Drüstania say, 'thank the winds' for that!"

"Tolvanen!" Voster said in greeting. "How is your arm feeling today?"

The D'harn waggled it and flexed his hand. "Good as new, maybe even better with Arondin's expertise in healing. Though I suppose you should know, after having him deal with all those burns. Have you seen him?"

Tollan spoke up. "Last I heard, he was tending to Niena."

"Hmmm, poor girl," Tolvanen said. "She still has not stirred?"

Voster shook his head, looking back toward the tent. "No. Arondin said this can sometimes happen when D'harnir who are new to magic overuse their power. He said he will attempt to wake her later on, if only to drink some water."

Tollan regarded Tolvanen with a raised eyebrow. "How is the construction going?"

"We are making fair progress," he answered, appreciating the interest. Since Molenia's unfortunate death in the siege of Por'monir, the surviving members of the Junir clan had unanimously agreed that Tolvanen should be the new patriarch. "Many of us argued against Shilvand and his teachings for a long time, and it pains me to see it take something like this to free my people from his grasp. Perhaps now we can finally return to the peaceful ways of Mishenna, apart from his influence."

Tollan tilted his head in skepticism. "I wouldn't count on it, even if I knew this Mishenna. Now the whole world knows you exist."

"We will have to convince them that at least some of us mean them no harm," Tolvanen said optimistically. "But for now, that wooded island across the channel will be remote enough to serve our needs, and the fish will provide enough nourishment until we can farm again in the spring."

Tollan grinned. "I suppose fishing must be pretty easy when you have magic. Just waggle your fingers and they swim right up."

Tolvanen frowned, making it clear that the idea was not in good standing. "Do not be so crass. The Codes tell us not to seek the suffering of any living thing. When we must kill, we can use magic to soften the blow, but to use spells to cause pain or death like Shilvand did is against our convictions."

Tollan winced, finding the reaction to his joke a little harsh. "Apologies."

Tolvanen's face softened. "It is fine. I understand you have mostly interacted with those who don't take Mishenna as literally as we do."

Kasdan called to them from outside Niena's tent. "Come quickly! She's waking up!"

Tolvanen took his leave and returned to the job at hand. Tollan and his father started back along the rocky shore. "What do you think of Kasdan?" Tollan asked him as they walked.

His father shot him a wry look. "I think he's sweet on our Niena. He's barely left her side this entire time."

"Yeah," Tollan said, having noticed it too. "But he's a good man. He did a lot for us while you were away, with no thought of reward."

"That's what happens when you're smitten," Voster said grimly, then laughed at Tollan's frown. "No, I've always liked him. I just don't like the idea of Niena being taken away from us for good."

Tollan fell silent, as there wasn't much more to say.

His father stopped him before they could enter the tent. There were tears in his eyes, and that was not a frequent occurrence. "We got interrupted back there, but I needed to tell you . . . I don't know what you've had to do to get here, or what you were ordered to do for the army, but I'm proud of the man you are, Tollan. You're mature beyond your years, and I guess I never wanted to let you go either."

Tollan said nothing, for nothing he could say was adequate. He folded his father into a hug, and let himself finally believe the words straight from his father's mouth. Despite all the mistakes they had made along the way, his father did love him.

When they came apart, Tollan reached up to wipe a couple of tears from his own eyes and covered the motion by scratching his ear, the one with the jagged scar. He looked at his father mischievously, recalling the story he had been told as a kid. "So, you mangled my ears with a pocketknife and then blamed it on me? Really?"

Voster laughed and tousled Tollan's hair like he used to. And this time Tollan didn't mind.

NIENA HEARD THE SOUND of crashing waves against the rocks and wondered if she was dreaming. Each wave was a step, and each step part of a long spiral staircase. Someone led her upward, someone she thought she ought to know but couldn't place where they had met. With wave after wave, step after step, she felt herself regaining her energy, coming back to her senses, and smelling the salty air of the sea.

It wasn't a dream. She was awake.

She opened her eyes, wincing at the invasive light. Arondin knelt next to her, arms outstretched over her chest and forehead, whispering an incantation. He was the presence she had felt leading her out of the trance-like state, back from the edge of oblivion.

How long have I been asleep? she wondered, noticing that her eyelids stuck together when she blinked. She remembered nothing after she and Tollan had pulled their father out from under the burning beam—maybe she had strained herself by using her powers so much.

Another familiar face came into view on her right. Kasdan got down next to her, his expression hopeful. "There you are," he said kindly.

Arondin nodded, removing his hands and smiling at her, though now he looked as tired as she felt. "You have been unconscious for days. We were beginning to worry, so I helped you along a little. But you still need rest."

Niena tried to speak but only managed a cough that tasted of smoke. Her throat was as parched as the Mersien Wold.

"Here," Kasdan said, producing a skin of the coldest, clearest water she had ever tasted. "Melted straight off the glacier a few miles from here."

Niena smiled her thanks at both of them and proceeded to swallow mouthful after mouthful until she had almost finished it. "W-where are we?" she asked, her voice scraping out. "Where is—"

Her father burst into the tent, with Tollan following right behind. They both wore bandages and other evidence of their narrow escape from Por'monir. "There's my little blossom!" Voster exclaimed in pride, squeezing in next to Kasdan and taking her hand in his. "How are you feeling?"

Niena cleared her throat. "Tired, but happy you're all here."

Arondin stood and allowed Tollan to take his place at Niena's side. "Yes, I believe I need to lie down now as well. You three, try not to tire her out any further."

Tollan knelt next to her, his dark eyebrows beetled in concern. "He said you would be okay, but I admit to not being sure I believed him."

"Hey, after that . . ." She trailed off in a cough and accepted another swig of water from Kasdan. "You think I'm going to let a little fatigue do me in? When do we leave?"

They all chuckled nervously, and her father spoke up. "Not until you're rested, and I mean fully. We caught a few runaway horses from the Drüstanian army, and the D'harnir were willing to let us keep two of them for the journey. They're building a way to cross the channel to a small island where they intend to weather the winter."

Niena looked questioningly at her father. "Are we going with them, Papa?" she asked, absently touching her mother's necklace.

"No, little blossom," he replied, smiling. "Tollan and I talked about it briefly, and ... Well, our home is back in Celwaith Tor. Anise is waiting for us, Tollan has a duty to the new king, and the people of the Barren Quarter need our smithy to stay open."

Niena breathed a sigh of relief. She didn't want to uproot her entire life, even though she supposed that's what had happened in the past couple of months. "Yeah. Though Anise is liable to flay us all alive when we get back."

Tollan laughed, a truly wonderful sound that Niena had missed dearly. "You don't know the half of it. At least Dad will catch the brunt of her fury though."

The corner of her father's mouth tugged upward. "And so I should."

Kasdan rose and began shooing them all out of the tent. "All right, you heard Arondin. Let her be. I'm going to refill her water."

"I'll come with you," Tollan said, patting his sister on the shoulder in farewell and leaving the tent.

"Kasdan," she called, and he held the tent open a moment. "Thank you."

Kasdan's bronzed face opened in a brilliant smile, before glancing away in embarrassment. He merely waved in reply and let the tent flap fall shut.

He is quite handsome, Niena thought.

Only she and her father were left in the small tent now, and he held her hand like he was afraid she might disappear into the ocean spray outside. "I spent so much time underground worrying about you and what they were doing to you," he said, his words measured. "Shilvand even came to me and told me terrible things . . ."

Niena swallowed, her throat tightening up again. "Papa, I'm okay. Or I will be. But—" She coughed again and tried to sit up a little. "But people died, and it was my fault. Yes, the D'harnir used me, but . . ."

Niena's father cradled her head with his other hand. "Make no mistake, none of that is your fault. Shilvand would have killed many regardless, and they didn't give you a choice. You did the right thing to get back to me."

Niena nodded, the thought entering her mind that although they would be heading home soon, nothing would ever be the same as before. And maybe that would be okay. "I love you, Papa."

He smiled at her, running his thumb through the blonde locks at the side of her head. "You know, I always call you a little blossom, but I never realized just how much you had bloomed. Your spirit reminds me so much of your mother. I know she would be proud of you."

Niena lay back and fell asleep again before her father left the tent, her mother's necklace draped across her palm.

After two more evenings and another round of Arondin's healing spells, Niena felt right as rain. The next day, the four of them embarked for Celwaith Tor, with all the preparations and rations that Tolvanen could convince them to take. Their father had accepted the bare minimum, knowing they would have ample opportunity to hunt while on the road.

It is a wonder how far one can travel by horse and not get tired, Niena thought, sitting behind Kasdan on a horse with a lovely cinnamon coat. They spent the majority of the ride exchanging their stories and experiences with each other, filling in the missing details.

Voster made sure to stop one last time at the old farmhouse, specifically for Tollan's benefit, and he happened to spot a stag past the edge of the clearing. Niena nocked and fired her father's bow without a second thought, and they ate extremely well that night.

Niena thought she saw the dryad Omeira smiling with a hand raised in greeting, but the vision faded when she focused on it. She chose to believe it anyway.

She also found herself spending more and more time with Kasdan as they proceeded south. He was a few years older than her, so they hadn't known each other well as children, but she could see where Keordi had picked up her hilarious and sometimes caustic wit.

Sometimes, Niena thought with a knowing smile, *siblings have more in common than they care to admit.*

It was the last turn toward home, where the North road met the East, that they learned it was not an average day in Celwaith Tor. The roads were deserted, not a single cart or a vagrant in sight as could commonly be spotted outside the capital. At points along their journey, they had encountered a few other Drüstanian soldiers, wounded men trickling in at a slower pace, but they knew nothing of any news.

Once they approached the city gates, gates which stood wide open with no checkpoint to enter, they noticed the sounds of a cheering crowd on the wind. Drüstanian citizens filled the streets to the brim, a sea of people leading up the tor to the palace.

"What do you suppose is going on?" Niena asked. She hated to expect the worst, but she had grown to distrust large public gatherings, given what had happened at King Pelendion's last two addresses.

Kasdan shrugged. "Look at all the people—most of them aren't even from the capital."

"Excuse me," Voster called to a woman wrapped in a shawl on the edge of the crowd inside the gate. "Can you tell us the reason for this celebration?"

"Haven't you heard?" she said, hollering back to them over the noise. "It's Anseldr's coronation day! The Scourge of the Elves is our new king!"

The group all exchanged glances at the title that had been bestowed by the public on Pelendion's successor. It struck Niena as a little ostentatious after the hard-won victory, but it made sense. The people had been forced to live in fear of the elves for so long, that any deliverer would be placed on the highest pedestal imaginable.

"Thank you, ma'am," Voster said. "We've been away for a while."

They pushed deeper into the city, through the Sunken Quarter and into the Barren Quarter. Even the side streets were packed with revelers —Niena had never seen the city so full. They passed the place where she had been accosted by rioters the night of the Wraelian Square bombing, and she marveled at how much had changed since then.

"I . . . think we had best wait until tomorrow to report in," Tollan said to Kasdan quietly. "I really don't want to go back to work today."

"Right with you there. Why rush it?" Kasdan asked, his eyes wide at the throng of people. "The day after next might be even better."

At long last, their horses spilled onto the street corner across from the smithy, and they all exclaimed in adoration at the sight. They tied the horses to the fence before opening the gate, which creaked at them in welcome. Voster and Tollan continued to the door, knocking and calling out when they found it was locked. Anise's muffled voice could be heard indistinctly from inside.

The door opened, and Anise let out such a shriek as Niena had never heard come from her before. She was dressed in plain clothes while her hair was done simply, with none of her characteristic faux finery. Tollan had told Niena what happened with the Denvald family, but the sight of Anise's transformation was still a shock. She bustled out of the house and gathered them all into an enormous hug before slapping Voster in the face.

"Don't you ever think of running off on me like that again!" Anise cried, then noticed at once how thin Voster had gotten. "Oh, dear, come in and I'll fix you all some flapjacks. You look half-starved!"

Niena and the others couldn't help but laugh as they followed Anise inside. She noticed before crossing the threshold that Kasdan hadn't come with them—he remained standing in the street, outside the fence.

"I should get going," he explained. "My family will be worried about me, especially if most of the army has already arrived and there has still been no word."

"Oh, of course," Niena said, going to him. "Family always comes first."

"And friends," Keordi said from behind her.

Niena turned to see her friend step out of the smithy. She must have already been there to keep Anise company. Niena's heart ached with how they had last parted, but she had already resolved not to stay angry with Keordi. After all that she had seen, the last thing she wanted was to widen a rift with her closest friend.

"I came to check on your aunt, maybe see if she wanted to go with me up the hill for the festivities," Keordi said quietly. "Niena, I don't know what to say. I have no excuses—you trusted me with that secret, and I should have believed you."

Niena reached up and placed a finger over Keordi's mouth. "Don't say another word about it. I forgive you."

Keordi's face crinkled up in a tentative smile. "You're sure?"

Niena nodded, the last part of the unrest in her heart melting away. "Not another word, remember? Now greet your brother, for pity's sake. He'll think you didn't miss him."

The two siblings laughed, hugged, and started down the street talking a hundred miles a minute. Niena was about to turn and join her own family indoors when Kasdan called after her. "Niena?"

"Yes?"

He came back over to the fence, leaned across it, and kissed her lightly on the cheek. Keordi's mouth dropped open in surprise, and Niena could already feel the heat go to her face. Not with embarrassment, but with something else.

"I hope that means you will come back to see me soon?" Niena whispered coyly.

Kasdan smiled, his white teeth positively beaming. "Hey, I've always been close by. As long as you don't get stolen away by any more mythical creatures in the meantime, I'll stop by tomorrow morning."

"I don't know if I can make that promise!" Niena said with a joyful wink, and waved farewell.

Niena watched Kasdan and Keordi go, and a lingering smile spread across her face. She heard Anise's shrill voice calling for her, so she turned and ran up the steps. The coolness of her mother's pendant lay against her chest, and the warmth of her waiting family's embrace surrounded her.

Anise had truly outdone herself. The place looked like the soldiers had never touched it. The attic had been emptied, and everything was set back in its proper place. What furniture couldn't be repaired had been replaced, and wonder of wonders, the grandfather clock was ticking. It felt like home again, but better.

Niena locked the door behind her, shutting out the noise of the celebration outside.

This was all the happiness she would ever need, she realized as she settled in at the dining table next to Tollan. Anise's cooking released the most delicious smells, and all the while she prodded Voster to tell her everything. He obliged and started at the very beginning with how he came to meet a lovely young elf maiden by the name of Tynathria.

Niena touched her mother's pendant, taking a deep breath and immersing herself in her father's story. She hung on his every word, welcoming the spoken memory of her mother into their home—every aspect of her, not just the simple parts. Niena resolved to follow her mother's lead and hide away her magical talents, at least for a time. It was not worth the negative attention it could draw to them, but she would still practice D'harna speech in private. She would be ready, in case their family ever needed her mother's healing or protection.

But she refused to think about the future anymore. The troubles of tomorrow would have to wait their turn for the joys of today.

The Cresthaven family had come home.

POSTLUDE

AS I LOOK BACK upon my life now, with gray hair and failing health, I see nothing but missed opportunities and empty promises. My father knew when to make a stand; I was lucky if I knew where to sit.

The regime installed by the Macula Society did not last, as one might expect. For all that they knew about the worldly sciences, they knew nothing about what corrupts the hearts of men. And now much of what came before has fallen into darkness. Our great libraries have burned, our great artisans have been murdered in the streets, and all that stands now is a flaming plinth, a memorial to the folly of power. It is a warning, for those with ears to hear it.

Only in the Union of the physical and the spiritual can healing be found, but no one yet knows the way. With understanding of the past comes a responsibility for the future, but few care to think beyond their next meal. That is why I have taken this writing upon myself, to share a little of the past and a little of the spiritual with anyone who might come across my humble watchtower one, two, three hundred years hence. Perhaps this humble chronicle and what little I can recall of the D'harnin Codes will help someone else to find their way in such a cold world. To remember what is truly important in life.

At the least, I am glad to have seen the first dawn of another new year. The world outside is cold, so very cold now, though I feel warmer for having written this. Time rolls on, whether we wish it or not, and mine is all but spent. Maybe you still have enough left to make a difference.

Peace and reconciliation to you all.

— Haron Geled, Last Scribe of the Union
1ˢᵗ of Numentia, in the 49ᵗʰ year after the Rift

THE END

GLOSSARY OF TERMS

(in alphabetical order)

- **BELVINT:** A small rodent that lives in the ground
- **CLAWCREN:** A vicious predatory bird with crimson feathers
- **DAST'REL:** The secret police of the Falir clan
- **D'HARNA:** The ancient tongue of the elves, through which spells are cast
- **D'HARNIN:** Of or pertaining to the elves, e.g. "elven"
- **D'HARN or D'HARNIR:** Elf or Elves
- **DRAKAINA:** Half woman, half winged serpent
- **FELINX:** A reclusive wild cat that prowls the mountains
- **GARISH:** A swarm of clawcrens
- **JARL:** Duke, appointed by the king to oversee a city and its surrounding lands
- **MANTICORE:** Chimeric apex predator of the wilds
- **MISHENNA:** The elven way of living according to the Codes
- **TOR:** tall or rocky hill
- **TRANCHEON:** A species of giant toad native to the swamp

PRONUNCIATION GUIDE

(in alphabetical order)

- **ALDREN:** AWL-dren
- **ANISE CRESTHAVEN:** ah-NEES KREST-hay-ven
- **ANSELDR ARVAD:** an-SELD-ur AR-vad
- **ANTON VERUNE:** AN-taan VEH-roon
- **ARONDIN JUNIR:** ah-RON-din JOO-neer
- **ASH'KIRAM:** ASH-kee-raam
- **BARANDINE:** ba-RAN-deen
- **BELVINT:** BEL-vint
- **BURTRAM:** BUUR-tram
- **CAPE VROSINGR:** kayp VRO-seeng-ur
- **CELWAITH TOR:** KEL-wayth tohr
- **CLAWCREN:** KLAW-kren
- **CORANNA ARVAD:** koh-RAAN-nah AR-vad
- **DANVAR:** DAN-vaar
- **DARAKH SHI'EV:** DAH-raakh SHEE-ev
- **DAST'REL:** DAST-rel

- **D'HARNIR:** dih-HAAR-neer
- **DISTERN:** DIS-turn
- **DRAKAINA:** drak-EYE-nuh
- **DRUINOR JUNIR:** DROO-in-ohr JOO-neer
- **DRÜSTALDA:** druu-STAAL-duh
- **DRÜSTANIA:** druu-STAN-yuh
- **D'SALNIR:** dih-SAL-neer
- **EMELINE ARVAD:** EH-meh-leen AR-vad
- **ENSDALE:** ENS-dayl
- **ERVAN GELED:** UR-van GEH-led
- **EVWOIN:** EV-wine
- **FELDRAM CRANDAS:** FELD-raam KRAN-das
- **FENDARAL:** fen-DAAR-aal
- **FINLEY CROSLOWE:** FIN-lee KROZ-loe
- **GADON SUNDER:** GAD-un SUN-der
- **GILBRANNEN FALIR:** gil-BRAN-nen FAH-leer
- **GÜTHANAS:** GUUTH-an-as
- **HALVANDR SENN:** hal-VAN-der sen
- **HARON GELED:** HAIR-on GEH-led
- **HELSFEN HOLD:** HELS-fen hohld
- **HEMILHET FALIR:** HEH-mil-het FAH-leer
- **HOLLYN:** HAH-len
- **KASDAN HARROWAY:** KAZ-dan HAIR-oh-way
- **KEORDI HARROWAY:** KYOHR-dee HAIR-oh-way
- **KIRAMET:** KEE-rah-met
- **LETACCIA DENVALD:** leh-TASH-uh DEN-vaald
- **MACULA:** MAK-yoo-luh

- **MAIVEY HARROWAY:** MAY-vee HAIR-oh-way

- **MANTICORE:** MAN-tih-kohr

- **MARLAPH STEMSON:** MAAR-laf STEM-sen

- **MARTON DENVALD:** MAAR-ten DEN-vaald

- **MERSIEN WOLD:** MER-see-en wohld

- **MISHENNA:** mih-SHEN-nuh

- **MOLENIA JUNIR:** moh-LEE-nee-uh JOO-neer

- **NERALIEL:** neh-RAH-lee-el

- **NIENA CRESTHAVEN:** nee-EN-uh KREST-hay-ven

- **NUMENTIA:** noo-MEN-tee-uh

- **OMEIRA:** ohm-EYE-ruh

- **OTHNIEL:** OTH-nee-el

- **PAMARTH:** pah-MARTH

- **PELENDION ARVAD:** pel-EN-dee-un AR-vad

- **PETRAS EMPTON:** PET-raas EMP-ten

- **PLINDRE:** PLIN-der

- **POR'MONIR:** POHR-moh-neer

- **RAULIN REEDS:** ROW-lin reeds

- **RUGER YORVIKSON:** ROO-ger YOHR-vik-sen

- **SERENIA DENVALD:** seh-REE-nee-uh DEN-vaald

- **SERIAH LE'SHOM:** ser-EYE-uh LEH-shoam

- **SHILVAND FALIR:** SHIL-vand FAH-leer

- **SILMON:** SIL-men

- **STENDEN ARVAD:** STEN-den AR-vad

- **STILBRY:** STIL-bree

- **TAFTLEY PINDARSON:** TAFT-lee PIN-dar-sen

- **TEMELIA MONIR:** teh-MEE-lee-uh MOH-neer

- **THAXON DENVALD:** THAK-sen DEN-vaald
- **TOLLAN CRESTHAVEN:** TOH-lan KREST-hay-ven
- **TOLVANEN JUNIR:** tohl-VAAN-en JOO-neer
- **TRANCHEON:** TRAN-chun
- **TYNATHRIA FALIR:** teh-NATH-ree-uh FAH-leer
- **VOSTER CRESTHAVEN:** VOS-tur KREST-hay-ven
- **WENDEBELL FARTHING:** WEN-deh-bel FAR-theeng
- **WELSEVIC:** WEL-seh-vik
- **WIRVANEN FALIR:** wer-VAH-nen FAH-leer
- **WRAELIAN ARVAD:** RAY-lee-un AR-vad
- **YODRIC KJORFALK:** YOD-rik KYOHR-faalk

ACKNOWLEDGMENTS

I first started writing AGAINST THE WARRING WINDS in March 2021. More than three years have elapsed while polishing the manuscript and pursuing different routes to publication, though it feels like mere months. While I could never have imagined founding my own publishing house at the time, I have learned so much along the way with assistance from so many wonderful people.

My gratitude goes first and foremost to God, for my creative gifts and each opportunity He has placed in my path to use them. He has led me down the right path for each season of my life to make me who I am today, even though in the moment it felt aimless.

To Sharon, my darling wife, for being supportive and patient with me while I worked long hours on this endeavor and talked incessantly of my plans. It wasn't long after we met that I started writing what would become this story, so you've been there every step of the way as the perfect partner and sounding board. I love you!

To my parents, who raised me the best they could and gave me an education to surpass the very best public and private schools could dream of offering. This book could never have been written, much less published, without the skills, responsibility, and work ethic you both instilled in me.

To my friend and best man, Caleb Brubaker, my fellow writer and storyteller for over twenty years now. Having our own apartment together was invaluable as I wrote the lion's share of the rough draft. Your friendship, feedback, and hearty discussion perhaps helped to shape this story more than anyone else's.

To my editor, Angela R. Watts, for your advice and willingness to answer questions throughout the publishing process. It never ceases to amaze me how you can be so young and yet so prolificly experienced at the same time.

To my family and friends who participated in beta reading, my aunts Karen Badger and Donna Chapman, Alex Peters, Sam and Rachael Miller, and Faith Landfair: thank you so much for taking your time to read and provide your critiques. This novel truly would not be as good as it is without your input.

To all those who backed or purchased this book sight unseen during the Kickstarter campaign, thank you for taking a chance on a fledgling author like myself. I am humbled by your support and adoration. Please flip through the next few pages to find your name forever immortalized here! Thank you from the bottom of my heart.

And lastly, to you, whoever may be reading this now. Thank you for being the kind of person who not only reads books, but reads the acknowledgments section! If you enjoyed what you read, please write a review on Amazon or Goodreads—even just a few words will go a long way to ensure others discover and enjoy AGAINST THE WARRING WINDS for themselves!

KICKSTARTER BACKERS

Thank you to all those who backed or purchased AGAINST THE WARRING WINDS sight unseen during the Kickstarter campaign. You took a chance on a fledgling author like myself, and I am seriously humbled by your support. The following section is dedicated to all of you, sorted alphabetically by last name or Kickstarter username. In any and all editions of this book to be published in the future, your names will be forever immortalized here.

But first, I would like to thank those who helped in other ways to promote the Kickstarter campaign. Fantasy authors Wayne Thomas Batson, Angela R. Watts, and Robert Mullin blessed me beyond measure with their endorsements. The Kress Cinema & Lounge in downtown Greeley, Colorado was incredibly gracious to provide advertising space on their movie screen. And Allison Skinner of the Phelps County Focus newspaper ran an amazing article to get the word out in my childhood hometown of Rolla, Missouri.

I could not have made this book a success without all of you.

- Joe & Sandy Abbott

C. JONAH ABBOTT

- Joyce & Gary Abbott
- Misty Arroyo
- Karen & John Badger
- Carla Bermudez
- Caleb & Veronica Brubaker
- Rachel L. Bundschuh
- Micah & Sage Burks
- Danyelle Butler
- Donna & John Chapman
- ChessCommands
- Covington
- Jaxtyn Delashmit
- Noah G.
- Nell Gillen
- Kelsey Gonzales
- Evelyn, Vivian, Etta, & Owen Gray
- Kenzley Harkins
- Troy Hively
- Grace Hoffman
- The Horton Family
- Reggie Hughes & Deanna Thomas
- Daniel & Courtney Jenovai
- Wyatt & Christina King
- Bonnie Lacy
- Ben Landfair
- Carol & Benny Landfair
- Janey & Allen Landfair

- Faith Landfair & Family
- Donald Lenhart
- Colin Letch
- Tristan Lietz
- Kristina Legkov
- Kie M.
- Jace Marrow
- Cindy Martindale
- Adrian McAuliffe
- Evelyn McClure & Walker Connell
- Z. R. McCormick
- Chase McGlinchey
- Rachael, Sam, & Alister Miller
- Tony Oliver
- Jamie Pedersen
- John Alexander Peters
- Petra
- Valerie Joy, Olivia, & Violet Rupe
- Adriano Scurto
- Jaclyn Soneff
- Danielle Stalzer
- Asakuno Tomohiro
- Giselle Trejo
- Steve Vanderheide
- Nikki Velasquez
- Efrain & Madison Villegas
- Angela R. Watts

- Philip Wilder

- Renee & Neil Youtsler

- Shelby & Brenden Youtsler

ABOUT THE AUTHOR

C. JONAH ABBOTT is a writer, artist, and the founder of Anointed Colony Media, a small publishing house dedicated to reclaiming entertainment for Christ and His Kingdom. His first short story, "The Codes of Binding," was second runner-up for the Baen Fantasy Adventure Award in 2021. When not daydreaming of Narnia and Star Wars, he lives with his lovely wife, Sharon, and her irascible feline, Shadow, in Greeley, Colorado. Thankfully, their dog, Winston, likes him well enough.

Follow C. Jonah Abbott on social media:
Gab.com/CJonahAbbott
X.com/CJonahAbbott

Publish with Anointed Colony Media:
www.AnointedColonyMedia.com

LIKE WHAT YOU READ?

NOW YOU CAN WEAR IT!

Anointed Colony Media is excited to announce a line of merchandise based on AGAINST THE WARRING WINDS! Featuring apparel, décor, and other lifestyle accessories, these items will allow you to show off your favorite new fantasy novel wherever you go! Ten percent of all profits will be donated to Alliance Defending Freedom.

Visit our store on Printful to browse the latest merchandise releases:

ANOINTEDCOLONYMEDIA.PRINTFUL.ME

ANOINTED COLONY MEDIA

9 798899 170750 3